My first wish
is that you
may really
enjoy this book·
and my next wish
is that you may
remember where
you borrowed
·it·

GENEVA PUGH

LIGHT IN THE SKY

LIGHT
IN THE SKY

BY

AGATHA YOUNG

RANDOM HOUSE

NEW YORK

To the memory of

BRIGADIER GENERAL LEONARD P. AYRES

who read most of this book in manuscript

To Marjorie *and* Robert Binger *heartfelt acknowledgment is made for their unflagging interest and encouragement, which transformed the labor of writing into an exciting adventure. Nor is any book of mine complete without most grateful thanks to my husband for his patience and for his critical judgment.*

This story is wholly fictional and only one minor character ever lived other than in the imagination. The whole district in which the mill lies is imaginary and the mill is not to be identified with any of those pioneer mills which did so much toward the post-Civil War development of Cleveland. The streets in this district cannot be found on any of the old maps of the city.

PART ONE

THE house stood in the bright sun of early morning, radiating newness and elegance like a grand lady in a new gown. The façade was full three stories tall, topped by a cupola of intricate design, bearing on its roof a final, ornate crown of lacy ironwork. The front of the house was a profusion of wooden decoration. Below each window acanthus scrolls unfurled, and above, each was crowned with a carved pediment. Double doors with elaborate filigree tops opened upon a high and narrow porch. Over the doors the writhing scrolls supported a cartouche, or shield, on which the letter F twined itself with many tendrils around the carved numerals 1872.

In the brilliant sunlight this mass of intricacy was striped with dark bars of shadow from tall fluted columns rising to the roof. The high front steps were slate-gray wood, and down the middle ran a strip of red carpet flanked by pots of flowers. More flowers cascaded from window boxes and poured from iron urns along the curving drive.

Back of this imposing façade the house diminished by stages, trailing out behind a number of successively lesser and plainer abutments, like a tall lady in a Paris gown trailing behind her bustle and train. On the lawn beside the final abutment stood a tiny structure on which had been lavished all the profusion of design which characterized the front of the house. A minute shuttered window was set in the side, complete with acanthus scroll and pediment. More lacy ironwork crowned the roof. It suggested some bit of trimming torn from the lady's gown and bore mute witness to a certain lack of faith in plumbing.

Inside the great house John Fenno woke early. He woke with a feeling of urgency and apprehension, and began to fight off the weight of sleep. He struggled to an upright position and his groping hand came in contact with the wooden side board of the bed. It came to him that he had missed no reveille, no saddled horse waited for him. He sank back on the pillow again, wondering at the way this illusion still occasionally returned to him even after seven years of peace. The fog of sleep drifted away from him and he opened his eyes and let his gaze wander around the room. Bright sun was spilling through the shutters making stripes and bars of light across the bed. His gaze came slowly to rest on Matild, still sleeping beside him. He stared at her curiously and dispassionately. Asleep, she looked like a stranger and he examined with cold detachment the way the chubby bulges of her face sagged when she slept. They looked like so many little half-filled pouches. This morning he felt no desire. When he did, he took her with his eyes shut, trying to keep himself partially in the daze of sleep. After all the years she still wept sometimes. He never comforted her.

He reached out, fumbling on the bedside table for his watch, tipping it to catch the light. Still early. Ten minutes before Ellen and Nora would carry his yellow tin tub into his dressing room. He closed his eyes, letting the fog of sleep come close to him, half listening to the sounds of the house. Someone was snapping a duster out a downstairs window. A brisk swishing noise was identifiable as Katie sweeping the stairs, and he wondered idly why women appeared to consider a dash of bad temper a necessary ingredient of good cleaning.

Various clinkings and clankings in the hall marked the progress of the two Irish girls with the tubs. These little domestic scurryings were abruptly drowned out by a hollow, thunderous noise in the hall outside his door—the stream of hot water from the cupboard taps hitting the bottom of a hot-water can. He sighed, pulled his feet over the side of the bed, sat up and rubbed his eyes. For some reason, that sound seemed to mark the official beginning of the day, the signal that tiptoeing could cease and voices need no longer be hushed. Then abruptly he realized that there really was urgency in this morning's awakening and the realization shook him a little. Sleep drained out of him altogether.

He sat still, fingers clutching the side rail of the bed, marveling that the import of the day could have slipped out of his consciousness. The meeting would be at eleven and he acknowledged to himself that he would be glad when the papers were signed, the mine his. There was something about young Hadley—(What was it the lawyers called him? Party of the second part)—that was too sharp for his liking. Backwoodsman, but with the native sense of a horse trader. He was driving a shrewd bargain.

Fenno reached out for his watch again, impatient at delay but unwilling to expose himself in his dressing room in night attire until he was assured the Irish girls had come and gone. Time dragged. Queer, how big industry sometimes went at things backwards. Here he was buying the source of the iron last. Mills first, then furnaces, then dock and ships, then a little stretch of railroad and now, last of all, the source. Busy years. Each step a triumph often hard won, but this, easiest of all since it took only credit, seemed to him the crowning achievement. It made the foundation complete. When that deal was closed, the base would be laid.

He got up and walked across the room and unlatched the shutters. Sparrows, startled away from their roosting on the acanthus leaves, flew about, circled and came back to light on the curling capital of a column.

"Shoo," he said automatically. The carvings tempted birds—a domestic problem. As he folded the shutters back into their niches in the wall, he remembered being told by the builders that foundations took longest of all. And they had to be solid. Were his? He pulled the window up and a little summer breeze blew over him, heavy laden with fragrance but laden also with soot, little round globules of it. He mashed one of them on the window sill under his finger, almost affectionately wondering if it had drifted perhaps from a stack of his mills —one of a forest of stacks along the curving shore of the glittering lake.

When he was sure that Nora and Ellen had taken their departure, he went in and began to dress methodically. He dressed with more than ordinary care, selecting the finest linen and anchoring the pearl pin in his cravat that customarily was reserved for Sundays. With the acquisition of the mines he felt he was reaching a goal; not the ultimate goal, but an important pinnacle in his career nevertheless. It was not in John Fenno to invite others to rejoice with him in his triumphs, or even to talk about them as triumphs at all, but in such private ways as this his lonely and austere nature celebrated.

He was standing before the glass, finishing a careful inspection of his perfectly fitting, if slightly somber, coat and his trousers with their muted stripes, when a commotion on the drive below drew him to the window once more. Pulling the lace curtain aside, he looked down and saw a buggy with the top down, rolling along between the petunia beds. One of the coach dogs was running beside it, barking joyously, and Fenno took mental note of this infraction of discipline. Coach dogs belonged in the coach house—never on the lawn.

One of the occupants of the buggy appeared to be Mark Sabin. Mark owned no rig of his own and now Fenno recalled suggesting that Mark could drive to the meeting with him if he liked. He had never gone to a directors' meeting before since his employer, Mr. Cushing, was himself a director. Mark had asked to be there and Fenno had told Cushing to let him come. Good training for a young lawyer. Fenno couldn't see who the other person in the buggy was and he pulled the curtains a little farther apart to find out. They were directly beneath him now, drawn up neatly in front of the red-carpeted steps. Some friend Mark got to drive him over, probably. Fenno took a second look and discovered the stranger to be a dark and rather formidable-looking young man whom he had seen with Mark once or twice before.

Fenno let the curtains fall and listened for sounds of activity in the bedroom. There were none and he opened the door. Matild lay on her back in the big bed under the carved walnut pears and grapes and stared at him expressionlessly.

"So you're awake," he said. She had no sense of time! He pulled out his hunter and snapped it open. "You'll be late again. Mark and some friend of his just drove in. They'll be wanting breakfast, I expect."

He went back into his dressing room, shut the door and stood undecided. If he went downstairs now, he would be forced to chat with Mark and this stranger until the others arrived. On the other hand, he did not want to spoil Matild by waiting for her. In the end, he picked up a copy of *Iron Age* from his table and began to turn the pages, intending to time his descent into the lower regions of the house to precede his wife by some minutes.

In the room next to her parents Willoughby lay on her side, watching through her long lashes while the Irish girls brought in her tub, but feigning sleep so she would not have to bother to say good morning. Being friendly with servants was, in her view, thoroughly middle class and she often pointed this out to her mother. Nora and Ellen, their starched uniforms rustling, were setting the high-backed tin tub on a huge piece of turkish toweling spread over the carpet. Willoughby watched in lazy comfort while they poured the contents of their tin water cans into it and set a towel, and soap in a saucer, near by. She closed her eyes when Ellen moved toward the window to open the shutters and she knew by the faint click that Nora was picking up the cup with the dregs of last night's bedtime chocolate. She heard them rustling together toward the door and suspected that, as they passed the bed, they gave her recumbent beauty a none-too-friendly look. She had the feeling they knew well enough she was awake.

When the door closed she opened her eyes. The sun was streaming slantwise in and pouring in with it were the smell of petunias and the heavy heat of the new day. She yawned and stretched luxuriously and then, throwing off the sheet, stood up with one lithe motion. She went to the mirror and peered in and smiled radiantly at what she saw. Somewhere she had read that youth had passed when a woman no longer looked alluring before her hair was brushed. This reflection of her tousled curls, her brilliant, somewhat scornful face and of her red mouth with its full, sensuous and seductive under lip was wholly satisfactory. The phrase that New York tattle sheet had used—yes—"the truly extraordinary beauty of Miss Willoughby Fenno."

Satisfied, she moved toward the window, her blue eyes bright with vitality and animal pleasure in the feel of her own body. Willoughby had more energy in her tall, beautifully rounded person than she could customarily expend, and the lack of outlet for this vigor often made her restless and irritable and on the prowl for excitement.

She looked out on the sun-parched lawn and the glittering gravel drive and sighed with annoyance. Another day of merciless heat with nothing to do but stay in the stifling, shadowy house. Another day of intolerable boredom when a few languid notes on the piano were enough to start the perspiration and not even her mother's dowdy friends came to call. She sighed again and closed the shutters a little way. Dear God, she almost envied Lettie and her eternal books.

No, she didn't. She wouldn't be Lettie—scarred up, awkward Lettie —for anything in the world. But there wasn't much advantage to being Willoughby Fenno either, not in this ugly, unstylish, backwater city. How she despised everybody in it! If she didn't escape soon . . . Exasperation was more than she could bear quietly. She left the window abruptly and, dropping into a chair in front of her dressing table, seized her brush. Not a man in the whole town was really interesting. She tossed her long hair backward and began to brush it with vigorous, sweeping strokes. Not a single man-of-the-world like the New Yorkers with their culture and their suave manners. Except Mark.

She stopped brushing and shut her eyes to think about Mark and saw him as clearly as though he were in the room with her. She saw his dark auburn hair and mustache, trimmed, as always, to perfection, and his thin body, broad of shoulder and narrow of waist, beautifully clothed in the height of fashionable taste. His amber eyes gleamed at her mockingly. Attractive, yes, when you thought about him as though you hadn't known him all your life. The brush began to move slowly. Was there anything to be gained by playing with this attraction a little, any thrill, any lifting of her boredom? Perhaps. A light shiver of physical excitement ran down her spine as she thought about his hands, thin, long-fingered and sensual.

The sensation was momentary and she swept the whole idea aside with vehemence. No solution to her problem, that. Her problem was as clear-cut in her mind as a military objective and it was not within the power of any Cleveland man, and most certainly not within the power of a young lawyer, to gratify her, however attractive he might be or however well qualified to dispel her boredom. Quite simply, she intended to marry, and so well as to insure herself an exalted position of wealth and independence. How she was to do this, cooped up in Cleveland, she did not know, but one way or another she intended to achieve this ambition—and soon.

She threw her brush with a clatter on the dressing table. Hard realist though she normally was, there was one thought which she avoided as though it were a sore spot. At twenty-two Willoughby did not like to think about her age. She skirted around the thought now, but the determination to escape her present life brought such a stubborn set to her jaw and a proud lift to her head that under her feminine beauty the resemblance to John Fenno was striking. Then, by one of those quick transitions which desperate longing makes possible, she was back in New York once more, feeling all through herself the glitter, the warmth and the excitement.

The sensation was only brief and a dark chilling shadow fell across the remembered glitter. She stood behind a portière in the house of her mother's friend, listening with drawn-in breath. They had not heard her step on the soft carpet, Mrs. Tilden and some unknown friend, but she knew at once by the lowered voices that they were discussing her.

"I'm sorry for Matild, really I am. I thought it would be so nice for Willoughby and our Annabelle to come out together—such friends at school —and the Fennos were most generous about the expenses of the ball, you know, because they saw at once the advantages of a New York season. But do you know, my dear, she attracts the wrong type of men, altogether the wrong type? She's so sort of full-blown and, well—lavish. The nice young men are afraid of her and the ones that aren't—elderly roués—positively, my dear. A very bad influence for our Annabelle. I'm sure I wish—if it hadn't been for their generosity . . ."

She began to dress hastily, as though by hurrying she could run away from her own thoughts. The image of Mark returned to her and this time it caused a ripple of unmistakable anticipation.

About the time she was adding the last quick, but expert, touches to her costume, Mark Sabin and Mike Brodi were putting their hats on the hall table and in these two dissimilar headpieces were to be seen many of the extremely dissimilar characteristics of their owners. Mark's was new, glossy and well brushed, and in the lining was the label of one of the best hatters in the country. It was tall to the point of being a trifle extreme, and the brim had a curve that was so dashing and at the same time so subtle in line as to make it unmistakably the hat of a man of the world. The luster of this hat was conservative but the material was patently expensive. Mike's hat came from nowhere in particular, was gray in color and had a low crown. Its shape had been undistinguished when it was new and it had acquired, with time, an even greater degree of shapelessness from having frequently been clapped on the head with too much emotional vigor.

The hands that laid them down were as dissimilar as the hats. Mike's fingers were short and strong, his palms broad and his nails cut straight. Mark's fingers were long and tapering and on the backs of his hands grew faint auburn hair. The nails were manicured into perfect ovals and buffed to a delicate sheen. They were clever hands, such as one might expect to find belonging to a professional gambler on the Mississippi river boats rather than to a young business lawyer.

Mark raised one of these long, but not in the least effeminate, hands and passed it over his auburn hair, looking sidewise as he did so into the hall mirror. Mark's hair was conservatively brushed this morning, in deference to the serious nature of the meeting, but he still wore it in the Paris way, so strange to Cleveland. This involved a long part from his crown to the nape of his neck from which the hair was brought forward, with the suggestion of a curl above his ears.

Brodi watched him with the amusement of a man to whom personal appearance means little. "I'm curious about this uncle of yours," he said.

"He isn't really an uncle, you know. Some sort of cousin."

"Well, whatever he is. I found out the other day that his Finnish dock hands are underpaid outrageously, compared to what other types of workers are getting. And they're overworked."

"So I suppose you are going to write one of your articles about them."

"I'm thinking about it."

"What on earth do you do it for? Articles like that don't pay and they don't help your confounded cause much, do they?"

"Not enough—but one of these days I think I'll take a more direct part."

"Labor leader?"

"Something like that."

Brodi was, as a matter of fact, already taking a more direct part, though he did not think it wise to confide in his friend Mark, and he had welcomed the chance to come here and make his own estimate of John Fenno.

Mark laughed. "You always were a queer bird, even in college. Wait for me in the living room, will you? I want to look over the papers I brought with me. The living room's in there—Willoughby calls it the drawing room. You'll probably find a newspaper around somewhere." Mark gave Brodi's square back a little shove.

Mark had no intention of looking over papers. His quick ear had caught the sound of someone singing softly at the top of the stairs and he knew it was Willoughby, for no one else in this house ever sang. For some time now, Mark had been a prey to the uneasy feeling that Fate was pushing him nearer and nearer to this girl. He was not in love with her. There was a detached part of him which kept him from being wholly in love with anyone; but debts, a great many of them, hard work, which he loathed, and lack of the luxuries which he loved pointed with inexorable logic to the advantages of marrying this heiress. Everything in him that was solitary, secretive and egotistical rebelled, but he had made up his mind, without committing himself to anything, even in his thoughts, to try his best to stir romantic feelings in her.

He struck a gallant pose at the bottom of the stairs, one slim foot advanced. He might have had a plumed hat in his hand. Gazing upward, he wondered whether she would be perceptive enough to detect anything new in his manner toward her.

She stopped singing when she reached the turn of the landing and saw him, and she smiled. She had a trick of turning on the full power of her beauty suddenly, and she did so now as she slowed her pace and came down almost languidly, as though to allow him time to admire the full perfection of her figure. His heart began to beat fast. Something electric, something which had never been in their relationship before, passed between them. He smiled and stretched out his hand to her.

To his astonishment she held out both of hers in a gesture that had in it a suggestion of surrender.

"Mark!"

It was a throaty sound with a thrilling quality that made his amber eyes flicker, and he forgot to reply because this was not at all the tone one used to greet a person who had always been almost one of the family. She laughed and gave his fingers a little squeeze.

"I'm glad we're alone," she said.

He came out of his daze. "We're not really, I regret to say. There's a friend of mine in the drawing room."

"Oh."

She came down the last step and started off, not toward the drawing room but toward the wide arch which led into the dining room, and he followed her, puzzled and a little fascinated.

The great dining room was deserted and the long table was set for breakfast under its protecting shroud of mosquito netting. The servants waited in the kitchen for the bell to call them to morning prayers. A faint smell of fried things which hung in the air in the midst of the room's grandeur offended Mark's sense of fitness.

She crossed the room to a corner well out of sight of the door, where a monstrous dish cupboard rose, tier on ornate tier to the ornate plaster ceiling. Here she turned around and faced him. She was laughing silently and her blue eyes were full of mockery and challenge. Her beauty had a shimmering, pulsating quality, an eagerness and vitality that almost took his breath. He snatched her hands and, raising them, buried his face in their palms. They were soft and perfumed and he felt desire stir in him. He noted the desire, as one might note a symptom, with interest and pleasure.

It was a long minute before he straightened up, holding her hands in fingers which were trembling a little. She was still smiling but the mockery was gone and an avid excitement had taken its place. They stared silently at each other. Both were filled with the strangeness of this love-making and of the excitement which, after all these years, they were finding in each other.

"It seems almost wicked, doesn't it?" she whispered.

"Don't spoil it by talk," he said, and took her in his arms.

Mike strolled into the drawing room, his hands in his pockets, and just inside the door he stopped to emit a low whistle. An amazing room—and one such as an assistant professor in a country college was not likely to encounter often. The colors were rich and dark—cobalt, plum, crimson, green and royal purple. He let his gaze wander from the oxblood-red vase with the three peacock feathers, to the Japanese fans on the draped mantel, to the dark green and heavily embroidered throw on the piano, to the Roman emperor's head etched on the glass globes of the gasolieres, to the eggplant curtains with their rich borders, to the woodwork lacquered maroon and black and gold below a Pompeian frieze.

Most of the furniture in the room was in the style which was just beginning to emerge under the name of "new Gothic," and its design was certainly more new than Gothic. It was, in fact, so very new that there was not another room like this in all of Cleveland. The tables were carved and gilded and inlaid. The chairs had little relation to the demands of the human anatomy, and they were upholstered in crushed velvet with what seemed to Mike a repelling plethora of buttons and tassels. Among these intricate objects, and as though put there to demonstrate a cultural breadth, were placed what Willoughby called "Louis pieces" and the whole was seasoned with various classical motifs and objects suggestive of the First Empire. In spite of these warring elements, the room had elegance, but as Brodi looked at it his face darkened. The cost of such a room would, perhaps, keep ten, no, nearer twenty, working families for a year. "My God," he thought, "I don't suppose I spent as much in a whole year at college as this fancy carpet probably cost."

Mike Brodi was an American of one generation's standing. Before that the blood was Polish and it still showed strongly on him. His most characteristic feature was his hair, which was the despair of the barber, for it was thick and wiry. It was cut straight across; indeed, there was nothing else that could be done with it, and the effect on top was rather like a section of black door mat.

When he finished his inspection of the room he went to stand in front of an elaborate, inlaid bookcase. This monumental piece of furniture was full of expensive tooled sets and covered by an ornamental brass grille, which his prying fingers discovered to be locked. At the moment when Brodi was squinting through the grille in an attempt to read titles, Lettie Fenno, upstairs in her room, seized a towel and patted her wet back hair. It was wet because, as she lay in her tub, she had been imagining herself to be the Lady of Shalott floating down the river in her barge. It made it seem more real to lie as flat as she could, even though, the tub being short, she had to hump up her knees to get her head down. She finished dressing, gave her flounces a shake, seized the book which was propped up on her dressing table and ran helter skelter down the stairs because she was still young enough to enjoy running for its own sake.

At the bottom of the stairs she stopped and her face took on a dreamy, almost rapturous look. She clasped the book to her flat chest and approached the drawing room with a curious slow motion that was a sort of bumpy glide and represented her idea of a stately tread. For this was not Lettie Fenno but the Princess Imogene, clasping white lilies to her breast, trailing her white Samite robes, and a knight in shining armor waited in the courtyard of her dreams.

Brodi took his hands out of his pockets and stared at her in astonishment. She gazed at this black knight and, clasping her lilies that were no whiter than her white arms, she murmured graciously in a voice like the soft sound of a woodland brook, "How do you *do?*"

"Hullo," said Black Mike, and continued to stare.

What he saw was a rather tall girl who might have been good-looking if it had not been for a long scar which ran from the outside corner of her left eye nearly to her mouth, and for a sullen, discontented look that was even more disfiguring than the scar. Her hair was brown, without much luster because she never brushed it enough. Her eyebrows met in a downward line across the bridge of her nose, giving her an almost angry look. She had the prominent Fenno under lip, but, instead of its being seductive and exciting, like Willoughby's, it was merely petulant. The hands that clasped her book so tightly were big and the sleeves of her ugly striped poplin dress were too short in the wrists. Her figure was good but her posture was affected by self-pity and boredom and sullenness and, because she had left off her hoops, her dress hung around her in draggled shapelessness.

All this Brodi saw, and under his bright stare, Lettie began to see it also. A slow and painful flush crept upward from her neck and burned unbecomingly in her cheeks. She began to turn her head stealthily to one side until the scar was hidden from Brodi's inquisitive black eyes.

"You can't be Willoughby," Brodi said.

She shook her head and gulped.

"Who are you, then?" This sudden seizure of self-consciousness disgusted one who did not know the meaning of the word.

"Leticia," she mumbled.

"Let—— What?"

"Lettie."

"Oh, yes. I guess Mark mentioned you, too."

From her quagmire of awkwardness she cast him a swift, upward look. She never looked at anybody directly but always upward, like this, from bent head, or sidelong with the scarred side of her face turned away. There was both admiration and misery in her eyes, though Brodi was not perceptive enough to see either, and she only embarrassed him a little without his understanding why.

"Nice place you've got here," he said conversationally. "Quite a room."

She looked around her blankly, as though she had never seen it before. Her mouth hung a little open and the flush came back to her face.

"I hate it!"

"This room?"

"No! The whole house. Everything. Everything!"

"Why, for goodness' sake?"

"It's hateful. Everything about it. I just hate it all."

The glitter in Mike's eyes grew hard with dislike. "I see. The bird in the gilded cage. Poor little rich girl. Too bad."

"It isn't that at all." Lettie Fenno saw herself so clearly in her dreams, and she felt that if only others would pay tribute to this true and beautiful inner self, then she could be gracious and charming. They failed, however, to see below the surface of Lettie Fenno and she became cross and sullen and moody. For this she felt that they and not herself were to blame. Nobody understood. Nobody! Her lips began to tremble.

"Being sorry for yourself isn't going to help. Unless you enjoy it— and I rather suspect you do."

"I don't enjoy it. That isn't fair. Besides . . ."

Lettie stopped, at a loss. No one had ever before challenged her right to be sorry for herself. That was the rock on which her whole nature was founded. Everybody she knew was sorry for her. They showed it, too, by all sorts of overkindness, which she dreaded but which fed her self-pity and made her dramatize herself. All but Willoughby, who nagged and nagged, but even Willoughby never made any direct reference to the scar.

Not at all remorsefully, Mike said: "Why do you keep your books locked up? Doesn't anybody read them?"

"Not those."

"What, then?" He reached out and took the book from her hands, *"The Fading Flower.* Is this the sort of thing you read?"

"It's a very beautiful romance."

"I bet. And you see yourself as the lovely but put-upon heroine who sacrifices all for love, dripping sentiment from every page!"

"I think you're simply horrid." She said it with so much spirit that

Mike raised his black eyebrows in surprise. Stepping past him with the scarred side of her face averted, she flounced down on the window seat and opened her book. Mike continued his inspection of the room exactly as though she were not there, sauntering around with his hands in his pockets and whistling faintly to himself. From time to time she stole a glance at him from under her sullen brows.

It was so that Mark found them when he strolled in, leaving Willoughby in front of the hall mirror, patting her hair.

"What a nice friendly scene," he said. "Have you two met?"

"No," said Lettie.

"Yes," said Mike.

Mark laughed. "Miss Lettie Fenno—she much prefers to be called Leticia, but her name is really Lettie—let me present Michael Brodi, affectionately known to his students, because of his winning charm, as Black Mike."

2

IN SPITE of John's admonitions, Matild was late for breakfast. She was often late, but not, as is usually the case with the chronically tardy, because she was either lazy or inconsiderate. It was only that time slipped through her fingers so easily and so unperceived.

At the top of the stairs she ran her finger along the banister rail and examined it for traces of dust. None appeared. Then the pattern of the carpet caught her attention and she stood still, regarding it with pleasure. She liked this carpet. It had a pattern of roses, many full-blown roses, intricately involved with a brown geometric design on a green ground. She liked to trace the curves and angles of the brown design, following it where it dived under the garlands of flowers and emerged again.

She had supervised the laying of the carpet herself—stood by while the workmen prepared the bed of rustling yellow straw, knee high, before they commenced to flatten it down. Now the carpet lay flat as it should, in the center of the passageway and down the middle of the stairs, but around the edges, where fewer feet passed, it still was humped up a little. Matild pressed one of the humped-up places with her foot and heard the straw under the carpet crackle. Whenever she could, she walked on these uneven places to flatten them, and now she began the descent of the stairs, walking slowly and precariously, as near the wall as possible.

On the landing she paused. Here was a long window seat with a dozen or more potted plants in saucers. Matild touched each one in turn, feeling the earth with her finger, turning each pot slightly to catch the light from a new angle and breaking off here and there a yellow leaf. At the exact center of the window seat stood a dome of glass which had once covered a clock on a mantel shelf and had since been converted into a Wardian case enclosing the delicate foliage of a tropical fern.

Matild leaned over the dome and peered inside. The miniature tropic world enchanted her. Large drops of moisture were gathering inside on the top of the dome. Later in the day they would fall, a tiny rainstorm, on the fern below. The case created its own weather. Matild thought that real rainstorms must be like that—drops of moisture gathering overhead on the blue dome of the sky.

She raised the glass of the case a little and sniffed with pleasure the smell of damp earth. She wondered why they were called Wardian cases. It was a new name. They were always called sweatferns when she was young, but Willoughby objected to that as inelegant. She didn't quite see why, any more than she understood why they all laughed when, forgetting the new name, she referred to it as her perspiration fern.

Reluctantly, Matild turned and continued her way down the stairs, the yellowed geranium leaves still clutched in her hand. When Matild was by herself she often became dreamy and slack, as though she undid some restraining hooks inside herself and let herself bulge comfortably. Her eyes never lost their look of strain nor her cheeks their deeply graven lines, but these things became filmed over with a transparent coating of a vague and rather wistful pleasure in the moment. Thus unhooked, she wandered slowly into the drawing room and was startled to see all the faces around her.

"Oh," she said, "oh, is everybody down? Am I late?" The little pouches in her face drew up and she hurried the last few steps, struggling to bring the invisible hooks together.

John Fenno scarcely gave her time to find her place. He stood by the mantle with the worn prayer book already open in his hand, and he began reading almost as soon as she came in.

"Almighty and everlasting God in whom we live and move and have our being . . ."

She rested a hand on the edge of the rosewood tête-à-tête and let herself down on her knees, heavily and awkwardly. The words were so wearily familiar. Before she composed herself to listen, she reached behind her and tucked the crumpled yellow geranium leaves into one of the many loops and swags of drapery that covered her hoop in a bunch behind. So wearily familiar, her husband's voice.

"To Thy watchful providence we owe it that no disturbance hath come nigh us or our dwelling; but that we are brought in safety to the beginning of this day."

Suddenly she was filled with a wave of hatred for her husband's powerful, sonorous and compelling tones. She knew so well just where the dramatic pauses would be inserted, just where the telling change would come, all so meaninglessly and hatefully well done.

". . . humbly beseeching Thee . . ."

Humbly! No one ever demanded grace with more assurance, more certainty of his right. It seemed to her that she could not endure one minute more of the lengthy prayers.

". . . for His sake who lay down in the grave and rose again . . ."

The first prayer was coming to an end. "Amen," she said crisply.

"But since it is Thy mercy . . ."

The second prayer. She tried not to listen. She slid her hand over her eyes and peered out beneath it at her kneeling family.

Lettie knelt like a child, with her elbows on the seat of a chair, her hands clasped and her eyes tightly shut. "She looks well from this side," Matild thought. "If it weren't for that scar she'd be almost pretty—only her skin is too yellow and her mouth droops so. Oh, dear. Why, her back hair is wet again. It was wet yesterday too. Whatever is she doing? I must speak to her. Oh, dear."

A part of Matild's mind listened to the resounding prayers. "Amen," she said mechanically in the right place and shifted her gaze to the stranger in their midst. "He's rather odd-looking," Matild thought. "What curious hair—all bristly and standing up straight. It looks as though it would scratch. I wonder if he would be interested in Lettie? It would be so nice if only somebody would."

Matild's eyes wandered away and fell on Mark. He was kneeling very straight and his head was only bowed slightly. His eyes were amber slits veiled by his long lashes and he was watching Willoughby, who was putting on a nearly perfect show of not being aware of it. There was something sensual and appraising about his look that, just to watch, gave Matild a tingling sensation and made her feel a vague shame. She had just begun to worry, though she was not quite sure about what, when prayers came to an end. John Fenno shut the prayer book with a clap, put it on the draped mantle shelf and, without further word to anybody, stalked off to the dining room. The others followed in a straggling procession.

John Fenno did not regard a meal as something to be enjoyed, except for a certain restrained appreciation of the quality of the food. Meals were simply occasions when the annoyances caused him by various members of his family were inescapably concentrated in one place, and so he stood behind his chair, waiting for his slow wife to be seated, with an air of martyrdom and without troubling to conceal his impatience.

The elation of his morning mood was gone, crowded away little by little by petty irritations that mostly had to do with Matild's ineptitudes. It was no new experience. He watched her pudgy hands disposing her ridiculous bundle of draperies with cold intolerance. They were all waiting behind their chairs and steam was rising from the oatmeal bowls all around the table. She was smiling in a kind of shallow, placid enjoyment of the moment, apparently oblivious that all their eyes were on her. She laid her hand with its puffy, short fingers on the table and twisted around to look up at Brodi, who was waiting to give her chair a final shove.

"I knew some Moodys in Boston when I was a girl. I wonder if they could be any relation of yours?"

Fenno felt a tension of exasperation that amounted to torture and some of the same feeling was expressed on Willoughby's face.

"Brodi, Mother, for goodness' sake!"

Matild looked reproachfully at her daughter and her lips worked as though she longed to reprove her, but she glanced up at the rather startling black and white face above her and her easy smile returned. "Excuse me, Mr. Brodi. I thought you might be. They came from Newton. No, it wasn't Newton, it was Newburyport. They were spending the winter in Boston. I forget why. I think we met at a church bazaar, but I forget for sure." She smiled vaguely.

Fenno clutched the sides of his chair and raised harassed eyes to Willoughby. They exchanged a deep look. Willoughby put her hand over her·mother's.

"We're all waiting, Mama." She pronounced it carefully, with the accent on the last syllable.

They sat down and Fenno picked up his porridge spoon and pulled his newspaper toward him with a sense of having gone through a physical ordeal. Morning after morning he faced the ugliness, the stupidity that finally reduced him to this detestable state of futile anger for which he hated himself and, hating, blamed her the more. Her faintly querulous voice broke in on him.

"John, may I have the horses today? I need to match some lace and . . ."

"No!" He dropped his spoon and clutched his napkin in both hands. Ah, he had hurt her. He watched her lips move and the familiar slight backward jerk of her head—as though you were thrusting her grievance too close into her face. He hadn't meant to speak so sharply. Well, no matter. But why, in God's name, need she get herself up to look like a half-filled sack of grain?

They were all chattering about something and he began to read the financial news, finding it, as he expected, highly satisfactory and restorative. Feeling better, he laid the paper down, seized a piece of corn bread, crumbled it into a saucer and urged a languid stream of maple syrup over it. Thanks to the financial upsurge reflected in the paper, he was savoring again the sense of adequacy and power that was his familiar relation with himself away from wife and home.

He spooned up the corn bread neatly and efficiently, keeping an eye on the folded paper. A minor headline caught his attention, and he stopped eating and frowned. The headline read, "Prosperity to End." He read the article through and looked up. Matild was launched on one of her interminable reminiscences of Boston; the rest were more or less listening. He looked at her hard until she felt his eyes and her monologue died away.

"Mark, listen to this. It says here 'In Wall Street men shake their heads at values and scrutinize the public credit. It is time to reef sail, they say, to get out of debt, to cast anchor and await the coming storm.' They haven't talked to us, eh?" Amusement crinkled the corners of his eyes.

Brodi looked up with quick interest. "It says that, does it? I've begun to think the same thing myself. I gather you don't?"

Ellen touched Fenno's shoulder with the edge of the large platter in her hands. He glanced at her, hastily captured the last drop of syrup, set the saucer aside and turned to examine the platter full of browned fish.

"These the trout I sent to Castalia for, Ellen?"

"Yes, sir."

"Good."

Waiting for his answer, Brodi thought he would probably never see anything more characteristic of Fenno than the careful choice of fish based on quality, the precise removal of the bones, the thorough buttering of the two halves. Portrait of a man paying tribute to value, he thought, and was abruptly conscious of the thickness of the carpet under his feet, the weight of the silver in his hand and the sheen of damask. His mild curiosity about an impressively rich and successful man curdled slightly with dislike.

Fish attended to, Fenno veered on him.

"I'll tell you about hard times, Mr. Brodi. There'll soon be no more of them. It's the natural course of civilization. We used to have famines —then the civilized world switched from agriculture alone to industry, and where there used to be famines there were hard times. Now hard times are on the way out. Why? Because industry is organizing into big corporations that can make things so cheap the whole world will want to buy—and supplying jobs so they *can* buy."

There was a general silence and Fenno regarded Michael with tolerant amusement.

"You in business, Brodi?"

"No, I teach history at Western Reserve in Hudson."

"Teacher, are you? History? History's changing. Being made by presidents of corporations and partners of banking houses now, instead of kings and generals." Interested in his own thought, Fenno leaned forward and put his fist on the table. "Who's back of war? Businessmen. Who's back of politics? Businessmen. They'll be the ones you'll have to teach about in future."

"I doubt it, Mr. Fenno."

Fenno raised an eyebrow, amused. "Why?" The gratifying thought had just come to him that he himself might reasonably be classed as one of the history-makers. Surely so, given a few more years.

"You forget human nature, sir."

"Human nature!"

Brodi smiled involuntarily. It seemed to him that Fenno could not have expressed more clearly in an hour of talking his doubts of that uncertain commodity.

"Yes, sir, human nature. The businessman will never appeal to whatever it is in people that makes them put up statues to history-book heroes. In fact, come to think of it, almost the only kind of success the world isn't just a little bit suspicious of is heroism and valor, and their suspicions of success in business and finance I take to be proverbial."

Fenno looked at him sharply and Brodi returned the look equably enough. Unable to discover malice, Fenno abandoned the conversation. Brodi, however, had more to say.

"The history of the future is going to be influenced by a different force. It's been gaining strength year by year. I'm talking about labor, Mr. Fenno, and the growing strength of labor, though you and I may not live to see history shaped for the common good of the common man."

Fenno gave him a brief look of contempt. There was some proverb

—folding his napkin and twisting it into the ring, he groped for it— Those who can, do. Those who can't, teach. Exactly! He stood up.

"Get up, Mark. It's time to go. Important day, my lad."

Outside the front door, heat and the heavy smell of petunias enveloped Mark and Fenno. At the bottom of the red-carpeted steps the shiny sides of the carriage gleamed conservatively. Sounds of altercation came from within—Matild's voice, which rose high and plaintive, as on the rare occasions when she was roused to real anger. The door flew open and Lettie burst out.

"Papa!"

"Well?" She was red in the face and the long scar scarcely showed.

"Papa, Mr. Brodi said he'd drive me downtown to get Mama's lace and Willoughby got Mama to say I couldn't go. It isn't *fair*. I can go, can't I, Papa? Can't I, Papa?"

"Lettie!"

"Please, Papa, it isn't *fair*."

"Go in the house at once."

"But . . ."

Abruptly Fenno seized her by the arm, whirled her around and thrust her through the door.

"We've spoiled her, Mark," he said, starting down the steps again, "because of that scar. It's got to stop. She'll have to learn to act like other people. Too bad, with your friend Brodi here." The high-pitched altercation was still going on inside. He closed his ears to it determinedly and marched down the steps.

" 'Morning, Joe. Going to be hot."

"It's hot already, sir, if you ask me!"

The front door opened a second time and Willoughby came out.

"Papa, just a minute, please."

He climbed in the carriage, sat down and faced her.

"Well?" How pretty she looked standing there in her frilly white dress on the red carpet! So all of a piece. No loose ends to *her*. Something resembling a smile settled on his face.

"Papa, Lettie ought not to go downtown alone with Mr. Brodi, do you think? And Mama says she can't spare Ellen this morning. I mean, isn't it time we stopped going out without a maid like anybody's children?"

"I don't know, Willoughby, is it?" Fenno was amused.

Willoughby threw up her hands in a mock helpless gesture and her dimples appeared. "Mama says it's just one of my Eastern notions, like dinner at night and gloves in summer, and she'd thank me to let her run her house and manage her own daughter and, besides, who's going to do Ellen's *work?*"

She laughed and Fenno laughed with her, for the mimicry was excellent. Mark sat quiet. The greatest drawback to romance for him had always been a certain detachment that made him observant of flaws and there was, now and again, a crudity in Willoughby, in spite of all her style.

"I should think you'd be qualified to know about such things, Willoughby. Get on, Joe."

Willoughby flipped a hand and a bright smile at them. "I'll tell her, then."

A picture of her standing there went with Fenno all the way downtown.

Inside, Matild and Mike were alone in the dining room. Mike drained the last of his coffee and put the cup down firmly on the saucer. He felt he must break away.

"It was nice of you to have me for breakfast," he said. Then, because he felt sorry for this feckless fat woman with the strained look about her eyes, he tried to please her by saying, "Miss Willoughby is very beautiful, Mrs. Fenno." Actually, he had disliked the girl on sight and so, characteristically, he tried to neutralize the compliment by adding, "Where did she get that extraordinary name?"

The pale eyes blinked at him and to his consternation the look of strain was intensified.

"My husband and I couldn't agree on a name, Mr. Moody. We couldn't agree at all. My husband is a stern man. I wanted to name my baby girl after my own dear mother. Her name was Verity."

Matild paused and Mike saw that her eyes were swimming with easy tears. Not knowing what to say, he said nothing and presently she sniffed and went on.

"He thought that was old-fashioned and—and not worldly enough. I used to try to resist him sometimes, in those days. We were going somewhere on a train just after she was born and we were arguing about it. Suddenly he got very angry and he said we'd name her after the very next station the conductor called out. It was Willoughby."

Mike crumpled up his napkin and rose. "Well," he said with forced cheerfulness, "you should be thankful, really. It might have been Ashtabula."

She turned her face up to him. She looked vague and a little frightened. She never was able to recognize humor. "Yes," she said. "I suppose so. I suppose it *might* have been Ashtabula—but nothing like that ever happens to my husband."

3

MARK SABIN was an Episcopalian, a Republican and a member of the Union Club. All these things he had become because they offered the greatest personal advantages and for no other reason at all. Mark seldom had any other reason for doing anything.

The fact that he was not well off was his most constant preoccupation, and he intended to remedy that defect by any means in his power. The law firm where he lent his able, if reluctant, assistance was the kind usually described as "old and established," a term which did not imply durability so much as it reflected the fact that its leading light, Mr. Cushing, had a long and honorable career behind him. Mark was uncomfortably aware of the lack of permanence in a situation such as this and he had begun to look, with furtive shrewdness, for a way to better his position.

The mill was, of course, the logical place for the meteoric career which Mark envisioned. He frowned, thinking about John Fenno's repeated refusals to take him into Fenno and Company in any capacity. When he thought about the alternative, marrying the glittering Willoughby, he had even now, and in spite of the stimulating interlude with her before breakfast, what Matild would have called a "gone" feeling in the pit of his concave stomach. He was already beginning to suffer from a certain amount of reaction, inevitable in a man who valued his freedom so highly. Moreover, on reflection, Willoughby's motives were not at all clear to him. He was enough of a realist to see that she was most certainly not in love and to suspect that marrying her might not prove so simple as her behavior had implied.

He sighed, put these thoughts away from him and gave himself up to the enjoyment of the moment, which is to say, the enjoyment of Mark in the setting of the moment. Driving with his uncle was always agreeable. He crossed his legs and dropped one tapering hand gracefully on his knee. Thus posed, he allowed himself the pleasurable awareness that they made an imposing appearance. The carriage top was folded back, exposing them to public envy, the cockade on Joe's hat stuck up with style and the sun shone on them benignly, if a little warmly. The beautiful, matched grays stepped high and the silver mountings on their harness shone. At the rear axle two spotted carriage dogs trotted. They might have been slaves chained to a chariot. Their heads were down and their red tongues hung out, and there was a grimness about them, as though they know the journey would be both long and dusty.

Mark tipped his hat a little farther over his eyes and glanced at John Fenno. A remarkable man to have given up his directorships and his interest in the wagon company that was making such a good thing out of the Western trek. He seemed to have come home from the war with fresh vigor, in spite of middle age. A remarkable man to have seen and seized opportunity the way he had, as though he had brought back from the Georgia campaign a special vision, and Mark asked suddenly, "What gave you the idea of going into the iron business, Uncle John? You never told me."

John Fenno pulled himself away from his own thoughts and a look of remembrance came into his eyes and softened them.

"Something General Sherman said. He was a great man. I was on his staff, you know."

"Was? He isn't dead, is he?"

"No, but a soldier can only become great in time of war. He said something like that himself, once. He's a queer man, too. I never quite understood him. It was one dark night when I was sitting in front of my tent and I heard someone groping around. Then a voice said, 'Is that you, Fenno? Got a match?' I lit the match and there stood the General in his long underwear with a big cigar in his mouth.

"We sat and talked and he said something like what I've just told you and that in the affairs of almost every man there is a tide which, taken at its flood . . . He said that, after the war, the country would be full of opportunities for making fortunes and that if a man could pick a tide which would rise high and roll far—I thought about that all through the rest of the campaign and then one day, the day of the Victory Parade of the Armies of the West in Washington, the idea came to me. I was waiting for the parade to start and passing the time by looking at some of the big guns built for the defense of Washington but never used. I got to thinking what a quantity of iron and steel-making facilities had been developed during the war and that they would be idle for a brief time—just long enough for a man to buy in advantageously, and then, with the growing West, the country would begin clamoring for iron. That's how it was."

"Interesting," Mark murmured, and silence descended on the pair.

The streets through which they passed had now degenerated into a dirty industrial district interspersed with weedy vacant lots. Beyond this in turn the carriage left the plank road, turned North and bumped and swayed over the dusty ruts of Mill Street. Here the Finnish dock hands, who kept themselves away from other nationalities, had built their shacks. Comfortable riding on Mill Street was impossible and both men were forced to sit up straight and grip the sides of the carriage. It was a physical relief to reach the end and turn into a cinder wagon road that wound along the top of the bluff above the lake and linked Fenno and Company with other industries closer to the center of the city. This road skirted a small, jaded and sooty park, a sporadic bit of civic planning already doomed by the demands of Cleveland's mushroom growth of industry for access to the lake front.

Mark pulled a monogrammed handkerchief from his pocket and fastidiously wiped the dust of Mill Street from his face and hands. The park was composed of stilted rockeries made from an unpleasant gray stone, rustic bridges with bark peeling off, and discouraged, un-natural-looking bedding plants set out in circles and half-moons and stars. The whole thing sloped rather perilously down to the railroad tracks and the glittering lake beyond, and Mark, pleased with the superiority of his artistic taste, felt that he would rather enjoy tipping it, like the shelf of an overloaded what-not, and watching the knick-knacks go tumbling down.

A freight train rumbled by on the tracks at the foot of the slope some hundreds of yards below them. The horses pointed their ears at it, pranced a little, but decided against making a real fuss and continued their way with slightly heightened mannerisms. Over the rumble of the empty cars Mark could hear the scream of the brakes as the train slowed for the siding at Fenno and Company.

These transitions seemed to have jolted John Fenno out of his preoccupation. Mark ventured on more conversation.

"What sort of fellow is this Sam Hadley, Uncle John?"

"Hadley? Oh, rough, I should say." Fenno seldom described people. They affected you favorably or unfavorably. They got in your way and they had to be brushed aside, or they were just there. In either case, the reason why they were that way did not matter and was certainly not of sufficient interest to talk about.

"Uncouth?"

"Some sort of schooling, I think. Didn't ask."

"Quite something to get left all that mine land." Mark spoke enviously, thinking about his unpaid bills. "His old man was just a trapper or a prospector or something like that, I hear. I wonder if he came by it honestly."

"Couldn't say. Title's clear—or Cushing says it is. *You* ought to know. Don't forget to check over your papers before the meeting. Have them in order."

"There aren't many. Mr. Whittlesey has the minutes. I have the sales agreement here." Mark touched his pocket. Whenever he could he avoided carrying the green baize bag, badge of the lawyer. "Mr. Cushing has his own copy. I have some extras."

"Extras? What for?"

"Mr. Cushing thought the Board might like to study them."

"Keep 'em out of sight. They've already agreed to the purchase. No use letting them reconsider. No reason why they should. I intend to run it through fast."

"All right, I'll hide 'em and warn the Chief. It was his idea."

"Cushing!" said Fenno, making the name sound derogatory. Cushing was the kind of lawyer who was half-pastor, half-doctor. His attitude was beginning to irk Fenno more and more. Mark did not miss the intonation.

They rode on in silence until they reached the door of the new red-brick office building which fronted on the lake. They stepped down with dignity. On the front steps Fenno stopped and, shading his eyes with his hand, gazed westward along the lake. The glitter of the sun on the water made it hard to see very far.

"Expecting an ore boat, Uncle John?"

"Yes, the *Willoughby Fenno* is due any time now. We're behind schedule and if the lakes close early . . . Sail is too slow, Mark. There won't be any left in the ore trade in a few years." He went inside and briskly climbed the stairs to his office. Mark, assuming a busy look, hurried toward the directors' room. Half-a-dozen frock-coated directors were already present, men of substance, having to Mark's observant eye a generic resemblance to each other and, Mark thought with satisfaction, the indefinable caste mark that he hoped was visible also upon himself. No one paid the slightest attention to Mark and he took a chair by the wall, not feeling entitled to one at the table, and sat stroking his mustache with one finger and watching the scene around him. Cushing was not present, but Whittlesey sat at one side of the long table, sorting papers into piles. "Funny old codger," Mark thought, watching with amusement while Whittlesey licked his thumb, picked up a piece of paper, hovered with it over this pile and that, and deposited it somewhere without conviction. "I don't believe he knows what goes on around him half the time. Rabbity. But a good Secretary-Treasurer, nevertheless. Completely under the weight of John Fenno's thumb, and pliable."

More directors were coming in, all men whom Mark knew by sight and reputation, and, enlivened by a new thought, he scrutinized them. Most of them were pliable—more or less. First-rank names, but first-rank men? Not quite, perhaps. If you were a John Fenno, was that altogether wise? Was it better to have a Board you could dominate, trusting to your own judgment alone, or a Board that would think for itself and might, as a corollary, be difficult to handle? But dismiss the thought. No point in questioning the technique of a success as brilliant as John Fenno's. These men all seemed to be a bit keyed up, and no wonder. Stimulating to find yourself a director of what was rapidly becoming one of the greatest iron companies in the country.

"Exception," Mark thought, gazing at the little man who stood in the doorway. "General Thatcher is neither pliable nor second-rate. I swear he wears lifts in his shoes. And I'd wager most of the people here think he's just the apple-cheeked little runt he appears to be— but look at those eyes." The General's eyes were not easy to look at, for he hid them carefully under his lids and disguised them with the merry wrinkles at the corners.

Cushing succeeded the General in the doorway, where he stood, baize bag in hand, peering about. "No generic resemblance there," Mark thought. "He's different from the other directors." Cushing's face bore traces of another kind of aristocracy, and his thin, delicate features and his Boston intonations set him apart as more cultured, more precise and more scholarly than the other men in the room. These traits manifested themselves even in the pince-nez he wore. They perched lightly on the thin bridge of his nose like a glass butterfly, conveying the impression that it was possible for them to remain there only because this was a man of controlled passions.

Mark knew that these glasses played a subtle role in his employer's relations with people. Seen through them, Cushing's eyes appeared to be keen and intelligent, but when he took them off, his eyes lost their brilliance, for without them he could not see. Then the world became private, himself enclosed in a mist in which faces were indistinguishable. Sometimes he found life easier when he could not see faces, and so he had formed the habit of taking them off whenever life pressed on him too greatly or whenever he found it necessary to express views likely to be received combatively.

Cushing took a chair at one end of the room. Mark, suspecting he was wanted, put himself in line of vision and was beckoned.

"Sit down, Mark. I want to talk to you." Cushing leaned forward and spoke guardedly. "I don't like this thing. The Company has too many commitments already. I've made up my mind to appeal to the Board not to carry it through."

"But, Mr. Cushing . . ." There was consternation in Mark's face and voice. With haste he modified them, remembering he was speaking to his employer, then, remembering he was also a member of the Fenno family, he frowned as disapprovingly as possible. "Uncle John already knows you disapprove, doesn't he?"

"My views have carried no weight with him."

"But, Mr. Cushing, surely . . ." A whole panorama of disaster opened before Mark. He wanted to say, "You can't go over his head to the Board. You'll lose us our best client." He wanted to warn Cushing that John Fenno was already displeased, and the impossibility of doing either diplomatically choked him. Moreover, what about Mark? Let that account slip away and just where would Mark be, he thought indignantly, and suddenly the whole world seemed to him insecure and terrifying. "Christ," he thought, "nobody gives a damn about what happens to *me*. I've got to fix something up for myself—something good."

Aloud, he said earnestly, "I'm sure you've done everything you could to dissuade him. Don't you think . . . ?" A lot of good the firm would be without that account!

"My position is one of double responsibility, Mark. Your uncle is my client, but I am also a member of the Board and in that capacity I am responsible, not to him, but to the stockholders."

Mark spoke with heat. "Still, I don't see . . ."

The glass butterfly glittered coldly. "You will find as you mature in the practice of the law that you will frequently be forced to decide a point of ethics against your personal advantage."

Mark sank back in his chair, sullen and resentful and still shaken by the feeling of insecurity. So what would become of him, he'd like to know. Damn Cushing! Have another try at getting taken into the Company? And why the hell shouldn't he have a job in the Company and a good one—the only male relative—why, he ought to be the heir, the crown prince. Anybody in the world but John Fenno would give him a handsome allowance, at least. And why didn't Fenno want members of the family in the Company? The whole thing willed to Willoughby, for Christ's sake! This feeling of desperation was almost more than Mark could bear.

He was prevented from further thought, however, by the noisy opening of the door. John Fenno strode in, went directly to the head of the table and looked around him imperiously. All over the room conversation stopped and there was a scraping of chairs. Knowing that he was not entitled to the elbow room of a director, Mark shoved his chair back from the table somewhat petulantly. His face was still flushed from emotion. The atmosphere became tense and expectant. Fenno was still standing, looking around him almost contemptuously. A grudging admiration stirred in Mark. "He has no respect for people he can control," Mark thought, "and no liking for those he can't."

His uncle's voice was deep with irritation. "Where's Hadley?"

It might have been a cue. Hadley entered without haste, smiled as though the scene amused him, and took the empty chair at Whittlesey's left. The chair creaked under his weight.

"Lord, he's big as a bear," Mark thought, and he crossed his long, well-formed hands on his knee and allowed himself a fleeting mind's-eye view of his own slim figure. The man's size and confident bearing were something of a shock, and evidently the Board felt it too, for there was a general heightening of the atmosphere. The director on Mark's left, a man named Brown, leaned over and whispered.

"Is that Hadley himself or a representative?"

"Hadley. " Mark felt sure of that though he had never seen the man.

"No idea he'd be so young. Looks like a tough customer. Where's his counsel?"

Fenno pulled his chair close to the table and leaned forward, about to begin.

"He's representing himself," Mark said hastily, and gave his attention to proceedings. Brown raised a surprised eyebrow and likewise bestowed attention.

Mark studied Hadley through eyes that were drawn down to slits and that gave him a craftier look than he normally allowed to appear on his face. Hadley was, indeed, as big as a bear. His coat had a loose fit made necessary by his bulging muscles and his free and careless manner of moving. He looked like a man of violent emotions but he looked, also, as though he could discharge himself of them easily. Grievances would not fester in him, but neither did he appear to be the sort who would mind treading on whatever happened to be in his path. His face was "open," but its openness came from a confidence that his own strength would win his ends without recourse to subterfuge.

After the first glance, Fenno had not once looked in Hadley's direction. "The minutes, Whittlesey." Fenno skewed sidewise in his chair and stared out of the window. Whittlesey began dipping in pockets and patting himself. Hadley smiled, picked up the glasses by one ear-piece and dangled them in front of Whittlesey.

The minutes proceeded, very dull, and everyone looked bored. The room was beginning to heat up. Whittlesey finished, rather pink in the face.

Fenno's voice sounded bored also. "Will someone move approval?"

"Move."

"Second."

"Ithasbeenmoved *and* seconded . . ."

It had a rhythmic beat, like the opening bars of a symphony. "Now they'll really begin to saw their fiddles," Mark thought, and glanced apprehensively at his chief.

Fenno was leaning forward, his hands folded on the table before him, his dark look holding their attention. "Impressive even in silence," Mark thought. "Damn him!"

When the quiet was absolute, Fenno spoke. "Gentlemen, we are here to approve the purchase agreement for the iron-ore mine land Mr. Hadley has inherited. Mr. Hadley asked to be present at this meeting. I saw no reason to object, especially as he has chosen to dispense with legal counsel and is representing himself. Mr. Hadley . . ." Fenno picked up a slip of paper and consulted it. "Mr. Samuel Hadley?"

"Just Sam." Hadley grinned.

"Mr. Sam Hadley . . ." Fenno again consulted the paper which he had too obviously not looked at before, "was born and raised in Michigan. He is twenty-six years old. In spite of his youth he fought in the war."

Fenno looked up from the paper in his hand and straight at Mark.

"He did not buy the services of a substitute, as so many of our gallant young men did." This was obviously not on the paper but an interpolation of Fenno's own. Mark flushed and picked a piece of lint off his knee with the utmost care. John Fenno continued reading.

"He fought on the side of the Union, a top sergeant of infantry, and was wounded. His father having died some months ago, he has inherited the ore property, the purchase of which we are met to complete. Gentlemen, let me present Sam Hadley."

There was something condescending about the way he said it. Hadley tipped his chair on its back legs and grinned broadly, looking with his confident stare from one director to another. He made no other acknowledgment of the introduction and Fenno continued at once.

"You are acquainted with the terms of the purchase. You have just heard it summarized in the minutes. Since Mr. Hadley is here, the agreement will be signed following formal approval. Will someone move . . . ?"

"Move it."

"Second."

Mark saw Cushing stir and heard him draw a fortifying breath, and his heart began to beat fast with apprehension. Here it is, he thought.

"Just a moment, Mr. Fenno. Gentlemen." Cushing took off his glasses and held them, almost delicately, by their gold nose-piece. He was looking not at the Board—which he could not see—but at some inner image of himself. "I have endeavored on a number of occasions to convey to Mr. Fenno my feelings about the wisdom of this purchase. Before we proceed, I feel I must lay them before the Board. Briefly, there seem to me ominous indications that the present prosperity cannot last much longer. With this purchase and our present obligations, the Company would be extended to such a degree that any sizable falling-off of business would be seriously embarrassing. I want to ask the Board to reconsider this purchase, or, at least, to postpone it until such time as the future appears more certain."

He put his glasses on his nose with a swift motion.

Fenno made an angry gesture and a dark flush rose to his face. "I had no idea you intended to take this position. You said nothing at all about it when I saw you yesterday. May I ask you why? I told the Board my intentions at the last meeting—you made no objection then. . . ."

"I have opposed the deal all along—you know that—though perhaps not as strongly as I should. But the real gravity of the situation has been growing on me slowly—the papers this morning—I did not decide to put my fears before the Board until now. I am sorry if you feel that I should have consulted you first, but I should have spoken to the Board in any case. And I hope"—Cushing swept the table with his glance—"I hope you will give it your most serious consideration."

Fenno was leaning forward, his hands gripping the arms of his chair. He stared at Cushing for a moment without speaking, and the veins in his neck looked swollen and dark. The atmosphere in the room was tense with the shocked realization of an animosity that went far deeper than the occasion warranted. Brown stirred uneasily and murmured: "It's getting so no one can have an opinion around here!" When Fenno spoke, his voice was controlled but full of cold and biting scorn.

"I get the impression, Cushing, that you waited to make these objections until the legal work was finished."

There were sounds of protest and chairs scraped. Mark's heart missed a beat and he tried to watch his uncle and Cushing at the same time. Whittlesey was on his feet, waving his hands like an orchestra leader. "Gentlemen, gentlemen."

All eyes were on Cushing. His hand was going, a little shakily, toward his glasses but something about the gesture, familiar as it was, riveted Mark's attention. "He's hurt," Mark thought. "Why, I believe he's a sensitive man, not up to this sort of thing. Confound him, he's a broken reed—and he looks old. I never saw that before." For Mark it was one of those fleeting, intangible moments in which some trivial thing changes our conception of a familiar person so that he is never again quite the same to us. Mark's attitude toward his employer had changed subtly but permanently. Mr. Cushing was no longer a respected superior. From now on Mark might work for him as before without visible change in their relationship, but Mark was on his own. The glasses fell to Cushing's lap and Mark's muscles jerked spasmodically.

When Cushing spoke, it was without anger. "Don't concern yourself about the legal fees, John. There will be none, if the purchase is not made."

"We'll take the vote." Deep resentment still sounded in Fenno's voice.

When the voting was over, there were two dissenters, Cushing and the man called Brown. Whittlesey concluded his hurried scribbling with a satisfied smile.

"It is my understanding the papers are to be signed now—a little ceremony—this great event." He dipped the pen in the ink and with a bow full of complacency, as though the achievement were his, he held the handle out toward John Fenno.

Hadley reached out and took the pen and put it down, scattering ink. Then he looked at the surprised faces around him slowly, with the same cold confidence.

"Since I talked to Mr. Fenno and Mr. Cushing, I've been thinking about this. I've been thinking I might as well have a job in the Company. That's valuable property I've got for sale. When the analysis reports get around, I wouldn't have any trouble selling. So I drew up some more papers—a new sales agreement—naming the job. If we're going to sign anything it'll be those."

Mark would have found it hard to bear the cold scrutiny that group of men directed toward Hadley. But Hadley was just sitting there, giving them back their stare without a trace of bumptiousness or bravado.

"Well, what *is* the job?" Fenno sounded impatient.

"Secretary of the Company."

There was something like an incredulous grunt from Whittlesey, as though he had had the wind knocked out of him. Someone laughed. Mr. Brown remarked severely, as though to a naughty child: "That is obviously absurd, young man." Hadley smiled at him.

"I can save you a lot of time," he said, swinging around to face Fenno, "by saying that the deal goes through that way or it doesn't go through."

It was Cushing, this time, who took on the duty of being placating. "That tone is hardly necessary, Mr. Hadley. I don't believe you realize how preposterous your suggestion is."

Hadley turned on him. "Now get this straight. I don't give a God damn whether you buy that property or not. I've been East long enough to find out I don't have to dispose of it to the first bidder."

Mark waited for the explosion from Fenno. None came. He was sitting back in his chair, looking at Whittlesey almost as though he were laughing at him. While Mark watched, the laugh became a reality, silent and with an enjoyment that chilled Mark. Whittlesey seemed about to choke. He was struggling to find words.

Fenno was smiling openly when he addressed the Board, all formality gone from his manner.

"I should like to suggest that Mr. Hadley leave the room while we discuss this. Whittlesey, will you show him the way to my office?"

For a moment Mark thought Whittlesey was going to refuse to leave. When he stood up to face Fenno, his hands were shaking.

"John, this outrageous . . . Surely you wouldn't . . ." He stopped. Fenno was leaning back in his chair, still with that chill smile on his face. Whittlesey turned away as though the look hurt him and spoke to the Board. "This is utterly preposterous . . ." Hadley stood up and took hold of his arm. Mark saw Whittlesey wince.

"Come on. Let them talk."

Whittlesey cast one more look at John Fenno and they departed. Fenno and everyone else turned around to watch them all the way out of the room.

When the door closed everyone talked at once. Fenno was still smiling a little when he said, "Let's have order, please." The outburst of talk subsided slowly.

"A little shake-up in *that* quarter wouldn't be a bad thing. Getting to feel a vested interest. Getting to feel secure. Shall we proceed? Let's see what's in those papers. Hand 'em to Cushing. I propose we make Whittlesey Treasurer only—at the same pay. Let him do both jobs as before. Give Hadley the title. I can deal with him later."

Someone protested. Someone else joined in the protest and someone said, "Why is this piece of property so valuable to us anyway? Why not another?"

Fenno's attitude astonished Mark. He would expect his uncle to be ruthless in his attitude toward even so old an associate as Whittlesey, but not to enjoy the process. He was startled to hear his own name.

"Mark, you've been up there. Is there any piece of property so well located in relation to our docks?"

Mark rose slowly with careful grace. He hooked his thumb through his fine gold watch chain and looked around the table before his eyes came to rest on Fenno. He spoke with suave confidence.

"No, sir."

"What's the grade from the property to our docks there?"

"All down hill."

"Any rises of any consequence?"

"No, sir. If you are thinking of narrow gauge, you could haul without power." It was all in the experts' reports, of course, but if his uncle wanted to hand him this chance to show off . . . Mark sat down, sweating a little.

There was more discussion, with which Fenno made no attempt to interfere. His attitude toward the Board seemed to imply that he shared a good joke with them. Perhaps this influenced them and perhaps there had never been any liking for Whittlesey among the members. The vote was almost perfunctory and Cushing was the only dissenter.

When Whittlesey and Hadley returned, Mark watched them cross from the door to their chairs and saw that in that fraction of time both men realized the outcome of the vote without a word being spoken. It seemed to him that Whittlesey shrank in size and that Hadley expanded monstrously until there were only two forces in the room, Hadley and Fenno. "They will clash some day," he thought, and fervently hoped that he might be present when that clash occurred.

The signing was brief. Whittlesey signed in tight-lipped futile anger. At the end, he had to be reminded to hand around the envelopes containing the fees. These caused a little stir.

"Gold!" someone exclaimed. "Double eagles."

"Why gold? With the country off the standard, it must have cost the Company something."

"This special occasion."

"Is it to be a custom, Fenno?"

John Fenno was smiling with the amused benevolence of a giver of gifts. Cushing and Hadley were talking together, and Mark stood by a window waiting for them to finish. Far out on the shining surface of the lake he saw a tiny white speck. On the docks below, groups of laborers were looking toward the west, their hands shielding their eyes.

"Uncle John, I think the *Willoughby Fenno* is coming in."

Fenno and several of the directors crowded around the window to see. Mark felt his sleeve pulled and turned to find Hadley beside him.

"You're Mark Sabin, aren't you? You know who I am."

The two young men solemnly shook hands.

"Successful meeting, Sabin."

"Mmmm."

"You're Cushing's assistant, I'm told."

"I'm in the firm." ("In," not "one of"—would Hadley catch the difference?)

"Look here, Sabin, I'd like to ask a favor of you. The Union Club seems to be the best place in town to belong. You're a member, aren't you? I've seen you there. Now that it looks like I'm going to be around town," Hadley grinned, "I want you to put me up for membership. How about it?"

Mark laughed out loud. Union Club, sanctum of Republicanism, big business and the trout fly. The idea tickled him.

"Sure," he said, "glad to."

Mark was under the necessity of waiting for his superior, which he found distasteful because, after this brief exchange with Hadley, everybody ignored him. The directors stood around in small groups, discussing the meeting, or began to drift toward the door and their own affairs. Mark leaned one shoulder against the wall, bit his mustache, examined one pale fingernail and sighed. After a minute his roving eye encountered General Thatcher's and he straightened up and bowed. The great man was standing by the directors' table stowing papers in various pockets, preparatory to departure. Because the General was alone, Mark decided to approach him. The General's diminutive figure stretched itself to the extreme of its height to receive this greeting and he wore his perpetual, deceptive smile, but his words were directed downward to Mark's somewhat lowly place in the hierarchy of business.

"Hullo, Mark. Surprised to see you here. Good experience, though."

"Interesting meeting, sir."

"Amusing. Most of 'em are pretty dull. My idea is that your uncle's got hold of someone in that young man who may not prove so easy to manage."

The General stowed his last paper, patted himself all over with an air of concentration, appeared to find his ballast in order and smiled again. The smile was far too well done to appear mechanical. "Good day, Mark."

Mark strolled back toward the window where, a moment later, Cushing found him.

"Ready, Mark?"

"Yes, sir."

"Let's be going then."

They kept silent until they had left the building and the cinders of the drive were crunching under their feet, when Cushing said, "I don't like any of this, Mark. I don't like what that young fellow did at the meeting and without telling anyone in advance. He obviously has plenty of nerve. Would you believe it, Mark, he had the gall to propose that I put him up for the Union Club? I'm afraid it gave me pleasure to refuse."

"Mmmm," said Mark. "Did he indeed, sir?"

They stepped into Mr. Cushing's sedate carriage and proceeded with dignity on their way. The horses were dappled gray and a little too fat, and the team looked as though it had not hurried for many years. When they entered the park, they saw ahead of them a carriage drawn up at the side of the road. The coachman was standing by his horses' heads, signaling to them with something that looked like a horseshoe in his hand. They pulled up beside the waiting carriage and the director called Brown, who had given his vote in support of Cushing, leaned out.

"Cast a shoe. Can you give me a lift to town?"

Mark politely transferred himself to the small seat facing backwards and Brown climbed in, the carriage swaying on its long, old-fashioned springs. This gentleman was still obviously stimulated by the events of the morning.

"Look here," he said, twisting sideways on the seat to face Cushing. "I'm glad I got a chance to talk to you. I'm not so much worried about the business outlook as you seem to be, though I don't think we ought to make this purchase. What bothers me is that Fenno is taking things too much into his own hands, railroading things through the board or downright disregarding the board's views. It's too much of a one-man concern. And another thing. There are no younger men in the Company to step up—unless you count that fellow Hadley they took in today. If anything should happen to Mr. Fenno . . ." Brown stopped abruptly and glanced at Mark as though he had suddenly remembered the relationship. "Thought Mr. Fenno looked tired today," he mumbled awkwardly.

They drove on in silence. Brown's remark about Fenno's appearance surprised Mark, for he had noticed nothing of the sort, but now he came to think about it, Fenno did look tired and sometimes he sighed, as though everyday things were an effort for him. Mark found himself wondering with keen interest what would develop at the mill if anything should happen to John Fenno. The way to catch a plum was to be under the tree when it fell. The question was, how to station himself under that particular tree? "Willoughby," he thought, "and some sort of job in the Company." Mark squirmed a little with the intensity of his emotions. Cushing was talking like a man thinking aloud and Mark gave him part of his attention.

"Fenno once remarked that Sherman wouldn't have had any prominence without the war. Something of the sort may apply to Fenno himself. Perhaps he would not have been so successful in any other times than these. But give him credit for perceiving that the great fortunes of this decade would be made in industry, not commerce, and for the ability to take advantage of what he himself likes to call the 'economic tide.' Would he have been the success he is without that tide? However, the ability to take advantage of it is greatness of a sort.

"Fenno's a new type in the American scene," Cushing continued. "His predecessors in the industry were the 'iron masters,' concerned chiefly with methods of production. Fenno apparently conceives of the head of such an organization as putting the emphasis on finance and business and, on the record, we'll have to say he's right. The old timers, like Huntington of Lake Furnace, for example, are failing because they don't see it that way. This tide that Fenno talks about has been running strong ever since the war, but some day we'll get a different set of economic conditions—a different tide. I wonder if it isn't about to change. And I wonder, if it does change, whether men like Fenno and ourselves have the qualities and the limberness to profit by the new direction. Maybe not. Maybe not."

"That's all too philosophical for me. I still say it's too much of a one-man concern, or maybe that's what you were getting at, too." Brown glanced at Mark again but Mark was presenting an abstracted exterior, as though he were not listening, and Brown appeared to conclude that if Cushing spoke thus freely, so could he. "I don't like it," he finished with emphasis, "but at the moment I'm damned if I can see what we can do about it."

4

THE medium of John Fenno's success might have been other than iron for all the affection he bore it, nor did he know much more about the process of making iron than when he first took control of Fenno and Company. Part of his success, moreover, could be attributed to exactly these characteristics. He believed that the old-fashioned iron master was certain to lose out in a business world in which competitive finance was becoming more important every day, and therefore he devoted himself to the business aspects and hired men to make the iron. He did this with some self-satisfaction, thinking of himself as a leader in establishing a new type of American industrialist.

Most of the task of managing the mill John Fenno had been able to delegate and the few duties that remained irked him. He intended to be free of them, also, as soon as he found the right man for the post of general manager. As the day of the directors' meeting wore on and he turned the events of the morning over in his mind, he became more and more of the opinion that he had found the right man in "that fellow" Hadley. There was a hardness about him that would make everyone in the mill, from laborer to scientist, knuckle down. And he was smart—too smart, perhaps. The way he had handled himself in the meeting had aroused not only Fenno's interest but considerable cynical respect as well. Fenno did not like Hadley, but Fenno had never felt any particular need for liking his associates.

Now at the end of the day he sat at his desk, scowling at a mote-filled beam of slanting sun, and thought about these problems, but it was only a superficial segment of his brain that planned and schemed. It happened to him often, as it was happening now, that a deeper stream of consciousness flowing through him kept him aware of the turbulent life of the mill without the awareness ever shaping itself into thought. In this way he often heard, without listening, the rumble of the mill, the clankings and the long-drawn hiss of steam. And at night, though he seldom looked at the sky, he was conscious of the light from the molten metal and the fires, which glowed there through the years, waxing and waning in prosperity and hard times, and the symbolism of the light stirred him. John Fenno was no poet, but the secret awareness, inside himself, of such things as these kept a part of him from hardening and tinged his ambitions with the kind of passion and urgency usually supposed to belong solely to the creative temperament. John Fenno was a hard man but he was also sensitive.

Today, for example, he was deeply aware of the coming of the *Willoughby Fenno,* like a calm and beautiful bird, across the shining surface of the lake, although, except for occasional quick glances from his office window, he did not watch her. In this clairvoyant manner he knew when she passed the breakwater into the calmer water. He knew when she was close enough for the stains of rust to be seen on her wooden hull and the cries of the sailors came to him faintly as they mastheaded the yards.

"A-hay! A-high! A-h-o-o-yo!"

He felt, rather than heard, the gentle bump as she touched the wharf and this secret part of himself felt the slap of the loops of wet rope as they fell over the bollards.

He pulled out his watch and glanced at it. A beam of sunlight struck the curved crystal, sending back star-like rays of brilliant light, and he moved it into the shadow. Five-thirty, and the carriage would be waiting. He pulled down the roll top of his desk, locked it, took his hat from the ledge on top and settled it firmly on his head. The day had tired him a little and it was very hot. He should have liked to carry his hat on the drive home and let the warm air blow through his hair and beard, but his nature forbade.

He walked slowly to the window and rested his hands on the sill, looking down on the activity of the ore docks. The *Willoughby Fenno* lay quietly now, her sails furled and her hatches open wide. Planks linked her to the shore and workmen with barrows swarmed over her like ants. Fenno listened for a moment to the distant rattle of the barrows and the jabbered Finnish, carried to him faintly on the summer breeze, and then leaned farther out the window to see if his carriage waited on the drive below.

There it was—and Willoughby, reclining with just the proper dignity on the fawn-colored cushions. He felt a glow of pride and pleasure. How self-possessed she looked and elegant, the little pleatings on her gown opening out like myriads of tiny fans. *She* never lost track of herself. Something very like the beginning of a smile softened John Fenno's features as he looked down at her. What absurd hats young ladies wore—this one, like an explosion of feathers. And style—the whole turn-out had style—even old Joe wearing the white gloves she insisted on. A pleasure to ride beside her through the city for all eyes to see. His glance strayed back to the *Willoughby Fenno,* looking a little blowzy now with the clouds of dust surrounding her, being ravished by the ant-like laborers. She was not good enough for such a name. There was talk of deepening the ship canal so that ships of greater draught could go through. Well then, a new *Willoughby Fenno,* steam, and the finest ship on the lakes. He shut the window slowly and slowly left his office, a little smile just touching the corners of his eyes and in them a distant look as of a man creating his future.

Mark was just leaving the building as Fenno reached the front door, and the sight of him dispelled some of Fenno's pleasure. What could he have been doing at the mill all day? Running up legal fees for that fellow Cushing? And Cushing himself must be somewhere about. Mark was making for the carriage and Willoughby. Neither of them saw Fenno and he stopped in his tracks, arrested by the expression on her face. That trick of hers of turning on her beauty when she wanted, as though some light in her were turned up—but for Mark? Surely not for Mark? A shaveling lawyer at nothing a year—she would have more sense. But a vague foreboding of trouble pervaded him and he continued to stand still, watching.

Under the radiance of that smile Mark's heart was beating a little faster and, being what he was, he hid it under mockery. Leaning over the side of the carriage, he gazed at her with theatrical adoration.

"Hello, Willie," he said, "you are more beautiful than the wings of the morning," and he smiled his insinuating smile. His feelings toward this girl were very mixed. The sun turned her hair into threads of gold. The logical thing would be to marry her.

"Don't be extravagant. And don't call me Willie."

"Aurora, Beatrice, Helen, Francesca, Aphrodite." (Ah, freedom!)

"Do you really like me, Mark?"

"You will find it graven on my heart."

"What?"

"Calais."

She slapped at him in mock annoyance and he seized her hand with fervor. On a hot day holding a woman's hand in a kid glove was like holding an oyster, and he let it go hastily. Why the devil couldn't he

fall in love with this princess, thereby making it easier to marry her
and inherit the kingdom? There was the faintest suspicion, moreover,
that she expected it of him—but on the other hand, it might be just
a game. He was thinking about his debts when he saw her eyes fasten
on something behind him and turned around to meet his uncle's cold
and distant stare.

John Fenno had listened to this exchange with the disgust of a
nature that did not know the meaning of flippancy and mistrusted sentiment, real or otherwise. Ignoring Mark, he addressed himself to his
daughter.

"I'm going down to the docks," he said. "I shan't be long." That
smile of hers would melt butter. Was it entirely for him? He turned
on Mark as one who warns an intruder away from boundaries.

"I expect Cushing will be waiting for you," he said.

He went slowly down the long flight of steps that descended the
bank to the docks. He was feeling the heat, the day had tired him and
the pleasure of the triumphant morning had completely deserted him.
Something he could not quite get hold of in that exchange between
Mark and his daughter still troubled him. Suppose she really were
. . . ? And he slowed his steps, considering this possibility.

In the back of his mind there always lurked, like a shadowy pit, that
disappointment—no son. It was all for her—for Willoughby. He had
always felt that in some way she would justify and repay him with her
own future, brilliantly, and now for the first time he realized that he
had never challenged this faith, never entertained the possibility of any
other outcome. But suppose she really had set her heart on Mark? Suppose he were to take Mark into the Company, make him his heir? A
swift vision came to him of Mark's alert and mobile countenance and
the mocking amber eyes. "He doesn't care about anything," he thought,
"but himself. An alien." He took out his handkerchief and mopped his
brow, realizing that in these things lay, in all probability, a problem
of the first magnitude. A matter of minutes ago there had been no
problem, then a look, half a dozen words and a dark and threatening
cloud hung over the future. Perhaps it was all in his imagination—the
heat.

The bottom of the flight of steps put an end to further thought. The
dock lay ahead of him, a hundred feet to the water's edge. Close to the
lake, piles of ore stretched away like a miniature mountain range. Most
of the ore was the bluish-brown hematite rock, with streaks of rust
in its heart. Bright flecks in the rock glistened like diamonds in the sun.

A few of the piles were the rarer magnetite, a sinister-looking black rock that assayed sixty per cent pure iron and had a strange magnetic power.

Fenno picked his way over the double line of tracks which lay close to the bottom of the bank and stood still looking around him, trying to discern in the swarm of workmen the tall figure of his dock superintendent, an ex-Army sergeant named Barnes. And as he stood there, something strange and unusual in the atmosphere of the docks began to invade his consciousness. Fenno was not, as a rule, susceptible to atmospheres, or perhaps it would be fairer to say that, when these peculiar emanations reached him he ignored them, feeling that susceptibilities of any kind were a confession of weakness. Now, however, with his apperceptions already jogged by the little scene on the drive, he failed to set up the usual barriers. He stood still and, as it were, sniffed the air.

Superficially, everything was as usual. Laborers milled about, jabbering Finnish, barrows rolled by, rattling when they were empty, rumbling when they were full, and over all this racket he heard the rhythmic screech of the winch. Though outwardly everything was the same, there was a tension in the air and it seemed to Fenno, as he stood still trying to capture its flavor, that something inimical to himself grew and surrounded him. Many of the Finns looked toward him as they passed, and he felt that when they did so, their heathenish jabbering increased. They were lowering, ugly-looking fellows with heavy shoulders and bulging muscles. Ordinarily they paid no attention to him on his occasional inspections of the ore docks. Now, as he began to move forward, searching for Barnes, they seemed to give him a wide berth and their lowering seemed full of animosity toward himself. He began to sweat a little and when he saw Barnes striding toward him, he stamped down a feeling of relief.

Barnes possessed the lean, loose-jointed hardness of body which is the especially American type of good looks, and he strode the wharf with the confidence of a commander on his own territory. His attitude toward Fenno was like that toward a higher officer who is both respected and liked, and it had in it a knowledge that in return he was relied on and trusted. Fenno, whose likings were few, liked Barnes. It was on the tip of his tongue to ask the fellow what was up and what the strange feeling in the air portended, but he was not given to asking questions. If anything were really wrong, Barnes, he felt, would tell him.

" 'Evening," he said, making it sound short and almost angry for the precise reason that he liked the man.

"Good evening, sir," said Barnes pleasantly, seeing through this subterfuge.

"I came to look at her." Fenno indicated the schooner with a motion of his head. "Full load, of course?"

"Full as she'll take."

"When will you get her unloaded?"

"About noon tomorrow I'd say, sir."

"That's a long time. We need to send her back. The season's getting on."

"We'll work at it. I hear you bought a mine?"

"Hmm. News travels fast. Where did *you* hear it?"

"I forget, sir."

Fenno gave him a sharp look and moved off toward the schooner. No harm done, but he did not like his affairs being discussed.

The two men walked slowly toward the ship. Fenno held himself erect and uncompromising, his chin firm set and the muscles in his jaw bulging a little because it seemed to him that the strange atmosphere of the docks moved with them and surrounded them. Barnes walked with the easy grace of perfect physical condition but Fenno thought he saw in him something watchful and alert. They stopped by the planking that sloped up to the deck and watched the barrows trundle by. A huge basket on a rope hung momentarily over the open hatch, then plunged into the dark hold. The rope grew taut, the winch screeched and the basket rose slowly, spilling chunks of the bluish ore. Shouting Finns seized the basket, dumped the ore into the barrows, grabbed the barrows and rolled them in single file down the planking, holding back with straining muscles against their heavy loads. The heat and the dust were stifling and the sun struck the lake with a hard and brassy glare that made the men squint.

Here, too, the tension seemed to grow in the air around them. A big, powerfully built Finn started down the planking, half-running, his muscles straining to break his heavy load. He looked toward them and it seemed to Fenno that his face was contorted in an ugly grimace. There was a sudden shout. The barrow swerved and Fenno felt Barnes' rough, quick hand dragging him back. The next instant the barrow broke from the Finn's grasp and hurtled toward them. Fenno stumbled and fell to his knees on the timbers of the wharf.

It was all over in an instant, and Fenno felt Barnes hauling him to his feet with strong hands under his armpits. A sense of evil violence hung in the air. The two men faced the crowd of laborers in the sudden silence, a silence in which, for a moment, no one moved. The barrow lay on its side, the ore spilled out, two long splintered furrows cut in the wharf by the iron legs. Half a hundred blank and expressionless faces were turned toward them. Barnes' face was grim. He took a forward step and pointed.

"Pick up that barrow."

The moment was full of intangible danger, a fleeting moment in which perhaps every man there knew that anything or nothing might happen in the next. Fenno stared back at the blank faces, his look as grimly expressionless as theirs. They all seemed frozen in the strange tableau, Barnes' arm still out, pointing to the overturned barrow. Then the big Finn stepped forward, grumbling, and righted the barrow with a jerk. Here and there a man moved and then the whole crowd was in motion again and the air again full of sound.

Fenno let out a long breath and stooped to brush dust off his knees. He felt his heart beating in hard, slow thumps that shook him. The two men moved away through the crowd that no longer took any notice of them but left, nevertheless, a wide path for their passage.

"Just what happened?"

"The barrow slipped, sir. An accident, perhaps."

Fenno's knees smarted and stung, and splinters pricked the palms of his hands. The sense of indignity at being seen thus on his knees began to seethe in him and to arouse his anger. He halted abruptly and faced Barnes.

"These fellows want a lesson," he said. "Rig the flares and unload tonight. We need the ore."

Barnes' reply came slowly: "They're in an ugly mood, sir."

"That's plain enough. What's the matter? What's it all about?"

"Well, sir . . ." Barnes hesitated, and his manner changed to a kind of embarrassed constraint.

Watching him, Fenno thought, "The fellow's got something on his mind and for some reason he's afraid to come out with it."

They were standing beside a pile of lumber near a resigned-looking horse which plodded round and round, supplying the motive power for the winch. At a certain place in the cycle, the winch screeched and the sound tore at Fenno's nerves.

"Well?" he said irritably.

Barnes took a resolution. "I guess you better know, sir. They are complaining on two counts. They want a shorter working day, ten hours, and they object to the Company keeping them on into the night to finish unloading a ship. We've done that quite a bit this season, if you remember, sir. And they want more pay. There is talk of a strike."

"So? Fire a few of them and they'll forget it. Do they think we're a gold mine? Have you talked to them?"

"I've talked to their foreman, that fellow Päkkä who speaks English. He got hurt last week and that's part of the trouble. They think it was Company carelessness and that the Company ought to pay his doctor."

"Nonsense. Fire a few of 'em and the trouble will stop."

"We will if you say so, sir, but I don't think it would do any good. It's the same on all the ore docks. They've been holding meetings. Maybe I should have told you before about what's going on, but I didn't want to because . . ."

"Because what? What are you trying to get at?"

Barnes kicked at the pile of lumber with the toe of his boot and kept his eyes away from Mr. Fenno's face. Barnes did not mind handing on responsibility to those higher up but, like a good top sergeant, he hated to admit a lack of knowledge of the affairs of his own command.

"There's something back of this, sir, and I can't find out what. They'd never think up things like that to complain about, unless someone put them up to it."

"Who'd be doing that?"

"I don't know, sir. That's just it, and when I tried to question Päkkä before that rope broke, he just suddenly couldn't understand English." Barnes flushed at the necessity for making this confession of failure. "If he hadn't got hurt, I'd have had it out of him right enough," he said grimly.

Fenno was silent, his eyes pulled together at the corners, considering. Once he glanced speculatively at the piles of ore. He was balancing the possibility of a strike against the approaching end of the season, when navigation would shut down and no more ore could be brought in. The present supply was fairly adequate, and the likelihood of any men as low in the human scale as these Finns being able to organize themselves into a strike seemed to him remote. Easy enough to smash them if they did. An altogether different proposition from the skilled workers in the mill, who called themselves the "Sons of Vulcan" and were growing more temperamental every day. He looked at Barnes with a hard and angry glance, from which the previous traces of friend-liness had vanished.

"Work the men tonight," he said, and strode off quickly toward the stairs.

The propulsion of his anger carried him to the foot of the steps before he was again aware of the angry mood of the men, but as he climbed higher he could feel their eyes on his back, and in his imagi-nation he felt that even Barnes was watching him.

When he reached the top of the bank, he did not turn his head toward the docks but strode along the railing toward his carriage with his face grim and set. If there were trouble, Barnes would have his hands full—maybe they all would. Barnes was probably giving them the order to work overtime this minute. And then a chill thought struck him. Preoccupied with his own anger, he had left Barnes to face those ugly fellows with that order, alone.

The thought stopped him in his tracks but he did not look down. Instead, he resumed his way again with the comforting reflection that to face them was Barnes' business, not his. Nevertheless, when he reached the shelter of a lilac bush which grew beside the railing, he stopped again and peered through its dusty branches at the dock below.

They were standing in one big group, Barnes out in front alone, and they were shouting, all those ugly faces turned one way, toward Barnes. And Barnes stood there alone facing them, lean and hard, his weight on the balls of his feet. Even from this distance Fenno could see that he was tense for expected action. They were pressing in on him, coming up on all sides of him, and Fenno leaned forward into the dusty bush, gripping the railing hard. What chance had Barnes if the fight were to start this minute? And it looked as though it might. It took courage to face them like that. They were surrounding him. The big brute on the side had something in his hand—what was it? He could not see. And they were all shouting. It was a stone and the fellow was raising his arm. If that stone flew, they'd all be on Barnes like a savage mob. A shout he did not hear burst from his own throat —"Barnes! Look out!"

Fenno had the impulse to run to Barnes' aid but he did not move. Barnes had both arms raised above his head and he was stepping for-ward against that angry crowd, forcing them with his body to yield or engulf him. And—they were moving back—not much, but a little— just those in the front ranks, moving back and crowding into those behind. And the fellow with the stone was lowering his arm.

Barnes was talking now—Fenno could not hear the words—talking with quick, emphatic gestures of his head and arms, and all the time he was moving forward step by step. The crowd was giving way before him, the backward motion translating itself from the front ranks to those behind and to those behind. The whole crowd was in motion now, scattering. The shouting changed to jabbering talk and an occasional angry cry. They were breaking up. Barnes was pointing to things now, giving orders. A few of the men started toward the schooner.

Fenno pulled out his handkerchief and wiped his forehead and looked with surprise at his hands, covered with dirt and dust. He cleaned them off as best he could. He felt dazed and drained, and his head throbbed. An ugly business, it seemed to him, and this was probably not the end of it. Barnes had courage. Fenno turned toward the carriage where Willoughby waited for him. She looked composed and smiling, unconscious of the drama below, unconscious of his thumping heart.

He got in beside her, careful to conceal his soiled hands. How pretty and cool she looked, refreshing to his spirit. For a moment he basked in it, letting her grace and beauty soothe him. They talked of trivial things, but as they talked that dark cloud of worry, which the events on the docks had dispelled, began to take shape again. He became more and more silent, watching out of the corner of his eye her easy pose, the fashionable angle at which she held her parasol, the toe of her slipper pointing out under the fan-like pleatings of her skirt, so perfect. She must not throw herself away. He could not believe she would, but . . .

"Willoughby," he said, and stopped.

"Yes, Papa?"

"Mark seems to be—well, he'll never break any records."

"Oh, don't worry about *him*, dear."

"Worry? I'm not worrying. What gave you that idea? You've got good sense."

"Yes, I've got good sense. I get it from *you*." She gave his arm the lightest of little pats as though to say, "We understand each other. We're alike, but we both want our own way."

He looked at her furtively. There was a faint, amused smile at the corners of her mouth. How self-possessed she looked! Would she share a secret with him if she had one? He doubted it. She must make a brilliant match, of course, some day, but one that would not take her away from him. Well, he was probably wrong about Mark, but he wished she were more communicative. Perhaps he did not show his appreciation of her enough.

"You've a birthday coming next month," he said almost gruffly.

"Yes, dear."

"What do you want? Something nice!"

"Pearls would be nice."

"Pearls? You *have* pearls."

"Not real ones."

"Real ones cost money." Lord knew how much. Something fabulous, he supposed.

"Of course they do, dear. That shouldn't bother *you*."

Flattery? Perhaps, but—why not? Wasn't she everything he had, everything he worked for? She was his achievement. She understood that—and him. He leaned back on the cushions, conscious of their comfort, conscious of the refreshing breeze of their motion and of the satisfactory impression they must be making in the streets of the city. He felt close to her and something like contentment pervaded him.

"We'll see," he said.

She smiled at him.

5

As dusty August gave way to parched September, Brodi found himself in a restless mood. Here was the summer nearly over and so little accomplished. Shortly he would be tied down by his teaching duties miles from Cleveland and not only was his article on dock labor not written, though he had hardly expected that, but the facts, the priceless hard-to-come-by facts which would make his work both valuable and convincing, were still largely beyond his grasp.

As he mounted the steps of the Union Club slowly, on his way to keep his regular Saturday luncheon appointment with Mark, something else was bothering him also. The thought that was causing the preoccupied scowl on his face was that no prosperity lasts forever and the current one was, in his opinion, about to burst.

So far as he could see, however, he was almost alone in expecting such a denouement. Wherever he looked, business activity seemed to be increasing, new enterprises were being launched and old ones expanded. It was as though everybody all at once wanted to remake everything on a new and grander scale—their businesses, their houses, even the way they set their tables and stocked their shelves. Everything bigger and more elaborate and more costly. The whole nation making itself over, he thought, contemplating all this with interest.

There seemed to him something feverish about it, something reckless. People on the street appeared to walk faster and talk as though they were moved by excitement. He had watched a group of them as he tied his horse to the side railings of the Union Club, a half dozen substantial citizens. They were mounting the steps of the club with energetic strides, talking in loud, positive voices, unaware of lesser men who might look at them with interest and some envy. Brodi had caught sight of Fenno in the midst of the group. They all seemed keyed up, as though for action.

The normal shadowy dignity of the club had given place to the bustle of lunch hour, and the clatter of dishes and cutlery reached Mike's ears from the dining room down the hall. Not being himself a member of the club, Brodi chose to wait in the unpleasant room dedicated to that purpose rather than make himself conspicuous by being alone in the members' lounge. He found this somewhat stilted apartment deserted. His appointment with Mark was for twelve-thirty and, as the hands of the clock which stood above a fireplace in which no fire was ever lit pointed exactly to that hour, it seemed likely to Brodi that he would have some time to wait. The room offered little in the way of interest or even comfort to those forced to cool their heels here, as though the club considered non-members a lesser breed not to be encouraged or coddled. Mike scanned the dog-eared magazines on the center table and, picking up the only one of recent date, which happened to be a copy of *Iron Age* that had somehow found its way here by mistake, sat down and held it open on his knee.

He did not read, however, for his thoughts still troubled him. Could he be mistaken about the portent of all this feverish activity? He thought not. The nation might be compared to a family in the process of renovating its house, throwing away old furniture and getting newer and more costly to replace it, refurbishing everything. But it couldn't go on forever. The time would come when things would be pretty well renovated. Then they would call a halt and all the carpenters and painters and cabinet makers would get no more work.

When that happened on a national scale, when a whole country called quits, what did you get? You got unemployment, you got hard times and one of those recurring economic catastrophes which paralyze business. And the more widespread the renovating, the greater the smash. If it could be foreseen, could it be prevented? Perhaps. Anyway, it was the only hope. *"Savoir pour prévoir, prévoir pour pouvoir."* If you could *prévoir* you could *pouvoir,* and Mike, sighing, paid silent tribute to the greatest good he knew, namely "facts." For facts, hard and cold, or whatever way you liked them, seemed to Mike the only approach to the problems of a troubled world, at the moment seemingly so unaware of its own troubles. Without facts no course of action could be anything but blind, and without facts the result of any course of action must remain in doubt. His belief in the virtue inherent in factual knowledge was the nearest Mike came to the possession of a faith. He picked up the magazine and riffled through its pages just as his privacy was invaded by a stranger.

The two men exchanged quick glances, found they were unknown to each other and behaved as men do in such a setting, exactly as though the other were not present. Something about the stranger interested Brodi and he studied him from behind the shelter of his magazine. He was well dressed, obviously by a good tailor familiar with certain caste marks in attire, but, except for his recognition of the authenticity of the general effect, these subtleties were lost on Mike. In some indefinable way, however, this stranger was no more like the men who frequented the club, when big business lunched out, than Mike himself. Not, Brodi decided, taking stock of the bold face, the almost pugnacious jaw, the keen but completely unintellectual cast of feature—not the Western Reserve type. A bruiser.

The bruiser scattered the magazines on the center table, looked hard at the one Mike was holding and sat down empty-handed.

"Did you want to see this copy of *Iron Age?*" Brodi had no intention of relinquishing it, but he was curious to see how the stranger would handle this recognition of his minor rudeness.

"Interested in iron?"

"Somewhat."

"Why?"

"As an economic indicator," and Brodi, suspecting the phrase would be over the stranger's head, grinned with enjoyment at his own snub.

The bruiser looked puzzled for a moment. "Know anything about it?"

"Quite a bit—from the economic viewpoint." And Brodi, tired of this exchange, glanced back at the page before him. He knew this type —aggressive to the point of quarrelsomeness. Under ordinary circumstances Brodi would have thoroughly enjoyed taking him down a peg but now, with Mark due to arrive at any moment, it hardly seemed worth while.

The bruiser shifted his considerable weight and put one big hand on the arm of his chair, the elbow sticking up. "If you know so much about iron, what's the year's production of pig to date?"

"National; 1,700,000 gross tons last report," Mike said without looking up.

"Ore?"

"What do you mean, ore?"

"How much ore will be coming down from the mines this season?"

Brodi raised his eyes and looked straight at the bruiser. "Nine hundred and fifty thousand gross tons—by the time the lakes close."

"Nine seventy-five."

"Nine fifty."

The two men glared at each other, Mike sitting back with his knees crossed, the bruiser on the edge of his chair, leaning forward, his elbow still making a right-angle triangle in the air. The look was a long one and, at the start, full of dislike on both sides. It was one of those looks which are apt to turn into a duel in which one or the other of the contestants eventually drops vanquished eyes, but something extraordinary happened to this one. It was as though, on closer examination, like recognized like, almost as though a mutual respect were being born and after it was over each one might perhaps have said, "This guy speaks my language." There was no loss of face involved, therefore, in ending the duel and it was the bruiser who did so. A broad grin spread across his face, which did not so much change his appearance as add to it certain characteristics which were not theretofore evident. It was a likeable grin, and, thought Brodi, "The fella would take advantage of you if he could, but he'd make no bones about admitting the fact. With the sort of confidence he's got he'd probably even call his shots!" And Black Mike grinned in return.

The bruiser rose and held out his hand. "My name's Hadley."

Mike rose too and accepted the hand. "I'm Mike Brodi. Glad to meet you." It was rather like two belligerent dogs coming to an understanding.

"You in the iron business too?"

"No, I teach school."

"The hell you say! What do you teach?"

"They call it history in the prospectus."

"Then how come you know so much about iron?"

"Economics, not iron."

"What's iron got to do with economics?"

"You're due to find out shortly—if a theory I have is right."

Hadley looked puzzled again. "I didn't know teachers took any interest in things like ore and pig."

"It's a trend. Who you with?"

"I'm general manager of Fenno and Company—as of yesterday."

"You don't say!" Brodi's black eyes deepened with interest.

"Know the Company?"

"Sure. You sweat your dock labor worse than anybody along the lake."

"Oh, that. We make 'em work." There was some pride in Hadley's tone. "We'll have a hell of a time getting in all the ore we need before the lakes close, at that. But I'm damned if I can see yet why a teacher should be interested in iron. I still say nine seventy-five."

"Want to bet? We'll know who's right in a couple of months."

"Sure. Ten dollars."

"Gold."

Mark, immaculate down to fawn-colored gloves, appeared in the doorway.

"Sorry to keep you waiting, Michael. Affairs, my lad. Affairs. Hullo, Hadley. What are you, a member in good standing, doing in this cubby-hole that we grudgingly allow to those beyond the pale?"

"Looking for the last number of *Iron Age*," Hadley said. *"He* had it." Hadley grinned. "How about drinks—on me? You're the only member of this damn club I know well enough to have a drink with yet—and the only bar I've ever seen where you can't get the fellow with his foot on the rail beside yours to talk to you. Don't you people ever talk to strangers?"

"It's the Western Reserve," Mark murmured. "I gather you two have met." And he led the way to the bar.

In the end Hadley stood two rounds, Mark one. Mark signed with a flourish, though he had in his pocket a request from the club not to sign any more checks until his dues were paid up. Brodi, because his name was no good on a Union Club chit, stood none. He could have eaten in Hudson for two days for what one round cost. They finished their drinks and made their way to the crowded dining room. Here the head waiter gave them a table in a corner for, after all, one of them had just joined and one of them wasn't even a member. Hadley, avoiding the overhanging fronds of a palm, sat down and shook out his napkin. Mark's amber eyes wandered over the room, for he was not one of those who is oblivious to surroundings and the opportunities they may hold. At the large center table he saw John Fenno and a group of businessmen, mostly directors. General Thatcher was sitting more or less in Mark's line of vision and Mark, waiting until he caught his eye, half rose and bowed. The little General took his cigar out of his mouth and nodded coolly. Hadley, who had picked up a hard roll, turned around to see to whom Mark was being courteous, saw the General, smiled and sketched a salute with his big hand. The General, apparently delighted, returned the gesture. This attracted the attention of half the men at the big table, who looked up curiously. Mark frowned.

This byplay was not lost on Brodi. He looked from Mark to Hadley and back again, and his curiosity rose. There was something deeply inimical about the two, Hadley bold and powerful and overbearing, Mark sly and swift and clever.

Mark spoke to Hadley and his voice was rather more suave and soft than usual. "Any more trouble with the unloaders?"

"No, a false alarm. But we're getting in some strong-arm boys in case of need." He turned to Brodi. "The damn unloaders are griping about their hours and pay."

Brodi, with uncharacteristic discretion, said nothing and Hadley turned back to Mark.

"I have a theory the trouble's caused by one or two ringleaders—that sort of thing always is—and I tried to get Barnes to tell me who they were so we could fire 'em. He looked me right in the eye and said he didn't know. 'The hell you don't,' I told him. 'You don't have to tell me, but fire 'em, see?' "

Brodi opened his mouth but shut it again. He hated subterfuge, however necessary for the good of the Cause, and, while acknowledging that there would be no good and undoubtedly considerable harm in revealing his association with these ringleaders, he simply did not like the position in which he found himself. From under drooping lids Mark flashed him a look and Mike flushed. The look said plainly enough that he, Mark, would not give his friend away, or rather, if Brodi had really read Mark's thoughts, would not be caught at it.

Brodi looked hard at Hadley. "A tough attitude toward labor never pays in the long run."

"Yea?" said Hadley. "Why not?" His tone was a nice mixture of interest and disbelief.

"Because, over the long period, you get more work out of healthy men than overtired ones and more work out of contented men than disgruntled ones."

"Yea?" said Hadley again, but this time the interest was entirely lacking. "By the way, Barnes warned the Old Man after that last bit of trouble not to take the carriage through Mill Street for a while. Too easy to scare the horses into a runaway, or something like that. I don't mind admitting I've been avoiding it myself."

"The girls sometimes go to meet their father in the evenings," Mark said.

"Well, they'd better not for a while."

Hadley looked up to find a harassed waiter standing at his elbow. "Steak," he said without looking at the menu. "Fried potatoes, coffee."

"Same," said Brodi.

Mark, however, reached for the menu and studied it carefully while the waiter shifted from one foot to another. "Is there an 'R' in this month?"

"Yes," the others answered.

"All right. Oysters and sherry. Do you have any of that old shipment of Amontillado? The new stuff tastes like olives. I want the old, understand. Then, let's see. *Coq au vin.* Corn—but cut it off the cob. No coffee until later. And no sherbet with the chicken. Of all barbarous customs!"

With this business attended to, they all seemed to settle a little deeper into their chairs.

Mark resumed. "Barnes is by way of being a favorite of Uncle John's. He's an ex-soldier and a good man on the docks."

"Well, if his bastards start trouble they'll have my men to deal with." Hadley spoke in the tones of a man who intends to bring a topic to a close. "What do I do with this?" He reached into his pocket, brought out a bent square of cardboard and tossed it across the table to Mark. "And what do the initials in the corner mean?"

Mark picked it up, read it and raised one sleek eyebrow. "An invitation to General Thatcher's ball next week. Was it sent to you?"

"Yes."

Mark turned to Brodi. "Don't look now, but the little man at the center table is General Thatcher. He's one of our directors, a banker —Fenno and Company banks with him. He's as rich as the inside of a dog, in fact it's a toss-up which is the richer, he or Uncle John. But he's had it longer so he's had more time to accumulate gaudy stuff. He's a dapper little guy who likes to have you think he is a great beau, but they don't come any stonier-hearted or shrewder."

Having delivered himself of this summary, that showed more insight into the little General than most of Cleveland's tycoons had acquired in a lifetime of dealing with him, Mark pulled an envelope out of his pocket, looked at it to be sure it was empty and began to write on the back. After an assiduous minute he put away his pencil and tossed the envelope across the table to Hadley.

"This is what you do about it," he said. "And the initials in the corner mean 'reply if you please,' only they stand for those words in French."

Hadley picked up the envelope and read the first two lines out loud:
"Mr. Samuel Hadley
Regrets that he is Unable to Accept"

He tossed the envelope on the table. "What the hell makes you think I'm not going?"

"Are you?"

"Sure."

Brodi, putting one finger on the engraved invitation, drew it toward him, picked it up, looked at it back and front, and smiled at this sample of the *mores* of what he and his undergraduate cronies had labelled so glibly the Capitalist Class.

"What do you wear to a thing like that?" Hadley said, pointing to the invitation in Brodi's hand and addressing himself to Mark.

"Evening clothes. Got any?"

Hadley roared with laughter. "Hell, no," he said. "I rented some once and they were too small across the shoulders, or something. Anyway, they split and the tailor said I damaged them on purpose, so we had a fight. It was quite a fight—he kept trying to get hold of one of his hot irons. Hell, no. No one has evening clothes in the mining country."

"Well, Vanetti will do it in time. Want me to go with you this afternoon?" Mark, whose bill with that gentleman was shockingly far behind, was not averse to being credited with bringing in new trade.

"Yea, would you? Be sure they're right then. There seems to be more to that kind of thing than I'd thought."

"Come along, Brodi?"

"No, thanks. Got an errand," Brodi said, thinking of the dreary reaches of Mill Street.

As they made their way out of the crowded club, Mark laid a hand on Brodi's sleeve. "Listen. I'm going to the Fennos for dinner tonight."

"Dinner?"

"Certainly. Willie thinks noon dinners are just a relic of the pioneers, so the Fennos dine at night, my lad, and Aunt Mattie hates it. But, as I was saying, I'm going there and I told 'em I'd bring you along."

"No, thanks. Sorry."

"No? Nonsense. You haven't got anything else to do and the food's good enough. And you can look at Willoughby. That ought to be enough for any man."

Mike made a sound between a grunt and a snort. The Fenno household and everything in it had left a bad taste in his mouth. He wanted no more to do with any of them, ever—aside from the dubious ethics involved in eating Fenno salt while inciting Fenno laborers to strike. He had done that once and his conscience bothered him.

"No, thanks just the same," he said.

When Brodi shook the reins or reached out and rattled the whip in the socket, the horse trotted. Otherwise, he plodded along at a sedate and jerky walk. Mostly he walked. Inherently he had no style. Every once in a while, when a fly lit on his forequarters, he would swing his head and swat at it viciously with a great rattling of curb rings, leaving a fleck of white foam on his side. He was chestnut in color but the heat of the day brought out the sweat in patches, turning his hair in those places to seal-brown satin. He gave off a warm, acrid odor which was wafted back to the buggy in rich waves. A livery stable hack was a luxury in which Brodi did not often indulge.

Long years afterward he was to remember this drive because of a curious illusion that came to him. It seemed to him that he was hearing the city grow. The air was full of the sound of hammers, clok, clok, clok. Every few minutes their beats synchronized, then lost the rhythm once more, clokity, clok, clok, clokity, clokity. The air was heavy with the smell of paint. Ponderous drays rumbled over the wooden paving blocks, light rigs rattled by, delivery boys shouted. And underlying all these immediate noises a distant, heavy, thunderous sound came from the heart of the city.

The full orchestra of prosperity. A man heard it only a few times in his life. It was an exciting thing. Every falling hammer, every turning wheel bringing nearer the fulfillment of someone's dream, making it possible for people everywhere, in all classes, to own things they never could afford before and to do things that formerly were denied them. Building a better and a happier country. A forward step in living standards, a new impetus to culture and art—all because, for some reason not adequately explained by the economists, there was work for everyone.

No wonder, perhaps, that men like Fenno dreamed about fantastic industrial empires. And while prosperity lasted, men always talked, as Fenno talked, as though the millennium had come to stay. It never had. No reason that he could see to think it would this time. Well, then, accepting the fact that it wasn't going to last, how could industrialists be prevented from getting panicky and cutting wages that in lots of cases wouldn't support life decently now. Bring it right down to cases, to, in fact, his special interest, the dock hands. They could get on—but only just—on their twelve cents an hour for their twelve-hour day, provided they could pick up other jobs now and then during the winter when the lakes were closed down. It wasn't much of a living, but they got by.

Could they get by on less? Say ten cents? That two cents might just stand off real hardship. They ought to strike for higher pay now in the hope that the cut, when it came, would be less drastic. But how could they strike with their leader laid up from an accident—their leader and the only one of them who spoke enough English to understand and pass on Brodi's preachings? See Fenno and reason with him? Useless without the backing of the strike—probably useless anyway. Thus Brodi's mind went over the now familiar problems without finding any solution. Brodi had passed the fringes of the town and the wooden paving blocks had given place to a plank road, uneven and noisy and emitting, as the horse trotted over it, little puffs of dust from between the planks.

The buggy dropped off the plank road onto the dirt of Mill Street with a jolt and he drew on the reins a little to slow his horse's pace so that the dust would not smother them altogether. There was no paving on Mill Street of any kind, only the dust that lay a good inch deep over the ruts of dried mud left over from last spring. The dust was a feature of life on Mill Street; it powdered the weeds in the vacant lots on either side of the road and discouraged the grass in the tiny, parched lawns in front of the houses. It penetrated the houses themselves and the women fought it with brooms and mops, just as, all the rest of the year, they fought the mud. The dust rose now around Brodi's slowly moving buggy, soft, powdery, insidious, so that the horse's legs, from the belly down, were lost to sight, and Brodi moved to the middle of the seat and drew in his legs to save the trousers of his best gray suit, even though the house he was seeking was only a little way ahead.

Mill Street stretched before him, drab and unattractive in the hard white sunlight that showed up mercilessly every detail of jerry building and poverty. The houses were small and some of them were painted only on the front. Most had small porches and pointed roofs but at the rear they sank abruptly to the dimensions of a lean-to so that, seen from the side, they appeared to be in a state of semi-collapse. Most of these houses had picket fences which were white before the dust reduced them to its own drab, but as the fences extended only across the front they served no purpose other than a futile gesture toward a better way of life.

These houses were built on flat expanses of what had once been rather poor farm land and now had grown up in teasel and various other weeds which were yellowing slowly from drought. Out of this waste land the Finns had carved themselves little vegetable patches, for these people, wherever they settled, seemed to have an urge to make things grow. The gardens were neatly laid out but they, too, were suffering from the long drought and they had the blowzy look of having passed the peak of the season's yield. Among the gardens were tethered goats and even a cow or two, for life without some semblance of farming activities was unthinkable to the Finns and these animals and the gardens, which were as extensive as the women could care for, represented many a wistful memory of other days.

Across the fields to Brodi's right and about a mile away, lay the outskirts of the city, approaching year by year a little closer, like a lava flow which would in time engulf fields and gardens and houses. To his left, but much closer, rose the black stacks and the long low bulk of Fenno and Company. Straight ahead Mill Street ended abruptly in the road that led to the mill, and through a fringe of straggly, wind-bent trees the lake glittered, gray-blue and metallic in the hot light.

Brodi passed at a snail's pace several vacant lots and drew rein at the third house on the right. There was no hitching post and no carriage block, for horse-drawn vehicles seldom had business on Mill Street and if they came through here at all it was merely as a way of reaching the mill beyond. Brodi, therefore, took the half round of cement on the leather strap out of the buggy with him and anchored his nag with that. A yellowish dog rose from a spot of shade and came forward to smell Brodi's trousers' legs, swinging his tail slowly as though he approved, in advance, of this stranger. Brodi snapped the strap to the ring on his horse's bit and, stooping, gave the dog's side a vigorous pat. A cloud of dust rose from the yellowish hair and Brodi clapped his hands together to rid himself of it. The dog barked once, as though this were a game, and then watched Brodi's retreating figure with disappointed eyes.

The front door stood partly open and, putting his round head to the crack, Brodi said in a loud voice, "Anybody home?"

"*Tule sisään,*" an even louder voice replied.

Interpreting this to mean that he was welcome, Brodi pushed open the door and went in. The room was neat with bare board floor, well scrubbed. On a cot in a corner a short, stocky man lay, a man with huge shoulder muscles and thick neck and hair almost as black as Brodi's own.

"Hi, fella," Brodi said.

The man smiled broadly and the smile broke his face into hard chunks of muscle and showed blackened, stubby teeth.

"Mike!" he said in a delighted roar. "Hi, Mike. How are ya?" He tried to push himself up on the cot with his arms, but a cloud of pain passed over his face and he sank back again.

"Don't move," Mike said, and crossing the room, he held out his hand with all the muscles of his palm tense to receive the Finn's stone-crushing handshake. "How are you doing, Päkkä?"

"Fine, Mike, fine. But God damn, she hurt."

"No wonder. You caught about a hundred pounds of ore on the back of your neck. What do you expect?"

The big Finn laughed as though this were the funniest thing in the world, his face all apart in the hard chunks again. "They can't kill Päkkä, heh, Mike? They can't kill Päkkä." Then he raised his voice to a bellow. "Helga. Helga. *Kahvia.*"

A door opened at the back of the room and a tall woman with a stony, expressionless face looked in. She saw Mike and her expression did not alter but a light came into her heavy eyes. She nodded once and disappeared. A strange apparition took her place in the door way. "The Witch of Endor," Mike thought and, rising, he placed another chair and went to lead the old woman to it. She shrank away from him, clutching at her stringy throat with a clawlike hand.

"You remember me, Mrs. Päkkä." Mike's voice was very gentle and full of a kindness that would have astonished his friend Mark. He stood still and held out his hand to her, waiting for her to get over her fright and uncertainty. She peered from under a fringe of gray, wispy hair first at Mike and then at Päkkä and then at Mike and suddenly she broke into a toothless grin that showed red gums, and came sidling into the room.

Päkkä roared with pleased laughter and slapped his leg under the coarse sheet. "Ma afraid of ev'body but you, Mike. Damn fine fella, Mike. Damn fine fella."

The old woman sat on the straight chair with her bony hands on her knees and grinned her toothless grin and blinked her rheumy eyes.

"Listen, Päkkä," Mike said, standing up and putting one foot on the seat of his chair and his arm on his knee. "We've got to put everything off till spring."

"You mean on counta I'm sick?"

"Yes, on counta you sick, you big so and so. It would have been all right before. The men were all worked up to the point where they'd have struck if Fenno had refused, and then you go and catch that ton of ore on the back of your fool neck."

"You ain't seen Fenno?" A dark cloud settled on the Finn's face.

"No, of course I haven't seen Fenno. What good would that do? He'll refuse, of course, and with you sick and not one of that damn crew of yours speaking more than three words of English . . ." He stopped. The stony-faced woman was standing at his elbow, holding out a plate with a thick mug of evil-looking brownish coffee on it. "Thanks," Mike said. He took the plate and, wiping all expression from his face, raised the mug to his lips.

"You ain' goin' have no strike?" The big Finn looked disappointed.

Mike took another heroic and noisy drag at the coffee. "What the hell good would a strike do now? A month ago, yes. There wasn't enough ore down from the mines to last the winter at that time. Then you had to get yourself hurt. Now . . ." He shut his eyes and took a big swallow of the coffee and looked hopefully into the mug. It was only half gone. "Now they've got near enough what they need so they'd tell you to go to hell and buy what little ore they've got to have from some other mill at a fancy price. The lakes close in six or eight weeks, don't forget, and you all get laid off for the winter anyway. No, wait till spring when they'll have to have the stuff in a hurry. We'll have a real hold on 'em then."

The Finn frowned ferociously, considering this, and one big clenched fist pounded the sheet rhythmically. Mike watched him with interest and his black eyes glittered and his thatch of black hair bristled. After a while the Finn looked up at him sidelong.

"Ve get 'em, yes? Ve get 'em then?"

"Yes, we get 'em then." Mike raised the mug and drained off the last of the coffee.

Driving wearily back toward the city in the reddish glow of a hot sunset, Mike found himself regretting that he had refused the invitation to the Fennos and marveling a little that he should have been asked. The invitation, he reflected, was probably Mark's invention. Fenno would certainly not ask him, though he had behaved as though Brodi's declared liberalism were no more than the yapping of a very small dog.

In the Fenno house Lettie was feeling the tempo of her life to be excitingly increased. Michael was coming to dinner. Lettie hugged the knowledge to her in secret. When she heard it mentioned at lunch— just casually mentioned—her heart had given a great leap and her blood had begun to flow faster so that it was hard to sit quietly with the fork in her hand, not giving anything away. She didn't want any more lunch after that. She wanted to jump up and dash around doing things, just anything, to release some of the excitement in her.

Willoughby said, "Oh, really, Mama. Why on earth? He's just a teacher." She said it in her most supercilious tone and Lettie gave her a dark glance under her drawn-down brows.

After lunch Willoughby went out, all dressed up in pale tan with green quillings and green feathers on her hat to match. She took Ellen with her over the protests of Matild, who thought that Willoughby's idea that she ought to have someone attending her every step when she went out was some of the worst of Willoughby's Eastern nonsense. Having Ellen away for hours at a time like that disrupted the work of the household. When the commotion that usually attended Willoughby's going anywhere had died down, Lettie sought out her mother.

Matild was sitting in the little rocking chair in the sewing room that opened off the landing. She had come here with some idea of sewing —there was always more than the weekly visitations of the sewing woman could handle—and perhaps she would put some of the ruching on the dress that was being made for Willoughby to wear to the Thatcher ball. She wished she could put some around the neck too—it was so very low—but Willoughby wouldn't let her. Matild sighed and fitted herself between the tight arms of the rocker.

When Matild saw Lettie enter she sighed, folded her lips and said nothing. Lettie walked past her to the bureau, picked up a box of pins and shook it, examined a piece of lace and threw it down, riffled through the pages of a Godey's and dropped it with a smack that ran all along Matild's nerves. Then Lettie wandered to the window and began making marks with her finger on the pane. This was too much for Matild's housekeeping instincts.

"Don't do that, dear," she said and sucked in her breath, instantly regretting having said it. This would ordinarily have been the cue for Lettie to say in an aggrieved tone that she wasn't hurting anything— that nobody ever let her do *anything* and the opening words of the inevitable scene would have been spoken. Matild was surprised and relieved, therefore, when Lettie merely crossed over to the cot and flounced down.

"Mama," she said, in what seemed to Matild's apprehensive ear a wheedling tone, "what are we having for dessert tonight?"

"Floating island, I think I told them, dear."

"Couldn't we have Spanish cream? Mama, couldn't we have Spanish cream?"

"Spanish cream's for Sundays, Lettie."

"But *why*, Mama?"

"Well, it's a lot of work," said Matild, floundering for a reason to defend this convention which in her mind needed no defending because it was a convention.

"Couldn't I just ask Katie and see if she would? I mean—company and all."

"It's just Mark and that friend of his."

"*Please*, Mama!"

"Well . . ."

Lettie pressed her advantage no further but, taking this for consent, said, "What centerpiece is Nora going to put on?"

"Let's see." Matild frowned with concentration. "I think it's the one with the pink roses embroidered on that we're using this week, isn't it?"

"The leaves are all faded, Mama. Couldn't we use the lace one?"

"The lace one! That's for very best."

"I'll just tell Nora." Lettie jumped up.

"As though she had springs under her," Matild thought, sighing and relaxing. Peace was cheap at the price of a lace centerpiece, but why should Lettie *care*?

Lettie allowed herself a whole hour to dress for dinner and she started early, for she wanted to be downstairs when they arrived. There were three dresses laid out on the bed, for she had not yet been able to decide which one she would wear. She was happier than she ever remembered being. It was wonderful—simply wonderful—and the last touch of good luck—how could she have forgotten about it until she saw Nora setting the table!—was that Willoughby was going out. She was dressing now.

Lettie sat before her hooded dressing table and pinned up stray locks of hair. They only let Ellen do her hair once a day to Willoughby's twice, but she had been very careful to save it. She did wish, though, they'd let her have puffs like Willoughby's, and not braids. But even so!

You look charming tonight, Miss Leticia, I don't see why they admire your sister so. She is merely pretty! Mr. Brodi, we are not friends. Your attitude— Oh, Miss Leticia, I spoke hastily. I can see now that . . .

Maybe it wouldn't happen just like that. But she would be scornful to him, cold to him and he would see how mistaken he had been. That was why it was so important to have everything nice, her dress and everything just so. And everything *was* nice and Katie said yes, she'd make the Spanish cream, only they'd have to have floating island tomorrow and like it, *she* washed her hands of it. And Ellen had promised to come in, when she was through with Willoughby, to hook her up and just *look* at her back hair. And—and, how could Michael help but be impressed?

Mr. Brodi, I thank you, but—we can never be anything but friends.

No, not even friends. He was simply *hateful*. She'd *show* him!

When she heard carriage wheels on the drive, she snatched up the aster she intended to be discovered in the act of smelling, ran downstairs pell-mell, dropped into a chair and, panting a little, tried to look as though she had been there a long time.

The sound of scraping wire reached her and she heard the faint jangling of one of the bells which hung from the coiled springs over the kitchen stove. Nora took forever to reach the door. Her heart was beating furiously and she raised the aster to her nose with fingers that trembled, but she was all ready to feign surprise and haughty annoyance when Brodi entered. She bent her head low over the aster.

"Hullo. Where's Willoughby?" Mark came idling gracefully into the room with his coat open, showing the most perfect devil-may-care waistcoat.

"Wh—Where's Michael? Mr. Brodi?"

"Couldn't come. Seems to find the atmosphere here inimical to radicalism. Where's Willie?"

It was awful. All through grace Matild kept stealing sidelong glances at her and Lettie knew that she was going to be questioned afterwards about why she had on her best dress. There was a great lump in her throat and she had to sniff and sniff until her father dropped his soup spoon with a clatter and said, "Lettie, stop that or leave the table." They were talking about Michael too and she wished they wouldn't.

"I'm so sorry your friend couldn't come, Mark," Matild was saying kindly. "Didn't he feel well?"

"No," said Mark, and smiled with one side of his thin mouth.

"What did you say he does?" said John Fenno, looking up from the gloomy contemplation of his soup. It was the only piece of biographical information about anybody in which he was the slightest interested.

"He teaches his own brand of history at Hudson, but the thing he's really interested in is the labor movement. Extraordinary chap in some ways. He drove all the way up to town just to see that sick Finn—that foreman who got hurt—remember the one who got in the way of the falling ore basket just before the last directors' meeting? That's where he went this afternoon—to Mill Street to see that fellow—Päkkä, I think his name is."

"What your friend Brodi, and others like him, don't seem to realize is that American workmen are better off than workmen anywhere else in the world. And instead of being thankful for what they have, they try to sap the very thing that put them into this position—the financial power of American industry!" Fenno gave his attention to spooning his soup as though the subject were closed.

Mark, however, had more to say and Lettie stared at him with big, mournful eyes. She was just Lettie Fenno once more, with the burden of all her old inadequacies and hates on her shoulders.

"He comes up once a week to see the guy. Shouldn't wonder if he were paying his doctor's bills too. He seems to like laborers better than people like ourselves. Always has, since college days when he used to make soap-box speeches to the Boston Irish. Amusing chap, though. He's writing an article about the Finns, by the way. About dock hands, really."

"You ought to stop him," Fenno said. "Crack-brained people, these radicals. I don't pay any attention to 'em." And he tipped his plate to get the last rich drops of soup.

Lettie was seeing a vision of Michael, the wonderful Michael, bending over the bed of the sick old Finn. Her mouth was a little open and she was gazing sightlessly at a scallop on the lace centerpiece. She jumped when her mother put her hand on her arm.

"Eat your soup, dear. Your Father's all through."

Lettie began to gulp the hateful stuff, her head bent, blinking tears. "Lettie! Use your spoon *away* from you, dear."

6

"I DON'T see why your father hates parties so," Matild said fretfully as she and Willoughby made their way toward the ladies' dressing room in General Thatcher's imposing house. "I think it looks queer for us to be here alone. And what in the world got into Lettie? Her dress was perfectly all *right* and her hair looked very nice."

"I'm sure I don't know." Willoughby's manner was indifferent, but she knew perfectly well that Lettie, at this moment, lay sobbing on her bed because she had not been able to bear the sight of Willoughby's radiant beauty. This knowledge did not disturb Willoughby at all.

The air in the ladies' dressing room was hot, and heavy with perfume rising from rustling silks and warm bodices. Billowing skirts filled nearly all the available space and the noise of high-pitched, excited feminine voices jarred on Willoughby's nerves. All the young girls seemed to be making a great fuss over each other and, while she waited for Matild to struggle out of her cloak, Willoughby's expression grew scornful. She had no girl friends and she did not want any.

"Do hurry, Mama, and let's get out of here." She tossed her cloak to the attendant and accepted in return a small square of paper numbered in gold. At the sharpness of her daughter's tone Matild's mouth set itself in the familiar lines of injured, stubborn protest and the little pouches in her face drooped dolefully.

"I won't have you speak . . ."

"Don't *mutter,* Mother. You'll have to fix your hair. It's all straggly."

Willoughby turned her back on her mother and began to edge her way through the spreading skirts toward a long mirror with gold carving on its top and a marble shelf at the bottom near the floor. Everywhere around her, pretty young things were rushing up to each other with cries of delight. "Oh, my dear, what a *darling* dress! What a *love* of a feather! What a *sweet* bouquet!" She despised them for their small-town deportment. Many of them were no older than sixteen, buds who wriggled and blushed with eager, timorous excitement. These especially she disliked and though she did not realize why, the fresh nubility of their youth made her want to snap at them when they showed a tendency to be deferential.

As she made her way with difficulty through the crowd no one rushed up to her. They nodded to her and, ceasing their excited chatter, became suddenly absorbed in arranging their bows and ribbons. She knew they thought her "fast." She calmly surveyed herself in the glass, taking her time, and she was quite aware that here and there around the room heads were turned her way and whispered remarks were being made.

"They're jealous," she thought, her mind aware at the same time of the chill around her and of the perfection of her appearance. "And I don't care," she told herself—nor did she, greatly.

She was entirely right. They were jealous of her poise, her easy ability to handle situations that made them blush and stammer, and of her clothes, designed and worn with so much surer a knowledge of style than their girlish fineries. But most of all they envied her incredible beauty. Probably there was not a girl in the room who at one time or another had not felt her dancing partner's hold on her small waist relax and, looking up, discovered him gazing at Willoughby's tall loveliness.

Willoughby dragged her mother away with difficulty from a chat with a friend, hurriedly tucked in the wisps of hair that Matild had forgotten and steered her, none too gently, through the crowd toward the door, noticing with a sigh that soiled marks were already appearing on Matild's white gloves. Willoughby's quick ear had caught the sound of violins tuning and rasping and she knew that in a moment would come that premonitory cadenza warning that partners for the next dance must be sought. At exactly that moment she proposed to make her entrance through the double doors of the ballroom, for it was then that people stopped flirting and talking and began to look about them, and then that their attention could most readily be captured. She propelled her mother's ponderous form down the long hall with such rapidity that Matild swayed from side to side like a ship wallowing in a heavy sea and at length pulled her arm rebelliously from Willoughby's hard grasp.

Willoughby let her go for she had business of her own. She stood still and, straightening her body until her weight fell on the balls of her feet, she pulled her shoulders back and raised her chin. Her bulky costume flowed behind her in graceful lines and the fine contours of her figure became apparent under the swags and draperies of her skirt. Her high breasts strained against her tight bodice and she looked like a figure on the bow of a ship proudly sailing into the wind. The petulance and irritation were gone and she glowed with an inner radiance as though, under the dignity of her pose, she were pulsing with provocative vitality. She paused only long enough to take a dance program with its tiny pencil from a silver tray and made her entrance. It was well planned and beautifully executed.

Seeing all this, Matild's mouth drew down at the corners and the pouches in her face grew hard with disapproval, but Willoughby had forgotten her mother. She was watching with secret excitement the impact of her entrance on the room full of people. Fans stopped fluttering and were used as screens for whispers as cold feminine eyes flew over every detail of her costume. Men searching their partners abandoned the search and came toward her, pulling their dance programs from their pockets. They pressed around her and over their heads she saw Mark idling composedly toward her. With a brilliant smile she handed him her card and he reached it back to her over the heads of the crowd with his name written on it in three places. A minute more and all the little spaces on her card were filled.

It was then that her watchful eye caught sight of General Thatcher, small, dapper and debonair in his evening clothes. He was bending over the hand of a flustered dowager in a headdress of quivering plumes. His apple cheeks glowed, the corners of his eyes were crinkled up in merry wrinkles and the toes of his patent-leather boots turned out like a dancing master's. The instant he saw Willoughby he dropped the dowager's hand and, leaving that astonished lady gazing after him, he crossed the room toward her. He came with the springy step that small men sometimes affect to create the illusion of height, his face wreathed in smiles. And as he advanced between the lines of gilt chairs against the walls, talking died out and turning heads followed his progress.

Everyone watched General Thatcher. The musicians, on the point of beginning the dance, watched him and violins came down from shoulders, waiting for the host to lead out his partner. His partner, General Thatcher's name scribbled on the card in her hand, sat by a potted palm and watched him, cold fury in her heart. The focal point of a hundred eyes, he elbowed his way through the crowd around Willoughby, bowed, took her gloved hand and led her out on the floor. And from the fringes of the crowd, his son, Bobby Thatcher, watched, his mouth slightly open and his brown, spaniel-like eyes liquid with disappointment.

Willoughby felt a delightful prickling along her spine as these many eyes stabbed her. She was very conspicuous and she loved it. She moved in the slow circles of the waltz, smiling faintly and making no attempt to minimize her height, confident in the knowledge that no one dancing with a man of General Thatcher's financial standing could look truly ridiculous, however short he might be. From time to time she bent forward to catch some remark, not bothering that she only heard snatches.

". . . lovelier than ever, Miss Willoughby."

She smiled tolerantly.

"Yes, my dear. Lovelier than anybody here. They pale beside you."

"How is your wife, General Thatcher?"

"Oh, Belinda?" For a moment the General seemed to droop. "Not well, Miss Willoughby. Not well at all. They used to carry her from her bed to a couch, you know, but now even that seems too much for her."

"Doesn't all this music disturb her?"

"No, my dear. She lives in a world of her own." The General brightened. "But don't let's talk about things like that. You're here to have a good time. That's what pretty girls are for! Come on, let's show these young fellows how to dance."

The General fairly pranced and for a few minutes he whirled her so madly that she could scarcely catch her breath against her tight stays. "The silly old fool," she thought. He seemed to be enjoying himself hugely, his apple cheeks bright and his smile as eager as a boy's. Willoughby didn't notice his eyes. Under the artless enjoyment of his expression, few people did. General Thatcher wore a perpetual smile but his eyes never smiled. They were swift and darting and cold, but so well hidden by the amiable wrinkles at the corners and by the drooping lids that few people took them into account in estimating him, and that was a mistake. "That funny little man," was a phrase often applied to General Thatcher by people who did not in the least suspect that, in point of fact, this was exactly what he found it convenient for them to think.

They slowed down and the General gazed up at her with delight. "You are so very pretty, Miss Willoughby. You don't mind if an old friend of your father's tells you so—where is he, by the way? But never mind that. Do you have a good time? Pretty women should always have a good time: Men should give it to them." And he squeezed her hand.

General Thatcher was a notorious hand-squeezer and cheek-patter, acting always on the prerogative of his advanced years, but there was something furtive and significant about this squeeze that made Willoughby look at him sharply under the veil of her lashes. His face was jolly but unreadable. She consulted her own thoughts carefully for a moment and then returned his squeeze with the faintest pressure of her hand. His eager smile remained unchanged and she could not for the life of her tell whether he had felt anything or not. "The old fool," she thought again and concentrated on trying to keep step with his erratic movements.

When the music stopped he almost split his gloves clapping. Then he shouted at her above the din, "The supper dance. Save it for me. I want you to drink champagne with me. Champagne is good for pretty women! I haven't said good evening to your mother yet. Where is she?"

His swift eyes searched among the dowagers and found Matild near the door. Willoughby sighed and followed him. For the supper dance, like the first, Bobby Thatcher's name was on her card, a privilege to which as her host's son he was entitled. She had been planning to elude Bobby and eat with Mark. The General bowed over Matild's hand, giving her compliments that made her blush with pleasure. Then he vanished with consummate skill and a moment later Willoughby saw him smiling before a young thing in pink organdy who couldn't be a day over sixteen, and his face was aglow with pleasure. "For Heaven's sake!" Willoughby thought.

Willoughby danced with most of the city's prominent young men until her feet began to ache and she felt she must have a respite and time for what Matild called "titivating." Without bothering to look in her program to see whose dance she was spoiling, she slipped out and started down the long hall humming "Pretty Bobby Shafto." Halfway to the dressing room she stopped to consider. She hated to face again the gossips and the refugeeing wall flowers gathered in that cloister. There was, if she remembered rightly, a conservatory at the back of the house beyond the dining room. She changed her course.

The huge dining room was deserted but there were sounds of feverish activity in the pantry beyond. The table, stretched out to its longest, was already loaded. There were molds of paté and great hams studded with cloves, their crisp fat cut into diamond shapes, and sliced so that the inside showed pink and appetizing. There were salads and boned capons in jelly, their nudity covered by large polka dots of black truffles. But the crowning glory was the centerpiece and Willoughby, enchanted, bent over the table to admire this in detail. There was, first of all, a great mound of candied fruit in jewel-like colors, resting on a nest of smilax leaves. The sugar crystals on the fruit caught the light from the many candles around the room and winked like diamonds. On each side of the fruit were six cock pheasants. They were complete in all their glory of iridescent feathers and gilded beaks, and their long tail plumes lay gracefully on the dark mahogany. Willoughby smiled with pleasure, knowing that at a touch the feathers would fall away, exposing the rich meat underneath all sliced and ready. She loved such elegancies as these.

Her eyes traveled around the big room from the fireplaces at either end, over the huge, sparkling chandelier to the long sideboard already crowded with silver buckets from which protruded the slim necks of champagne bottles. Outmoded in style this room might be, but rich, rich. She wondered how much money General Thatcher had. More than her father, perhaps, and only that sick woman who never came out of her room and Bobby of the calflike eyes to enjoy it all. Willoughby saw herself sitting at the head of the beautiful table, her neck and wrists sparkling with jewels that made her beauty a hundred times more beautiful. *The young and incredibly lovely Mrs. Thatcher entertained* . . . She sighed and, reaching out, selected with care a bonbon shaped like a rose.

She wandered on and found the conservatory, its entrance a tunnel of potted palms. The conservatory was deserted and moist from the small fountain that plashed in the center, and it smelled of damp earth. No wonder nobody came here, Willoughby thought, secure in the knowledge that her curls could defy damp, and she smiled maliciously, thinking of the havoc wrought in Lettie's hair by even the lightest summer shower. A small mirror hung over a settee and, stripping off her gloves, she peered into it critically. From a pocket under her blue satin polonaise she drew out a piece of chamois and a round pillbox full of rice powder. "Heavens," she thought, "if any of the old cats caught me using powder! Ah, lovely! Really lovely!" She tried out several expressions and finally smiled at her reflection as ravishingly as at a lover.

A low and rather bold laugh startled her and she whirled around. A stranger stood in the doorway and she thought in that quick moment, as she recovered her composure, that he was the biggest man that she had ever seen. The muscles on his shoulders bulged so that they made his fashionable and obviously new dinner clothes seem effeminate. He was leaning against the door frame with one hand in his pocket—no gentleman stood thus in the presence of a lady—and he looked her over so appraisingly that she felt her blood begin to tingle. Having finished his scrutiny at leisure, he pulled his hand out of his pocket and came toward her, smiling.

"Haven't we met somewhere before?"

There was something overwhelming and masterful about him. She backed against the settee. "No," she said. "Not anywhere. Never." And as he continued to smile at her, she added, "You know that perfectly well." At that he laughed loudly.

This was the moment to sweep haughtily past him, but he stood between her and the door. She opened her fan with a jerk and began fanning herself rapidly, her eyes blazing with indignation.

"Well, we've met now," he said lazily, "so don't get excited." His smile broadened. "If I'd known there was anybody like you in this town, I wouldn't have waited this long to meet you. Sit down. And let's make friends." He gestured toward the settee behind her and, seizing a little chair by its fragile back, swung it around and set it down with a thump not a foot from her.

How rude! How presumptuous! But while she was putting on this display of anger, she was feeling a sensation which interested her tremendously. This was a delightful tingling of the nerves, half anticipation and half a titillating fright, and with it a shortness of breath as though she had been running. It was exciting and made her feel more alive than she had felt for a long time. She lowered her lashes and looked him over calculatingly and her look, though veiled, was as bold and free of self-consciousness as his own. But when she raised her eyes to his, she saw there an expression that was so hot and at the same time so full of a detached amusement that the flesh at the back of her neck crawled, her sensual mouth opened slackly and she thought that never in her life had she felt so exciting a sensation. Without realizing what her face betrayed, she sank to the settee with a carefully careless grace. He sat down at once and inched the frail chair closer.

"I was watching you making faces at yourself in the glass. You're a damn pretty woman."

"You shouldn't spy on people." The fan fluttered.

"I'd spy on you any chance I got. Anywhere. You're lovely."

"I've heard that before, lots of times."

"I've no doubt you have, but you're hearing it from *me* now!" His eyes swept over her again.

Willoughby's pulse was still racing and she was suddenly very much aware of the low cut of her gown in front, to which Matild had objected almost with tears. She stole a downward glance under her lashes at her own white bosom. Only the topmost part of the full curves of her breasts could be seen and only a hint of the hollow between them. She drew a deep breath and her breasts rose, straining against the bones in her bodice. She looked at him sidewise and saw a deep glitter in his eyes. She laughed suddenly with pleasure and exhilaration.

He leaned forward, half rising from his chair, and a delicious fright ran along her nerves. "Sit down," she said. "Sit down." He leaned back in the groaning chair. "Here, take this." She thrust her fan toward him.

He took it and she noticed that his hands were unmanicured and broad across the palms, as though at some time he had worked hard with them. He turned the fan about curiously, examining the delicate ivory filigree of the end pieces.

"What do I do with this?"

"Fan me, please. Here, open it, silly. Like this." She reached out to show him and her hand touched his. He gave her a swift look and then dropped his eyes to the fan.

She laughed happily. "You look as though you'd never held a fan before."

"I never have, and that's a fact."

He raised the fan and batted the air a few times, smiling with amusement at himself as he did so, while she leaned back luxuriously and gazed at him, her blue eyes wide. The currents of air stirred perfume from her gown and she knew by the quick flare of his nostrils that it had reached him.

"I've never seen you at any of the dances," she said, lowering her eyes demurely.

"I've never been to a dance before."

"You never . . . ? Why, for goodness' sake. Where have you been?"

"The woods in Michigan mostly."

"Don't you even dance?"

"Not what you'd probably call dancing."

"Why don't you learn, then?"

"Will *you* teach me?"

"Perhaps." She looked at him swiftly, an intense and flashing look, and lowered her lashes quickly.

"How about a lesson right now?" he said, standing up and holding out his arms to her.

"No. Get me a glass of champagne first, and we'll see."

He came back with two glasses and a whole bottle. She sighed happily and settled herself against the pillows of the settee. Willoughby loved champagne, but no lady ever drank more than a sip or two. This man looked as though he wouldn't know so very much about ladies. She held out her hand for the glass and took a deep swallow. His wine was gone before her glass was half empty and he held the bottle out to her invitingly. She let him fill it to the brim.

"Silly stuff," he said, watching the bubbles break on the surface of his glass. He made no further comments and they drank in silence, sharing enjoyment. At the end of his third glass and her second he made a face and, taking her glass from her, set them both on the floor.

"I don't know whether I like being rich or not. This stuff tickles my nose. Rye's my drink."

"Are you rich?"

"I'm going to be. *You* like it though—I can see."

"How do you know I'm rich?"

"I can tell by the smell. You always can. What about that dancing lesson?"

He got up and held out his hands to her and she let him pull her up from the settee. The sound of the orchestra was coming to them faintly. She took his hand and put it on her waist, a waist made small and firm by the lacing of her stays, and he instantly tightened his arm and drew her close to him.

"No, no," she said, struggling free. "Not like that. You hold me loosely."

"With all that air between us? It seems a shame. What next?"

"Listen. *One,* two three. *One,* two three. Do you hear it? A long glide and two short ones, like this." She stretched out her foot and laid it along the inside of his, giving it a little shove. The motion brought her leg close to his and with a thrill she felt the bulges of his muscle under his trousers. They glided awkwardly a few times and she kept her leg pressed close to the inside of his. The champagne warmed her blood and filled her with a reckless excitement. He was holding her close to him now and she made no protest, yielding to the intoxication of his magnificent body and to the feelings within herself. She closed her eyes. Her face, turned up to his, was pale from her sensual abandon and her parted lips were red and moist. Without her becoming really aware of it, their gliding stopped but their bodies swayed together in time to the music. She was lost in an ecstasy that took no account of anything but herself. Suddenly he put both arms around her and, pressing her tight against him, kissed her upturned mouth with a violence and a passion that swept through her like flame.

The unexpectedness of it brought her back to reality and a sense of her surroundings. A feeling of outrage followed the first shock. This was not playing the game as it was known in her world. To be kissed by a stranger and in such a manner! Kissed, perhaps, but only after long preliminaries of artful tantalizing on her part and desperate pleadings from the man. But even then, never pressed so tight that the animal heat of his body warmed hers and the beating of his heart speeded the tempo of her own. Anger seized her and she struggled to free herself.

In another part of the house, while this was taking place, Mark was searching for Willoughby. He watched the dancers from the doorway of the ballroom until he was convinced that she was not among them. He turned away and began to saunter with an indolent air into room after room, where he found a number of couples engrossed in each other but no sign of Willoughby. Inevitably, his quest led him through the dining room which was beginning, now that the supper dance was near, to attract a few hungry people, and from there, at length, he drifted toward the conservatory.

He was about to enter this ornate place when the looking-glass on the far wall gave him a sudden view of two struggling figures—Sam Hadley holding Willoughby tightly in his arms. Even in the dim image in the glass, Mark recognized Willoughby instantly and with one quick motion leaped back from the doorway and concealed himself behind the bulwark of palms.

Peering through the fronds, he watched the struggle, and all the casualness of his manner was gone. Hadley, the great oaf from the mines, mauling Willoughby! The thought of rushing to Willoughby's aid never entered Mark's head, for he gave Willoughby's resistance about the weight it deserved; but suddenly he was seized by an anger against Hadley so violent that he trembled. In that minute Willoughby seemed to him infinitely more desirable than she had ever been before, and Hadley assumed the form of a rival, a threat, a dangerous menace to be fought with every sly and clever and subtle method he could devise. Without consciously realizing that he had taken a resolution, Mark determined to make Willoughby his.

Another sort of man might have interrupted this scene. Not Mark. He held the fronds of the palms apart with thin, twitching fingers and watched and smoldered and planned. Hadley held Willoughby tightly, his lips pressed hard against hers with a strength that startled and finally frightened her. She twisted and turned, she tried to free her hands, but his arms were like bands of iron, and he pressed his body into hers in a way that made her blood run hot at the same time that it filled her with rage. She tried to move her head but his mouth clung to hers. Finally, with a desperate effort, she managed to turn her face a little to one side, not much, but just enough, and with savage joy she sank her teeth into his lower lip.

He let her go, then, shoving her away from him violently so that she stumbled over her flounces and almost fell.

"You—you—you unspeakable *brute!*"

He was holding his handkerchief to his lip and his eyes glared at her over it.

"We've got names for women like you in the mining country—names I guess rich girls don't get to hear."

"What do you mean, names? You insulted me!"

"You asked for it."

"I did not." She wanted to run out of the room and leave him and never see him again, but her knees felt weak and trembly. The trembling spread all over her and for a moment she was afraid she might be going to cry. She went to the settee and sat down quickly, forgetting for once in her life to be graceful.

In spite of his anger, Mark could not help enjoying her discomfiture, and he smiled a little and prepared to make his presence known. Before he could come out of his hiding place, however, he heard quick, light steps approaching, and he shrank back, hoping fervently the palms would conceal him. General Thatcher appeared and, though he passed close to Mark, he was looking straight before him like a man with a purpose and Mark, to his great relief, remained undiscovered.

Mark did not wait longer, but when he was beyond the range of vision of those in the conservatory he walked slowly with bowed head toward the dining room, a man deep in thought, reviewing in his mind his resolution to win Willoughby and the money that would come to him through her. Now that the resolution had been taken, the difficulties he was sure to encounter were, for the first time, presenting themselves in force to his active mind. He frowned—and the frown was like a slanting exclamation point, betraying tension and determination.

General Thatcher made his entrance into the conservatory, dandified and smiling.

"Miss Willoughby, my dear!" He crossed the room to her, with his hands held out. "Miss Willoughby! It's the supper dance. Have you forgotten? I've been hunting you. Can't miss my chance to dance with you and take you in to supper, now can I?"

"I'm tired. I don't want to dance."

"Good. Splendid. We'll just sit here and talk, and you can tell me what you think of all these young fellows."

He sat down beside her and then, seeming to see Hadley for the first time, he leaped up and held out his hand.

"Ah, Sam, my boy! So glad you could come tonight. You've been keeping Miss Willoughby company? Splendid! We must have a talk by and by—after supper." Still holding onto Hadley's hand, he maneuvered skilfully toward the door so that there was nothing for Hadley to do but follow.

The General rejoined Willoughby, sat on the edge of the settee and carefully raised the knees of his trousers between his thumbs and forefingers.

"What luck for an old man finding the belle of the ball all alone like this. I've got an idea. Let's have supper here, just the two of us. An old fellow hasn't any right to keep you all to himself I know, but I've got you now."

"Delightful," Willoughby murmured, still dazed. The General sped to the door. "Goodness," she thought, "he darts around like a dragonfly. He makes me tired." The General was bawling for food in a parade-ground voice that, coming from so small a body, made her want to laugh.

"Bring us pheasant—lots of pheasant and salad. For two. And . . ." His eyes flickered over the champagne bottle and the glasses on the floor. "More champagne."

Two hours later Mark stood on the front steps, and the confusion of departure was all around him. The dispatcher bawled numbers into the night. Carriages dashed up, their wheels crackling on the gravel drive, took on loads of gaily laughing people and moved away toward the remote iron gates where the night digested them one by one.

Mark tossed a fold of his opera cape behind his shoulder with irritable grace. He made a striking picture standing there in the spill of light from the lanterns by the door. His evening clothes were perfection and worn with an air that no one else in the city could quite achieve. His vest was pinched in at the waist rather more fashionably than most; a delicate design done in fine silk braid outlined his lapels and his cuffs, and the narrow stripe down the side of his trousers was of gleaming satin. His tall hat was perched at an impeccable angle and his hair was brushed into intricate, overlapping waves of the utmost elegance.

He was thinking about Willoughby and wondering what had transpired after he had left her, and Hadley, with the tittuping General. He rather regretted that he had not waited to see. And he stared morosely at the drive, goaded by the thought that, in the pursuit of a pretty woman, it is never wise to dawdle lest you find, as sundials say, that it is later than you think.

There seemed to be some trouble on the drive and the starter was yelling hoarsely, "Number fifty-nine. Number fifty-nine is blocking the way!" Some stoppage seemed to have occurred in the orderly process of digestion.

"Hullo," a voice said at Mark's elbow.

Mark turned. "Oh, hullo, Hadley," he said coldly. "Enjoy the evening?"

"Well enough. Considerably, as a matter of fact. Say, who is that tall girl standing down there by the carriage that's holding things up?"

Down on the drive Matild's purse had slipped from her hand during that difficult moment of hoisting herself into the carriage. It had fallen behind the wheel, and Joe, the coachman, was trying to retrieve it with the butt end of the whip while Willoughby stood by, bored and indifferent.

Mark laughed, not very pleasantly. "Don't you *know*? That's your boss's daughter."

"Huh?"

"Willoughby Fenno."

"Jesus," Hadley said softly.

PART TWO

7

WHEN Lettie thought about having to go to the Thatcher ball her stomach felt cold and the palms of her hands grew damp with apprehension. Her father made her choke down some dinner but when she went upstairs to dress she felt weak and shaky. Parties were torture to Lettie. Her cheeks would flame in an agony of shyness when she made her awkward curtsy and held out a limp hand to be shaken. She would have to sit with her mother and hear her say, "Lettie, sit up straight and don't look so sullen. You'll never get a partner that way." And she would try to look like the other wallflowers sitting among the potted palms, straining to appear bright and eager and as though they were having a wonderful time, desperation in their eyes.

She hated having to be thankful for any partner at all, even the youths who were dragooned by their mothers into dancing with her and who made no attempt to conceal their unwillingness. She hated to watch Willoughby waltz by. When she could escape to the dressing room it was a blessed relief and she stayed there as long as possible, pretending to be very much absorbed in fixing her hair.

While she was getting ready to put on her ball dress she felt really sick. Little waves of prickly damp chill ran over her body and she wondered hopefully if she might be catching something. They'd be sorry then. She wanted to be sick. Her shoulders drooped and her under lip hung slack and heavy as she made a half-hearted effort to fix herself up. "I wish they'd leave me *alone*," she thought as she struggled into the too-girlish dress that Willoughby said was "suitable." "I wish I was dead!" A great lump hurt her throat and she blinked back tears.

Even then, it might have been all right and she might have gotten through the evening somehow if Willoughby hadn't come and stood in the doorway, radiant as a star. Lettie gazed at her slackly for a moment and then despair overwhelmed her and a horrible awareness of herself, and she threw herself face down on her bed and burst into sobs.

She was still lying there, sobbing and beating the counterpane with her fists when the front door slammed behind Willoughby and her mother, but she held her breath to listen to the sharp sounds of the carriage wheels on the drive. There was something so final about that sound. Now that they were gone and the lights and music of the party beyond her reach, she felt regret. This time it might have been different. She started to cry again but since there was no one to hear her, the stormy bitterness abated and she cried quietly, in sorrow for herself.

There is, however, very little satisfaction to be had from tears which are shed alone and after a while Lettie's gave way to sniffs and silences. The house was very still. At this hour she knew the maids would be lingering over their supper and her father would be smoking in his study with the stack of papers on his knee which were his excuse for staying away from the ball. She wriggled into a more comfortable position on the bed and lay for a while in the mental vacuum of emotional exhaustion, scarcely feeling her own body, as though she were floating. Then she heard loud voices and they startled her but it was just Ellen and Nora coming up the stairs to turn down the beds and talking because they did not know that she and her father had stayed home from the party. She heard the rustle of Ellen's uniform approaching her door.

"Miss Lettie! Holy Mother, you startled me. Are ye sick, now? Nora, come here, it's Miss Lettie."

Lettie rolled over on her back and weak tears oozed out of the corners of her eyes.

"Your poor dress, Miss Lettie. Shall I help you out of it? There now, you just lie still—and you missing the party and all. Does it hurt anywhere?"

Lettie shook her head and gulped. Their kindness made her feel sorry for herself again. They put her to bed as though she were really ill and she lay limp in their hands. Nora took the pins out of her hair while Ellen washed her face with a cool cloth and made little clucking noises to her as though she were a child, and when they blew out the lamps and left her lying in comfort on the big square pillows she was filled with a soft sadness that was very consoling.

Now, in the dark, Lettie entered a different world. It was a world to which she often fled for she could move about there freely with sureness and confidence, without the dreadful consciousness of self, without fear and without the scar. This dream world was her refuge. There were many different stories which she told herself, stories which never progressed very far in plot but which she told over and over. She was always the central figure. Sometimes she was herself, Lettie Fenno, to whom wonderful things happened. Sometimes she was an altogether different person, the Princess Imogene or the heroine of a book of recent reading or a singer, like Jenny Lind, accepting the applause of thousands, or even a sweet-faced nun in a cloister.

Recently, however, these dreams had failed to nourish her and gradually she had worked out a new one. In this dream she was always patient and sad and, in spite of the cruelties of her family, who did not appreciate her, she suffered in silence. No one guessed the grief in her heart because it looked to everyone as though she had a life of ease and luxury—poor little rich girl—when all the time she longed to give her life to the poor.

Here her dream became slightly confused with the legend of Saint Teresa as related to her by the pious Irish girls. When her basket was uncovered, however, there were no roses but the richest food from her own table. And it was Michael Brodi who stepped forward from the crowd to defend her—against what, was not quite clear.

"Michael," she whispered, "Heaven will reward you."

"I do not want my reward in Heaven, Miss Lettie, I want it now."

Taking her heavy basket on his arm, his black eyes burning, he raised her hand reverently to his lips. And Lettie, seeing him look at her thus, turned away to hide her tears.

Tonight, however, she varied her dream a little. She saw herself kneeling by the bedside of the sick Finn, an old and feeble man with a long beard who gazed at her with worshipping eyes. A shaft of sunlight, coming in some mysterious manner through the ceiling, illumined her kneeling figure while the sick man's family stood in shadow and admired her. And Michael entered.

It was at this point that the idea came to her. Perhaps it had been lingering on the periphery of her consciousness, waiting for a chance to move in, but its advent was like a shock. Why not take food to the old man, real food in Katie's market basket? She sat bolt upright staring into the darkness. Michael would be sure to hear about it—perhaps he might even find her there—and then he would admire her and realize how wonderful she really was and be so sorry for the mean things he said to her. Perhaps he would tell her so and she would scorn his apologies—*"You do not understand"*—and he would feel dreadfully and she would never speak to him again.

Sitting in the dark with her arms wound tightly around her knees, she began to plan. Katie's market basket and a damask napkin to cover the things inside—and . . . But how could she get there? They wouldn't let her use the carriage—they wouldn't let her go at all. She'd have to go in secret. A livery-stable hack and driver—how much did that cost? There were five dollars under the tissue paper in her hat box. The difficult part would be getting the food—she couldn't just ask Katie for it—and then getting out of the house without being seen. Her thick brows drew together in a frown of concentration as she considered these problems.

Finally she decided that, in the matter of getting out of the house unseen, she would just have to rely on luck. But the food—most of the jellies and preserves were in the cellar and the stairs went right down out of the kitchen and the kitchen was never deserted for a moment in the day time. For a while she thought she would have to give up the whole beautiful plan and then a startlingly simple solution occurred to her. She could get the food now, while the girls were in bed and her father way off in his study absorbed in his work. She could hide it all in the back of her wardrobe until tomorrow.

She pushed back the covers and sat on the edge of her bed, feeling with her toes for her slippers. She found her robe and put it on and, her heart beating wildly, she opened her door and tiptoed out into the hall. Everything was quiet; the only sounds were the slow ticking of the old clock on the stairs and an occasional creak or snap as the new house got on with the slow business of settling itself. A faint light came to her from the gasoliere in the hall, turned to its lowest, and as she began the cautious descent of the stairs she saw a pool of yellower light from a lone lamp left burning in the drawing room.

Anyone watching Lettie then, as she furtively stole from step to step, might have been truly astonished at the change which had come over her. The droop, the hang-dog air, the sullen look were gone. Lettie's shoulders were lifted by excitement, there was a gleam in her eye and an eager flush in her face.

She crept into the dim dining room, her eyes wide at the monstrously distorted shapes that familiar things assume when they consort with shadows. She did not allow herself to be afraid, but all her senses were sharpened and alert. The leather-covered pantry door had a new clamminess under her hand and its creak was like a midnight graveyard sound. The pantry was dark with an abysmal kind of darkness and the steady drip of a faucet into the sink was not a sound but something felt by all her nerves. She drew in her breath and hastened toward the kitchen door.

She almost backed out again in terror for here the darkness was lighted by an eerie red glow that brought her heart to a standstill until she realized that it came from the banked-up fires shining through the crevices in the great iron stove. She hastened to grope for a match where she thought they ought to be, in a tin holder tacked to the wall above the varnished wainscoting. By its light the room ceased to be a cavern in some strange hell and her nerves returned to normal sufficiently to allow her to experience the faint revulsion which comes to those who strike a light in a deserted kitchen. An aroma hung in the air, compounded of frying pans and oil lamps and yellow soap. She took a candle in a tin holder from a shelf and lit it just as the match was about to burn her fingers. She picked up Katie's basket from under the marble-topped pastry table and opened the cellar door.

Here her courage almost failed her for this part of the house was unfamiliar and the stairs, beyond the yellow circle of her light, went down into black nothingness, and, new as the house was, a damp smell rose from the sandstone walls. Her robe trailing on the stairs, she went down while great shadows leaped and danced and the candle flickered from mysterious drafts.

The cellar was partitioned into rooms and she had no idea where she would find the shelves of preserves. The first room she tried held the quiescent furnace, a Fenno pride, raising octopus arms. She backed out and shut the door. The next room was the laundry, smelling of soap and dampness. The next held long racks of lath, already filled with apples and hard pears. She paused for a moment to consider the wisdom of plundering these or the long bins of potatoes and squash which lined the walls, but she remembered that the true heroine carried only delicacies to the poor and she turned away.

The last room was the one she sought and in the uncertain light she saw a padlock hanging from the hasp. Remembering too late that her father had ordered this door to be kept locked, she could have cried. In bitter disappointment she reached out to touch the padlock. Matild had been here last to dole out supplies to Katie, and Matild was never on good terms with locks. This one came off in Lettie's hand.

As she pushed open the door a wayward draft flickered her candle. A drop of hot wax fell on her hand and the shadows leaped and danced more wildly than ever. She had to reassemble her courage before stepping inside. She moved with the utmost caution for she was right below John Fenno's study now and the slightest sound, the slightest clink of glass or scrape of shoe would surely reach him. Nevertheless, it made her feel safer to realize he was there, just over her head, and she advanced into the looming shadows with more confidence.

This was a big room, half given over to honeycomb racks from which protruded the necks of wine bottles, the other half covered with shelves on which stood many rows of preserve jars and jelly glasses. On the floor in front of the shelves crocks of pickles were lined up and in the center of the room stood a group of barrels. These were the pigeon barrels and on the point of setting down the basket and the candle on one of them she paused to consider the advisability of starting her looting here. Thoughts of dipping into the stiff salt and drawing out the flattened brown forms deterred her. Besides, wild pigeon was so common, everyone ate them. Perhaps the Finns ate them too. Perhaps, when the birds appeared over the city in a cloud so dark it blotted out the sun they, like everyone else, rushed to the rooftops with sticks and brooms and shovels to knock the birds from the sky.

She turned her back on the pigeon barrels and tiptoed across the room toward a sturdy door. A duck, she felt, would be the thing, a duck with feathers of bronze and shining green and soft, limp neck. She muffled the latch with the palm of her hand and the thick door swung open, wafting toward her such a wave of chill air that she clutched her robe close to her. She returned for her candle and stepped inside. All the iron hooks were empty, hooks which later would be full of hanging forms, pathetically head down, ducks and pheasants and quail and perhaps a deer or two.

She sighed and looked around her curiously for she had never been in this ice room, which was so much bigger than the one in the old house. The ice, put in before the house was even finished, was low now. Once the chunks had lined the walls from floor to ceiling but now they were mere mounds under the covering of sawdust and burlap, trickling away into the drain in the floor.

Lettie went out and shut the door, thinking about the thing that happened last fall that made her father so angry and his friends laugh so hilariously. She herself could see nothing funny about it. The ducks were always left in their crates until her father came home from the marshes, when he and Joe, in mufflers and overcoats, would unpack them, tie their legs together and swing them from the iron hooks. Last fall Fenno had shipped home a case of a hundred ducks. Matild should have known they were ducks, for the marshes were productive of nothing else but good fellowship and head colds. But the case said plainly, as she later pointed out with tears, "Rare Old Wine," so she sent it to the wine room where, after a dormant period, it made its presence known.

Still shivering a little, Lettie began the business of filling her basket, walking along the shelves and taking down jars at random without bothering to read the labels. When the basket was nearly full she stood in front of the wine racks for a moment, deep in thought, and then carefully pulled out a bottle from a corner near the floor where she hoped it would not be noticed. She did not read the label of this either. It was champagne.

The load was heavy and the stairs were steep. She held the candle in one hand and the basket in the other and her long robe got under her feet at every step, but this was a state of affairs she took for granted. Climbing stairs with both hands full was simply something women, in the nature of things, could not do and had seldom been able to do, for that matter, at any time since stairs were invented. Wishing fervently for pins, she inched her way up and reached the top at the cost of a torn hem. There she abandoned her candle and the rest of the way was easy.

She slept much better than usual and woke early to a sense of excitement. Immediately she began to think about what she would wear that afternoon. It was most important, she felt, and nothing she owned was right. All her dresses seemed like ugly, school-girlish things, and she spent some minutes in intense hatred of Willoughby, who bullied Matild into accepting her ideas about what was suitable for a sister she intended to keep out of the young-lady class as long as possible. What the occasion called for, Lettie knew, was a dress with a train, a train that rustled like Willoughby's dark green silk. She loved that dress with its taffeta underskirt and the sea-green velvet bows for trimming. If she could only wear it, just this once.

Then at lunch a wonderful thing happened. Her father, it seemed, was staying at the office late, even though this was Saturday, and that would leave the carriage free all afternoon. When Willoughby heard that, she decreed a round of calls for herself and her mother that would fill the whole afternoon. Lettie listened to them bickering about it with her head bowed so that they would not see how excited she felt. Afterward, she watched their stylish departure from behind the lace curtains in the drawing room, so anxious to have them gone that she jumped up and down with eagerness, like a child. The grays tossed their thorough-

bred heads and their silver bits tinkled like bells. The carriage began
its stately progress and the two Dalmatians took up their places docilely
at the rear axle. Lettie dropped the curtain and ran from the room.

In the hall she almost collided with Ellen.

"Why, Miss, whatever is the matter? You look all excited."

"Nothing, Ellen, oh, nothing."

She dashed up the stairs and Ellen gazed after her, thinking, "Now
whatever? She looks all different and if it weren't for that scar, now,
she'd be quite pretty, she really would."

Lettie went straight to Willoughby's room, just to look at the green
silk with the sea-green velvet bows, nothing more. She took it off the
pegs, thrilled by the lovely rustle of the taffeta and, holding it up to
herself, crossed the room to Willoughby's long mirror. Green was more
her color than Willoughby's, really. It made her eyes almost green and
little lights in her hair, that she had never noticed before, gleamed
reddish. She turned her head slightly so that the scar would not show
and smiled at herself in the glass. Then with one swooping motion she
gathered the dress into her arms and ran from the room.

The dress didn't fit her very well, Lettie had to admit that, but it
was not so bad, really, except just in front. The square neck, too open
for a street dress, according to Matild, was stiffly boned to the shape of
Willoughby's rounded breasts. On Lettie there was a rather appalling
void between the edge of the dress and Lettie's flat chest. She stood
as straight as she could and took a deep breath, but the void remained.
She was ready to cry with vexation but the dress was lovely, lovely. If
only they would let her wear the little ruffled pads with which other
girls of her age remedied the shortcomings of nature. She didn't even
own any. Then she rushed to her dresser, pulled open the untidy top
drawer and, seizing a handful of handkerchiefs, she began cramming
them down the front of the green dress. The effect, she felt, was dis-
tinctly better, and if she remembered to take deep breaths and hold
them as long as she could . . .

Her hack drove into Mill Street at a leisurely pace and the driver
turned around to look at her.

"This is Mill Street, lady. Where do you want to go?"

"Oh," Lettie said and with a sick feeling she realized that this all
important detail had slipped her mind. "I—I don't know," she said
weakly and felt the self-conscious blush creeping over her face. She
sank back in the corner of the carriage. The driver was looking at her
so strangely—all the men loitering around the door of the livery stable

had looked at her the same way. She felt the buoyancy of her adventure departing and her inadequacies and miseries returning to her.

"Don't you know what house it is, girlie? This is a pretty tough street."

"Just let me think a minute. I—I'll remember the name in a minute. It's somebody that's sick."

The driver turned his back and the horse drooped his head and swished at flies. She searched her memory frantically for Mark's words, "A foreman by the name of—of—Päkkä!"

"The name's Päkkä," she said, "but I don't know just where he lives. He's one of my father's foremen, you see," she said, struggling for her lost dignity.

"Yea? Want to ask that woman where he lives?"

The driver pointed with his whip toward a thickset woman who was coming down the path toward them. She was dour-looking and she kicked out her skirts ungracefully as she hurried along. Lettie seized the side of the carriage in both hands and leaned out.

"Excuse me, please. Can you tell me where Mr. Päkkä lives?"

The woman stood and stared at her, a heavy surprise in her face giving way to a stony look of unmistakable hostility.

"Päkkä. Mr. Päkkä. Do you know where he lives?" Lettie asked politely but the unfriendly look upset her and she felt the clammy perspiration start under her armpits.

After a long cold stare the woman turned around and pointed a work-roughened hand and without looking at Lettie again she resumed her way.

"Thank you," Lettie murmured to her retreating back.

"I guess she meant here," the driver said, drawing up. "Look, girlie, it's none of my business, but do you think you ought to go in there alone?"

Fright was beginning to mix itself with the uncertainty in Lettie's mind and she felt herself sinking once more into her familiar morass of inadequacy and self-torment. Her bright dream and the magic release it brought her from herself were gone. There was desperation in her eyes but she lifted her chin in a way that she imagined looked like Willoughby.

"I know what I'm doing, thank you."

The driver shrugged and she lifted her basket with hands that trembled.

Crossing the dusty path, trailing Willoughby's green gown in the dirt, she regained some composure. Now everything would be all right. Now they would all turn to her with gratitude. Perhaps there would be tears in the old man's eyes. Perhaps he would even take her hand and kiss it. What should she do then? *"Do not thank me, I am but the —but the—I but bring you these gifts from a full heart."* She raised her hand and knocked.

Somewhere inside a dog barked and a shrill, harsh voice called something unintelligible. "Goodness," she thought, "don't they speak English?" This was another contingency she had not foreseen. There were sounds of heavy steps inside and the door was thrown wide.

A woman stood there, a woman who, in appearance, was very like the first one Lettie had spoken to, but bigger and even more stolid. Her arms were bare to the elbow and glistening with water as though she had just pulled them out of a washtub, and the muscles bulged like a man's. She looked Lettie up and down with a cold, impersonal curiosity that made the flesh on Lettie's spine crawl.

"I've come to see Mr. Päkkä," she began. "I've brought him these." She lifted the basket a little.

The woman glanced at it and, turning her head, called out something in Finnish to someone inside. Then she resumed her cold scrutiny of Lettie. Her eyes came to rest on the scar and in their dull depths Lettie saw the first spark of animation. She turned her head and the woman moved a little and continued to stare at it, and suddenly Lettie wanted to turn and run. She wanted to throw herself across her bed and cry and cry, but before she could take more than one backward step two more women crowded past the tall one in the doorway, flanking Lettie on either side.

One of these women was short and fat with a dirty apron covering an enormous abdomen. She smiled at Lettie, revealing the lack of three front teeth, and the smile was more frightening than the tall woman's cold stare. The other woman was old and bent and yellow. Her whitish hair hung down in wisps, and patches of parchment-colored scalp showed through it here and there. A strange, sickening odor of age, food and disease surrounded her. These women were so far beyond anything in Lettie's experience that they seemed scarcely human to her, as though they must be devoid of normal feelings and outside the bounds of ordinary behavior. She would have been quite incredulous had she been told that, since she was to them an equally strange being, they regarded her in much the same way.

The woman with the missing teeth spoke. "Vat you want?"

"I—I'm Lettie Fenno. I'm Miss Leticia Fenno," she said in a strangled voice. "I've brought some jellies to Mr. Päkkä."

The fat woman said something to the other two in Finnish and they all began talking at once in strident voices. Through her confusion Lettie thought she heard the name Fenno several times. Then they stopped their jabbering and all three stared at her again with their stupid, dull eyes.

The rest of it happened so quickly that Lettie was taken by surprise. The big woman reached out and grabbed the handle of the basket. Lettie, terrified by the gesture, hung on and the big woman with a jerk wrenched it out of her hand. She saw the damask napkin pulled off and the fat woman, plunging both hands in the basket, raised the bottle of wine and a jar of jam with guttural sounds of delight.

"It—it's for Mr. Päkkä," Lettie said.

At that all three turned on her, fairly screaming, and again Lettie heard the word Fenno. Trembling, she backed away and then, her nerve giving way entirely, she turned and fled. At her first step the old woman reached out with a quick motion and snatched one of the sea-green velvet bows on her skirt. As she ran Lettie felt it tear away.

On the last of the shaky flight of steps she tripped and would have fallen but a strong arm caught her. She gasped with terror and tried to break away but the arm held tightly and, raising her head, she found herself staring into Mike Brodi's bright black eyes.

"Michael, Michael," she cried and burst into tears. She felt his strong hand close hard around her arm. "Stop it. You're not hurt."

But she could not stop. The fright, the disappointment and the disillusionment crushed her and she wept stormily.

"Stop it! Don't be a baby. Nothing happened to you. Is that your hack? Answer me!"

She nodded and continued to weep. He propelled her down the path toward it and she stumbled along blindly, with her gloved fist in her eyes like a child. He fairly shoved her in and spoke to the driver.

"Wait here a minute. I'll be back."

Lettie threw herself into a corner of the rig and abandoned herself to her tears, only half aware that the driver was staring curiously at her.

Michael was gone more than his stated minute and when he returned he tossed the basket and the napkin on the floor of the hack.

"Here you are," he said. "I let the old lady keep the bow—she's stroking it as though it were a kitten's fur. She's not all there but she's harmless. What did you do to them? And for Heaven's sake, stop crying!"

"What did I *do* to them?" Lettie wailed. "They attacked me!"

"Nonsense."

"They did, I tell you. That awful woman grabbed the basket and—and—they tore off Willoughby's bow."

"*Willoughby's* bow." Brodi laughed loudly. "I told you the old woman wasn't right. You could have seen that. And that stuff in the basket was for them, wasn't it? I bet you told them your name was Fenno, too. You go home and get out of that ridiculous dress and wash your face. I'll go with you if you'll stop that crying. I'm going that way anyway."

"I hate you," Lettie said sullenly, moving over to make room for him.

When they had left Mill Street and were trotting along the plank road at the speed peculiar to livery-stable hacks hired by the hour, he said to her, "I've got a handkerchief if you haven't. And would you mind telling me what you thought you were doing, anyway?"

Blushing furiously, she dipped down in the front of her dress and brought up one of the many handkerchiefs. Brodi grinned.

"I—I wanted to help you."

"Help me, for Chri—— What do you mean?"

"Mark said you were trying to help Mr. Päkkä."

"I'm trying to help him and the rest of the dock hands make trouble for your father."

"For father? What's the matter with Mr. Päkkä? Is it father's fault?"

"Yes, in a way. A rope broke and a basket full of magnetite dropped on him. It caught him on the shoulders and it's a wonder it didn't break his neck. They should be more careful about their ropes. But you still haven't told me what you thought you were doing."

"I hate everything at home so."

"What's that got to do with this ridiculous performance?"

"I want to help the poor."

Brodi put back his head and roared. "Poor little rich girl!"

The difference between Brodi's reception of her charitable deeds and her imaginings suddenly overwhelmed Lettie and she began to cry again. He reached over and pulled her hands away from her face.

"Lettie, or Leticia, or whatever your name is, stop it!"

She gazed at him with liquid eyes. Then she sniffed and said in an aggrieved tone, "But I thought *you* wanted to help the poor."

Brodi sighed with fortitude. "Listen. And try to understand, if you

can. There are two ways of helping the poor. One"—he raised his
hand and took hold of a stubby finger—"Charity. Direct relief. Jellies,
God save the mark, to guys like Päkkä! *But*—are you listening? That
doesn't do anything to remove the causes of poverty. Take 'em a ton
of jelly and the poverty's still there. Now, two." Brodi pointed the other
finger at her. "The other way to help the poor is to remove the cause
of poverty. That's not easy. In fact the only way I know of doing it is
to influence the thinking of lots of people—public opinion—so that
they'll want to do away with poverty by changing economic conditions
that bring it about. Get that?"

"I think so," said Lettie meekly.

"Now the first kind of charity I don't care anything about—in fact,
I think it's dangerous both to him who gives and him who takes—
but you wouldn't understand that and we won't go into it. What I am
interested in is the forming of a public opinion that won't tolerate
the abuses that bring poverty about. There are a lot of others who
think the way I do—and there'll be more. Now, listen. There are
several ways of rousing people against these abuses. One of 'em is to
tell them that the abuses exist and what they are and how they should
be remedied. I do that by writing articles. Another is to rouse the
working men to fight for their own rights and the astonishing thing
is that you have to start by telling them what their rights are. Are you
still following me?"

"I think so," Lettie said again, more doubtfully.

"All right, then. Your jelly is worse than useless. And, in addition,
Päkkä is working for me to stir up the dock hands in your father's mill
to demand better hours and pay. I've picked them out as a sort of
experiment because they're the largest group of unskilled labor around
here. Now don't you feel pretty silly?" Brodi showed his even white
teeth in a broad grin and his black eyes gleamed with amusement.

There was silence for a while and Lettie said in a small voice, "I
want to help you."

"Are you crazy? It's your father and people like him I'm working
against."

"I hate my father. I hate them all. I want to help. Please!"

Brodi laughed shortly. "You saw what happened to you on Mill
Street. You couldn't deal with the Finns."

"Please. Perhaps I could help about the other thing." Lettie's face
was flushed with eagerness and, momentarily forgetful of self, she
looked straight at him. Animation brought color to her cheeks and she

was, if not pretty, at least far better looking than normally, but Brodi, full of contempt for her and what she represented, did not notice.

"What other thing? The article? My God, no. For that I have to gather facts—hundreds of facts about the Finns and how much they earn and how many weeks they work and how much a family spends for food and that sort of thing. I need help, right enough, because I can't find out all I need to know and teach at Hudson too, but you have to have a person trained in research to do work like that and you . . . What kind of education have you had? Any? Why, you don't even know what a fact is. Thanks just the same," he added with irony.

They rode in silence. Lettie, with face averted, gazed over the side of the carriage. Black Mike brooded over his own thoughts with a ferocious scowl on his face. It was so that they arrived in front of the Fenno gates. Lettie gathered up her train, sniffing from time to time as though tears were again imminent, and scrambled out without looking at Brodi. He made no move to help her but he reached her basket over the side.

"Here, don't forget this. And how about paying for this conveyance you hired?"

"Oh!" Lettie thrust a trembling hand in her pocket for her purse.

When she looked up again he was smiling at her not unkindly. "Don't feel too badly, youngster. It isn't all your fault."

"Come to think of it," he reflected as the hack bore him toward the livery stable, "very little if any of it is her fault."

8

ON THE second Sunday following the Thatcher ball, John Fenno
stood at the bottom of the red-carpeted steps, his big gold hunter
in his hand, alternately looking from its face to the front door. Matild
was late, though she knew perfectly well he hated to troop into church
after the services had begun. The carriage waited in the drive, Joe
nodded on the box, the horses drooped their heads to the extent that
their check reins would allow and the two coach dogs lolled on
the lawn, their noses on their paws. In the back of the carriage Willoughby and Lettie sat, Lettie on the narrow seat with her back to the
horses and Willoughby reclining on cushions and holding her head
a little stiffly to keep her creamy complexion from the October sun.

The air was clear and cool after rain and the end of the long drouth.
A wind across the lake, blowing the land mist southward, carried to
them something of the freshness of the forests and hills of Canada.
Some exceptional quality in the air turned shadows a deep blue and
brought objects into so sharp a focus that the scene might have been
a stereopticon view with the lens turned so that every detail stood out
more sharp and clear than reality. A puff of the cool wind lifted ribbons
on the girls' dresses and waved them like tiny flags. Lettie pulled her
cloak around her for the air was chill after the long weeks of heat, and
Willoughby raised her gloved hand to tuck in a vagrant curl. John
Fenno sighed, dropped his hunter into his pocket and clasped his
hands behind his back. He hated waiting.

Time passed; you could almost feel it ticking away and John Fenno
paced five deliberate steps east, turned, paced five more west, pulled
his watch out again and snapped the case open irritably.

"Lettie, go tell your mother to come at once."

He watched her sternly as she climbed down, pouting, and then
he circled the carriage slowly, inspecting it carefully. He found no
flaw. Sun gleamed from the silver on the harness, the body of the

carriage was bright with polish and the horses' coats shone. All this alleviated somewhat his irritation. He came to a halt by the horses' heads, admiring their slim legs and their sleek bodies. Mince pricked up her dainty ears and stretched her shapely neck toward him, pushing out her upper lip in hope of sugar. He stepped back to avoid getting flecks of foam on his frock coat. Joe spoiled them, in all likelihood. Mince took a step toward him and Docket, abruptly aroused from torpor and becoming aware of the possibility of profit, stretched out his neck also, edging toward Mince. They both reached for him. He felt the stirrings within him of a strange impulse to stroke their long, eager faces and discarded it sternly, keeping his expression stony. But their attentions flattered him, making him feel queerly warm and a little foolish.

Mistrusting these unfamiliar sensations, he walked away, conscious that both horses had turned their heads and were gazing after him, ears forward and disappointment in their velvety eyes. He had never thought about them as anything but a fine pair of horses but—they liked him, it seemed. It made him think well of himself. Belatedly Joe came out of the coma in which coachmen seem to spend so much of their waking lives, and pulled them up.

Fenno looked at his watch again, his exasperation returning. What could Matild be up to? Putting on her gloves, probably, with the slow care he had chafed at so many times. He could see her in his mind's eye, smoothing out the wrinkles slowly, almost sensuously, deriving some kind of physical pleasure from the feel of the kid, intently fastening the buttons, concentrating on each little plop as they came through the tight holes. Matild found a sort of refuge in things like that, into which she could escape and shut out the world.

A tinkling of bridle chains made Fenno glance up quickly. Mince and Docket, sharp ears forward and heads turned toward the distant iron gates, were watching a rig turn in the driveway. Willoughby was watching it too with one graceful violet-colored gloved hand on her breast, the other clasping a prayer book from which dangled violet ribbons suspending a gold cross, an anchor and a heart. He walked around to the back of the carriage to see who it might be. Queer, he thought, how you could tell a livery-stable rig as far as you could see it, though if anybody asked you how it differed from any other kind of rig, you couldn't say.

The occupant of the rig was visible now, sitting forward, the reins held loosely and the rig sagging one-sidedly from weight on the springs.

Hadley! Fenno frowned. What was the fellow doing, coming to the house? Did he think he'd be welcome? Something to put a stop to, once and for all. Behind him, Fenno could hear Matild and Lettie in the hall, Matild's voice high and querulous. He walked briskly down the drive with some intention of keeping Hadley and the family separated.

"Morning," he said as Hadley drew rein beside him. "Just leaving for church." He stood close to the step of the rig so Hadley wouldn't get out.

But Hadley did get out. "Good morning, Mr. Fenno," he said. "I brought you a telegram that came to the office." He twisted the reins around the whip handle and jumped dexterously over the wheel on the far side from Fenno. He pulled a blue-and-white envelope out of his pocket and advanced, holding it out and smiling as though he had won a minor victory.

"I was down at the office when it came. Thought it might be important."

"Thanks." Fenno turned it over in his hands and while he did so, Hadley studied him curiously. He did look tired. Perhaps, after all, there was something to this rumor of ill health. Two directors had found occasion to question Hadley about it. Something to keep in mind, he decided. Queer that Fenno wasn't training anyone to take over after him, but lots of men made that mistake.

Fenno thrust the telegram in his pocket. "They don't seal these things very well. What were you doing at the office?"

"Working—looking things over. Lots to learn."

Fenno looked at him sharply and, turning his back, started toward the carriage. Working at the office, was he? First time anybody but himself had ever done anything like that on a Sunday!

"Thanks," he said again over his shoulder, meaning to make it sound like a dismissal.

But Hadley was greeting Matild, and Fenno put a hand on the carriage door, doing his best to convey impatience.

"My name's Hadley, ma'am. Sam Hadley." He stood before her, hat in hand, and she looked up at him rather distraught and obviously wondering whether this was another face she was supposed to remember. There were so many.

"Oh, yes," she said vaguely and then, feeling this to be somehow inadequate, she added still more vaguely, "We were just going to church."

Hadley cast a quick look over his shoulder and met Willoughby's startled and hostile gaze. He smiled broadly and Willoughby turned her head away, chin in air.

"I was just going to church myself, ma'am."

The little byplay escaped Matild. She looked up at Hadley, blinking earnestly and trying her best to place him. Her bad memory for faces troubled Matild and because she was really sorry about her shortcomings she said, "Why don't you come to church with us, Mr. Badney? I'm sure there is plenty of room. Lettie, just run in and tell Nora to tell the stable boy to look after Mr. Badney's horse, dear."

When she turned from watching Hadley fasten his nag to a ring upheld by a brightly painted iron jockey planted by the steps, she was aware of hostility. John and Willoughby were staring at her, though why they should do so, she had no idea. Certainly it was nothing that she had *said*. With an injured and quite audible sniff she swayed toward the carriage.

"We'll be too crowded," Fenno said.

"That's absurd, John. Lettie can just sit with us."

"All right, all right. Anything to get started. Will you please get in?" And now Willoughby included her father in her reproachful glance.

Fenno grasped Matild's arm to help her in, none too gently, and felt her wince and draw away. Hurt her, had he? He swung himself in quickly and took the seat opposite her, clenching his teeth against his seething irritation. There were moments, such as now, when she failed to perceive a meaning with which the atmosphere fairly crackled, when he found her close to intolerable. At such moments he actually enjoyed the minor hurts he gave her, regarding them as richly deserved. He looked her over with cold malevolence. She was staring at nothing, her lips trembling and her pale eyes swimming with the injured self-pity that only made his exasperation the greater.

She made room sightlessly for Lettie who squeezed in between them, sullen because of the dagger glances from Willoughby in defense of her flounces. Nor did she see that Hadley, who was sitting beside John with his hands on his knees, was apparently missing nothing. Fenno continued to stare at her coldly, knowing from weary experience what the pattern of the next few moments would be. They jogged on in silence, the Sunday air full of the special quiet that comes after the church bells have ceased to ring. Matild blinked, sniffed, her lips ceased to tremble and she smoothed at her dress with the palm of her pudgy gloved hand. Then she looked straight at him, her glaucous eyes full of hurt and reproach, and said in a voice that quivered with injury, "You didn't tell us what was in your telegram, John."

Forgiving him, trying to make a martyred peace, crawling back to be kicked again. His eyes were full of contempt and distaste.

"I don't know what it is. I haven't opened it." Nevertheless, he reached in his pocket and pulled out the telegram. He looked at the uncertain seal and glanced beneath his brows at Hadley. The fact that Hadley was looking at him with interest disconcerted him a little and he frowned at the telegram as he tore it open. Then he looked at all of them with sudden animation.

"It's from Jay Cooke."

"Who is Jay Cooke, John?" Matild's voice was flat and perfunctory.

"Good Lord, don't you ever read the papers?"

He commenced reading the long telegram to himself, annoyed with himself that he had expected them to share his interest.

"Would like opportunity to discuss many matters with you. Am informed you have industrial development of the country at heart and feel we may find meeting ground of common interest in opening of the West along Northern Pacific route. I have nothing specific in mind but feel we might find mutual benefit in discussion. My private train stops at Cleveland two-thirty P.M. Monday. Will you join small party for short stay at Gibraltar, island retreat at Sandusky?

Jay Cooke"

Fenno folded the telegram thoughtfully and slipped it back into his inside pocket. "Nothing specific in mind." He wondered. An unlikely telegram, if that were really true. An attempt to see how the land lay, obviously. Now what could he be after? Monday was tomorrow—rather sudden. Didn't want him to have time to think, probably. Good thing Hadley *had* brought it around.

"Was it good news, John?"

"Jay Cooke," he said coldly, "is the country's greatest financier. He financed the war. We probably couldn't have won it without him."

"Isn't he building the Northern Pacific Railroad, Papa?"

A smile came into Fenno's eyes, Hadley grinned and Willoughby looked rather smug.

"Yes, and opening up the West, planting towns along the line of the railroad. He sends agents abroad to persuade immigrants to come to this country and settle along the road, because a railroad in a wilderness is no good. You have to have a population to make it pay. Clever idea, making the road and the trade for it to live off, both." Fenno chuckled appreciatively and Willoughby laughed with him.

Matild broke in, peevish because of this harmony. "What in the world can he want with you, John?"

Fenno's irritation returned. Why shouldn't Jay Cooke want him? Why wasn't it natural that Cooke should want to meet and talk with a man of his stature and prominence? Helpmate! How little she knew or cared about his life and his achievements, taking it all for granted. No, not even that, not even seeing how much there was to take for granted.

"We're going to be very late," he said crossly. "There isn't a carriage on the street."

They were indeed very late. He suffered the ignominy in a stoic silence, surrounded by a palpable aura of wrath. The General Confession was over and the reading of the Psalm was begun. With an outstretched arm he held them motionless at the back of the church until the rustling and sighing swept over the church that is the prelude to the reading of the First Lesson. He dropped his arm then, as one might let down the bar of a gate and, preceding them down the aisle, stood sternly to one side while they entered the pew.

The Fenno pew was the first one on the right, under the pulpit and Mark was already in it, prayer book in hand and on his face the watery, cautious smile which passes for welcome in a church. He shared the Fenno pew for reasons of economy and he went to church regularly because he felt it to be a social benefit he owed himself. The Thatcher pew was the first on the left, under the lectern. In it Fenno saw, by some abnormal process of second sight for he scorned to look anywhere but straight ahead, Bobbie Thatcher with a rapt expression as though he had just watched the passage of an angel. Beyond him was the General, faultlessly attired and looking as though he had considerably more eye for titillating detail. "Even in church," Fenno thought disgustedly, rather ashamed of an impulse to look around for the cause of the smirk, unaware that it might be Willoughby.

The position in which he found himself, pilloried, as it were, for the whole congregation to stare at, was loathsome. A prickling sensation across his back made him square his shoulder blades for martyrdom. They were staring at Hadley, of course, wondering—all sorts of things. A deep instinct to keep his affairs out of the public eye made him suffer at this present exposure. The feeling of being far too un-pleasantly conspicuous was not even alleviated by the picture his second sight presented him of Whittlesey, reared back as though some-one had stuck something unpleasant under his nose.

They all dropped to their knees, briefly, perfunctorily, and then Fenno swept the prayer books in the rack toward him preparatory to finding places and dealing them out, but there were only three—one for Matild, one for Lettie and one for himself. Willoughby and Mark were already supplied. That was how Hadley happened to share a book with Willoughby. In entering the pew she had tried to avoid him but in the limelight they were all a little rattled and Matild had plunged in next to Lettie instead of taking her place beside her husband. That brought Willoughby and Hadley together and a frown of annoyance to Willoughby's face. Hadley did not ask to share the book, even by a gesture. He simply reached over and seized one side of it, smiling and practically leaning his big body against her. She gave him a glance of reproval.

They raised their voices in song.

> "Nearer my God to Thee,
> Near-*er*-er to Thee . . ."

The pressure of Hadley's body increased meaningfully and she moved a little away. Down the row of bowed heads Mark's half-closed eyes shot amber fire.

> "Still all my song shall be
> Nearer, my God, to Thee,
> Nearer to Thee."

Willoughby's soprano lifted, clear, efficient and almost true. At the faultiness of the last note Mark shut his eyes and compressed his shoulders slightly.

At the beginning of the second verse Hadley reached in his pocket and pulled out a pencil. Holding his side of the book with his left hand, he wrote rapidly at the top of the page, "When am I going to see you?" Willoughby, seeing this, looked up indignantly—and caught sight of Mark. That gentleman had not missed one stroke of the pencil though he was too far away to read the words. He was plainly angry. Mark jealous! The idea pleased her enormously and Hadley, seeing the pleasure, and misinterpreting the cause, wrote "Rudd's for tea— today at four." She shook her head slightly and he wrote "Yes," and underlined it. To this she made no reply. She felt Mark's eyes on her.

Throughout the rest of the long hymn her thoughts were busy. Hadley would go to Rudd's—she was sure of that. And of course she wouldn't, and he would just wait and wait. Then such a delightful idea came to her that she wanted to laugh aloud. Mark was coming home to dinner and if she left her hymnal lying around, he would be sure to look into it. He would be wild with jealousy and he might even go to Rudd's to prevent her being alone with Hadley. That would infuriate Sam Hadley. She would go, and almost any way it worked out would be fun. Willoughby's voice soared into the last phrases of the hymn exultantly.

Neither his family nor the service kept Fenno from speculating about the telegram in his pocket. So absorbed was he that he saw none of this byplay, though he was literally brushing elbows with Hadley. By the time they had begun, at the rear of the church, to take up the collection, Fenno had decided that there was something that he very much wanted to say. Not in the carriage—Fenno belonged to the old school that would sooner swear in the presence of ladies than talk business in their hearing. The taking of the collection was a mundane recess, full of whisperings. Very well, then. Frock-coated figures were already passing wooden plates along the pews behind them and, leaning toward Hadley, he said in a low voice, "I have a job for you. I want to see what you can do with it."

Hadley leaned closer. "Yes, sir. What is it?"

The sound of silver changing hands was getting closer and Fenno spoke hurriedly. "There's a small plant up the river, the Lake Furnace Company, making rails."

"I know about it."

"Good."

The wooden plate appeared under their noses and Fenno reached in his pocket. As a regular pew-holder, he was supplied once a year with a packet of small white envelopes in which to seal his offering. Each envelope was printed in lavender with a cross and a dotted line on which the donor might, if he saw fit, sign his name. The envelope John Fenno drew from his pocket read "John Fenno and Family" in a bold hand. He waited while Hadley dropped a folded bill on the plate, tried to see the denomination, failed, and added his envelope to the brimming collection of bills and small change and envelopes like his own. Glancing up, he saw that the arm which held the plate belonged to Whittlesey and he nodded briefly and resumed his talk with Hadley.

"I'm going up to Sandusky tomorrow afternoon. Now I want you to do two things." Fenno held up two fingers and took hold of the first. "One, find out if there is any concern west of here making rails."

The black-coated figures with the plates were forming at the rear for a triumphant procession down the aisle and Fenno spoke rapidly. "Two." He transferred his hold to the other finger. "Go to Huntington, president of Lake, as my representative and start negotiations to buy the Company."

The organ pealed, the procession started forward, an altar server, who was a neighbor in private life, came down with a heavy silver plate to receive the offering and the congregation rose. Under cover of the general stir Fenno raised his voice.

"Understand, we may not actually want to buy Lake. Probably couldn't get it cheap enough. Old plant anyway—been going since the twenties."

The procession passed them and Fenno noted that one of Whittlesey's shoes was squeaking.

"This is the situation. I want to be in a position to say to the people I'm seeing that negotiations are under way to buy a plant that is now producing rails. Understand?"

Hadley nodded as they sank to their knees.

The remainder of the service Fenno passed in astonishment and malaise. The astonishment was with himself that he should have entrusted such a mission to Hadley when Cushing would have been the logical choice. Perhaps better to involve Cushing also, now he came to think about it. Where was his pew? Over there in the east transept somewhere, but the man didn't seem to be there. Very well, then, let it rest. He'd tell Mark about it after dinner.

The cause of the malaise he did not know and, not liking to acknowledge feelings that could not be captured and tabulated, he dismissed it. But the thought stayed with him that Hadley had exhibited no surprise at the projected trip and had asked no questions.

The service was over at last, and Fenno stood woodenly while his family filed out of the pew. As they were going out the church door Matild pulled at his sleeve. She was breathing in little gasps from the exertion of walking down the aisle.

"John, do you think it would be nice to ask Mr. Badney to dinner?"

"No!"

"But his horse is at our house and Mark is coming. Won't it look queer not to ask Mr. Badney? He might like Lettie, you know, John."

"No!"

She made a little motion of resentment with her lips but said no more.

They drove home in almost complete silence and when they got there they all went in the house without waiting while the stable boy brought around Hadley's rig. He said good-bye formally, making clumsy and good-natured bows that quite charmed Matild. He offered Mark a lift and was refused with a rather annoying smile and the news that Mark was staying to dinner, and he tried to catch Willoughby's eye and failed.

He had just gathered up the reins and the whip when Fenno appeared on the top of the steps.

"Hadley, one thing more."

"Yes, sir."

"Better see Huntington this afternoon. No good wasting time."

"Yes, sir," Hadley said in exactly the same tone and then, for no reason that Fenno could see, he put back his head and laughed.

Fenno went glumly inside. Here he was, entrusting confidential affairs to a man he suspected of opening telegrams! He must be bewitched. The man had no more ethics than a dog, probably, but he was smart—too smart. And Fenno renewed his resolve to oust him as soon as things at the mill quieted down a little.

Sunday dinner was the climactic orgy of the domestic week for which Matild planned far in advance. Sitting alone in her room with the folding shutters closed against the glare, her closed eyes shutting her into her private world, she fanned herself with one of her innumerable paper fans and balanced the merits of roast and Yorkshire pudding against goose and sherry gravy. But her planning always tended to melt into day dreams, comforting day dreams of family harmony in which she was the central figure, surrounded by love and admiration, so different from the reality.

She never lost hope that these dreams, which moved her so that sometimes real tears came to her eyes, might some day come true. She rocked and fanned and her tired face with its little sagging pouches was soft with emotion, and the irritability and strain that customarily resided there dissolved. No one in her family had seen her face like this for many years.

They were not noble dreams but to her they were beautiful and full of comfort. In them she saw all their faces turned toward her, lit with love and the respect for which she longed. In her dreams they sat at table and even John Fenno was interested in what she said. They all listened to her without the mockery that hurt her so, and Willoughby's blue eyes were full of remorseful love. "Oh, Mama, forgive me for all I have done to you. Teach me to be like you, so gentle, so kind."

Matild rocked back and forth and there was a soft smile on her face. She saw herself smiling in her dream and knew they were all touched to the heart by this sad sweet smile, ennobled by her forgiveness of them all. She was no longer at the Sunday table; she lay on her big bed, gently dying, and they stood around her with bowed heads, sorrowing. John took her hand and raised it tenderly. "Don't leave us, Matild. Stay with us for we need your noble guidance and the example of your forgiveness."

Matild dreamed this scene over and over again, drawing comfort from the supremely egotistical moment of death, the decision between roast and goose still unmade. When the great moment of the Sunday dinner really arrived, she strove so hard to make the dream of their respectful love come true that she talked with breathless nervous gasps between her words and a dark stain of nervous perspiration began to spread across her plump shoulders through the purple silk of her best dress. Willoughby, cool and fresh, ate with a disdainful daintiness that Matild ignored but felt, nevertheless, to the quick. John Fenno brooded over his plate in sullen silence, his eyes carefully away from her flushed face. In her heart she hated them and cried out to them with a terrible need for their love and because she knew no way to reach them or to find any outlet for these devastating emotions that shook her so, her hand trembled and her pale eyes were agonized with strain, and she lashed out at them feebly with an irritability that gave her scant relief.

Today, the sherry gravy was bitter and she missed the solace of her coffee. They had coffee in the living room now and she must pour, though the handle of the big silver coffee pot burned her hand until the tears almost came. And there were her mother's cups, the fragile, beautiful things, tiny bowls without handles, that she loved because they were like part of her dear mother. Never in all these years had they been used; never had anyone touched them but herself. She stopped the black stream of coffee when she saw them and, casting an angry look at Willoughby's amused face, she set the coffee pot down hard. The ruffle in her sleeve swept over the tiny cup and flooded the tray with coffee. She rose, clutching her sleeve.

"I . . . don't want any. I'm going upstairs."

She moved toward the door, her heavy body swaying. They would follow her now, surely they would follow her and bring her back and be kind to her.

No one moved and she mounted the stairs slowly, pulling herself from step to step with her plump hand clutching the banister rail. John Fenno's voice came to her.

"What on earth is the matter with your mother?"

And Willoughby's clear tones. "I don't know, I'm sure, Papa. The heat, perhaps. May I give you some coffee?"

Matild sank wearily into the little chair in front of her dressing table and patted away the beads of perspiration on her forehead with her crumpled handkerchief. Her hand reached out to the table drawer and her little secret store of rice powder. The drawer was full of many things and her hand with its short, fat fingers hovered over them, touching them here and there. She began to set them one by one on the table top, gently and lovingly. Her things, a broken brooch, some hairpins, a bit of jet trimming, one pale-blue kid glove, the other lost some happy evening long ago—things treasured for thrift, things treasured for memory, the things of yesterday and the useful things of today. They never hurt her, these beloved things of hers, and her lips moved a little as she piled them on the table top. Just so, long ago, a little girl had whispered to her doll and hugged to herself the warm comfort of the inanimate thing. The lump in Matild's throat hurt her. She unrolled the blue glove, smoothed it on her knee and rolled it up again. A weak tear brimmed over and tracked an irregular course down her face. She sniffed and wiped at it with the back of her hand. Matild's tears were always weak and snivelling. She had not cried lustily for many years.

She heard John Fenno's step heavily climbing the stair and her lips tightened as she bent over her things, feeling her husband's presence, injury and rebuke in every line of her. John Fenno stood beside her, looking down at her silently, a baffled expression on his face. He was trying to see in her heavy dowdiness the trustful, rather timid girl he had married. These occasional attempts to recreate her youth were the nearest approach John Fenno ever made to tenderness. He sighed and, going to the window, pulled the shutters open and stood there looking out. He did not like to look at her. He wondered where along the way he had lost the plump, pretty Matild of long ago. He did not know. He only knew that he had discovered gradually that she could not be molded. She had, in fact, stood in her tracks with a kind of bewildered stubbornness, and refused to be led or coerced or driven into becoming something other than herself. He sighed again and spoke to her over his shoulder.

"I've been having a talk with Willoughby."

Matild bent down and peered into the table drawer, discovered a coverless box filled with beads and fished it out. She raked them over with her finger. The rattle of the beads jarred on Fenno's taut nerves and he whirled around to face her.

"I'm talking to you, Matild."

She sighed, put the box down, and sat, not looking at him.

"I've been talking with Willoughby, I say. Her birthday is Tuesday. I'm going to Sandusky with Jay Cooke tomorrow afternoon."

Matild's hand stole out toward the box of beads and he paused, looking stern. She set the box in the drawer quickly and folded her hands.

"Yes, John."

"I probably won't be back before Wednesday and I have arranged for Mark to stay here while I'm gone, so you'll have a man in the house."

"But, John, if you do that, you won't be here for her birthday."

"That's what I want to talk to you about. I may get back, but if I don't, she'll understand. Now about her present. She says she wants a string of pearls."

"She has a string."

"No, real pearls. I'd like you to see about getting them for her."

"Not *real* pearls, John?"

"Why not? I can afford them."

"But John . . ."

"What's the matter?"

Her face was flushing slowly and the strain in her eyes made her look as though her eyebrows were being pinched, and she mumbled something he did not catch.

"Why shouldn't she have pearls? I don't want any niggardly little string, understand. You'd better not get them by yourself. Get Mrs. Tenney or Mrs. Hay to help you. Go to Cowell's and let Mark talk to them about the price. Pearls cost money. They're an important purchase. They'll have to be insured. What are you upset about?"

Matild's hands were moving tremblingly among the things on the table top, scattering them.

"You never bought me any pearls," she said faintly.

"What's that? You won't have any trouble, with them to help you. Let Mrs. Tenney pick them out. I'm going to wash."

Matild still sat, clutching her treasures in two hands gone suddenly damp, staring down at them without seeing them. From the next room she heard the splash of water in the china bowl. She sniffed and blinked, and a tear ran crookedly down her face. She wiped it from the corner of her mouth with her wrist, and her eyes filled again. She began tremblingly to stow her possessions in the drawer. They were just things that cluttered up her life, her bitter, wasted, loveless life. She could have found it in her heart to burn them all.

Down went her head on her arms on the open drawer and she sobbed, not for today alone, but for the barren yesterdays and the bleak tomorrows.

After a time her sobs grew less and she dried her eyes. She pushed the drawer shut, got up more cumbersomely than usual, went to the water pitcher and dipped a corner of a towel in the warmish water. Her throat still hurt her. She held the wet towel to her eyes, hating the runnels of water that leaked down her face. Behind her she heard her husband come in and knew by the sound that he was rubbing his face and hands dry, vigorously. He did not say anything and presently she heard the door of his dressing room shut and, after a moment, the distant slam of his study door.

Downstairs Mark was glad to be left alone, or approximately alone, for there was only Lettie, reading in her favorite corner of the window seat. They were all upstairs, even Willoughby, who had gone to change her dress before going out on an expedition she did not explain. Mark put his hands in his pockets, which pushed his coat tails back at a jaunty angle and humming Handel, "Did you not hear my lady . . ." in a most nonchalant manner, he wandered out into the hall.

He was just in time, for Ellen was gathering up Willoughby's hat and gloves and prayer book from the table where she had tossed them.

"Just a minute, Ellen. There's something I want to look up."

He took the prayer book from her, turned to the section of hymns and let the gilt-edged pages fly under his fingers. He found what he wanted without trouble.

"All right," he said. "Thanks." He handed it back to her and went off toward the study, the single, slantwise furrow, like an exclamation point, marking his forehead.

There was really no reason for Willoughby to change her dress, which she called her toilette, except that the mock solemnity of her church-going gown did not seem right for a tryst. And this was certainly a tryst, she thought, smiling at the novelist's words. Blue, then, sky blue, the exact color of her eyes, of broadcloth so fine and silky that it might be satin. A vine embroidered in dark blue edged the skirt and crept up the front toward her tiny waist. The same vine was repeated in miniature around each of the three deep flounces of her sleeves and on her shoulders, like epaulettes. Dark blue lace nestled in the deep neck line and fell in a shower, like a Spanish mantilla, from the back of her absurd but charming hat.

Rudd's was deserted except for a family party way at the back of the raised section where the little marble-topped tables were set. The crowd would come later after the fashionable hour for driving up and down the Avenue. She stood in the front of the store between glass cases of chocolate and pastries and looked around her but Hadley was nowhere in sight. She glanced at the tiny watch with the dark-blue enamel back which hung on a chain around her neck. Four-ten. She had timed herself well and he should certainly be here. Vexed and in something of a quandary, she stared down a Napoleon slice, as though she bore it some special animosity, considering the advisability of walking out. An insult, nothing less, to be kept waiting.

The enticing smell of chocolate and cake surrounded her. One cup of chocolate, perhaps, and when he came she could be properly distant and make it clear that people waited for her, not she for them. Glad that there was no one to see her here without escort, she strolled to the back, mounted the three red-carpeted steps and sat down at a tiny round table in one of the flimsy gilt chairs to which caterers are addicted. Waiting for her order of hot chocolate and macaroons, she looked at herself with pleasure in the mirrors. There were many of these, in gilt frames, on both sides of the room, and she saw herself sitting there, very stylish and self-possessed, repeated in diminishing form down a long vista of blue gowns.

The chocolate came in a tall, thin china cup with a pink rose on the side. She picked up her spoon and daintily stirred in the glob of floating whipped cream, watching the door, her blue eyes a cold fury that boded no good for Sam Hadley. Then she postponed her anger in favor of the delicious chocolate and, raising the cup, took a slow and appreciative sip. The blue figures in the mirrors on either side of her raised cups and sipped in synchrony like a well-trained *corps de ballet* and on each appeared a tiny mustache of white.

She patted her lips with a corner of her napkin and broke off a piece of macaroon with a vicious snap. All her anger boiled to the surface again, made the more intolerable because there was nothing more to wreak it on than the macaroon. Her foot in its delicate bronze slipper began a staccato tap on the iron base of the little table and she sipped the chocolate almost with violence, forgetting to enjoy its flavor. Then she put her cup down hastily. Someone was coming in the door. She lowered her eyes and became completely absorbed in the dregs at the bottom of her cup.

"May I join you?"

Blue eyes opened wide as she raised her head. Mark! He waited for no invitation but dropped into the slim gilt chair opposite her.

"Fancy finding you here." Mark bowed across the table, taking her all in with one sweeping glance.

"Yes, I was hungry."

"Don't explain, my dear. It's so seldom convincing." He snapped his fingers for a waiter. "I'll have *café au lait.*"

He went into a longish dissertation about having the milk hot and when he turned back to her his yellow eyes were dancing with mockery, but he only remarked that coffee pots should have straight handles sticking out from the sides because the other kind made such an ungraceful line of a person's arm when pouring, especially a woman's arm. She sipped the last drops of chocolate and nibbled her macaroon while he talked on, weaving her pretty compliments.

Whenever Willoughby thought he wasn't noticing, she glanced at the door. She hoped fervently that Hadley would come—what on earth could be keeping him?—and find her enjoying herself with Mark. She practiced looking as though she were having a delightful time.

Mark, however, saw her swift glances. "She's looking for him," he thought. "Where the devil can he be? She's angry at him now. Good. Very good. Mark, my lad, if you play it right, this is very much to your advantage," and he reached out and stroked the back of her hand lightly with his finger tips.

She waved him away. This time she was looking at the door quite openly. Mark turned and looked too. A very small and ragged boy was coming through, clasping a gray florist's box that was nearly as long as himself, and several waiters were converging on him, flapping their aprons as though to shoo him back to the street. A shrill treble, very much on the defensive, reached them.

"He said to give 'em to the lady. The gentleman said to give 'em to the lady and this letter too. He said she's been waiting for him." He did a complicated maneuver with the long box and his cap and drew an envelope out of the latter. "Her name's on the letter, I guess." He held it out to the semicircle of waiters. One of them took it, glanced at it and came rather hesitatingly toward the table. The small boy followed him.

"Are you Miss Fenno, ma'am?"

Willoughby held out her hand for the note while Mark pointed to a chair. "Put the box there, son. Here, wait a minute. Take this." Mark, who economized only in small ways, handed the lad a dime.

The boy looked at the coin in his hand. "Gee, thanks. The Mister gave me a quarter, too. Gee, thanks."

"All right, run along."

Mark watched with half-shut eyes while Willoughby read the note but her face gave nothing away. She folded it neatly and slipped it down the front of her dress and it seemed to Mark that her cheeks were pinker than usual but from what emotion, he did not know.

The note said, "Dear Miss Fenno: I'm sorry as hell (hell was crossed out heavily) that I've been delayed by some business your father asked me to do for him when he came back out on the porch after you had gone inside. Wait for me, please. I'll be there quick as I can. We could go for a drive if you like. I want like everything to see you—so wait. Yrs. Sam Hadley."

"He could have come on time," Willoughby thought. "Business shouldn't stand in the way. He could have come on time."

She leaned across the table and smiled ravishingly. "I've finished if you have, Mark. Do you think we could get a rig somewhere and drive on the Avenue a while?"

"I've got the Tenneys' runabout outside."

"You've got a nerve. Why didn't you take ours?"

"Uncle John is getting a bit cool about that. I'd better let up for a bit."

"All right. Let's go, then."

She stood up and began putting on her gloves. Mark stood up also and stooped to pick up the florist's box with distaste plainly on his face.

"Oh, leave those," she said. "Just leave them there."

The runabout was gay with red wheels and a cream-colored cushion on the high seat which was surrounded by a shiny brass railing instead of a back. This fashionable turnout was hitched to a small mare whose coat was the color of a pair of chamois gloves. Her mane and her tail were both uncut and very long and flowing and the same light cream color as the cushions. Mark, who was secretly a little afraid of horses, thought of this one as a "stepper" for, though she was small, she was full of spirit and very feminine. She was tied to a long, horizontal pipe that served as a hitching place for the patrons of Rudd's and she hated to be hitched. When Willoughby and Mark came out she was making little restless backward and forward motions that threatened to dash the delicate red wheels into the surrey behind her.

Getting into a high runabout is a feat requiring grace and agility, for the step is a piece of iron not much bigger than a piano pedal and a quick transfer of hands at the psychological moment, to a lady's waist, is required to boost her. Willoughby leaped upward with the requisite grace and just the proper turn of her body to bring her skirts swirling in a froth of blue around her feet. In mid-flight upward she saw a buggy turning in just three places beyond them and in it Hadley, his aston-ished face turned up toward her.

Her heart gave a little leap. Could she pretend she hadn't seen him? Yes. And the timing would be perfect if only they could get away before he could hitch.

Leaning over the side, she said to Mark, who was pulling on chamois gloves and meticulously turning them back at the wrists, "Mark, do hurry. The sun won't last much longer. People will be leaving the Ave-nue. Do hurry."

Through her lashes she saw Hadley scrambling out of the buggy, which tipped and swayed under his weight. Mark leaped in and gathered up the reins and the red-handled whip and they began to back out of the narrow space. The mare made a great fuss about it, curving her hind ankles, swishing her blonde tail and tossing her head, behaving exactly as though backing were beneath her socially.

"Oh, hurry, Mark," Willoughby said, watching Hadley make a quick twist of his hitching strap around the pipe and come running toward them.

"Bad place here," Mark muttered, wishing the mare had a more phlegmatic disposition and keeping a worried eye on the back wheels of the neighboring surrey.

Hadley reached the curb just as Mark cleared the surrey and swung them out into the roadway, but a basket cart full of children coming to Rudd's for a treat had to be skilfully avoided and Mark did not see Hadley.

Willoughby saw him. She raised her eyes and looked straight at him as though she had never seen him before, just as the mare, finished with the ignominy of backing, took a forward leap and whirled them away. She saw incredulous surprise on his face, a fleeting look of hurt and then a black look of anger so intense and threatening that she clutched the brass rail and a shiver ran through her and she was glad of the swift pace of the mare, carrying her away.

Hadley watched them all the way out of sight, the cloud of anger dark on his face. "By God," he said to himself. "I'll fix her. The bitch." Then he looked around him as though surprised to find himself standing there, shrugged and moved toward his rig.

"Maybe she didn't get the note. That was it. Give her a break. She was a lady, or supposed to be! What was the matter with him, anyway? Why should he give a damn? Listen," he said to himself, "you got plans. You got ideas. And mooning around after the boss's daughter isn't part of 'em. You didn't come out of the woods to sit around parlors and crook your finger through the handle of a tea cup. You came to get in on the big time and the big money, a clean fight in a man's world. No women, Sam, my friend. No women."

Unaccountably he was trembling a little. "Hell," he thought. "I need a drink," and turning his back on his rig, he pushed open the door of Rudd's. The air, full of the smell of chocolates and pastries, seemed sickish to him. God, what a place! A woman's place. He strode to the back, up the red-carpeted steps, jerked out a gilt chair and sat down. The vision of Willoughby's blue eyes and her parted lips and the feel of her body in his arms, twisting and turning to be free, engulfed him and he stared morosely at the table top. And he'd had an idea he had made her want him. Hell, he knew he had. He felt it when he held her in his arms. Well, to hell with it. Let her play around with that sly devil, Mark. He was just the sort to marry the boss's daughter. Let him. "You're going to keep clear, Sam, my boy. Damn clear, from now on. She didn't get the note—sure, that was it."

"Your order, sir?"

"Rye. Make it double."

"We don't serve drinks, sir."

"What kind of a place is this? Beer, then."

"We don't serve beer, sir. Coffee, tea, chocolate, sarsaparilla, root beer."

But Hadley did not hear this chant. His eyes had fallen on a long gray florist's box on the chair beside him.

9

THE directors' meeting was just breaking up but Fenno did not linger to talk to anyone. He went slowly up the stairs, deep in thought. For sometime now there had been something new in the attitude of the board he did not like. Today, whatever it was had seemed to him about to come out into the open. They had not actually opposed him on anything but the atmosphere of rebellion was there and he had sensed it immediately, even in the way they drew their chairs up to the table. It had seemed to him almost as though they were looking for a chance to oppose him, and therefore he had said nothing at all about his plans to meet Jay Cooke and what might develop from them, and nothing at all about further expansion. If they were feeling rebellious, let them learn about all this when it was too late to rebel!

He entered the anteroom and old Williams rose deferentially. Barnes was there also and Fenno nodded to him, at the same time pulling out his watch.

"I have to catch a train pretty soon, Barnes. Is it anything important?"

"Well, no, sir, not exactly. The men are in an ugly mood but I don't look for real trouble this close to the end of the season. It's hard handling them with Päkkä laid up."

"Then what's on your mind? I understood you thought Päkkä was the ring leader."

"Yes and no, sir. He's the one that stirs them up, all right, and I'd fire him quick if there was anyone else who spoke English like he does. He's a fine worker, too—best of the lot—keeps 'em all working by his example. But I can't help feeling there's someone behind him. He wouldn't think up all those things about wages and hours by himself. Maybe it's somebody who doesn't even work at the mill. You wouldn't have an idea, would you, sir?"

"No, you'll have to find that out for yourself. I'll talk to you when I get back."

Fenno went into his office, pulled down the top of his desk, locked it and went to look out the window to see if the Company hack was waiting for him. There it was and there, too, were most of the directors standing in groups around the drive, talking. Fenno watched them thoughtfully. They usually hurried away. Perhaps there really was something afoot. The sight of them there, conspiring without him, gave him a swift spasm of loneliness. He would rather not encounter them just now but there was no alternative. He turned away and picked up his bag.

At the bottom of the stairs he found Thatcher and Brown deep in talk, and something about the way they broke off convinced him the talk was about him.

Brown said, glancing at the bag in Fenno's hand, "You are going away? We were coming up to have a few words with you."

"Sorry, I haven't time. I'll be back in a couple of days."

Thatcher said nothing and his round face was as inscrutable as ever. Fenno was almost through the front door when Brown said, "How are you *feeling*, John?"

"Why, all right, thank you." Now, that's queer, Fenno thought as he climbed into the hack. He could feel himself the center of attention of all the directors, who lingered talking on the drive.

The train came in with a rush and a roar of wind that swirled John Fenno's coat-tails around him and he clutched his hat and squinted his eyes against the rain of cinders as it rolled to a grinding halt. The display of headlong power exhilarated him, as though the train were a monster being with difficulty halted expressly for him. He was, in point of fact, the only passenger and this, in addition to the ornate appearance of the special train, made him the center of attention of the loafers on the station platform. Disapproving both of his own exhilaration and of the loafers, he frowned and stood his ground, not sure where to board this thing of gilt and glitter.

The problem was immediately solved for him. A colored porter clinging to a brass rail of the last car dropped to the platform and came toward him all wreathed in servile smiles.

"Mr. Cooke' train, sah. You Mr. Fenno, sah? Jus' le' me have yo bag. This way, sah, if you please."

Fenno mounted the steps and entered the car with rather more hos-

tility in his manner than was his wont because he was about to encounter strange men in an environment not his own. Just inside the
door of what appeared to be an exceedingly elaborate smoking car he
stopped, being unwilling to conciliate the unknown by advancing to
meet it. Let the unknown come to him. It came in the form of a young
man who was seated with a group of older men at the far end of the
car and who, on sight of Fenno, stood up and advanced, all smiles and
with outstretched hand.

Taking the proffered hand unwillingly, Fenno noted that, though
the young man's manner was deferential, there was in it an unmistakable emphasis on social equality. "Not a secretary," Fenno's mind said,
noting also that his rather conspicuous charm failed to be fully cordial
since it was too obviously both a technique and a defense. Fenno's mind
finished the classification. "Bright young assistant," he thought. "Annoying type. All big men seem to have 'em. Perhaps I should." He
allowed his hand to be wrung with a somewhat bad grace, looking
over the young man's shoulder the while and so occupied with wondering which of the men at the other end of the car was Cooke that he
scarcely heard the greeting.

"Mr. Fenno, of course? My name's Van Rensselaer. We are delighted
to have you with us. Mr. Cooke was most pleased that you could make
the trip."

"They always manage to have aristocratic names, these bright young
fellows," Fenno thought, presenting this one with a cold fraction of
his attention.

His coat and hat were whisked off and he found himself going down
the aisle in Van Rensselaer's wake. The far end of the car was separated
from the rest by two partitions which jutted out into the aisle. The
tops of these were of ground glass and on each was a design of a stork
standing on one leg, between columns with Egyptian tops. On the
other side of these partitions was a round table covered with a green
rep cloth and surrounded in part by a semicircular leather bench and
in part by arm chairs. Eight men sat at the table and they all stopped
talking at Fenno's approach and stared at him with a careless scrutiny
that was almost insulting.

To stares Fenno was accustomed and, whether they were admiring
or full of animosity, he rather enjoyed them for they had in common
the knowledge of his preeminence. This was something different. The
looks these Eastern financial men directed toward him not only con-
veyed their solidarity as a group, but made him both angry and self-

conscious. John Fenno had never been aware of provincialism in himself but something very like that unpleasant feeling assailed him now.

He noticed with disapproval an air of careless expenditure about their dress, a certain tightness of fit and a tendency toward checks. "A flashy lot!" A coterie with its own sartorial standards, he concluded, aware to the marrow of the blackness of his own attire but impressed in spite of himself by the obvious authority and sureness of their manner.

As he walked slowly down the aisle an insidious sense of his years stole over him. Not that they were younger than he. Most of them were, in fact, about his own age but they had a trimness about them that comes to a middle-aged man of affairs only as a result of considerable concentration on the subject. Their waistlines were the product of the massage table.

Having thus, in the time it took him to walk twenty feet, weighed them and been weighed, he was introduced around the table. His greetings were gruff and he did not offer to shake hands. For that matter, only one man offered to shake hands with him and eyeing him Fenno thought, "He's no more one of them than I am," and submitted to having his hand pumped up and down. Kingston, the fellow's name seemed to be. No one had answered to the name of Cooke. "Where is he?" Fenno thought, sinking into a chair beside Kingston that the bright young man was shoving against the backs of his knees. "Where the devil is he? He should have been here to meet me!"

Talk broke out again just as though it had never been interrupted by his arrival, rather noisy talk in which several of them seemed to be joining at the same time. Fenno couldn't get the drift of it and Kingston seemed to be saying something to him behind the shelter of his hand.

"What?" said Fenno. "I can't hear you."

"I say they're talking about whether the Northern Pacific should go into the market to borrow at whatever rates would secure loans."

Fenno nodded and sat back. Kingston had said "they," not "we," confirming Fenno's suspicion that the fellow was an outsider like himself and Fenno, resolving on a cautious coolness toward him, returned his attention to the financial men.

They were talking with a volubility and with an amount of laughter to which he was unaccustomed. "I still say"—one of them cut across the flow of talk—"that the money market will stay too tight unless the Treasury can be talked into buying about three million of governments to ease it up."

There was a general laugh at this, though Fenno could not see that anything funny had been said. "If that's all that's worrying you," someone else interjected, "the Treasury will come through all right. Cooke is seeing to it himself. Didn't you know he's had Secretary Richardson visiting him at Ogontz?"

"Where the devil *is* Cooke," Fenno thought, and promptly forgot him in his growing interest in what these men were saying. The more they talked the more apparent it became that they felt they had the Administration in their respective pockets. Government, they appeared to regard as a kind of partner of big business, a junior partner, like someone taken into the firm because of useful connections but from whom the firm's real secrets are hidden. "Everyone knows these fellows rig the market," he thought, "but they seem to think they boss the government too," and his blood began to run fast with excitement. With government itself as a partner, anything might be accomplished! He looked around the group from face to face, smiling a secret smile because he knew, and they did not, that he was going to use them for ends that they did not even suspect. If it was a contract they had gotten him here to sign, the details now seemed trivial to him. He knew in advance that he would sign it. For the first time he became really curious about what manner of person Cooke might be.

Young Van Rensselaer was sitting at his elbow and Fenno turned sharply on him. "Where is Mr. Cooke?"

"Ah, sir, I was going to mention that." Charm flowed from the young man like soft cream from a pastry tube. "Mr. Cooke told me particularly to tell you how greatly he regretted not being able to come himself on this trip. Assistant Secretary Richardson—a most important matter, I assure you, sir. Mr. Cooke said to tell you that he had hoped to give himself the pleasure of making your acquaintance but—you know how it is." He waved conciliatory hands.

A deep flush of anger mounted to Fenno's face and he gave the bright young man a baleful look.

The charming smile did not waver. "Mr. Cooke's associates are fully empowered, sir. In fact"—his manner became tinged with the confidential, as though he were taking Fenno into a very special secret—"it sounds like disloyalty to say it, but I don't mind telling *you* that you will find them better posted on the details of anything you may want to discuss than Mr. Cooke himself."

At this time-honored formula for guarding the great, Fenno snorted. "Young whipper-snapper! Does he think I'll fall for *that?*"

After this the whipper-snapper retired to a seat by himself, where he began to deal with a pile of telegrams that seemed to have come aboard at Cleveland. One of the older men joined him there, and their earnest mumblings formed a counterpoint to the bright talk at the round table. At Elyria the train pulled off on a siding for the purpose, Fenno was told, of exchanging more wires with Cooke and to receive market quotations. One of the telegrams contained greetings from Cooke to Fenno. On being told this flattering news, Fenno made no comment at all. As a result of the delay, they had dinner on the train and by the time they pulled out of Elyria, dark had come.

The dinner consisted of too much Frenchified food. Afterwards Fenno left the smoke-filled car and went to stand alone in the vestibule, where the air was cool and fresh. The night was very dark and he could not see the landscape but it seemed to him they were running through flat country, perhaps in the incipient beginnings of the great plains. From time to time cinders rattled on the roof of the car like sharp gusts of hail and the whistle wailed eerily, the sound trailing off into the night.

Fenno's mind was fixed on a bright future, much as, long ago, he had gazed on visions while he stood beside the great guns in Washington, but now there was a change both in the dreamer and in the dream. Time is like a tide slowly seeping out, eroding, carrying away, but leaving behind strange odds and ends and the tide of the passing years, having washed over John Fenno, left him both less and more than he had been. He stared out into the night with a face grown somewhat thinner, as though the softer substances were by degrees washing away, leaving the rocky prominences of the bone structure a little nearer to the surface. In the process, positiveness had given place to sureness. The jaw was grown more square; the eyes were not perceptibly more sunken under the brows but their expression originated from deeper within. The face was more controlled, more dominated by the mind, as though physical prime were giving place to mental prime. And with the process of change a visionary quality that was never quite there had become more conspicuously absent. It was the face of a determined man who was reaping both the penalties and the rewards of his determination.

The difference in the dream was that now John Fenno was more concerned with difficulties and details than the younger man had been. With his eyes on the hills he was more keenly aware of the steepness of the path. He had just followed that path to Washington, where he was becoming a familiar of Cabinet members, when a sound at his elbow startled him. No start of John Fenno's ever reached the surface and this one began and ended on the inside.

"Black as a hat here," the source of the sound said. "You're Fenno, I take it? I can't see for sure. I'm Kingston."

"Good evening," Fenno said with marked uncordiality. Kingston was already docketed in Fenno's mind as being too garrulous, too insignificant and too omnipresent. "Likes to hear himself talk," Fenno thought, "without anything to say." At that moment Kingston was saying it and Fenno gave him grudging attention.

"They'll get around to talking business with us tomorrow, I suppose."

"Us?"

"I'm in the iron business too. You may not know me but you probably know my Company, Federal Iron, in Trenton. I know who you are, of course. Everybody in the industry does. Can't have a success like yours without creating a lot of envy among us old timers, you know." He laughed good-naturedly.

"I didn't know you made rails."

"So you figured out that's what they're after, too? I don't—any more than you do. Look here." He hitched himself a step nearer to Fenno and poked a finger at the spot where the top button of his coat should be. Fenno, feeling his proximity, stepped as far away as the cramped vestibule would let him. "Let me give you some advice. I'm nearer New York than you are and I hear things maybe you don't. Did you ask yourself why they want to talk rails with a couple of concerns that never made them? Because the money market's tight, just as they say. That's why. And they wouldn't have to pay a couple of newcomers as promptly as those they're doing business with—and maybe owing money to now."

"You surely aren't meaning to imply that the credit of Cooke and Company . . ."

"I'm not implying anything. I'm just watching the terms of the contract, that's all. Maybe the money market *will* be better in the summer. Maybe this high-powered Treasury deal will fix everything up rosy—or maybe we were just intended to think so. Well, I've got to find that lad and get him to send this wire for me as soon as we pull in. See you later."

Fenno stared out at the dark fields. Could there, he wondered, be anything in what the fellow said? No whisper of doubt about Cooke and Company had ever reached him before. No, the more he thought about it the more absurd it seemed. The very size of the firm, meshing, as it did, into all sorts of enterprises here and abroad, was a guaranty of its reliability. Were Cooke and Company to fail to meet its obligations, thousands of companies and hundreds of banks would suffer. Suppose, for argument, that such a situation could exist. It would take on the character of a national disaster so far reaching that the Government might well lend aid to prevent such a catastrophe. That kind of thing was over for good and all. There were too many new elements in American business nowadays for any return to the recurring hard times of former decades. The size of such firms as Cooke and Company was one of these elements, surely. The settling of the West another and likewise the unprecedented demand for machine-made goods of all kinds. People were not going to go back to the old simple way of living any more and so hard times were gone.

"Thing of the past," he said aloud to the darkness.

The tiny nucleus of doubt lodged at the back of his mind was no more irritating than a cinder in a shoe.

10

O N THE afternoon of John Fenno's departure, Ellen was opening florists' boxes in the pantry under Willoughby's supervision. Though the Fenno house stood on three acres of what had once been good farm land, nobody in the Fenno family cared for gardening and the flowers in Willoughby's rather lavish arrangements were what Matild called "boughten." Today the flowers were a riot of late-season color with the toughened look of having withstood some frost, the welcome and unexpected produce of Indian summer. There were smoky red and purple salpiglossis, long spikes of crimson snapdragon, fuchsias curling back their slim petals from their deep blue bells, late delphinium and purple asters. Ellen lifted them gently from their tissue paper and laid them on a tray.

"Shan't I bring the vase in here, Miss Willoughby, where it won't make such a mess, the stems and all?"

"No, thank you," Willoughby said and pushed open the pantry door.

Ellen gave her retreating back a look and, picking up the tray, followed her.

Willoughby was in a venomous mood which had been building up all day from an accumulation of little things which all added up to make her life intolerable. In the first place, her father going off in all that luxury on the private train and meeting the millionaire financiers was too great a contrast to the stagnation of her present life. Then, oh, so trivial but so exasperating because it was occurring constantly, like the drip, drip of a leaky faucet, Matild had come home from a shopping trip with six inches of draggled petticoat flounce trailing out from under the back of her brown cashmere. "Oh, she's a *disgrace*," Willoughby thought, clenching her fists and feeling that Matild's forgetfulness in the matter of tying petticoat strings was more than her nerves could stand.

Then, just as she was preparing to go somewhere—anywhere—out of the house, Bobbie Thatcher had arrived. He sat on the front of a chair and gazed at her with his dying-calf look, explaining, while his blushes grew brighter, that she had come between him and the pages of his ledger until work was useless.

"I had to see you, Willie," he said eagerly. "I'll get the devil, too, if Father finds out I left the bank."

She turned on her charm for him while she raged inwardly, and she did it so well that he stayed for two boring hours and left at last in a daze of bliss. The effort added much to her nervous tension and she indulged in a good slam of the front door behind his back. "He's like a wriggling little white mouse," she thought. "Imagine *him* being the heir to a fortune!"

Those were tangible irritations. The business about Lettie was nothing you could put your finger on. Willoughby plunged a stalk of larkspur into the Lowestoft vase on the table before her, pulled it out again and cut off part of the stem with a vicious snip of the scissors. Ellen immediately went after the fallen bit of stem like a retriever and Willoughby turned toward her.

"Leave me alone, please. I can't do anything with you watching me. I'll ring when I'm through."

Ellen went, leaving her grievance hanging in the air like a cloud. "Lord!" Willoughby thought. "Lord!"

She was by no means insensitive to Lettie's moods. There was a part of her, a very secret part, that always quivered a little when Lettie's despair became violent. Perhaps if she had had nothing to do with Lettie's scar—but that was ridiculous. That was Fate. She did not blame herself in the least—not in the least, and the secret sore spot in her was unconnected with conscience.

She shoved the stems of the flowers down into the vase with fingers that trembled a little. Lettie was different. The change had come, so far as Willoughby could make out, right after the Thatcher ball. She was more secret, more shut inside herself than ever and her unhappiness, instead of being generalized and all-embracing, seemed to be focusing on something special. Willoughby found it peculiarly exasperating that she did not know on what. She stood back to examine her arrangement, frowned with distaste, jerked the flowers out of the vase and began all over again. Lettie was slipping through her fingers. Lettie was—she could swear it—leading a secret life. The symptoms of this were elusive. Willoughby's tongue lashings seemed to be losing some of their power to hurt, as though a part of Lettie were beyond her reach. And there was that queer business of the torn-off bow on her green dress that nobody seemed to know anything about. Heretofore Willoughby had always been the dominating factor in Lettie's life, as she was in her mother's and, for totally different reasons, in her father's also, but now some subtle instinct told her this was no longer true.

Willoughby was not doing her best by the flowers, for the suspicion that she might be losing her hold on anyone, even a Bobbie Thatcher, even a gauche and miserable younger sister, was intolerable to a nature as possessive and as in love with power as hers. "I'll teach her," she thought, without any clear idea of what she meant. "I'll teach her!"

Then, too, she was jumpy every time the door bell rang, for though it was only yesterday that she had seen that big lunkhead, Hadley, she felt certain all last night and all today that he would make some sign, more flowers, a note, something. She would know how to deal with that and while she jabbed flower stems into the vase she recited a whole string of epithets, among which "impertinent" and "presumptuous" were featured. Nevertheless, it was frustrating not to have anything with which to deal.

Under all these exasperations ran a deeper trouble that she could not bring herself to face. It was all summed up in the date, tomorrow, her birthday, another year gone by, another year added to her age. Suddenly she was seized by a violent rage against the inevitability of time, against her life, her boredom, even against herself. It boiled up in her with irresistible force, breaking through the bounds of her control. She seized the vase in both hands, raised it and threw it with all her might. It fell on the hearth and shattered into a hundred pieces. But even this outburst was not enough to relieve the tension in her and she began to pace the room violently, with long strides that jerked the train of her dress in angry susurrations.

It was so that Mark found her. Coming down the stairs with cat-like lightness, his slim shoes scarcely rustling the straw under the carpet, he stood in the drawing room door and watched Willoughby rage up and down the room with a little one-sided smile of amusement. She caught sight of him on the turn and he sauntered into the room.

"Why all the emotion, Willie? It's becoming, but—why?"

"Don't call me Willie."

"Venus, my love, balm of my heart, what is it?"

She flung her arms wide. "Everything! This town, my life, you, everything. Oh, Lord! *Dieux,*" she amended. Willoughby was trying to train herself to use French expletives.

"Me?" said Mark, but the momentary astonishment faded from his face. She didn't mean it, of course. How could she? But the remark gave him a shock in view of his intentions toward her.

"Yes, you! You're always the same. You bore me!" She turned her back on him, walked to the window, jerked the lace curtain aside and stood staring out, seeing nothing.

Mark strolled toward her and, raising his hand, brushed aside the curls on the nape of her neck with his long fingers and kissed the white skin. She whirled on him with a gasp and he put an arm around her. He did not kiss her mouth. Instead, he pulled aside the ruffle which edged the deep V-neck of her dress and, bending, kissed the hollow between the swelling curves of her breasts. To his relief, she did not pull away but he felt her go tense and he moved his head a little so that his lips touched the side of her breast. Then with a sudden motion, his hand slid down inside her dress and, cupping her breast, he pressed it hard against his mouth. Just as suddenly he released her and stood back, smiling.

"You're not bored now, are you?"

Her face was a conflict of emotions and she sank down on the window seat. *"Dieux,"* she said faintly.

"You liked that! The trouble with you is, you've never been loved by hands like these." He held them out toward her. "You've never been loved by someone who knows how to make love, who knows all the subtle secret things to do to give you pleasure. Every woman should be loved well, loved with art, once in her life so she knows what it can be like." His eyes, as he bent over her, were amber slits and his mouth under his mustache was moist and bright red.

Mark had a plan, carefully thought out, as were all Mark's plans. He must have Willoughby—his mounting debts, if nothing else, demanded that. He dared not risk a refusal. "But," he argued to himself, "she wouldn't refuse if she were compromised— If I could get her to bed she couldn't refuse." This invitation to stay at the Fennos' was an opportunity not to be missed. His nerves tingled, but less with desire for her than with the excitement of the game.

She closed her eyes and a little spasmodic tremor passed over her. Pin points of light appeared in the amber. "I've got her," he thought. "If I'm careful, I've got her."

"You and I," he said, and his voice was a soft murmur. "Why shouldn't we give each other pleasure?"

Her eyes were still shut and she tilted up her face toward him. He smiled the one-sided smile that made him look cynical and a little hard. "You want a kiss, do you?" he thought. "Well, you can just go on wanting it. I won't satisfy you, my dear, until you're so crazy for it you'll beg me." He took her hand, opened the fingers, ran his palm softly over hers once and, raising it to his lips, held it there. Again the tremor passed over her but he had the eerie, clairvoyant feeling that in her mind he was someone else. The tip of his tongue slid between his teeth and explored her palm but a little perspiration broke out on his forehead and his face flushed a dark red.

He heard the heavy step coming down the stairs before she did and he released her hand with a little squeeze. He bent close and whispered.

"Tonight, in the study, after they've all gone to bed. I'll be waiting for you."

She opened her blue eyes and looked at him, rather dazed and far away. He shoved his hands in his pockets and whistling a tuneless, sibilant air through his teeth, began to examine with a great show of interest an oil painting of Cleopatra on a barge surrounded by slaves with peacock feather fans in their hands. The slaves looked astonishingly like American Negroes.

"Willoughby? Willoughby? Are you there?" Matild sounded a little breathless. Her big bulk appeared in the doorway. "Why, Mark! Oh, yes, you've come to stay. I forgot. Oh . . . !" Matild had caught sight of the shattered vase.

She swayed across the room and, putting one hand on the arm of a chair, eased herself down on her knees beside the hearth.

"Oh," she said. "Oh. It was my mother's. My darling mother's."

She raised her head and looked at Willoughby. Tears swam in her pale eyes.

"How could you, Willoughby, how could you!"

"It slipped. I couldn't help it. It's a hideous old thing anyway." Willoughby rose and swept with injured dignity from the room.

Mark, trapped, and not liking his aunt in her lachrymose moods, or in any other for that matter, sat down at the piano as the surest way to avoid the necessity for giving sympathy. He shot his cuffs, held his slim hands poised for a moment over the keys and brought them down in the opening notes of a gavotte by Rameau. He played with considerable virtuosity, color and perhaps more dramatic effect than the composition required. As he played he became interested in his own performance and, having reached the end, he played it again, listening critically and experimenting with a somewhat different interpretation. Both times the work had brilliance but no feeling. When he finished he was pleased to note that Matild had taken herself off.

Mark and Willoughby got through an intolerably dull dinner somehow, helping themselves along by frequent furtive exchanges of meaningful looks and Willoughby almost persuaded herself that she was not giving a thought to Hadley. They had coffee in the living room and three of them, Mark and Willoughby and Lettie, were silent and withdrawn into private worlds. Matild, reminded by the tragedy of the vase, droned on and on about her girlhood home in Boston but no one really listened. Lettie, more sallow and round-shouldered than usual, might as well not have been there at all and once Willoughby came out of her thoughts long enough to study her with a look so cold and contemptuous that Mark, intercepting it, shuddered involuntarily and had to give time to rallying his resolution.

". . . and cups didn't have handles then, or at least ours didn't—wasn't that funny? And Mother used to wash them herself on a stool in front of the fire in a silver punch bowl with a towel in it on account of chips—just the cups, nothing else, of course—a lady couldn't—but all ladies did cups—and I'd sit and watch her rings sparkle in the firelight." Matild's breathless, monotonous chant went on and on while the others sipped coffee in silence.

". . . and the century plant—when it bloomed—or maybe it was a night-blooming cereus or—I don't know—something rare—Mother put two little flags in the ground by the gate and a lantern on a pole and dozens and dozens of people came to see—just dozens and dozens."

Willoughby yawned behind her hand and Mark glanced for the twentieth time at the ormolu clock.

The evening ended at last and they were all shut away in their own rooms, closed in with the dark and their own thoughts. The whole house was dark and quiet except for the steady tick of the old clock on the stairs, a calm, unhurried tick as though the clock were like an old, old man who has seen so much of life that nothing can disturb him or excite him ever any more.

Lettie clutched her pillow tight with both hands.

I'll go back there—I won't be afraid—I'll ask those questions at all those houses—I won't be afraid but they all speak Finnish—what shall I do? I won't be afraid—how much do you earn in a year, please?—how much money do you save?—how many months do you work?—are you a citizen? —it's for Mr. Brodi, you see, please—Michael, Michael it's for you.

Matild was not really thinking because it was more like a dream, only it wasn't really a dream either for she could make things come out the way she wanted them to, only it was as real as a dream. The old clock on the stair was ticking calmly and unhurried. She could hear that, only it was all mixed up, for she was hearing it long, long ago, lying in her bed and listening for the rustle of silk and the light tap of a small heelless slipper on the stair. She saw the wavering light first, the uncertain light that grew stronger as her mother came up the stairs. She came so softly because her little Mattie might be sleeping and she shielded the candle flame with her hand. She bent over the bed and the faint, fresh smell of lavender came with her. But Mattie was not asleep. She was lying awake just for this and she reached up her arms in the soft dimness. Matild raised her old and brown-spotted arms and her mother, holding the silver candle stick so the wax wouldn't spill, bent and kissed her cheek and Matild's cheek was wet.

Mark had not been granted the grandeur of the guest room. He sat now on the edge of his cot in the sewing room. His coat was off, his collar and tie loosened and he held his head in his hands. The scent of a pomander ball stole out of the wardrobe and a dress form loomed in the dark monstrously, with something nightmarish about its deadly femininity, or perhaps Mark was feeling overwrought.

Jesus Christ, I can't go through with this—she'd never let me call my soul my own—you've got to, my lad, before someone snaps her up—Hadley will get her if you don't—but surely she wouldn't marry that lout and I'll get her tonight—and after—not so much work—time to enjoy things a little— enjoy things, Christ! when you're owned body and soul?—but perhaps it wouldn't be so bad—away by yourself sometimes—New York—concerts— alone.

Willoughby was trying to see the time by tipping her little clock toward the dim moonlight, but it was no use. She'd have to wait for the hall clock to strike again. She stood by the window looking out on the night. A radiance of moonlight spilled patches of silver on the lawn and crowned the trees with a misty luminance. The branches swayed and bent from some unseen breeze and the patches of silver light flickered and danced. It seemed to Willoughby that she and the silent house were floating through space, the trees, the lawn, floating rapidly as though she were feeling the motion of the world itself. All outdoors, even the curving driveway and the flower beds, were transfigured and alive and waiting as though in expectation of revelation and all around were the sounds of the night, the myriad of tiny voices rising like a hymn to glory. She closed the shutters quickly, glad to shut out this heady festival and return to the limits of her own world.

The important thing is not to think—not to let your mind dwell on things —how can I help it when the only eligible man I know has white eyelashes and blushes like a school girl?—maybe I'll be driven to it—what is it like to be in bed with a man?—what would it be like to be in bed with Bobbie Thatcher? he'd suck in his breath and feel with his hands—what would it be like?—don't think about him—keep your head and get a man of the world—with money—money—money—how sick is Mrs. Thatcher?—invalids live forever, don't they?—suppose she outlived the General and then Bobbie would get all the money and you couldn't marry your stepson, or could you?—why doesn't he have money?—or even Mark—how could you help thinking—maybe Mark could stop the thoughts for just tonight—his hands—not let him go too far—just make me stop thinking about things for a while.

The old clock on the stairs began a low whirring sound that meant it was gathering its forces to strike the hour. Willoughby stood still, listening, and continued to stand there deep in thought after the booming notes had died away. Then she went purposefully to her dressing table and took the pins out of her hair rapidly. It fell about her shoulders in a soft cloud. She raised the skirt of her dress and began pulling at the tapes which held her hoops and petticoats. They fell to her ankles and she stepped out of them, leaving them on the floor. She paused to think again, with her hands held flat against her bodice, then she raised her skirt once more and with rapid, jerky motions, began pulling out the lacings of her corset. A little smile dented the corners of her mouth.

Mark was lying full length on the study couch with his hands behind his head and his ankles neatly crossed. It was a peculiarly uncomfortable couch made of slippery black leather which bulged between the buttons with which it was studded in what looked and felt like black cobblestones. There was no back or side but one end rose in a slope which was too steep for comfortable reclining and not steep enough for sitting. For whatever purpose such a thing might be designed, Mark thought, it was certainly not for love.

The study was as dark as a cave and when Mark heard the door handle turn he rose and felt for a match. When it flared she was standing close to him, smiling as though it amused her to find herself there. Mark held the match high and stared at her and for just that instant he was forgetful of everything but what he saw. In this queer light she was more beautiful than ever, with a beauty that seemed to Mark beyond human experience and he began to shake a little, feeling all physical desire drain out of him. He put out the match flame.

"If I'm to love you, my dear, it will have to be in the dark."

"Why?"

"Because a few flaws are needed to make a lover feel superior. Come here."

He felt for her wrist and drew her down on the couch beside him. She seemed stiff and unyielding. "She's trying to figure that one out," he thought, "to see if it was meant to be a compliment." He turned and put his arms around her. She resisted him a little and he pulled her toward him, discovering suddenly that, in spite of her resistance, her body was soft and pliable under his hands as he had never felt it before. The discovery was a distinct shock and for an instant his exploring hands were still. "She's left her stays off—for Heaven's sake! Now what am I supposed to make of that?" Perversely, he was not altogether pleased and he was faintly shocked. That she had thought about this tryst beforehand in such detail offended, not so much his sense of propriety, as his sense of the artistic.

He slid his hands over her to make sure he was not mistaken. His detachment vanished. His hands wandered downward, sinking suddenly around her slim waist. Perfume was rising from inside her dress and he drew a deep breath, letting his senses lose themselves in exquisite pleasure, letting himself forget everything else. She moved away from him as though she were aware of his abandon and was alarmed by it and she pushed his hands off. He raised his head, outraged that she should break the spell, and seized her tightly by the arms.

"Let me go, Mark," she whispered fiercely, pulling away from him.

Suddenly he was filled with a wild desire for her that was not pretended and that was both fierce and animal. He threw himself on her, forcing her down with the weight of his body. She fought him, twisting and turning, but after a moment he felt her go limp. He put his hands on either side of her face and kissed her violently. Her mouth was warm and soft and yielding.

That had happened an hour, two hours, ago, for what time it might be now, Mark did not know.

He had been very sound asleep and he woke slowly, struggling up from the depths. For a minute he did not know where he was and then the bumps in the couch, pressing into his side, brought him to himself, and with full wakefulness a tingling wave of apprehension swept over him. He must ask her now, while she was still under his spell and under the spell of physical love.

Willoughby was still asleep and he lay listening to her soft, relaxed breathing, staring into the dark, his heart beating in quick jerks. Was it, perhaps, not as dark as it had been? Could they have slept the night through? Surely only a little time had passed. His watch was in his vest pocket, just out of reach on the chair, but he could not grope for it because her head was pillowed on his arm and he could not bring himself to wake her. Not just yet—not for a few minutes. He needed time to pull himself together and renew his resolution. He began to enumerate to himself all the advantages that would accrue to him as John Fenno's son-in-law. A place at the mill at which he need not work too hard—and in time actual ownership of the mill, through her, would come to him. Money. No more debts. Position, luxury and the things he loved.

He found that his body was tense all over and his teeth were clenched so tightly that they ached. He forced himself to relax and to lie calmly, though he was sweating with emotion. He hated her for sleeping so peacefully. And now he discovered that he was excruciatingly uncomfortable. Every remnant of physical desire was gone, and he longed passionately for cool sheets and a soft pillow under his head. He wondered again if it might not be better to postpone this business, ask her another day, but he knew that was not wise. Once let her regain her poise and her normal perspective on life and he might not be able to persuade her. He drew a long and shaky breath and tried to pull his numb arm from under her head.

She stirred and he knew her eyes were open. "Darling!" he whispered in as ardent a tone as he could manage, his mind still filled with his longing for bed and solitude. He propped himself on one elbow and reached out his hand and touched her forehead. It felt sticky with damp curls plastered to it, and he hastily rubbed his palm on the couch. "Darling," he said again in exactly the same tone.

She murmured something undistinguishable and he took a final grip on himself.

"Willoughby," he said, putting his arm around her and holding her close to him. "Willoughby, I love you and I need you, always. Willoughby, my darling, you are mine now and I want you for mine for ever and ever. Willoughby, will you marry me, dear?"

She was wide awake. He felt her alertness and he waited in an agony of suspense for her answer. When none came he bent and kissed her cheek. "Darling, we've had each other and we know now how wonderful it can be. I'll love you like that always, only it will always be better and better."

She laughed softly, a contented sound and, he thought, the most completely feminine sound he had ever heard. "I don't want to make up my mind now, Mark. Besides, what makes you think it would be you?"

"But Willoughby, after *this!*" He was genuinely shocked and it was audible in his voice. He hastened to add, "I can't possibly live without you *now!*"

She laughed again, a little ruefully. "I really didn't mean this to happen. But don't rush me. I have to make up my mind, I tell you. It might not be you at all."

"But Willie, for Heaven's sake. You can't marry anybody else *now.* You're mine, Willie."

"We'll see."

"Willie!" he said imploringly. He was really worried.

She was enjoying herself and suddenly he hated her. She said thoughtfully, "I might marry you some day. Don't rush me, I tell you."

"Willie, *please!* After tonight . . ."

"You haven't any money, for one thing."

"You'll be rich some day and I intend to make money."

She made a derisive sound.

"Willoughby, will you *please* listen to reason?"

She was sliding off the couch, and he knew she was groping on the floor for her dress. He sat with his head in his hands, trying desperately to think of a way to appeal to her, but he could not, and he listened with a sinking feeling to the sounds of her hasty dressing.

"Willoughby!" He reached out in the darkness to snatch at her, but she moved away as though she had guessed his intention.

"Good night, Mark." The door closed with finality behind her.

He sat on the edge of the couch feeling miserable and desperate. "For Christ's sake," he said aloud with a great deal of emotion. Then a cold feeling hit him in the pit of his stomach. "She can't be thinking of Hadley, can she? He'll try to get her, that's sure—but, by God, he won't. By Christ, he won't! I'll get her if it's the last thing I do." He groped for his clothes.

11

O N HIS return Fenno went straight to the mill where he replied to Williams' greeting with a monosyllable and, avoiding the eager eyes of those who waited in the anteroom, walked rapidly into his office and shut the door. Behind that barricade he discarded his brisk manner and his scowl and, as he slowly took off his coat, he looked around him. The place seemed to have grown smaller while he was away, smaller and not so impressive as he had supposed. He surveyed the room with a calculating look. A partition could come down here, his desk could go over there in a more commanding spot. The door opened and Williams' head appeared.

"Mr. Hadley to see you, sir, and several others."

"Let them wait."

"Yes, sir."

Williams also seemed to have grown deficient in size and dignity. Williams, with his worried frown and his old coat, should go and be replaced by someone on the order of that young ass on the train perhaps, who could impress visitors and make them feel uncomfortable. Great times lay ahead and they should have their proper setting.

As Fenno took out his keys and unlocked the roll top of his desk, something like a smile affected the normal sternness of his face. The smile, it is true, amounted to no more than a softening of the facial muscles, a slight twitching of the lips, but as he threw back the top of his desk and sank into his leather chair, there was about him an air almost of geniality. He was experiencing one of life's rarest pleasures, that is to say, he found himself in the position where, as a result of his own achievements, he could reshape his life to a large extent, sweep away annoying limitations and begin to live some of his dreams.

He swung his chair to face the gray lake and the corners of his eyes drew together while a look of seeing distant horizons came into their depths. John Fenno was as nearly a happy man as was possible for a nature such as his. He was enjoying the warmly gratifying knowledge that he had associated with important people and his world would shortly be apprised of it. No one but himself, moreover, need know that the encounter was not wholly satisfying.

His eyes came down from the heights and, as he contemplated the nearer scene, their far-seeing squint vanished. There was work to do, and a decision arrived at on the train must be reviewed before the door was opened to Sam Hadley. With a businesslike manner he took out a cigar, lit it and, leaning back in his chair, watched the involuted ribbon of blue smoke rise upward. The fellow was a good worker—give the devil his due. He had, in fact, a positive genius for getting things done. That would be missed, particularly now with this new contract. On the other hand, the overbearing confidence was a constant annoyance. He was not slick like Mark, but smart, and the smartness was a constant . . .

With something very like shock Fenno broke off the train of thought. His mind had been about to say "a constant threat."

A threat to what? Himself? Ridiculous! And Fenno, not liking the thought and not caring to look into the dark depths of his own motives and emotions, told himself that the whole trouble was the man needed watching. In the months ahead there would be no time for that! Fire him and be done with it.

Fenno was reaching out to bring his hand down on his bell to summon Hadley when his door opened and Williams' deferential head appeared.

"General Thatcher and Mr. Brown to see you, sir."

"Show them in." They didn't waste any time, those two. He wondered what it could be they wanted.

Greetings were disposed of, chairs drawn up and cigars proffered and declined. Fenno sat down, unconsciously employing, as he did so, the mannerisms by which the man in the swivel chair betrays his feeling of advantage. There was a pause and Brown and Thatcher glanced quickly at each other. General Thatcher nodded almost imperceptibly, giving the lead to Brown. The nod was not lost on Fenno, who had long ago learned that the spokesman is not necessarily the one who will say the things of import, and he continued to keep his eye on Thatcher.

Brown hitched forward in his chair and took a deep breath. "There's no use wasting time, John. Thatcher and I have been talking. This is a good deal of a one-man concern—always has been. We've been thinking it's time to get in some young blood."

Fenno looked from one to the other. "Things are going all right. When I feel the need of new blood, I'll get it."

"We'd like to see you do something about it now. There's that fellow Hadley, of course, but he strikes me more as the type you could use in the mill rather than in the office as Secretary."

"He may be better than you think," General Thatcher said.

Fenno made no comment and Brown continued. "Most of the directors feel as I do. That's why we're here—to tell you there is this feeling in the board."

"Thank you—but the running of the mill is in my hands and it will have to remain there. I must point out that the internal management of the mill is outside the province of the board."

"Listen, John." Brown's tone was placatory. "We're not trying to run the mill. But you're not immortal, you know. It's the province of the board to look to the future. Don't forget we've got a lot of money invested in this company."

"Just who are 'we'?"

"The General, here. Cushing. Myself. Several others. Most of 'em, in fact."

Thatcher spoke. "There's been talk of bringing it up in meeting. I'm sure you agree that would be undesirable from any angle and we thought perhaps we could forestall that by this talk. My reasons for urging this step are a little different from the others'. I think that young fellow, Hadley, is a good man. But he's the kind that might get a bit too big for his breeches, if you don't watch out. A good horse needs a check rein more than a poor one. You can keep him in his place of course, but another bright young fellow in the organization might give him a little wholesome competition—keep 'em both on their toes."

"I don't like that young fellow," Brown said dogmatically. "Tried to hold us up."

There was a silence filled by Fenno's swift thoughts. The signing of this contract was going to force the Company to expand once more and in the restive mood of the board, it might well be that the support of these two, and especially Thatcher, would be helpful, even necessary, to raise the money. There would be no need to keep Hadley if he took in some other young man, even though Thatcher did seem to be partial to him. Perhaps a concession now . . . Aware that the silence was lengthening out undesirably, he said, "There aren't many of them who know this business that we could get away from their present jobs. The war took its toll, you know."

Brown was quick to sense a yielding on Fenno's part. "He wouldn't have to know the business—at first. You yourself didn't and you've always been more of a businessman than anything else. There's that young man in your own family, Mark Sabin."

"I've always been against taking members of the family into the Company."

"It has its advantages. He's very prepossessing. And he's a lawyer. He could handle small matters and cut down on our expenses a bit. Fees to Cushing's firm were pretty steep last year."

"I don't think much of Mark," Thatcher interposed.

Again there was a silence. Finally Fenno said, "There may be something in what you say, Brown. I'll see about it. Yes, I'll see about it. And since you're here, it is a good opportunity to discuss another matter in which I would like your support when it comes before the board."

Having said this, Fenno wondered if he had made too plain the fact that he was proposing a trade. No matter—Thatcher would see that anyway. "I've just been to Sandusky, talking with the Cooke people. I signed a contract with them to make rails."

"Rails!" Both Fenno's visitors said it in unison. Brown brought his clenched fist down hard on the arm of his chair.

"By God, John, you can't make rails with the set-up you've got here! You'd have to install more converters or buy a better-equipped plant. That would cost us a lot of money before we could deliver the first rail. You'd have to borrow money again." Brown shot a swift look at Thatcher, the banker, and mumbled, "This is just the sort of thing the board objects to."

For a moment the air bristled with antagonism which Fenno, for his own ends, made a swift attempt to eliminate. "The approval of the board is not necessary to legalize a contract to deliver material," he said mildly. "It *is* necessary to ratify the purchase of an additional plant, which may be the wisest course to follow."

Brown cut in angrily. "You had no right to make a contract which depends on plant expansion of any kind without consulting the board."

"I admit an outlay for this purpose may be necessary if we are to fulfil this contract. The fact that the contract has been signed is being published in New York this week, incidentally. This is a great opportunity for the Company and I'll be willing to go into that in as much detail as you like whenever you like. But I'll say this—the necessary expansion gives weight to your suggestion that we take on a new man."

Fenno paused to let this remark settle. "I'll want your help in getting the board to ratify the plant purchase if such a purchase is necessary. I don't think, as a matter of fact, that there are likely to be any dissenters, except perhaps Cushing, especially if you gentlemen give this your support. I would not like to ask the board to vote you down—and the Company is already committed to making rails, remember."

General Thatcher's round and rather too pink cheeks rose in curves that obliterated any expression but a sort of benign dandyism. "Another loan would put control of the Company in the hands of the bank," he said gently.

"Temporarily. Only very temporarily."

"Oh, certainly."

Abruptly Thatcher rose, smiling. "Well, John, we've taken too much of your time, I'm afraid. I'm glad to hear that you agree with us about the need for new blood." He stretched himself to tiptoe on his small and shining shoes. "And since the contract is signed and the announcement being made, why, I think we could go along with you if it's necessary to purchase more plant."

Brown, looking bewildered and a trifle resentful about this outcome, rose also but he was prevented from saying anything by the effusive nature of General Thatcher's farewells.

Fenno went with them to the door. "May I ask you gentlemen to keep all this among ourselves until a meeting can be called?"

When they were gone, he sank wearily into his chair. For a gloomy moment it seemed to him that he often felt tired without reason these days. He sighed and, remembering Hadley, he again stretched out his hand toward the bell.

Hadley entered with an easy self-confidence that was an instant annoyance to Fenno. There was, moreover, something very like challenge in Hadley's bold glance.

Fenno pointed to a chair beside his desk and, omitting any kind of greeting, said sternly, "Sit there."

The chair Fenno indicated faced the windows and caught the glare from the lake. Hadley put a big hand on the back and swung it, as though it weighed nothing, just far enough over so that Fenno was forced to move around and partially face the light. The maneuver had every earmark of being merely thoughtless, but Fenno had an irritated conviction that it was not. There had as yet been no exchange between them and Fenno was already deeply angry.

"How did you make out with Huntington?" Fenno managed to keep most of his anger out of his voice. Hadley seemed to be smiling a little.

"He was in a lather to sell. I think he was mystified but he smelled out a good price. Strange as it seems, I don't think it ever occurred to him to go after the business of making rails for the Northern Pacific."

"And how did it occur to *you,* may I ask?"

Hadley said nothing. Leaning back in his chair with his hands on the arms, fully at ease, he favored Fenno with a smile that just avoided being insolent. Fenno stared at him blackly and growled something in his beard.

Hadley's smile broadened and when he spoke, his tone implied that he would overlook the interruption. "Their rails are part iron and part steel—Booth rails, they call 'em. Moreover, there's no place west of here making enough rails to count. You wanted to know that, I believe."

Fenno turned his swivel chair away from Hadley and, seeing the lake there beyond his windows, he gave it one of those unconsciously anxious glances frequent among men who depend on these uncertain waters. The lake was flat and lead-colored under a lowering sky. There were no waves but here and there the surface heaved threateningly like a pot about to boil. Fenno turned away and, worrying with a part of his mind about the impending end of the navigation season, he gave his gaze back to Hadley. Get the fellow's report in full and then fire him. Tell him to get out at once. It would be a positive pleasure. Some of Fenno's geniality returned. He crossed one knee over the other and broke off the ash of his cigar into a bowl on the desk.

Hadley was still grinning and sitting back comfortably as though to allow Fenno ample time for these mental asides. He did not speak until he felt quite sure that he had all of Fenno's attention. Then he said, "It would take four to six months to install converters here—nearer six. I've been looking into it. Besides, our mill is too small. We'd have to build. Whatever you do, you'll have to put up more of your own stock as security for the loan to the Company—over fifty percent of the stock all told, I should think. You're pretty well extended now."

"It would be safe enough. You needn't lose sleep over that, Mr. Hadley." Fenno's manner was reproving. "The bank won't sell me out, and bear in mind, if you please, that Thatcher is one of our directors."

Fenno thought well of his own strategy in arranging that the president of his bank be also one of the Company's directors, and the satisfaction that it gave him made him for a moment almost affable.

"Did you ever stop to think what a great invention credit is? Couldn't expand without it. We'd still be in the dark ages."

His geniality vanished and his stern mood returned so incisively that Hadley was reminded of a clam shell suddenly shutting down. Fenno continued coldly, "You realize of course, Mr. Hadley, that we will be in a position to pay off enough of the loan to satisfy Thatcher when the first lot of rail is delivered."

"And paid for."

"Certainly, and paid for." A look of shrewdness came into Fenno's eyes. "I don't suppose Huntington let slip what he would want for Lake, did he? I think I remember telling you not to go into details."

"We didn't talk price at all, Mr. Fenno, but—fact is, he doesn't own control of Lake Furnace."

"Who does?"

"I do."

"What!"

"I do, sir."

"Look here, Hadley . . ."

"I think I'd better explain."

"I think you had!"

"You told me to see Huntington on Sunday afternoon. Well, he wasn't in. Gone duck shooting. So the first thing Monday—and this is why I didn't get to the office before you left—I looked him up. As I say, he was in a sweat to sell, though he tried hard enough not to let me see that. Something about the way he acted made me smell a rat. Why the hell should he be so anxious to sell unless he was in difficulties of some sort?

"So after I left him I asked around a bit and I found he doesn't bank with the Thatcher crowd—had a big loan at the Second National. I also found out what you probably know already, that Lake hasn't been doing so well the last couple of years—bad management probably, and it must have been pretty bad at that. Must have been or he couldn't have failed to make money, the way things have been booming in the business the last few years."

"Get back to the point, Mr. Hadley."

Hadley smiled a little and continued his story in a rather more leisurely manner than before. "As I say, he had a big loan at the Second National and they'd been threatening to sell him out. I guess they figured too that any fool who couldn't make money in these times wasn't a very good risk. Anyway, they jumped at my offer to buy."

"*Your* offer to buy!"

"They asked me if I was acting for you, and I just smiled and said the deal was to go through in my name, so of course they assumed it was for you."

Hadley paused and contemplated the angry, mottled flush which had risen on Fenno's face before he continued.

"I'm quite a capitalist, you know—thanks to you. I'd no idea things like that could be done so easily. Why, I went in there at eleven o'clock, signed a few papers, and by twelve I was out again, owning control of the damn thing!"

"Mr. Hadley . . ."

"Just a minute, sir. Let me finish."

Hadley tipped his chair back until it rocked on its hind legs and then let it come down again with a crash that jarred Fenno's already taut nerves.

"I asked them not to say anything to anybody about the deal until you got back, not even to Huntington. They were so glad to get out from under that they'd have agreed to anything within reason. Why, the vice-president shook hands with me about six times and followed me all the way to the door."

"This has gone far enough, Mr. Hadley!" Fenno had pushed himself part way out of his chair and the mottled flush had turned to a deep, burning red. "This is the most completely outrageous breach of faith . . ."

"Mr. Fenno . . ." Hadley raised a hand in a gesture that was almost a threat. "Will you please let me finish! You'll have to hear all about this sooner or later and it might as well be now. With no one else listening in. Now listen—I don't intend to hold you up. Sit down, will you?"

Fenno sat down again with a growl but he kept his hands on the arms of his chair, elbows up, as though he might at any moment rise in his wrath. His eyes blazed at Hadley in silent fury.

"I don't intend to hold you up. You can have Lake for exactly what it cost me and you can tell the directors I was acting on your orders—pressure of time, need for secrecy, all that sort of thing. Or . . ." Hadley's chair teetered back on its hind legs and he smiled broadly again. "If you don't want Lake—if you're not afraid of the time clause that is probably in your contract—if you are willing to build and install equipment and wait six months or more before you get into production—and if you don't care whether or not the world knows I put over a slick one on you—why, then, at the very worst, I own Lake and I'm in business for myself. I'm making rails *now,* not six months from now. Think it over."

"You infernal blackguard!"

"I wouldn't say that, Mr. Fenno. The whole thing is perfectly legal. If you want Lake you get it for the same price you would have had to pay Huntington. If you don't—all right. Then we're competitors and you know me well enough to know that I'd be quite a thorn in your side. You'd better not answer me now. If you do, you'll only tell me to go to hell and regret it the minute you cool down. Remember, the directors can think I was acting for you. But a blackguard, Mr. Fenno. Certainly not!"

Fenno was on his feet, filled with an anger so terrible that he was visibly shaken with it. His eyes blazed and one hand groped for the side of the desk and clutched its support. Hadley rose too and watched while Fenno struggled to down his rage and speak. When the words came they were thick and blurred with passion.

"Get out of here!"

And having said that much he seemed unable to say more.

Hadley walked around to the back of the chair he had been sitting in, folded his arms and leaned on it. "There is just one more little thing, Mr. Fenno." His voice was calm, his manner easy and pleasant. "You may get to wondering why I've done all this. Well, here's your answer. If you take over Lake from me you will, of course, want a general manager for both organizations. I'm your man. That would be in the purchase agreement."

Fenno had begun to tremble. He still clutched his desk, leaned on it, rather, and his face was purple. He seemed unable to speak. Hadley watched him with an expression of triumph that faded into interest and finally into concern.

"Are you all right, Mr. Fenno?"

Fenno straightened his shoulders, the trembling stopped and his eyes deepened. "Get out!" he said in ringing tones.

When the door shut after Hadley, Fenno leaned with both hands on the edge of his desk and let himself down into his chair slowly and carefully. Nothing else in the world existed but the heavy beating of his heart. It was beating slowly, too slowly, but each beat was like the stroke of a hammer under which the blood in all his pulses leaped. Before his eyes there was nothing but a red blur and when he closed them the red blur was still there. Beyond that there was nothing at all, no thoughts, no sensations. He sat very still, his big frame jerking slightly every time it felt the hammerlike blows of his heart.

After a length of time that was entirely vague to Fenno the door opened and Williams' anxious head appeared. Remotely aware of him and guided by the instinct to conceal his trouble, Fenno leaned forward in his chair and with hands that felt like lead slowly drew a piece of paper toward him, picked up a pencil and began to make marks. "Get out," he said over his shoulder. The words had a queer familiar ring as though they were not words at all but echoes. His head seemed to be entirely hollow except for the sound they made. He repeated them to himself again and again and little by little thoughts and memories began to build themselves up around them until the whole of his mind was clear again.

He rubbed his hands across his eyes and looked around him. He seemed to be alone in the room. With trembling fingers he drew out his watch and snapped open the case. The red mist was gone and after a moment of concentration he saw that the hands stood at five-thirty. He put it away and, gathering his forces, rose to his feet. He took hold of the top of the desk to pull it down, his eyes falling on the pieces of paper, and he looked at the meaningless, straggling marks with detached interest. "Must see a doctor," he thought vaguely, closing the desk and putting on his hat and coat. He still felt rather giddy and the effort of stooping over for his bag daunted him.

In the anteroom he found Williams alone. It had been full of people, surely. Williams was standing respectfully behind his desk.

"I sent them all away, sir. Said you were too busy to see anyone."

Fenno scowled at him. "Get my bag."

The carriage was there waiting, as it should be, and for the first time in his life Fenno allowed himself to be helped in. During the long drive home he leaned back and, whenever he thought no one could see him, he closed his eyes. He mounted the red-carpeted front steps slowly and went slowly into the hall. Willoughby was playing the piano in the drawing room and, throwing his hat and coat on the hall chair, he stood still to listen. He was no judge of music but the air she played was sweet and soft and lilting like a summer breeze and it carried balm to his spirit.

After a time he walked slowly into the drawing room and when Willoughby would have stood up to greet him he waved a restraining hand at her.

"Don't get up. Go on playing. I like it."

She began to play again and he walked on past his accustomed chair by the fireplace and let himself down into a corner of the frivolous little settee that Matild called the *tête*.

The music flowed and danced around him. He was tired beyond thought, tired to the point where the circumstance of victory or defeat had no meaning. He let his heavy hands drop to his sides and his eyes closed. After a while the music stopped and he opened them again. Willoughby was coming toward him, the rustling of her skirts making an accompaniment to the tune which still went on in his head. And she was smiling. Without knowing that he did so, he smiled at her and a great wave of warmth and satisfaction and pride in her rushed into his heart.

He laid his hand on the seat beside him. "Come and sit down."

"Daddy, they're beautiful!"

She hadn't called him Daddy for years. Not since she was a little girl. She was holding her chin up, stretching her beautiful throat.

"What?" he said. "Oh, the pearls."

He had forgotten about them. He leaned toward her to examine them, feeling a need to scowl.

"They seem to be all right," he said. "You must keep them in the bank when you don't use them. They cost a lot of money, I suppose."

"I'm sure they did, dear. They're lovely."

She laid her hand on his knee and then swiftly she bent to kiss his cheek.

He wanted to say something gruff but there seemed to be something stuck in his throat. He cleared it noisily and, putting her hand aside, he rose.

"Must go to my study," he mumbled and walked rather quickly out of the room.

The next day he refused to see Hadley and he sent for Mark. Then he had Williams prepare a memorandum to Hadley directing him, as Secretary of the Company, to call a meeting of the board to act on the purchase of Lake Furnace, Hadley's appointment as general manager of both organizations and Mark's appointment as Secretary.

12

IN NOVEMBER Lettie returned to Mill Street and because she always overdid her emotions, she went in much the same spirit that one might go to the guillotine. Päkkä himself opened to her desperate knock and regarded her with hostile, beady black eyes, his powerful body planted belligerently in the doorway.

Looking more frightened than she knew, she said to him, "You speak English, don't you, Mr. Päkkä?"

"Yea, yea. Vat you vant?" Päkkä moved restlessly and Lettie retreated a step.

"I'm a friend of Mr. Brodi's," she said hastily.

Suspicion spread over Päkkä's expressive face. "Ain't you Fenno? Ain't you name Fenno?"

"Yes, I'm Lettie Fenno but I'm a friend of Mr. Brodi's. Really I am."

"Yea?" The little black eyes were taking her all in with remarkable shrewdness.

"Yes, truly. Let me talk to you. Please."

"You a friend of Mike's? You—Fenno—really friend of Mike's?"

"Yes, I am," Lettie said firmly.

Suddenly Päkkä smiled and his face broke up into the hard chunks that made her think of the piles of rock ore on the docks. "You a friend of Mike's. That's funny. That's very funny." He pointed a thick roughened finger at her. "You say it. I believe it!"

He beckoned her into the house and, turning toward the door of an inner room, shouted something in Finnish. The tall woman who had so frightened Lettie on her first visit appeared. They conferred for some time in Finnish while Lettie stood awkwardly waiting. Plainly Päkkä was trying to win the woman over, for she glanced suspiciously at Lettie now and then, shook her head and appeared to argue. Then greatly to Lettie's relief, she went out, shutting the door behind her, and Lettie realized that Päkkä was pointing to a chair and inviting her to sit down.

"Thank you," she said, sitting nervously on the edge of it and holding her pocketbook tightly in her gloved hands.

Päkkä sat down opposite her and put his hands on his knees. "You Mike's girl?" he inquired sociably.

"Oh, no, Mr. Päkkä!" Lettie blushed scarlet.

"Vy not? Mike fine fella. Mike damn fine fella."

Lettie's confusion overwhelmed her and Päkkä stared at her, his bright black eyes shining with interest.

"You not his girl—you his friend. All right. Vat you vant? But you make mistake," he said earnestly. "Mike fine fella."

Lettie was uncomfortably aware that the door had opened a crack and that a wild and crazy eye was peering out at her. "It's that terrible old woman," she thought, and she went tense all over with a fear she had made up her mind to conquer.

"I want you to help me, Mr. Päkkä." Lettie tried not to look at the door but it was hard to resist the fascination of that horrible eye.

"Me? Sure. Sure. I do anyting for Mike. Anyting."

Lettie drew a deep breath and sat up very straight. "It's like this, Mr. Päkkä. Michael—Mr. Brodi wants . . ."

The explanation took a long time and at the end of it they were both exhausted. Lettie was worn out with trying to make him understand what she did not fully understand herself, why Mike wanted all those questions asked and answered. Päkkä was worn out with his many protestations of help and with his puzzled eagerness to comprehend what was wanted of him. "Why," Lettie thought, "he's just like a great big dog trying to guess what you want him to do. I *like* him!" And suddenly, without knowing that she was going to do it, she smiled.

The change in her was startling. The sullen look, the droop, the sidelong glance for just that instant vanished. Päkkä's black eyes gazed at her wistfully. "You sure you're not Mike's girl? I tink Mike, he need a girl." Lettie laughed. The door opened and the old woman slid into the room, her felt slippers making a whispering noise on the board floor. Lettie took firm hold of herself and managed a smile in the old woman's direction. She was rewarded with a toothless, bleary grin and a noise that sounded like a cackling hen.

Lettie stood up to go. "Thank you, Mr. Päkkä. I'll be back as soon as I can and we'll start the work together. I just don't know what I'd do," she said impulsively, "if you didn't speak English so well."

She was not to get away so easily. Päkkä again raised his voice in loud Finnish and after a minute the stony-faced woman appeared with a piece of board on which were four mugs of the muddy black coffee. "Poor thing," Lettie thought, "she doesn't even have a tray and the mugs don't match and they're all cracked but one."

They drank the frightful stuff standing, all but the old witch, who nursed her cup in a far corner. "I like them," Lettie thought, raising the unblemished mug to her lips, and she found the idea so surprising that she repeated it to herself. "I like them!"

She left, hugging to her something even better than that warming thought. Stepping with care through the mud of Mill Street on her way toward the horse car, she said to herself solemnly, "I believe they like me."

The wind off the lake blew cold against her back and bits of hail stung her cheeks, but her heart danced because these strangers seemed to like her. "I really think they do," she said to herself, trying to be judicial about it. "Mike's girl. Oh!"

In Lettie's state of mind the shabby yellow car might have been a fairy coach and the four steaming cart horses that drew it, spirited and beautiful steeds. She waded through the slush, climbed aboard and settled herself primly on a seat. Today was the first time she had ever been in a car by herself and though her feet, resting in the matted straw, were numb with cold, she was perfectly happy.

The work proved very hard to do. Päkkä took a winter job as a night watchman, and so he was only free to help her in the late afternoons. Then she herself found it difficult to get away from home without arousing suspicions. Nevertheless, little by little the task progressed. She bought a notebook and at the top of a page she wrote the name of a family, or at least the English equivalent of what their name sounded like to her. Underneath she listed, in what she felt was a very neat and systematic manner, all the questions which she could remember Mike's enumerating to her and as many more besides as she could think up. She left out some important ones and asked some which were no use at all. She got her answers in the best way she could, through Päkkä's interpretation, and it never occurred to her that there might be a recognized technique for putting questions of this sort. She did not even have more than the vaguest idea why Mike wanted them or how he was going to use them. It was enough for her that his wanting them gave her a chance to work for him, and on the whole hers was not a bad piece of work.

She kept at it with a persistence which she had never shown about anything before. In times of discouragement she often cried into her pillow, but she never gave up, though she was close to it often enough. The work dragged on during all the rest of November and well into December and still only the houses on one side of Mill Street had been visited. Päkkä was tireless and cheerful and friendly, and though he was completely confused about the purpose of their work, the idea was firmly in his head that it was something which his idol, Black Mike, wanted. Before very long he and Lettie had become fast friends. Lettie frequently showed him her notebook, which he could not read, but he took such a keen interest in watching the blank places fill up that he did much toward bolstering Lettie's determination. Before very long she found herself liking this Finnish laborer with a warmth of simple friendliness which she had never in her life felt for anyone.

During all this time Black Mike was in Hudson, struggling with real success to put the breath of life into the dead pages of history. Mike regarded each new group of students as the stupidest collection of lunk-heads ever foisted off on a long-suffering teacher, and this year's crop was no exception. He bullied and browbeat and fascinated them into hard work and they adored him. Once in a while he gave Lettie a brief thought which was a fairly even mixture of contempt and pity. He had, of course, no idea what she was up to, and would have been astonished beyond words by the alliance between herself and Päkkä.

Lettie asked Mark about Michael as often as she dared, but Mark knew no more than she. "He'll show up," Mark told her, "probably in the Christmas vacation. Why do you want to know?"

Lettie was changing. The discontented, mournful look was absent most of the time and though she still kept her head down from habit, the dullness was gone from her eyes. Instead of slumping when she stood and dragging resentfully along when she walked, she held her shoulders back and she moved as though she had a purpose. The trans-formation in Lettie's life was in the process of transforming Lettie. Her father and mother were so used to seeing her that they never saw her. In Willoughby, however, there was a raw spot that sensitized her to Lettie's moods and Willoughby sometimes watched her sister with a sort of hard and glittering speculation.

The grim task that Lettie had set herself was slowly forming her character. In these days she rarely drifted into the slack self-indulgence of her day dreams. The old, impossible romances in which she was the heroine no longer nourished her. She rarely felt sorry for herself. This was the more remarkable because it was her own voluntary doing, but fortunately she never saw it in this light and so, for once in her life, she did not dramatize herself.

In one respect she remained unchanged. Any notice of her scar was still torture to her and threw her into agonies of self-consciousness. Facing the curious stares of the Finns was the hardest part of her task and she did it with shrinking and despair, but who shall say what constitutes courage? She could tell by their gestures and even by the tones of their voices when they were asking Päkkä about it, but he never told her what they said and she never asked him.

Though she did not realize it, the scar was a help to her because it convinced the Finns that this Fenno, this being from another world, could also suffer misfortune. Once one of the women gave her a jar of some repulsive, homemade brownish substance that smelled like suet, and indicated with gestures that she was to rub it on her face. Blushing and miserable, Lettie took it because she was too polite to refuse and she rubbed it on her scar in secret every night until the stuff became undeniably rancid and had to be thrown out.

One Sunday about two weeks before Christmas Mark came to dinner and, sopping a piece of Yorkshire pudding daintily in gravy, he said casually, "That friend of mine, Mike Brodi, that Lettie admires so, is in town. He's staying at my boarding house."

"*Lettie* admires!" Willoughby said scornfully.

Matild looked up, interested, as she always was in any little item of news. "That's nice. Wouldn't you like to invite him here for Christmas dinner, Mark? He could go on to the theatricals at the Thatchers' with all of you afterwards—though why, with poor Mrs. Thatcher so very ill . . ."

"No," Fenno said, laying down his fork. "You are not to bring him, Mark. I strongly disapprove of his radical views . . ."

Lettie's heart was beating so hard she scarcely heard the rest of it. Her father was saying something like "I believe in ignoring these radicals. It's what hurts them most." She put her hands under the table to hide their trembling.

She did not dare leave the house until the next afternoon, and then she went skipping along over the icy walks with her precious notebook rolled up inside her little round sealskin muff and a pink glow in her usually sallow cheeks. She had walked most of the way there before she remembered to walk with dignity, like a grown-up, and to keep her hoops from bouncing. The last few weeks had given her a good deal of practice in meeting strangers and so she stood on the front porch and explained herself to Mark's landlady with a degree of dignity and composure that established confidence at once in that lady's suspicious mind. She even smiled at Lettie.

"I'm sorry he's not in, dear. I'm Mrs. Simmons. This is a man's boarding house and as a rule young ladies aren't allowed, but you look all right to me. You get so's you can tell after twenty years in the business. You can wait in my parlor if you like."

"She *does* look like a spider," Lettie thought, following her. "A fat brown one. I wonder what on earth she does to her hair to make it look like that."

Lettie was not sufficiently familiar with landladies to recognize the type, of which Mrs. Simmons was a singularly perfect specimen. The hair that Lettie remarked was an improbable shade of reddish brown, frizzled and dry. Her dress was over-trimmed and dusty and her many chains jangled on a large bosom that appeared as hard as rock. Her heart was kind but subordinated to business interests. She talked to Lettie over her shoulder as she ballooned toward the parlor.

"Most of them says they're sisters and I say to 'em, 'No, you can't come in here, into a decent boarding house kept by a decent widow woman.'"

"Why not?" asked Lettie innocently.

With her hand on the door knob Mrs. Simmons turned to gape at Lettie. Then she laughed, and it was the kind of laugh that even a child in a well-bred household recognizes as concealing something mysterious and dirty, and it embarrassed Lettie.

As they entered the stuffy parlor a lean Irish setter rose and came to meet them, swinging a pendent tail.

"Meet the old lady," Mrs. Simmons said. "Bess. Mr. Simmons used to raise hunting dogs, God bless his soul. The little fella there is the last of Bess's litter. I've sold all the others."

"Oh!" said Lettie, gazing in rapture on Bess's offspring. "The darling!"

The darling was having difficulty with his feet. They were outsized feet on long and wobbly legs and the back ones seemed to be wanting to go in a direction at variance with the front. After several steps in as many directions the puppy collapsed altogether and sat on his haunches, smiling at Lettie as though life were a huge joke. Lettie ran to him.

"May I pet him, Mrs. Simmons? Would you mind if I petted him?"

Without waiting for an answer she squatted beside the puppy and put her hand softly on his red hair.

"Sure you can pet him. Pick him up, if you like. Bess won't mind. If you'll excuse me, I'll go and see to things."

Left alone with this delight, Lettie got up again, put her muff and the precious notes on the table, stripped off her gloves and, stooping, picked up the puppy with both hands and carried him gingerly to a rocking chair. She had never before in all her life held a puppy and it made her feel trembly and weak with tenderness. "Oh," she whispered, "how wonderful," and she bent over until her cheek rested on the small silky head. Bess rose and thrust an enquiring nose into Lettie's lap.

"It's all right, Bess." Lettie stroked her too, feeling her heart big enough to love the whole world. Apparently satisfied, Bess withdrew and flopped loose-jointedly at full length in front of the Franklin stove. Followed some active moments during which the puppy tried, with commendable singleness of purpose, to eat the buttons on Lettie's cuff and then with no warning at all he was asleep, with his huge paws thrust out in front of him and so limp that for one awful moment Lettie thought he had died. She sat as still as she possibly could so as not to waken him, and heat from the little bundle of red fur came through her skirts and warmed her and suddenly, for no reason at all, there were tears in her eyes.

The door opened and someone came in. "Shush," she said, without looking to see who it was. "You'll wake him."

Brodi laughed.

"Oh, Mr. Brodi—do be still."

"Puppies don't mind a little noise. What on earth are you doing here?"

"Oh, *don't* wake him. I'm sure it's bad for him."

But the puppy was awake. He rose on the precarious footing of Lettie's lap, thrashing his skinny tail for balance, yawned and then sat down on his haunches, his insouciant look giving way to an absent expression of inward concentration.

"Watch out!" Brodi said from the depths of experience.

Lettie leaped up and deposited the puppy hastily beside Bess and returned to her chair with a crimson face, trying to hide a large wet spot on her skirt.

"They do leak." Mike laughed.

"I've brought your notes." Lettie hid her confusion in disentangling them from her muff.

"What notes?"

"Oh, I forgot you didn't know—we've been working on them so long. It's a surprise. It's all the questions you wanted about the Finns."

"What on earth?" Scowling darkly, he took the proffered roll.

"Just open it and see." Lettie's voice was eager with excitement. "I've got Mr. Päkkä to help me and I've worked ever so hard. We did it all for you and it took ages and ages."

Brodi wet his thumb and threw back a few pages. "The Cajender family raised thirty cabbage plants last year." He laughed. "That's not exactly the kind of information I had in mind, but thanks anyway. There's a lot of it, isn't there? I'll look it over when I get time, but you'd much better just forget about it. Now, for goodness' sake, don't cry."

But for once Lettie was very far from tears. "You'd *better* look at it. There's weeks of work there. Hard work, too."

"It was nice of you to try. Thank you. I didn't mean to be rude. I'm sure you tried very hard, but I'm sorry you did because I'm afraid, as I told you before, that there isn't anything you can do to help. I'm honestly sorry."

He stopped because it seemed to him that, for an instant, he saw in Lettie's face a shadowy forecast of the way she would look when she was older. "She might even have a strong face," he thought in surprise. "The chin—it's faintly like her father's. Why, exactly, should I find that touching?"

Not being greatly interested in the subtleties of his own emotions, he made no attempt to answer his question. Instead, forgetful of the sloppy notebook he still held, he watched with surprise the unmistakable signs that Lettie was very angry. Her show of spunk gave him pleasure.

"I do think you're rude," she said. "I think you're horrid and, what's more, I think you're stupid."

"Stupid?" Brodi's pleasure evaporated and scorn took its place.

"Yes, stupid! Here you have a willing worker—two of them, because you ought to count Mr. Päkkä—and instead of saying to yourself 'Here are two people that I can get to help me,' you just say that I'm not fit for anything but silly love stories, I haven't any education, I'm a poor little rich girl, I haven't been trained to do your work. All right, why don't you train me? It can't be so hard, and the choice is not getting your work done at all. *I* think it's important, too. I'm willing to help.

I'm willing to work really hard. Why don't you train me? Yes, I do think you're stupid—and probably conceited too."

Her voice broke on the last word, and she snatched up her muff and ran for the door. There she stopped. "Oh," she said. "Oh, I forgot!"

"Now what," Brodi thought. "By God, I didn't think she had it in her!" And he watched her with a considerably heightened interest.

She came quickly back into the room. She wore an expression of comic haughtiness but she did not so much as look at him again. She hurried past him to the stove in front of which Bess lay sprawled, the puppy asleep in the curve of one of her fore legs. There Lettie squatted down awkwardly. "Good-bye, puppy," she said, putting out one hand and patting the astonished little animal on the head. "Good-bye, puppy."

"I'll be damned," Brodi thought. "I'll be damned. Like a child—and a minute ago she was as grown-up as anybody. At that age you don't know where you stand from one minute to the next." He thrust his hands in his pockets with characteristic vigor and watched her leave the room with her chin in the air, not knowing whether he was amused or annoyed or downright angry.

When Lettie reached home, she flew to her room and threw herself on her bed, sobbing. Her world was in pieces, her wonderful world of interest and adventure, and now there was nothing left but her old life, more dreary than before. She wished fervently that she were dead. She went down to dinner because she had to, a pale ghost, too full of despair to feel much hurt when her father spoke to her angrily and Willoughby pointed out her shortcomings with sarcasm.

That night in their room Matild said to John, "I think she must be sick." She said it through a mouth full of hair pins. This habit of hers of putting hair pins in her mouth disgusted Fenno and irritated him to the end of his endurance.

"What?" he said, though he had heard her well enough.

She took the shell pins out of her mouth and put them in a damp pile on the dressing table. Fenno averted his eyes from the pins and stared with loathing at the spot on the back of her head that was beginning to grow bald.

"I *said* that I think Lettie must be sick."

"Take her to a doctor then." Fenno, dignified even in a nightshirt, strode to the bed, got in, rolled on his side and pulled the covers up to his neck.

Matild took Lettie to see the doctor the next afternoon, even though Willoughby, who wanted to use the carriage herself, said that in her opinion Lettie wasn't sick at all but just acting like a fool—as usual. Lettie went with her mother with an air which implied that nothing which could happen to her would ever matter any more, and Willoughby was left pacing restlessly up and down the drawing room with no outlet for her nervous energy. The carriage was scarcely out of sight when she saw, through the lace curtains, someone on foot turning in at the gate. She hid herself behind the heavy draperies and peered out. For one wild, thrilling minute she thought it might be Hadley—"And about time, too," she muttered before she realized that this man was short. And he was close to the house before she saw that he was—of all people—that schoolteacher friend of Mark's.

"Well!" she thought, "I suppose I did impress him, though he took his time about coming back. I'm just the kind of person who would impress—no, dazzle is the word—a backwoods schoolteacher," and she laughed, feeling both pleased and scornful. She started toward the front door, pursing her lips. Her mouth, she felt, tended to be just the smallest shade too large. "Prunes and prisms," she whispered. This piece of abracadabra was her method for counteracting nature. "Prunes and prisms. Prunes and prisms."

She threw the door wide. "How do you *do?* This *is* a surprise."

"Hullo."

"Won't you come in?"

"Thanks."

"Your hat and coat?"

"Can't stay."

"Oh, don't keep them *on*."

"Can't stay. Just came to see Lettie a minute. Miss Leticia—whatever her name is. Will you tell her?"

"Lettie!"

"Yes, Lettie." He bristled inwardly with dislike. "Surprised, are you?" he thought. Enough of his dislike showed in his face so that she took refuge in her most queenly manner.

"My sister is not at home." Then, remembering the probable boredom of the afternoon, she added, "But won't you come in and talk to *me?*"

"No, thanks. Just tell her I called, will you? She's a remarkable girl."

The door shut behind him with a distinct slam. He ran his hands through his stiff hair and clapped his hat on his head with vehemence, annoyed that he had been so aware of being an inch shorter than the beautiful Willoughby.

Brodi walked away, nursing frustration. When a man has admitted to himself that he has acted like a fool and then nobly resolved to eat humble pie and apologize, it is very upsetting to be prevented from putting the program into effect. But this was only a small part of the emotions which were stirring Black Mike so profoundly. He jammed his gloveless hands into his overcoat pockets and hunched his thick shoulders, wincing inwardly. "The fact of the matter is," he told himself, "it's a good job she did—a wonderful job, all things considered. And sticking to it like that makes it a miracle. She was scared, too, but that didn't stop her. And I laughed at her. Jesus!"

This was old familiar ground, for Brodi had been saying much the same thing to himself ever since the evening before, when he had picked up Lettie's notes and glanced through them, at first casually and then with a growing interest that, in the end, amounted almost to excitement.

In this mood of self-chastisement, Mike swung along, finding an angry pleasure in facing the biting wind. When he reached the center of town, he heard his name called and looked up to see Mark standing in a doorway, stick under his arm, pulling on his gloves.

"Hullo," Mike said. "What are you doing downtown at this hour?"

"New clothes in honor of the new job." Mark jerked his head backward at the tailor shop behind him. "Vanetti's so impressed he's being quite decent about credit. How about a drink? This cold sears my soul."

They carried their drinks from the bar to a far table, and after the first warming swallow and the sigh of satisfaction which followed, Mark said, "You look stirred up. Is anything the matter?"

"The matter is I'm a damn fool. Mark, Lettie Fenno is a remarkable girl."

"Lettie! Have you gone crazy?"

"No. Listen to this, but for God's sake, don't spill it to her Old Man."

Mike told his tale with heat and passion. "Do you realize what nerve it took for a girl who has been sheltered all her life to do a thing like that? And to stick to it the way she did—why, it's the most remarkable thing I ever heard of. I've never had a student who could have done it. And, what's more, I think the girl has a mind—if she only had a little training, but look at the atmosphere she lives in. Character and brains all in the same person. I wish I could teach her for just one year." Mike took a violent swallow of his drink.

Mark laughed uproariously. "That's the funniest thing I ever heard of. Lettie! Love is certainly blind."

"Love! Have you lost your mind? I'm not in love. She's just a youngster. I admire character and intelligence wherever I see it and I tell you, to find it in such . . ."

"Love," Mark said positively. "And I've never heard anything so funny in my life. I might have known that a guy like you would fall in love by the intellectual route. I suppose that's why most intellectuals have such dowdy wives. Mind first, body a poor second. If it were me, now, beauty, style." Mark kissed his finger tips and threw the kiss into the air. "I suppose you'd rather teach a woman something out of a book than go to bed with her. That's where I do my teaching. Bed. But Lettie, for the love of God! Hey, bartender. Two more."

"You have me entirely wrong. Just because I happen to take an intellectual interest in a girl. Why, I've only seen her about three times —but you don't have to know her to know what a fine youngster she is. Yes, by God, I *do* know her. I know her better than you do, and better than that damn family of hers. I tell you . . ."

Mark's hilarity hit a new high.

Some two hours after Brodi's call Lettie and her mother returned from the doctor's. All of Lettie was one vast droop. She dragged herself aimlessly into the drawing room, where Willoughby was playing scales in a peculiarly staccato and irritating manner.

When Lettie came in, Willoughby stopped playing. "Mother," she called, "what did he say was the matter with her?"

Matild was halfway up the stairs and she hated being yelled at because she hated the exertion of yelling in reply.

"Nothing. Not a thing. Says she needs an interest in life. I should think a girl of her age could find enough to do without any trouble at all. I'm sure when *I* was her age . . ."

The tone of Matild's voice, as it died away in the distance, made it plain that this argument had been going on all the way home in the carriage.

Willoughby seemed to find the situation funny. "Well?" she said with a laugh, whirling around on the piano stool with a great froth of skirts and looking at Lettie's despairing figure with a quizzical kind of superiority that she took pains to make as exasperating as possible.

"Well what?" Lettie walked to the window and stared dismally out at nothing.

Willoughby did not at once reply. She was smiling a little, though she did not know it—the rigid smile that sometimes accompanies cruelty. She felt with a kind of instinct that Lettie was at the end of her rope and the knowledge exhilarated her, as though this were a moment for which she had been waiting.

And Lettie was like a rabbit caught in the corner of the garden wall. The atmosphere of the room was thick with her desperation and the panting of her heart. She turned away from the window, glancing at Willoughby and shrinking into herself afterwards as though she expected the lash of a whip. She started to walk, almost to sidle, from the room. Willoughby rose and stood in her path.

"Just a minute, young lady. I want to talk to you."

Lettie stood obediently, but her lip began to tremble. She might with justice have cried out, "Why do you hate me so? What have I ever done to you?" And someone wiser than herself might have said to her, "Willoughby doesn't hate you for anything you did to her but because of a wrong she did to you, a far more malignant kind of hate, human nature being what it is." As it was, Lettie simply stared at Willoughby out of a sodden face that was all eyes, and the great scar burned so red that something inside Willoughby cringed at sight of it and her words took on a tone of harsh hysteria, as though she were the attacked and not the attacker.

"You've been up to something and I want to know what it is!"

"Leave me alone."

"You little sneak. I know you have. Tell me or I'll fix you right."

"Leave me *alone*, can't you? It isn't any of your business—it isn't anybody's business." Lettie made a dash for freedom but she was not quick enough. Willoughby caught her arm and jerked her around so that they were facing each other once more.

"Come here. I'm talking to you. You're up to something and I'm going to know what it is."

"Let go, will you?"

"Tell me!"

"I won't. I haven't been doing anything wrong. Let me go."

"I think you *have* been doing something wrong. I think you've been sneaking off with that fellow Brodi."

"Let me go."

"Don't fool yourself—he doesn't care a thing about you—not a thing. How could he? *I'm* the kind men care about. He's just after money and you think it's you. It would be *me* he'd be after, only he knows

I wouldn't have anything to do with him." Willoughby was so absorbed in her own tirade that she did not see the blaze of anger take fire in Lettie. Before Willoughby knew what was happening, Lettie jerked her arm free, took one backward step and smacked Willoughby in the face.

The blow was so swift and, from such a source, so unexpected, that Willoughby was taken entirely unawares and Lettie was running from the room before Willoughby could react in any way. Then she picked up her skirts and ran after her, screaming in fury, until the stairs and her tight corsets took all her breath. She arrived at Lettie's door just as it was slammed in her face and she heard the key turn.

13

THE next day Lettie was still in black disgrace, shut in her room on bread and water—a revival of a childhood punishment dictated by John Fenno which made Matild feel obscurely embarrassed. Lettie had endured a tirade from her mother and she had listened to an appeal to what Matild called "my darling child's better nature." Immediately following their quarrel Willoughby had taken to her bed, upsetting everybody with demands for pillows and cologne and shaded lights, but she had recovered in time to go to a party where she danced until two in the morning. Today, overflowing with restless vitality and irritated because the Irish girls, who were really fond of Lettie, went tiptoeing around the house as though someone were ill, she insisted on dragging her mother off down town to do Christmas shopping.

Before leaving, Matild looked into Lettie's room. She did not admit to herself that she longed to have Lettie throw her arms around her neck and say, "Mother dear, I'm sorry I hurt you. Please forgive me and love me." But she did rather expect something of the sort to happen. When it did, she would call Lettie "my own dear little girl" and maybe they'd both cry a little.

"Lettie," she said to the crumpled heap on the bed.

There was no reply.

"Lettie, your mother is speaking to you, dear."

The crumpled heap heaved but kept silent.

"Very well, Lettie." Matild's bosom swelled with the hurt and the anger of the scorned. "I'll lock you in so you can just think of what a bad girl you are."

The door slammed and Lettie raised herself and looked at it from a strained face full of hate and despair. Matild went downstairs with her lips folded grimly and so intent on the hardness of her lot that she passed the geraniums on the landing without noticing that the bud she had been watching for days was finally showing color.

Whenever Willoughby left the house, a peace seemed to descend on it, though actually everybody in it was less guarded about making noise. The peace had been pervading things for about half an hour and Lettie was lost in constructing a tale of her own death that was more touching than any of the previous ones, when she heard a conspiratorial tap on the door and the key turned in the lock. When the door opened, Ellen appeared, an expression of suppressed excitement and stealth on her Irish face.

"They've gone, Miss." She said it in a whisper, though "they" were halfway down town as she spoke. "It's a surprise we have for you in the kitchen. Come on quick, now, Miss."

"Cookies?" Lettie's tone said, "What were cookies to one with a foot, at least, in Charon's boat."

But Ellen only said, "You'll see," in a way that sounded so mysterious that Lettie rolled off the bed. Her dejected attitude, however, made it plain that she could never again be coaxed into an enjoyment of cookies. Ellen went ahead, her stout button boots squeaking and the starch in her voluminous apron crackling like fire in paper. Lettie dragged along her burnt-out grief, preternaturally aware of the house and its furnishings. She felt as though she had shrunk in size, and the dislocation of her every-day life made the rooms through which she passed both utterly strange and piercingly familiar.

"I won't eat them," Lettie thought. "I'll say thank you very much, but I won't eat them."

At the kitchen door Ellen stood back, letting Lettie open it for herself. At first glance Lettie saw only Nora and Katie standing on either side of the big kitchen table with its red and white checked table cloth—and then she saw the puppy.

"Oh!" she cried. "Oh!" and she hurled herself forward.

It was the same puppy, the puppy of her dreams. He sat in approximately the middle of the checked table cloth, his feet wide apart and his small brow furrowed with anxiety to understand this strange world in which he found himself. There was a large bedraggled red bow around his neck, on one end of which a paw was firmly planted. He had obviously been chewing the other. This gave him a raffish look, though he was clearly eager to please and anxious to look on the brighter side of life even in adversity. The red ribbon was run through the corner of an envelope which stuck up over one skinny shoulder blade and on which was written in a bold black hand, "Merry Christmas to Lettie."

"Oh, the darling." Lettie spoke in a choked voice. She dropped to her knees in front of the table, clasped her hands and began to cry.

Katie clucked disapprovingly. "Here, here, there ain't nothing to cry about now. Ain't he the cute little thing though? Just look at them big feet now, like blacking boxes at the end of his little legs. A fine big dog he's going to be, and he's all yours."

"Oh, is he *really* mine?"

"It says so, don't it, on the card? Merry Christmas to Lettie, it says, plain as day."

Lettie put out a hand and at sight of this strange white object approaching him the puppy rose unsteadily on all fours, backed a wobbly step or two and, in response to some instinct stirring in him, he barked. It was a faint but mighty sound, a miniature explosion from which he recoiled, collapsing with great suddenness to a sitting position. His small face had a comical look of such surprise and pleasure at his own achievement that everybody laughed, including Lettie.

"There, see what a fine dog he is, Miss," Katie went on, "as Irish as they come, as Irish as a shamrock, the little mite. Somebody loves you, that's sure. And what will you be naming him, Miss? He should have a fine Irish name, a fine Irish dog like that."

"Shamrock! I'll call him Shamrock, Katie. How's that? Here Shamrock, Shamrock. Oh, isn't he a love?"

Nora sniffed audibly.

The puppy rose and, with great thrashing of his skinny tail for balance, made his way more or less in Lettie's direction. She was delighted.

"See? He knows his name already. Oh, Shamrock, you darling!" She buried her face in the puppy's lean but silky red side. Ellen watched this display of affection with anxiety.

"What *I* want to know, Miss, is, what is your father going to say? And Miss Willoughby, for the matter of that? Do you think they'll be letting you keep a dog around the house to chew things up? You know they won't, Miss, so you better not let yourself get too fond of him."

Lettie raised her face from Shamrock's side with such an expression of tragic dolor that Katie intervened.

"There now. There now. Don't be getting upset. Maybe something can be fixed up, though I wouldn't be knowing what. Let's call Joe."

"Joe's off driving the ladies," said Nora, who clearly was less moved by Shamrock's charms than the other two girls.

"That he's not. Don't you remember he has to go early for Mr. Fenno the night and they went in a hack. And for all the fuss Miss Willoughby made about it you'd a think they'd went in a cart. I'll call him."

Katie was "going steady" with Joe and so she had a sixth sense which informed her of his whereabouts throughout the day. "Joe, Joe," she bawled from the back steps. Nora looked pained.

Joe came in, stamping and stomping the way men do in kitchens, and Shamrock wabbled across the table to greet him, trailing the end of ribbon.

"For gosh sake." Joe put a finger behind a small ear with a sureness born of experience and understanding. "Where'd he come from? Cute little devil. Good points, too." And he swept Shamrock skyward by the scruff of his neck, letting him dangle and turning him about appreciatively.

"Oh, don't!" Lettie cried in agony. "You'll hurt him."

"Not a bit, Miss. That's the way their mothers carries all young things. Their skins is loose apurpose."

Lettie gathered up Shamrock and began to croon. Katie watched Joe with pride and proprietorship. Nora glared at Katie and, turning her back, began to bang pots and pans around in the soap stone sink with great energy. Katie ignored her and spoke to Joe.

"Now you, you've got to think of something. It's Miss Lettie's dog —a present from her fella." She gave Lettie a sly look. "Her father'd never in the world let her keep him. What are we going to do, now? We can't let them break her heart."

Joe raised a slow hand and removed the cloth cap with the pendent ear muffs that he wore around the stable, and then he looked at Katie and for a lethargic man it was an astonishingly sly, quizzical look with a great deal of admiring affection in it and it caused Nora, who was watching out of the corner of her eye, to sniff again.

Katie bridled. "Think of something—you!"

Joe folded his cap carefully. "We could—" he spoke slowly, thinking as he went along—"sort of tell Mr. Fenno I'd gotten the dog from a friend. We'd play the little fella up as a thoroughbred—which he is— and say how lucky I was to get ahold of him. Mr. Fenno might fall for it if I said what a good hunting dog he'd make—and of course he'd be Miss Lettie's all the time, only nobody knowing. If anything will get

Mr. Fenno, it'll be the little fella's points. Mr. Fenno likes quality," said Joe, exhibiting insight. "I'll fix a pen for him in the stable. Here, Miss, there's a letter or something inside this envelope."

For Lettie it was a wonderful, glorious time but she was torn between the desire to read her letter, which she knew must be from Brodi, and to follow Joe and Shamrock to the stable. Finally Ellen resolved her difficulty by pointing out that the letter would keep and if she wanted to go to the stable, she'd better hurry for she only had a little more time before she would have to be locked up again, "And when they come home," Ellen said, "you act all innocent, Miss, or our skins won't be worth *that*. Saints preserve me, I'm conniving at crime, as they say."

And so Lettie rushed to the stable and gathered up armfuls of straw for Shamrock's bed and held wire while Joe built a pen in a corner of the carriage house, until Ellen called her in.

Being locked in her room again seemed like no punishment at all. She sat down with her letter on the cretonne-covered shoe box by the window and read it over and over until she knew it by heart and could repeat snatches of it to herself whenever she wanted to feel the warm glow the words gave her.

Brodi's script was bold and undecorative, made up of vigorous strokes and dashes in exceedingly black ink, all so like Brodi that it gave Lettie a rather awestruck awareness of his personality.

"Dear Lettie," he wrote. "You are entirely right, I was stupid!" (The exclamation point bit into the paper but it failed to convey to Lettie any of Black Mike's shock at that discovery.)

"Oh, no," Lettie murmured, "you could never be stupid, Michael."

"You have done a fine piece of work. Perhaps it is not just what a trained worker would have turned out, but that isn't the point. You have done amazingly well and under circumstances which command admiration. Confound it. That sounds snobbish and superior and I don't feel either one. You took me down a peg or two and I needed it. So thanks, Lettie. Thanks for the work and thanks for the lesson.

"I know you want to carry the work on—I even think that, now you have opened my eyes, I can guess how much you want to do something that is somewhat more important (I hate the word 'worth-while') than you can manage when you are limited by the activities of your home. Unfortunately, there are some obstacles in the way, though they have nothing to do with

your ability to do the job. You have demonstrated that. Perhaps these difficulties are insurmountable—perhaps not. Anyway, we ought to talk about
them. Why don't you lunch with me on the twenty-fourth? Mark says nobody ever lunches anywhere but Rudd's. *I've* never been there, but let's try
it. One o'clock? He did say something about the club but I'm not a member.
Don't bother to answer this—I'll just wait around in hope.

"I'm sending along this little fellow because I thought you took a mutual
liking at my place and because I hope his ingratiating ways will soften your
heart enough so that you can forgive me for acting like an ass.

Y'rs,

Mike."

"Oh, Michael, Michael," Lettie whispered rapturously, pressing this
scrawl to her breast.

Some time later the Fenno carriage passed the jolts of Mill Street
and Joe took a resolution. He waited, however, until Fenno's ruffled
temper might be expected to be soothed by the smooth riding of the
plank road before he inclined a deferential shoulder in Fenno's direction and spoke over it.

"I've come by a very fine young hunting dog, sir, and I snatched
him up quick till I got a chance to talk to you about it. Seems like
everybody takes his own dog to the Marsh nowadays and this fella
would make the others look like curs, so I just got a corner on him
quick till I got a chance to mention it to you, sir."

"I don't want any dogs around, Joe. What do you mean, a corner?
You haven't been promising anybody any of my money, have you?"

"Oh, no, sir. Certainly not. Fact is, I got him on a bad debt—cousin
of mine," said Joe, inventing wildly and fervently hoping for the best.
"Worthless fellow. Knows dogs, though. Raises 'em. Fine breeds."
Joe flapped his arms ever so slightly to keep the perspiration, which
had started out under them, from staining his livery.

There was silence from the back seat and just as Joe was wondering
how to break the terrible news to that poor kid, Miss Lettie, Fenno
spoke.

"I can't afford to buy any more dogs, Joe. You'd better sell him
somewhere else."

"Well—fact is, he's a cute little codger—sort of warms up to you, and
the best points I ever see in an Irish setter. I thought maybe, if you'd
like to use him for hunting in return for his board, I'd kind of like
to keep him around for company and train him free times."

The silence on the back seat this time lasted all the way home, lasted, in fact, until they were turning in between the high iron gates and Joe had despaired again.

"Where is this dog you were talking about, Joe?"

"In the carriage house, sir."

"All right, I'll drive back there with you."

They walked to the back of the carriage house, followed by the two Dalmatians, who still had a tolerant, if mild, curiosity about the new-comer. Shamrock came to the front of his pen, ignored the Dalmatians, and putting his front paws on the wire, stretched up toward Fenno. Both men stood looking down on him in solemn silence while Shamrock panted in wistful charm and drooled an enormous tongue.

"Humph," Fenno said at last. "Maybe you know about such things. Feet seem too big to me."

"They grow up to their feet, sir. It's a good sign—my cousin says."

Silence, during which Shamrock drooled and yearned and Joe, as he claimed to Katie afterwards, aged ten years.

Fenno turned away. Over his shoulder he said, "Very well, keep him if you like. Call him Rover. Good name for a dog."

The morning of the twenty-fourth finally came. "It's the most exciting day of my whole life," Lettie thought, sipping the dregs of her morning coffee. The front door had just slammed behind John Fenno and the house still seemed to tremble slightly. She glanced apprehensively toward the morning paper which hid Willoughby, and spoke to her mother.

"Mama, I want to go down town to get some secret things all by myself. May I please?"

The paper came down with a jerk. "*You* want to go down town. *I* want to go down town just as soon as the carriage gets back."

"Couldn't you go together, dear?" Matild sounded tired and pla-cating.

Willoughby put on an expression of exaggerated patience. "I can't be waiting around for Lettie. I've ever so much to do."

"Shall you be back for lunch? It would be nice, with so much for the girls to do the day before Christmas, if you and Lettie could just lunch together down town."

Lettie stopped breathing.

"I don't know *what* I'm going to do, Mama. I can't be pinned down. I'm not going to nurse-maid Lettie. Let her eat alone or come back here." Willoughby threw the paper on the table and stood up. "I'll want Ellen with me to carry things, of course." She sailed from the room.

"Oh dear!" Matild put her fat hands on the table cloth. "She *knows* I can't spare Ellen. If she'd just *say* she'd stay down town and you'd stay down, I'd just have a bite on a tray. Nora's so cross I'm afraid to go into the kitchen. Christmas is *so* much work. You couldn't stay down *alone* could you, Lettie? Usually Willoughby doesn't think either of you should lunch alone but—"

* "Don't worry about me, Mama. I'll walk and I may be late but I'll just fix myself something when I get in." Lying like this made her pound, but she didn't feel the least bit guilty.

A few minutes before one Willoughby stood on the sidewalk in front of Rudd's and said crossly to Ellen and her armful of bundles, *"Now* what's keeping Joe?"

She was not nearly as cross as she sounded, for many people in the Christmas crowds were staring at her and she loved it. She was too skilled, however, to let her pleasure be evident and she played her role of haughty impatience most convincingly. The stares were understandable, for real beauty was a rare thing before the cosmetic trade began wiping out distinctions of age and class. Moreover, in a day when women cultivated the meek and drooping look of a wood violet, Willoughby held her chin up and her shoulders back.

She turned and looked thoughtfully at the door of Rudd's. Perhaps the best thing would be a good lunch—it was sure to be awful at home. But eating alone. Everyone always wondered *why.* She glanced back toward the street and saw General Thatcher a second after her retina registered an image of Brodi pushing open the door of Rudd's. "That fellow in Rudd's—how odd. Sometime it might be fun— Anyway, Lettie shouldn't have him."

General Thatcher saw her a hundred feet away. "Magnificent," he murmured, and gave directions for his carriage to draw up to the curb beside her. His carriage was a closed one with a low-hanging belly of impeccable sheen, and he popped his head out of the window "for all the world," Willoughby thought, arranging an expression of pleased surprise, "like Punch out of his box. All he needs is a false nose and peaked cap."

"My dear," he trilled. "My dear. How delightful. Are you on your way home and would you let an old fellow like me drive you?"

His quick eye, darting about, lit on Ellen and her arms full of bundles. "Your maid could take the car," he added.

Willoughby gave him an upward look. "How sweet. Would you? How very nice! Ellen, wait here for Joe, please."

The General was out of the carriage in an instant, bowing and smiling and pulling off his chamois gloves to take her hand and help her in. "He uses too much toilet water," she thought, presenting her tightly gloved hand and showing just a trifle more ankle than was strictly necessary. The inside of the carriage smelled of the coals in the foot warmer and also faintly of the General. She put her muff to her face and said, "How is dear Mrs. Thatcher?"

That question was asked the General forty times a day and his expression of grave concern was instantaneous and unfailing, but it seemed to Willoughby, who did not realize this, that it was wholly mechanical. "Why," she thought, "he doesn't *care*," and hastily checked a pleased smile.

"Poorly, poorly," he was saying. "The doctor says—but never mind. The robe. Let me tuck it around you. There!"

He leaned over her and tucked her in, intimately and at great length, and she gave him a warm smile of thanks, whereupon he seized her hand in both of his and fairly bounced on his seat with rapture.

"Miss Willoughby—my dear Miss Willoughby, this is delightful. But your poor hand will be cold!" And rather to her dismay he dragged it down under the robe and held it in a grip that she could not break without making a point of issue.

"And how is your father, my dear, and that bright young man— what's his name?"

"Mark?"

"No, no. Don't let Mark fool you. He's not bright—he's smart, and there's a difference." He peered up anxiously into her face. "But you're not—? Perhaps I shouldn't have said—? There isn't anything between—?"

"No, of course not," Willoughby said firmly.

"Ah!" He seemed immeasurably relieved. "I'm glad to hear it."

"Why?" Willoughby asked, opening her blue eyes wide in dewy innocence.

"Because I'm an old fool, I guess," he said, slipping off the hook. "But let's not talk about Mark. I've got you all to myself now, with no good-looking young fellows about."

The General let go her hand and patted her knee in the most fatherly manner. "I don't see enough of you," he said. "Not nearly enough."

"I must come to see Mrs. Thatcher," Willoughby murmured.

"Mrs. Thatcher isn't—but you could come to see me!"

The General pulled his hand from under the robe and waved it. When he put it back again it came to rest, by the merest accident, a trifle higher than the knee. Willoughby tensed a little but she smiled at him and lowered her lashes.

"That will be lovely."

"We can sit by the fire in my little study and you can pour my tea. Do you think," he said, bringing his hand to the surface in a gesture of supplication, "that I could make you happy for an hour or two?"

"Of course, General." "Without a chaperon," she thought. "Risky—but worth it?"

"Ah, my dear," his hand descended, lighting even farther up the curve of her leg. "We could be real friends, you and I, couldn't we?"

Willoughby did not reply for she was experiencing a form of panic. She was sitting so far into the corner of the carriage that she could not retreat one inch, and she held herself rigid. For once in her life she was not at all sure what course to take, for the General was not behaving in the least in the way that she had imagined. And he kept harping on the privileges of his age. "If he calls this being fatherly!" Willoughby thought, squirming with emotions she did not dare express.

The General's quick eyes were sweeping over her and suddenly, before she had time to rally her forces, he gave her leg a little pinch and withdrew his hand. She shrank into her corner as far as she could, really fearing its next descent, but he did not so much as look at her again. Slipping on his chamois gloves, he folded his hands on the robe and began to chat with animation and complete formality about the theatricals which were to be given at his house on Christmas evening.

The sudden change left her more baffled and uncertain than before and, perversely, she liked it no better. When they reached her house he merely touched her fingers and stood holding his hat while she mounted the steps, as stiffly as though he were reviewing troops. She walked slowly through the hall, puzzled and dissatisfied, and when her mother called downstairs to ask if she had seen Lettie, Willoughby snapped at her.

Meanwhile, Lettie arrived at Rudd's so absurdly early that she had to walk around and around the block before she dared go in, but by some miracle she and Willoughby did not meet. On the last lap around she was suddenly convinced that she would be late and she rushed the rest of the way, arriving just before the hour.

Brodi was there, his hands in his pockets, idling down the long aisle of glass cases, gazing at the candies and fancy pastries with a sociological interest that turned to amazement whenever his eye lit on a little flag bearing a price. He reached the end of the aisle and turned back just as Lettie came eagerly forward.

"Hullo," he said, taking his hands out of his pockets. "You're prompt. You must know my weakness. It's nice of you to come. I wouldn't have blamed you if you'd never spoken to me again."

"Oh, Mr. Brodi—of course I came and, oh, Mr. Brodi, he's wonderful!"

"The name's Mike. What's wonderful?"

"Shamrock. Shamrock's just simply wonderful—Mike."

"Shamrock? Oh, the little dog." Mike laughed. "How did you happen to call him that? But don't tell me now. We're blocking the passage."

He took her by the arm and led her up the steps toward a table at the rear. He held out a chair for her rather awkwardly and sat down himself, cautiously, after a dubious look at the spindly gilt legs. Then he sniffed the air, which was warm, perfumed and heavy.

"This is quite a place. Say, what's the matter?"

A very great deal was the matter for in the midst of taking off her gloves Lettie was being engulfed in a wave of her old self-consciousness. She bowed her head so he would not see her misery. Her heart was racing so fast it was hard to breathe, cold drops of sweat ran down inside her bodice and every muscle in her flat chest was tense.

Brodi's black eyes studied her for a moment, then he said, "Have you ever had lunch alone with a man before?" All the normal roughness was gone from his voice.

She shook her head.

"Well, I've never had lunch alone with a girl either, so we're both in the same boat."

She looked up, startled, and met such a bright look of self-mockery in his coal black eyes that she smiled in spite of herself. At that he laughed and suddenly, as quickly as it came, all her miserable shyness left her and she laughed too. Then a wonderful thing happened—they were laughing together, laughing now for no reason at all but delight in sharing the laughter.

They both hitched their gilt chairs a little closer to the table and Lettie said, very grown up, "I think we ought to eat now, don't you?"

"If *you* think so. What shall we eat?"

They both picked up their menu cards but Lettie simply could not bring hers in focus.

"What do you eat in a place like this?" Mike said.

"Well, Willoughby always has cream soup with a glob of whipped cream on it, and chicken salad with mayonnaise, and a pastry."

"How awful. Must we?"

Lettie giggled. "Let's not."

"What, then?"

"You choose."

"Shall I? Promise to like it?"

"Promise!"

She sat quietly while he frowned over the menu. The world was flooded with happiness now. She looked at him proudly, smiling a little. How nice the furrows in his brow were—so even, like those brackets that appeared in the back of the copy book along with other samples of fancy penmanship that you suspected not even the teacher knew how to make. Like brackets with balanced curves, only lying down. "Horizontal," she said aloud, startled by her own memory of the word.

"What?" Mike looked up.

"The wrinkles in your forehead—like horizontal brackets."

Mike touched them with his forefinger, running it down, smoothing them out, but the shadow of them remained.

"Don't," Lettie said. "I like them." And, miraculously, they were both laughing again.

"Look here—we've got to get down to business. That waiter over there disapproves of us. How about cold chicken for you, cold beef for me, pickles, salad, coffee and worry about the dessert later?"

Getting no reply, he looked up to find Lettie gazing at herself in the wall mirrors that caught up and threw back their reflections from both sides of the room. She had a look of fascinated horror. "Poor little kid," he thought, "a thousand faces and a thousand scars." He crooked his finger at the supercilious waiter, gave his order quickly in a low voice and then laid his hand gently over Lettie's.

"Why are you so self-conscious about your scar?"

She looked at him in consternation and swiftly down again with the habitual sidewise turning of her head. She started to pull away her hand but he grasped it firmly.

"Lettie, look at me. No, don't turn away. Look at me. No, not like that. Right at me. Right straight at me."

Her eyes faltered and came to rest on his grave black ones.

"There," he said, and his eyes began to smile. "Now you'll never be afraid to look at me again, will you, Lettie?"

He squeezed her hand a little to make her reply. She shook her head wordlessly, her eyes swimming with tears.

"All right. I just wanted to show you you could do it. Friends have to be able to look each other right in the eye. Now let's get down to business and talk about this work of yours—"

He did talk about it, long and earnestly, and the gist of it was his fear that if she worked with him her family would find it out. "I tell you," he said, "I don't want to be responsible for getting you into a row with that father of yours."

"But I'd be responsible, not you, Michael." It made him tingle strangely whenever she called him Michael, for no one but his mother had ever used that name.

Each time she brought forward her argument he sighed and began again. Finally he said, "Hell, I don't know who I think I am to tell you what you should or shouldn't do. Let's make sure you really know what you're doing, though." Then he told her something about the social ostracism of those who work for the cause of labor. "At the very least," he said, "they'd think you were queer."

"They think so now." And delightfully they were laughing together again.

"No, but listen, Lettie—what would they do to you if they did find out?"

"Oh, Father would have a tirade and Willoughby would jaw at me and Mother would cry. They might even send me away to school again."

"A strict school where you'd have to wear a hideous uniform and say 'Yes, ma'am' and 'no, ma'am.' My God, they might even make you curtsy."

"They make me curtsy now!"

And again they were laughing as though that were very funny, but Mike sobered quickly and looked both serious and worried while he pushed the last bite of cream puff—Lettie's choice of dessert—around the plate on his fork to collect the last bit of chocolate.

"Michael."

He put the cream puff in his mouth and looked at her enquiringly.

"Let me ask *you* something. Suppose you were me—I—which is it?"

"I," said Michael automatically.

"Suppose you were I, Michael. What would *you* do?"

He looked at her very solemnly for a long time and then he grinned, rather sheepishly, with his head on one side, and the look somehow reminded Lettie of dear, darling Shamrock, and her heart got as soft as the cream puff.

"Michael, what would *you* do?"

"I'd tell me and my good advice to go to hell and I'd help me to do a job of work."

14

CHRISTMAS in the Fenno household was a grim festival. There was a rule that no presents were to be opened until after breakfast, and breakfast was a precise half hour later than usual. There was no tree. Matild would have liked one, remembering how her mother let her help to make the garlands of pop corn and how together they hung the necklaces of sugar beads and the candied apples and peppermint sticks, but years ago John Fenno had declared that a tree was a fire hazard and she had long since ceased to plead.

Lettie, as the youngest, was supposed to open her presents first, while the others sat in rather supercilious maturity, demanding the proper show of ecstasy and gratitude. Each year Lettie tried miserably to oblige them, conscious of nothing so much as the size of Willoughby's pile compared to her own. Most of Lettie's presents were prosaic things intended for use, or they were utterly silly, like this year's silver filigree bouquet-holder, with a ring that went over her arm, to carry to the parties she hated. Her father always gave her a check in an envelope, which he took back at once and put in his pocket to be deposited in some mysterious thing called her investment account. Willoughby's presents were mostly "suitable" gifts from admirers and she laughed at them affectedly. Matild's never took long for there were just three. John Fenno took his to his study unopened and never commented on them afterward. The servants' Christmases had been gotten out of the way the evening before; such things as flannel petticoats and cotton stockings and mufflers and a small, clean bill for each.

After this orgy of good will, the family went to church and the servants toiled over the preparation of a stupendous dinner. In the afternoon Willoughby and Mark departed together to gatherings which always seemed to take place in other people's houses, John Fenno went to his study and shut the door and Matild went upstairs, ostensibly to write notes but actually to loosen her corset laces. That left

Lettie alone to stare out of the window at the gray sky and the dirty, crusted snow and to listen with longing to the gay sound of sleigh bells on the Avenue beyond the iron gates.

This Christmas was blessedly different. She could hardly contain herself until after dinner. As soon as she was alone, she raced upstairs and pulled three packages from the wardrobe. These she bore triumphantly to the carriage house. One was a huge bone for Shamrock, with so much juicy red meat still on it that Joe, when he saw it, would not let Shamrock have it all at once. One was a lovely cap with ear flaps for Joe, all made of real seal skin that had cost her all her savings. The third Joe promised to deliver to Michael himself, and it had caused Lettie a lot of worry until she hit on just the thing. Etiquette demanded a present that she had made herself and, the time being so short, she was in despair until she thought of the slippers which she had embroidered for her father last year and which he had never worn. She stayed in the damp carriage house so long she almost had a chill but that hour with Shamrock and Joe beside the two carriages, with their shafts turned back like arms thrown up in astonishment, was her real Christmas.

In the evening Mark took the ladies to the entertainment at General Thatcher's. It was his first appearance at a large party since becoming Secretary of the Company, and he wore resplendent new clothes. Lettie went also and to her surprise she found that she only dreaded it a little. It was Willoughby who was irritable and dissatisfied with her appearance. "That," Lettie told herself, "is because she is not the chief performer," and she giggled and thought about her own exciting affairs without realizing that, for the first time in her life, she had laughed at Willoughby.

General Thatcher's ballroom was filled with rows of chairs and Mark and Willoughby, exchanging a quick look of understanding, lost Matild and Lettie expertly in the crush by the door. Mark touched Willoughby's elbow.

"Look, Willie, let's go up there at the side where we can get out if it's too unbearable. Have you ever heard Claudia sing?"

"Don't call me Willie. Screech, you mean. Of course I have. You can't escape her."

Willoughby was darting quick looks all over the room. If he came to the other party surely he would come tonight! Her heart was beating so fast she had to open her mouth a little to breathe.

"Sour grapes."

"What?"

"I said, sour grapes. You'd give anything to be in Claudia's place."

"Do you think I'd stand up in front of all those people and make a fool of myself?" *Maybe he's just late. Maybe he's at the buffet getting a drink. I'll have to watch the door.*

"I certainly do. At the drop of a bonnet."

"Don't be horrid or— Oh, good *evening*, General."

"Ah, Miss Willoughby! Mark! How fortunate. How lucky. There are three chairs right here. May I presume? You can't sit on *both* sides of her, Mark, you know. Ha!"

Willoughby's smile was ravishing. "Of course, General. Please do." "He always wears an imaginary sword and spurs," she thought, turning around to adjust the back of her chair as an excuse for sweeping a look toward the door. As she sat down Mark sighed heavily in her ear. She giggled—the sigh said so plainly that now, with the boopety little pipsqueak with them, they couldn't make fun of the performance, which was the only fun two worldlings like themselves were likely to get out of it. She opened her fan with a snap and winked at him behind its shelter.

A footman carrying a snuffer on a pole began putting out lights in the fabulous antique crystal chandelier. He was red-faced and nervous, and General Thatcher watched him with an eye as cold as ice, obviously concerned about his crystal. Some young boys at the back began to applaud and make whistling noises, and the General smiled frostily. A man with a roll of music climbed the steps to the platform and, sitting down at the piano which stood to one side, shot his cuffs. The boys applauded again and the frost in the General's smile thickened.

The red rep stage curtains parted and Claudia Ranleigh McQueen came through. "God, what names," Willoughby thought, wondering if she dared look at the door again. Claudia was small and dark, and she had the kind of plumpness that draws attention to seams and buttons and, like so many plump people of both sexes, she always had her clothes made a little too tight. She bowed to the audience, frowned in the direction of the redoubled cat-calls, touched her bosom lightly and opened her mouth twice, experimentally. "Exactly like a goldfish," Willoughby whispered to Mark. Next Claudia dropped her hand to the piano and raised and lowered her bosom several times. Mark snickered and Willoughby could tell by the slight quiver in the General's shoulder, pressed against hers, that he had heard. She tried to kick Mark and missed. The lights in the chandelier were out now and in the faint glow of the wall lights, and some improvised footlights, Claudia stepped forward.

"Merry *Christ*-mas," she intoned, turning a bright, synthetic smile like a searchlight on the audience. "I will now sing you—ah—a very sad and beautiful bal-had. This bal-had will then be enacted for you in—ah—pantomime while I—ah—sing it again, verse by verse. It is the story of a young—ah—bride who, on her wedding night, plays hide and seek, that is to say, she wanted to hide—"

In the semi-bloom it was not easy to tell where the laughter was coming from, but the light on the stage was strong enough to see the wave of scarlet rise from Claudia's bursting bosom upward to her face.

She finished hastily. "They didn't find her for years and years—in a chest. She was dead."

The applause from the masculine part of the audience, especially from the stags by the door, was thunderous; that from the female contingent, arid. Under its cover Willoughby looked backward and instantly her face was as red as Claudia's. There, leaning against the wall and towering above everybody else, was Hadley and by one of those wordless passages of feeling she knew that he knew she was looking for him.

After that the scene around her was a blur and she heard not one word that the affected Claudia sang. It was not until the red curtains parted with a series of spasmodic jerks that she came to herself and even then she was more conscious of the General's leg pressed hard against her than of the scene on the stage.

> *"The mistletoe hung in the Castle Hall,"* sang Claudia
> *"The holly branch shone on the old oak wall;*
> *The baron's retainers blithe and gay*
> *Were keeping their Christmas holiday.*
> *The baron beheld with a father's pride*
> *His beautiful child, young Lovell's bride—"*

The parted curtains revealed various friends and neighbors, very self-conscious in costume, sitting around a banquet table. They were frozen in the stiff postures of a tableau. Bobbie Thatcher, obviously representing young Lovell and very unhappy in a tarlatan ruff, held a goblet raised in a toast to his bride.

"Why," Willoughby whispered to Mark, "it's that little, washed-out Prissie Daniels." Prissie was one of those anemic-looking blondes with transparent skin and fly-away hair, and what little personality she had was swamped under a massive wreath of white roses and yards of net veil. The scene faded and Willoughby saw herself walking up an aisle to soft music, tall and stately, her beauty mysterious under a mist of tulle, radiant as a star. Prickles ran up the back of her neck. She could almost feel his eyes on her and, taking a breathless resolution, she turned around.

He was still leaning against the wall looking, as she knew he would be, not at the tableau but at her. When he saw her turn, he grinned at her and the grin was self-confident, amused and contemptuous. It was cut short by a commotion at the door. The red-faced footman was pushing his way through the crowd and from his manner it was obvious that something was amiss. Everybody turned around to watch him, even the actors in the tableau strained to see, especially Bobbie, whose raised hand holding the goblet began to shake visibly from strain and fatigue.

Before the footman was halfway to the front of the room, General Thatcher rose. "Excuse me," he said, edging past Willoughby. "I believe I'm wanted upstairs."

There was no one to see, as he ascended among the shadows of the grand staircase, how diminutive he looked wearing the imaginary sword and spurs.

The theatrical performance proceeded under a good deal of strain, for everyone was preoccupied by the knowledge of the General's absence and of the sick woman upstairs. Willoughby's fan fluttered nervously and then stopped while she tried to hear the whispers of the two women behind her.

". . . really devoted to her. These parties help him bear . . . A love match, you know, a little nobody—an invalid since Bobbie was born . . . getting worse year by year . . . They say—"

Claudia continued to sing, her voice grown thin and a little tinny.

> " 'I'm weary of dancing now,' she cried;
> 'Here, tarry a moment, I'll hide, I'll hide!
> 'And Lovell, be sure thou'rt the first to trace
> 'The clue to my secret hiding place.' "

The fair-haired Prissie went through the motions of the pantomime and her glances toward Bobbie were so realistically lovesick that they filled Willoughby with disgust.

The whispering behind her began again. ". . . what a sweet couple.

They say the General favors the match . . ." Willoughby began to fan again as though she were stifling.

Bobbie's eyes were more constantly on the door than on Prissie. He kept lifting his chin in an agonized sort of way and it was easy to see that the tarlatan ruff had already scratched it raw.

"They sought her that night and they sought her next day!"

Claudia's voice was really showing strain.

> *"They sought her in vain, when a week passed away!*
> *In the highest, the lowest, the loneliest spot,*
> *Young Lovell sought wildly but found her not."*

And the pantomime limped on, seeming, as this form of dramatic art always does, to involve a great deal of shuffling and stamping and breathing. The red curtains closed and opened again, the actors indicating the passage of years by hastily applied lines of grease paint and white cotton beards, but no change of costume.

> *"At length,"* sang Claudia who was now visibly wilting, *"an*
> *old oak chest that had long lain hid*
> *Was found in the Castle—they raised the lid—*
> *And a skeleton form lay mouldering there,*
> *In the bridal wreath of the lady fair."*

At this point the lid of the Thatcher silver chest was raised and Prissie's wreath and a skeleton borrowed from the medical school were held up to view while Bobbie, flinging one last look toward the door, pretended to faint.

Nobody paid any attention at all to the final scene. Just as it started the General returned and sibilant rumors flew around the room. General Thatcher did not, however, rejoin Willoughby. She was torn between a desire to look around again, which would have been easy since many heads were turning to look at Thatcher, and haughty resentment at Hadley's mocking look. She was very conscious of the vacant chair beside her and she hoped with violent intensity that he would join her in the intermission. She would, of course, tell him in a sweet but reproving tone that the chair was being held for their host.

All these turbulent emotions failed, however, to absorb her completely. A part of her had departed with the General and, while he was upstairs, had hung suspended with an urgent question. His prompt return had seemed to answer that question and now she felt flat and, in a sense, cheated. The lady upstairs took such a very long time about dying.

The red curtains were pulled together for the intermission and applause burst out. "Now," Willoughby told herself. "Now he'll come." But it was a fat woman, smelling too strongly of lily-of-the-valley who crowded past Willoughby and Mark to take the empty chair. Willoughby pulled her draperies away from the encroaching flesh with an angry gesture. She glanced at Mark, but he looked debonairly at ease in his chair and clearly had no intention of leaving it.

"Mark," she said, "I'm dying of thirst. Would you? Perhaps there's punch."

Mark rose and bowed, and in spite of her agitated state she noticed that he no longer looked wholly elegant, even in his new clothes. "Just a shade—just the slightest bit slick," she thought. "My goodness—is he the kind who will wear checked vests when he's sixty?" "Don't," she said aloud, "ever twirl the ends of your mustache."

"What?" He was puzzled.

"Nothing." She leaned toward him and whispered, "You *could* bring champagne if you put it in a punch glass so the cats . . ."

He was gone and she became one burning concentration again. Minutes passed and she longed to look behind her. Surely he would come! She fluffed out the flounces of her skirt over the empty chair like a mother hen, to protect it from seizure by anyone else. The minutes dragged and her disappointment began to turn to anger. The thing, she thought, was to go back there herself on some pretext—the cloak room—sail part way past him, see him suddenly, feign surprise.

She was gathering up her things to execute this maneuver when her flounces were pushed aside and Hadley dropped into the chair beside her. He sat on one hip, one arm thrown over the back of her chair, leaning a little toward her, and his attitude seemed to preempt her, to exclude everybody else, positively to envelop her, and she experienced again the sensation of being overwhelmed and breathless.

"Hullo," he said, and his voice sounded accusatory.

Now was the time to put him in his place, to crush him with her superior perfection, her worldly grace. Her mind's eye saw him confused and awkward, conscious of his backwoods origin, and she began to gather herself for the attack. Her chin went up, a cold light filled her blue eyes, the angle of her head was a masterly rendering of sarcastic scorn, and she seemed to withdraw herself from him until she was positively remote.

He watched her with a gleam of amusement and the easy grin that she had come to think of as hateful. When she was just about to speak, he forestalled her.

"Why didn't you wait for me at Rudd's that time?"

His tone was calm enough, but there was a cold anger just under the words that made her want to back away. She took refuge in evasion.

"Because Mark came and said I was wanted at home."

"That's a lie." He was still grinning at her and his voice was still soft, but she felt hardness under the surface.

"It isn't a lie."

"It is. You left because you're spoiled, too spoiled to wait half an hour for a man—because you're too . . ."

Mark's voice cut in. "Good evening, Hadley. I believe you have my seat." Mark held two glass cups full of champagne and his temper was frayed to the breaking point by the difficulty of getting them through the crowd.

Hadley looked up slowly. "If it's yours—I have." He made no move to get up.

"All right, then, if you'll please get up. I've brought Miss Fenno some champagne."

"That's right," Willoughby thought. "Tell the world about it."

"Give it to her, then. I happen to know she likes it."

Anger was not becoming to Mark. It disturbed his suavity. Some of the champagne spilled on his cuff and Willoughby tittered nervously.

"Get up!"

Hadley seemed to settle more solidly into his chair. Willoughby half rose and sank back again helplessly. People all around them were looking, attracted not so much by the words as by the sudden tension in the air. The latent animosity between these two had flared and, like lightning around a rod, the atmosphere crackled with it.

"Get up. You're making a nuisance of yourself—pushing yourself in where you're not wanted—here, the mill, the club—God damn it!"

There was a dead stillness around them and Willoughby, her nerves tingling, was conscious of being the center of drama. A surge of excitement and joy went through her. "They're fighting over me. Me!" Willoughby could feel the cushiony flesh of the woman next her pressing against her shoulder in her anxiety to miss nothing. Willoughby heard her panting breath. The dowagers in the row behind—she could not see them but the perfume they wore was suddenly stronger and mixed with it there was a smell of age as their bodies gave off the heat of excitement.

Hadley said nothing at all. He crossed one knee over the other, laid his hand caressingly on it and leaned back at ease, but he looked at Mark through half-shut eyes with such cold contempt, such scorn, that Willoughby felt a tremor of fear run down her spine.

The effect on Mark was instantaneous. He stepped back, his eyes widened with a wild look and, with a gesture as though he were warding off a blow, he let fly with the glass cup in his right hand. It caught Hadley on the chest and splattered over Willoughby. Hadley was on his feet instantly, but before either man could make another move General Thatcher was suddenly there, affable, apple-cheeked, bouncing.

"Ah, an accident. Champagne—a shame, but it doesn't really spot, you know."

He was between Mark and Hadley like a wedge. "More champagne, that's the thing. You get it, Mark." And before Mark had time to gather his routed senses he found himself whirled around and propelled a dozen feet into the crowd, which closed around him. Like a flash the General was back, a huge handkerchief in one hand, patting at Hadley's shirt front, while the other pressed him down into his chair.

"Just a little accident—a very little accident." The General blocked one end of the row like a cork in a bottle, leaning over Hadley solicitously. "Here, Sam—Miss Willoughby needs help. Take this." He stuffed the handkerchief into Hadley's fist. "A very little bit got on her too. Dry her off, my lad."

Willoughby laughed from sheer joy and malice, yielding to Hadley's ineffectual dabs at the front of her dress. "The silly old fool," she whispered to Hadley. "Wouldn't he be surprised if he knew what really happened?"

Hadley stopped dabbing and looked at her in astonishment. "You really think so?"

When they looked up again, an additional chair had mysteriously appeared and the General was comfortably seated in it. "Shush," he said. "The show's about to begin again. Christmas carols this part is. Just Christmas carols. I love 'em. Peace on earth good will to men," he chanted softly, and nothing could be seen of his eyes but the slits with the merry fan-shaped wrinkles at the corners.

In spite of the General's admonition to "shush," Sam bent low over Willoughby and whispered.

"May I take you home?"

She came very close to betraying her excitement, for a ride home in the dark with this man would certainly give her alluring and dangerous thrills. Just the thought made her feel weak with pleasure. She dropped her long lashes and let these sensations flow through her for a fleeting second, unaware that her face had taken on a sensual expression. Her mouth was slightly open, her lips were full and moist, and Sam, watching her, flushed and his own face reflected the intensity of his desire. Then all that was strong-willed and Fenno in her rose to the surface as she realized that this was the chance that she was waiting for, the perfect chance to revenge herself and put him in his place.

She opened cold blue eyes and gave him a look of scorn. "Certainly not. Most certainly not."

All during supper the little General stuck like a burr to Hadley, and Willoughby, eating ice cream with angry jerks, watched them where they sat in a far corner of the dining room, deep in talk and apparently enjoying themselves thoroughly. Bobbie, without the ruff but bearing the scars, was bending solicitously over the back of her chair and excitedly breathing down her neck in a way that made her want to scream. A few feet away, Prissie sat with the bridesmaids of the pantomime, nibbling and casting murderous looks at Willoughby.

A little further down the room, Matild was eating steadily and placidly, sending Lettie on frequent trips to the table for titbits. "She doesn't know about the fight," Willoughby thought, watching her. "No one would dare tell her. Bobbie doesn't know either, I guess," and she suddenly knew that all other eyes in the dining room were avoiding her. "They've always hated me," she thought defensively. "There isn't a girl in this room who could have two men fighting over her," and she lifted her head proudly. But something inside her shriveled and her mind slid away from the knowledge that now, at last, their envy and jealousy and hate had something to fasten on. Their enmity seeped through her as she sat there eating her ice cream in little dabs off the tip of her spoon, feeling Bobbie's stealthy touch on the back of her neck, and she was almost overwhelmed by loneliness and a sensation very like fear.

She whirled around toward Bobbie so suddenly that he drew back. She put her fingers on the hand with which he held his own saucer of pink ice cream.

"Bobbie, I like you a lot."

"Oh, Willoughby, do you? I thought . . ." His rapturous trembling dislodged his spoon, which fell to the floor and, as he stooped for it, his ice cream almost slid off the plate. He straightened up, pink with confusion and joy. "Oh, Willoughby, I didn't think . . ."

"Silly boy." She swallowed and made herself look at him. "Of course I do. Let's see a lot of each other. Let's be very gay and go to lots of places together. Let's go everywhere."

PART THREE

15

S AM HADLEY lived in two rooms in a boarding house run by one of
the many respectable widows with which the War had left Cleveland well supplied. Though he had been living there some months,
these rooms bore but slight trace of his occupancy, for he was, and
would always remain, one of those men who never impose their per-
sonalities on their surroundings. This was in part because he had no
tastes of his own, all forms of décor being more or less alike to him,
and in part because he had the personal neatness and dislike of superflu-
ous possessions that come of much living in camps and out of knap-
sacks.

His rooms, then, were exactly as he had found them, which is to say,
clean and a little shabby, and he had added to them, in addition to his
clothes in the wardrobe and in the bureau drawers, a hair brush, a
clothes brush and, on the sitting-room mantle shelf, a precise row of
specimens of rock ore and an ornate Confederate cavalry saber. There
was also a small stack of reading matter, mostly periodicals and clip-
pings garnered throughout the week, but these rested beside his half-
eaten breakfast on a table in front of the fire. Each week Hadley made
this careful collection of things he felt he should read and Sunday morning he placed the pile beside his breakfast and, while he ate, he grimly
worked his way toward the bottom.

Having demolished ham and two fried eggs and about a third of the
literature, he found the next item on the pile of papers to be a slim
periodical bound in the kind of apricot-colored rag paper which warns
the experienced reader that only the most polished of intellectual-liberal
views will be found within. Someone had sent it to Hadley with a
check mark opposite an article entitled, "The Workingman in the Industrial Revolution." The name of the author was Brodi, and Hadley
had a vague feeling that he had heard it somewhere before.

Wondering about this, he laid the magazine, open, beside him, holding it that way with his coffee cup and the butter dish. Then he made a quick but thorough inspection of the rest of the breakfast, holding up to look at it in turn a bird-bath shaped dish of baked beans, a half-dozen baking-powder biscuits, a pitcher of maple syrup and a slab of cold apple pie, for the New England traditions persisted in Cleveland in a number of strange ways. Without much enthusiasm he made himself a sandwich out of a biscuit and some beans, and turned with a sigh to the article. He did not want to read it, but he had not yet grown out of a slight feeling of awe of the printed word so that his reading was not as discriminating as it might have been. Moreover, the checkmark was bold, black and compelling.

He took a bite of biscuit and read:

"A country which passes through a phase of hard times, like a country that goes through a war, is never the same afterward. This is true in spite of the avowed wish of most of the population to return to the good old days and, considering the number of times that the good old days have failed to materialize after one or another of these catastrophes, the obtuseness of the wish is something at which to marvel."

At this point the author rolled up his sleeves and got down to business in a manner of which Hadley, consuming his biscuit, thoroughly approved. He said hard times were imminent and he marshalled his reasons for thinking so with such logic and force that Hadley suddenly found himself reading with absorbed interest while his coffee cooled.

After that bit about the coming of hard times, Hadley's interest slackened a little, for the article turned out to be about the workingman in these times of stress and for this Hadley cared rather less than a fig. The workingman, Brodi argued, is the real sufferer in hard times, for the easiest way for capital to retrench is to cut wages and fire labor. Labor, however, from the time of Watt Tyler has done everything in its power to resist this summary treatment and, as soon as the economic skies have cleared, labor has put up a fight to better itself, which not only has met with progressively more success over the generations but has caused capital a great deal of well-deserved grief.

The rest of the article was a plea to industry to recognize that an aftermath of labor troubles, so-called, would be the inevitable result of the coming hard times and at this point Hadley's interest revived again. The author suggested that industry, instead of bemoaning the economic disaster and wasting wishes for the return of the good old days, put in some solid thinking about how essential retrenchments could be made without taking it out of the hide of labor, for only in that way could the aftermath of costly and wasteful friction be avoided.

"How the Hell do you do that?" Hadley wanted to know, reaching blindly for a cold biscuit.

The article went on to tell him. It said flatly that the ancient belief that if wages were raised, prices had to be raised also, was not true, as was the belief that wage levels could not be maintained in the face of shrinking commodity markets. Ninety-nine times out of a hundred, it declared, ways could be found to manufacture the product more cheaply without lowering quality. Efforts should be made to develop new markets, especially foreign markets. Profits to owners and stock-holders should be cut down for the period of stress and the whole manufacturing establishment, from front office down, should be scrutinized for possible operating economies.

The windup stated with vigor that such things would prove far cheaper to capital in general in the long run than any protracted struggle with disgruntled labor. It prophesied, finally, that if such steps were not taken before the storm hit and wages were again lowered below a decent relation to living standards, the country would shortly see the worst wave of labor troubles in its history.

Hadley whistled, took the periodical out from under its restraining crockery, and looked at it back and front. Michael Brodi. A light began to dawn, but it hardly seemed possible that the fellow he had met with Mark at the Union Club could be the author of this article, for it seemed to Hadley highly improbable that writers were likely to be encountered thus casually, like normal people. Worth talking to, that chap. Taught somewhere—Hudson? Hadley held up the apricot-colored magazine and meditated. Then he slapped it down, rose and went out into the hall. Mrs. Adams would know how far Hudson was and how you got there. The guy had something to say!

In the hall a mental image of his landlady rose before him, gray-haired, five feet one, straight as a birch on a New England hillside, of an uncompromising and slightly acid gentility. The vision made him aware of his coatlessness and of his shirt, open at the neck and devoid of tie. Going back into his bedroom, he remedied these defects and returned to rap with meekness on her door. The door opened and she stood there, spare, neat, and a little chill. This almost strange woman was, perhaps, the only person of whom Sam Hadley stood in awe.

"Excuse me, ma'am. Could you tell me how I get to a place called Hudson and how far away it is?"

"I believe I can, Mr. Hadley. It's east and quite a bit south and . . ."

Half an hour later Sam was on his way in a livery-stable sleigh, sitting sidewise to accommodate his long legs, with a worn brown robe made of shoddy over his knees. He was still half-incredulous that a teacher in a country academy could have anything to say about the problems of industry that would be worth listening to, but the article, in spite of its pro-labor bias, had really fired his imagination.

"To hell with labor. Lower costs, new markets—that part was all right, though likely the fellow wouldn't have any particular ideas how you did it. He did sound as if he had really thought about the coming of hard times though. . . ."

Presently Sam's mind slid off these matters and, without his being aware of the transition, he found himself thinking about Willoughby. Perhaps "thinking" is too strong a term, for it began with something more like feeling, a stirring awareness of her that filled him with a restless vitality and a sort of anger. The perfection of every line of her; the grace, the mockery of her manner, her sureness, the worldly sophistication that showed itself in the most casual of her gestures affected him as they might had she been present. He moved his shoulders uneasily, for these emotions were so strong that he felt the need for some physical outlet, and he flung out his hand as though he would sweep all these attributes of hers aside—which was, in point of fact, exactly what he yearned to do.

These qualities of hers seemed to him the purest of artificialities designed, perversely, to hide something underneath. What that something was, he possibly could not have put into coherent thought, but he felt its vitality, its violence, its ruthless selfishness as though these things were a challenge. Now, transported a little out of reality by the rhythmic motion of the sleigh, he let go some inner grip on himself and imagined himself striking her, mussing her hair, tearing her dress, insulting her, ruining her perfection and uncovering her hidden nature so that their real selves could stand face to face.

In something of a daze he realized that he had reached the outskirts of Hudson and that the gate to the campus was on his left. He tied his rather apathetic horse to a long horizontal pipe, which seemed to be intended for hitching, and entered the campus, feeling an impulse to tread lightly on these special grounds. Having entered, he stopped for he had been so absorbed in his thoughts that it never occurred to him until just now that on Sunday Brodi might not be on the campus. He looked around with some curiosity. His woodsman's eye noted that there was a good deal more snow here, back from the lake, and already it had the watery look of the late season. It was criss-crossed in every direction by tracks. Quite a number of people seemed to be about, flowing toward the various gates. "Chapel," he thought. "Perhaps he *is* here," and Hadley moved forward. He asked a number of persons where Brodi might be found and none knew, though one of them remarked that since chapel was compulsory for the faculty it was just barely possible that Brodi had been there. All these people semed to be teachers and they all struck Hadley as either waspish or vague. They made him feel alien. On a chance, he struck off across campus toward the chapel.

He admired the compact, athletic figure swinging toward him even before he realized it was the man he sought.

"I read your article, so I thought I'd drive down."

Brodi, shaking hands, looked surprised, gratified and interested, all by one trick of his black brows.

"Can we talk somewhere, Brodi, if you've got time?"

"By all means."

They headed toward one of the square brick buildings, not hurrying, but saving their talk. A number of college boys passed them and they seemed to Hadley, whose youth had been far from sheltered, to look both soft and immature.

"I don't believe I was ever that young."

Brodi grinned. "*I* was."

All of the boys greeted Brodi with enthusiasm, seeming to put themselves forward for his notice.

"It's Black Mike— Hullo, Mr. Brodi."

There was affectionate proprietorship in their manner and a kind of deference which youth gives only when it feels it has good reason. A ball flew through the air, a boy reached for it and missed it and it rolled to their feet. Brodi scooped it up and, holding it close to him, looked all around with comic stealth before he threw it back, a long throw and an accurate one. It was entirely obvious that ball was a forbidden Sunday sport.

"I'd let them play if I had my way," Brodi said, opening one half of the double doors into the forbidding building. They went into a wide corridor that had dismal, chocolate-colored walls and floor boards tracked up with melted snow. The place was dank and had a physical smell.

Brodi opened a door and stood back to let Hadley through. "Let's go in here. I've got an office of sorts but it's quite a ways."

Hadley found himself in a deserted classroom and he looked around him with the touch of pleased sentimentality which is part of an adult's rather fatuous attitude toward his own school days. Brodi pulled a chair with a bulbous arm out of line, invited Hadley to take it and himself sat down on the edge of the platform.

"Better keep your coat on. No fire in the stove on Sundays."

"I'm damned if I know why I'm here, really." Hadley's smile was disarming and frank, and Brodi returned it with reserve, but under these amenities both men were as busily sizing one another up as two dogs that sniff and sniff. "There's no point in asking you if you meant what you said, for you wouldn't have written it otherwise."

"That's right."

"You didn't say when these hard times are going to catch up with us. There isn't a cloud in the sky right now."

Brodi thought for some minutes, shifted his position and spoke earnestly. "Prophecy's ticklish business. You can't really know—a guess founded on your best judgment is the best you can do, of course. On the other hand, I don't believe in hedging. Fall or winter's my guess. It's up to you to give that guess its proper evaluation. I told you much the same thing at the Union Club that time, if I remember rightly."

"You did but I sort of forgot about it. Seeing it in print makes more impression. And say, that reminds me. I owe you ten dollars. I remember the whole thing now and, by God, you were exactly right about that tonnage—though how you knew beats me."

He fumbled with his pocket and brought out a ten-dollar bill. "No, wait a minute—the bet was in gold, wasn't it? I don't want to short-change you." He turned out a handful of coins and raked through them. "I usually have one or two because I'm a director of both Fenno and Company and Lake, and the Old Man's been paying the fees in gold lately. Funny bit of swank with the country off the standard. I'm always afraid of passing the damn things for pennies. Here you are."

Brodi took the little coin with a grin.

"The point is," Hadley went on, "if what you say is true, there are a lot of steps an outfit like ours should be taking right now."

"How does Mr. Fenno feel about it? Same as he did?"

"I guess so. I want to do my own thinking first, then I'll tackle him." For a brief instant Hadley looked dejected. "There seem to be a hell of a lot more complications than I suspected when I got myself into the iron business."

"Most men in your position ignore 'em—or don't know they're there."

"*You* fixed it so I do know and I can't ignore 'em." His eyes traveled around the shabby room with the torn maps, the dirty blackboard and the film of chalk dust over everything. "I'm tempted to ask a personal question."

Brodi laughed. "It's a means of support and gives me time for writing and other things. I rather like to teach, as a matter of fact. By the way, I'm trying to organize your dock hands."

"Lay off. We've got a union in the mill—Sons of Vulcan they call themselves—gives us trouble enough. Those bohunks on the docks aren't skilled workmen—they're just cattle. Why should *you* care?"

"That's just it. The skilled workmen have been busy for the last ten years organizing themselves into unions. Fine thing, but they're getting to be as exclusive as gentlemen's clubs. The dirt laborer is the forgotten man. Everyone kicks him around."

Brodi paused, but his thought hung unfinished in the air and Hadley waited.

"Look here, Hadley. I want to put my cards on the table. I'm using your dock labor for a kind of sociological experiment, if you want to call it that. I think maybe I want to be a labor leader of a new type. I want practice before I can step out into the field that really needs the missionary work—the organizing of national unions. But skip that. Anyway, I've been preaching to the dock hands that they have a right to a living wage—not charity—that the old saw about employers' and employees' interests being identical is rot and that they'll be healthier, happier men on the eight-hour day and should fight for it. We'll fight for ten hours as a starter. Believe it or not, they'd been stepped on so long they were almost hard to convince.

"They are about ready to fight for their rights, though, and shortly I'm going to Fenno as their spokesman and propose a ten-hour day and a raise in wages from twelve to fourteen cents an hour. I'll try to convince him that he'll actually get more out of them on that basis—which I believe to be true. Starvation wages and slums never produced profits, and where I see those things I know the cause will always turn out to be one of three things: stupidity, bad management or a shaky financial structure.

"We'll force the issue this spring when you people need ore badly. That's good strategy and then, if we win and the crash comes in the fall and you fellows begin to talk about cutting wages and lengthening hours, the poor devils won't, with luck, be any worse off than they are now. If we don't get the kind of deal we want, we'll strike."

Hadley stared at him with an alert hostility through which shone something like amazement. "You're frank! Why?"

"You're too new at the game, I gather, for the industrial pattern of thought to have become a habit with you. I want to convince you I'm right."

"Hell, you can't do it. All you've done is give your hand away to an opponent. It's no advantage to you if I tell Mr. Fenno what you say. We'll fight you and we'll lick you—easy."

"That may possibly all be true, but it'll be a fair fight."

"You'll be fighting Fenno, not me."

"Maybe this time, but not in the long run. I'd judge Fenno to be too rigid to change with the times. He'd crack. From what little I've seen of you I'd guess it would be important to have you thinking my way." He leaned sidewise and pulled a cheap watch out of his pocket. "It's past dinner time. There's an eating place of sorts down the street—how about having dinner with me and listening to my side of the case?" Then with a grin, "I promise to leave humanitarian considerations out of it and rest my case solely on the proposition that the so-called reforms I propose will result in better business and more of it. How about it?"

"All right. You won't succeed, but all right." Hadley reached for his hat and stood up. "You're the damnedest school teacher I ever saw."

Some two hours later, Hadley turned his sleigh homeward. A damp wind was blowing, cold and raw enough but with something soft and alive in it too that stirred the blood with a feeling of expectancy, as though this wind might be the forerunner of a distant spring. Hadley made himself as comfortable as the sleigh would allow, liking the feel of the wind in the roots of his hair and around his collar. One of these days, soon perhaps, the piled-up yellowish ice in the lake would begin to move, stirred by this wind and by the mysterious currents that had lain dormant all winter. Here and there bits of blue lake would appear and the ice would move slowly out from shore to hang, perhaps for days, like a white line on the horizon. Before it was quite gone the ships would put out, plying back and forth. . . .

Sam stretched his big frame. He had the feeling that this had been an exciting day and his muscles were as tense as though the excitement were physical. "Jesus, what a fella *he* is!" He took the whip from the socket and put one foot on the cracked leather dash.

"All right, giddap. We'll go tell the Old Man about this." He flicked the horse's rear scientifically until that flaccid animal was convinced that a semblance of sustained speed was the best policy. "Wait till Monday? And miss the chance of seeing Willoughby without letting her think that I went on her account? Oh, no."

The drive seemed endless and before he reached the outskirts of the city he had to stop and light the candle stubs in the lamps. The south wind had done its work and, nearer the lake, where the snow fall was always lighter, the runners rasped from time to time on the bare gravel of the road. Supper was just over when he arrived at the Fennos' and the family had dispersed, as they so often did after meals, not being a family that took any pleasure in each other's company. When Sam announced his call as business, and Ellen led him through the drawing room toward the study, Lettie and Mark were the only ones present. Lettie sat curled up in the window seat and when Hadley smiled at her she returned the smile tentatively, after a brief hesitation. He remembered that when he had last seen her she had the expression of a kitten expecting momentarily to be drowned. She seemed to have lost the look, or most of it. Mark sat by the fireplace reading a paper. "Hullo," Sam said and, getting no reply, he grinned. So they were still not on speaking terms except in office hours. That type cherished a grudge! He passed on to the study.

During the brief instant Hadley was in the room Mark did not move a muscle, but everything about him seemed to become more intensified, from the elegant detachment of his pose to the gleam of his pointed shoes. The studied carelessness of his cravat became more so; even the seal ring with its somewhat mythical crest which he wore on his little finger was somehow augmented. Not that Sam was aware of any such nuances. This aura of Mark's reached him only in a fleeting sense of his own bigness, barely touching his consciousness but conveying a vague and rather pleasant impression of himself as a hearty and powerful sort of individual.

Fenno was reading the paper and smoking a cigar. He put the paper down quickly with an air of guilt at having been caught in self-indulgence and looked at Sam sternly.

The look did not dim Sam in the slightest. "I was passing, Mr. Fenno. Something has come up." The open and rather ingratiating smile spread over Sam's face. "The fact is, I've been listening to a lot of talk and I don't know whether I'm bewitched or whether what I've been hearing is sound business sense.

They talked and Sam found himself, to his own surprise, urging that Fenno and Company open the season with the experiment of the ten-hour day on the docks. He did it rather well, considering that the whole of him was tense with listening for any sound that might imply Willoughby's presence in the house. He left out, meticulously, and for what reason he could not himself have said, any reference to Brodi's connection with the dock hands. "Let Brodi fry his own fat," was the way he put it to himself as he watched Fenno's irritation rise. Thereafter he listened patiently to remarks about "inexperience," "long years of dealing with labor," "fool ideas of people with no practical experience," "margin of profits," and an almost plaintive disappointment that Hadley should, after making a promising start, be so easily led astray.

"You're the boss," Hadley said at the end of all this, "but I can't help thinking there may be something in what these labor fellows say."

Fenno's reply was like the sound a candle makes when the wick has burned down to the point where the flame is drowned in the liquid wax. Sam rose reluctantly, seeing no way to prolong the interview, and at that moment the door flew open violently and Willoughby came in with a great sound of silk and commotion. Seeing Hadley, she did all kinds of subtle things to herself that transformed her in the flash of an eye into the languid, haughty and bored beauty. She greeted Hadley with a frosty disdain which, illogically, pleased him but made him long to do her some violence.

"Pa-*pa*," she said, turning a shapely back on Hadley, "I'm off to the concert. I thought I was going with Bobbie but for some reason General Thatcher has come instead. I thought perhaps you'd like to say good evening to him. Mark's got him now."

"Thatcher? I suppose so." Fenno rose. "He probably thinks you've been seeing quite a lot of his son lately."

General Thatcher was standing in man's immemorial spot, in front of the fireplace. He had kept his overcoat on and his gloves were in his hand. Mark, standing beside him, was being effusive.

"Evening, General." Thatcher held out his hand. Fenno gave his reluctantly, because he never liked to give anything of himself to others, even his hand to shake.

There was an uneasiness between the two men. Hadley's presence seemed to help them.

"Hadley's been trying to tell me we ought to coddle our dock hands."

"That wasn't quite it, Mr. Fenno."

They both studied Sam gravely and their scrutiny made him feel foolish. Thatcher mumbled something about "lots of unrest—the war gave 'em fancy ideas."

"The bastards," Mark put in, and they transferred their grave stare to him. He flushed. Willoughby appeared, swathed in furs, and her presence was a relief to everybody. She held out her arm toward Mark, indicating a gaping glove button, and he bent dutifully over it while she chatted brightly, unaware of tension, as though going to Sunday religious concerts with General Thatcher were the most natural thing in the world.

All the way to the concert the General chirped and tittuped, as Mark would have described it, and Willoughby's puzzlement grew, but he did not offer to explain why he had substituted himself for Bobbie. She slid into her seat with a great deal of preoccupation about her furs in order to avoid having to meet the frosty looks around her. "This won't help," she thought. "They'll start talking again. Just when they were beginning to be all right on account of my going around so much with Bobbie." She settled herself, smiled meltingly at the General, hit him a playful blow on the arm with her purse because his response was too enthusiastic, and ignored him to examine with interest the backs of the heads in front of her. This was a pleasing occupation for it never failed to bring her a sense of her own superiority.

The smile on her face became fixed and the enjoyment drained out behind it. Three rows ahead of her Bobbie Thatcher was making his way past the obstructing knees and just ahead of him walked Prissie. Bobbie was stumbling blindly, unaware of angry looks, unaware, it almost seemed, of where he was, flushed with unmistakable misery and defeat.

Prissie carried her pale, pointed face high under her fluff of fly-away hair. She looked around her with arrogance, the special, brittle, defensive arrogance of the wishy-washy in a moment of triumph. "Now what's come over her?" Willoughby thought and in that instant Prissie saw her and gave her a smile, small, mean, victorious. Willoughby looked quickly at the General with alarm in her eyes and a sense of impending shock filling her. The General was leaning forward a little, breathing through his mouth and watching Bobbie with the intent, held-in interest that is sometimes on the face of a parent who watches a child take its first faltering, unaided steps, determined not to lend a helping hand. In his case there was nothing kindly about the look; it was as though he were saying in effect those unsympathetic, doom-filled words, "For your own good." If there were anything stony in the General, however, Willoughby, who was never sensitive to emotion in others, failed to see it. To her there was just the General, leaning forward and for once in his life not smiling.

What Willoughby did not know was that in the afternoon of that same day the General had what he would have described as a "little talk" with Bobbie. For this purpose he went to sit behind his very large table desk in the dark and imposing library. The chair behind the desk had an extra large cushion on the seat and, though the General's feet did not quite touch the Turkey carpet, this fact could not be seen. His arms were thrust out straight; his doubled fists rested, wide apart, on the desk top. Bobbie sat opposite, just out of the pool of yellow light from the student lamp. His head was bowed and his hands were clasped in the attitude of a prisoner listening to his doom. When the General finished speaking Bobbie looked up wildly.

"But Willoughby *is* a suitable match, sir!"

"When I say it is time for you to make your choice and settle down, I am not thinking of Miss Willoughby."

"But Father . . ." Bobbie's tone was imploring, desperate.

"Miss Willoughby is not the kind of girl I want for my daughter-in-law."

There was a moment of dreadful silence before Bobbie again raised his eyes to look at his father and this time they were filled with a horrified suspicion. But his father's eyes, wide open now as they seldom were, appeared so steely cold and implacable that Bobbie, flushing painfully, shifted his miserable gaze to his tightly clasped hands.

"I love her, Father."

"Nonsense. Infatuation. Puppy love. Control it. You must. I tell you that you must. *I* tell you." He gave the "I" the despotic over-emphasis of the small in stature.

"Father, I tell you there is not another girl in the whole world!"

"There is Prissie."

"Prissie!" The name was a wild wail.

"An altogether suitable young person."

"But I love Willoughby, I tell you. I love her. I won't give her up."

The scene went on and on, and Bobbie's importunities were like waves beating on rock. At the end Bobbie's resistance broke, as it was bound to do before a stronger will than his own. Bobbie sobbed, miserable, shattering sobs with his head on his arm while he beat one tortured fist on the desk. Watching all this, the General never moved but when it was all over and Bobbie, gulping back subsiding tears, nodded his weak capitulation, the General's eyes were hidden once more by the curve of his apple cheeks and he was once again kindly and buoyant.

Now, feeling Willoughby's look, the General turned to face her all aglow.

"There's Bobbie and Miss Prissie. I didn't tell you but I want you to be the first to know of my pleasure. They're going to be married, but we mustn't tell anybody—not just yet. We must let Prissie be the first to do that, mustn't we?"

Going home in the dark carriage, Willoughby let the General kiss her.

Matild was not exactly waiting up, but when she heard Willoughby's step she came out of the door. She was sallow and puffy with sleep, her gray hair in wisps, her gray flannel gown rumpled, "like something you find under a stone," Willoughby thought, turning her back on her.

Over her shoulder she said, "Bobbie and that Prissie are engaged."

"Really, dear? How nice! I thought perhaps you—he didn't seem—so pink! Prissie? Prissie who? Oh, yes. Her father's the banker. A rival of General Thatcher's, I believe. A thorn in his flesh, I think your father said. When is it to be? The wedding, I mean."

Willoughby gave her mother a rather startled look before she went into her own room and shut the door.

16

MAY of 1873 was exceptionally cold and rainy, or possibly people merely thought so, for the feeling that the weather is not what it used to be seems to be universal. Spring usually comes late to Cleveland, with many false starts and disappointments, and so in May, when the tulips at last come into bloom, they are apt to be caught in wintry, penetrating rains that bow their heads with a weight of water and turn their petals to pale transparencies.

By this time of year the ore boats were plying the lakes, but they did so with a nervous awareness of the sudden force of spring storms, prepared to scuttle to the nearest harbor at sight of a bank of cloud; for these lakes are more treacherous than the seas and their storms come with far less warning. These spring storms are not like those of summer, over in an hour. They may last for days, a week even, and bring with them a chill which is all the more disheartening because of the feeling that by rights warmth and sunshine should be the order of the day.

On this particular Sunday there was, in addition to the chill, a steady downpour of rain that gurgled in the down-spouts and made the wooden roads slimy and dangerous. There were no afternoon pleasure drivers on the Avenue, and Clevelanders of a certain social standing sought to escape after-dinner boredom by going to the only entertainment in town, an exhibition of rather heterogeneous paintings. The General was there because he was one of the financial backers and Willoughby was there because it was the fashionable place to be. Hadley went out of simple curiosity to see if he could discover in the paintings half the things Mark said were there. Mark was now occasionally speaking to Hadley of things not connected with business, but he did so in a manner that was intended to be rather insulting and about the paintings Hadley suspected himself of being the victim of a little leg-pulling. Mark himself was not present because, sincerely loving art, he had seen the exhibit on the day it opened.

Hadley glanced sidewise at a picture and quickly away again. The painting represented a woman most self-consciously asleep on a hard-looking couch of vaguely classical design. Her draperies had slipped, uncovering various parts of her, and this Sam found embarrassing. It made him, in fact, somewhat indignant, and he glanced around to see how other people were reacting to this blatant display of indecency in a public place. There were several women in the crowd and they were apparently quite unconcernedly examining the painting and, since they were to all outward view respectable females, this horrified Sam. "Jesus, you'd never see anything like that in the mining country. The nice ones would at least look the other way." He caught sight of General Thatcher a little way off, looking at him. Sam moved toward the General hastily, without noticing the quality of the General's smile change from amusement to welcome. Both expressions were valid enough, for the General really liked Sam. He stretched himself upward a little as Sam approached, and suggested that they sit down together, away from the crowd.

"I dislike crowds that smell of damp wool," he said, perching uncomfortably on the edge of a circular seat which was covered in red plush. The seat had a high, cylindrical back from which sprouted a potted palm. "Everybody seems to be here. Have you ever noticed that people always go to the same place at the same time, like chickens when something at the other side of the run attracts their silly attention? How are things at the mill?"

"Tolerable. I'm expecting some trouble from the dock hands."

"There was something or other last season, wasn't there? It came to nothing. This won't develop either, you'll see. That kind of labor's easy enough to handle. It's the skilled workmen and their trade societies that are the fellows to watch out for. They got too strong during the war. We have a little edge on 'em now, but in my view they'll take the first chance to try it again."

"Yes, you're probably right."

Both men stared morosely at the brown and blue and white tiled floor.

"What in hell *is* democracy, General?"

"How should I know? The party in power says it's one thing—the party that isn't says it's something else. I suppose it's what you like to think is good for the other fellow. It's treated *you* all right. Do you happen to know if Fenno plans to do anything about getting Cooke to pay up? I don't like to ask the question in a meeting—not yet."

"He doesn't take me into his confidence about that sort of thing."

"He should."

"I guess he always was the kind to play 'em close to his chest. Mark may know. The question would get back to Mr. Fenno, of course."

"Precisely."

A silence again developed, filled largely by the disagreeable, scratchy noise of feet on tile. When the crowd thinned out for a moment they could hear the heavy rain drumming on the skylight. The General's quick glance darted here and there in the uneasy manner often acquired by prominent men fearing to be buttonholed by undesirables. Abruptly he sat forward, his hands grasping the edge of the seat and this, as much as his tone, warned Sam that the interview was about to end. The General spoke with the augmented affability with which a busy man closes a conversation.

"Very nice to have run into you, Sam. Gives me a chance to say I've watched your work at the mill and I'm pleased that you're there. New blood, you know, though I don't imply Fenno's getting on. Couldn't do that. Same age myself. Anything I can do for you, let me know. Feel free to drop in at the bank any time. Like to keep posted on things. Like to talk to you."

Suddenly he became remote. He stood up, very straight, very military, and his smile went on as though someone had turned a switch. Rather amazed, Sam followed the direction of the General's smile and saw Willoughby bearing down on them.

"Magnificent," the General murmured.

Her skirts made a sound like poplar leaves in a wind.

Willoughby had, in point of fact, been more or less lurking behind them in a most uncharacteristic state of flustered indecision. She had not expected to meet Sam in a place like this, and to see him there suddenly before her made her feel oddly tremulous. "Just once since Christmas night," she thought. "That time he came to see Father—the night that Bobbie, the little beast! Oh, what a *mess* life is—waiting around— waiting around." She looked at the General with hatred, as though his wife's lingering on were his fault. "Oh God, I'm bored with it all—I hate it all—why doesn't something *happen?*"

She shifted her gaze to Hadley. "He *is* exciting—it might be chic to be seen in public with an ex-woodsman—to take me places now that Bobbie . . . *That man with the beautiful Miss Fenno? A new man at her father's mill. A diamond in the rough but a coming man, they say. . . . So charming of Miss Fenno to sponsor him socially.* He *is* exciting. He hasn't been near me all this time, but then, I haven't *really* tried to fascinate him. Every single time I've seen him he's made me so mad. What on earth can they be talking about? Well, if they're not going to separate . . ."

She adjusted herself with little pats and preenings and swept toward them into the General's line of vision, and she was the image of surprised pleasure.

"Why, General. Sam." She extended one hand to Thatcher and put the other familiarly on Hadley's arm. "The show is a great success, General. Sam, you have been neglecting me."

"Neglecting you!" Sam swelled with righteous indignation.

"Oh, but you have! You thought I was angry with you, stupid, but it was Mark . . ."

"I know darn well you were."

"General, don't let him be angry with me." She leaned toward Thatcher with a charming gesture of pleading. Her blue eyes were gay and she pursed her lips in a way that was at the same time rueful and intensely provocative.

Something about the way she did it made Sam violently and unreasonably angry, though at the same time he was in every part of him conscious of the curve of her breasts under her tight bodice and of her small waist around which he could so easily throw an arm. "If she were my girl," he thought, "then, by God . . ." and he scowled at her, clamping his jaws so tightly atogether that the muscles below his cheeks bulged.

"I've got to go," he said. "Excuse me."

He took his arm rather roughly from her grasp but she seized his coat sleeve again in a tight grip.

"No, no, Sam. General . . ."

But again the General's restless eyes were on the distance and as Willoughby looked at him he stiffened up, like a man preparing for something. Coming down the long room, hurrying toward them, Willoughby saw Bobbie with Prissie straggling in his rear. They were making what time they could through the crowd, and urgency and alarm were on every line of Bobbie's too expressive face.

"Mrs. Thatcher," Willoughby said half aloud, while her clutch on Sam's sleeve tightened convulsively. She was filled with a wild excitement which almost betrayed itself.

Bobbie was panting for breath. He looked at his father imploringly. "Father, you've got to come at once!" He was so obviously unable to handle himself in a crisis that Willoughby longed to shake him.

The General merely nodded and, taking Bobbie by the arm, turned him about. A wail from Prissie stopped him.

"What about *me?*"

"You stay here, my dear."

"Alone?" Her spider-web hair was slipping down; she was pale with emotion and fright and, at the prospect of being deserted, her lip began to tremble. The look the General gave her had little patience in it.

"Miss Fenno and Mr. Hadley will see you home."

Willoughby gazed after the General's retreating back and even her excitement was not enough to prevent a feeling of shock at the complete disappearance of the bouncing, pink-cheeked little old fool she knew.

Sam was looking after him too. "You can see why the little man could command troops."

Willoughby gave him a look and transferred her attention to Prissie. "What happened—do you know?"

"It's Mrs. Thatcher. She's sinking fast. We were sitting by the fire at their house when the nurse came running down. Oh, I should have stayed so I'd be there now. I should be with Bobbie in his great hour of need."

"Nonsense." Willoughby was crisp. "Don't cry in public and, for Heaven's sake, tuck your hair up. Sam, have you got a rig? I sent the carriage home. Come on."

She took Prissie by the arm with rather unnecessary firmness and, collecting Sam with a look, made for the nearest door. "I hope to God," she thought, "Joe has sense enough to go home. It would be just like him to sit there in the rain with the harness getting soggy and water running off the horses' tails all *night*. But let Sam go off with Prissie alone? Oh, no indeed!"

Prissie jerked her arm free, reared back and gave Willoughby an insulted glare.

"Oh, come *on,*" Willoughby told her impatiently.

"Don't be so—so . . ."

"Executive," Sam supplied. "No hurry, ladies. There isn't a thing you can do."

"Oh, isn't there?" Willoughby thought. "We can get rid of this sniveling little fool and then, Sam, you and I . . ." But with a start she realized that if the General were going to be a widower, it might not matter about Sam now, or Mark, or Bobbie or anybody else.

"Things do happen," she said complacently and, catching an astonished look from Sam, realized that she had let her satisfaction betray itself.

"What?" Prissie said irritably.

"I said—" Willoughby spoke loudly and spaced her words as for a deaf person, making them sound as lugubrious as possible—"things—do—happen."

They drove in silence, squeezed together in the stuffy buggy. The rain protector slanted from the dash upward nearly to the level of their eyes and it was buttoned securely to the sides. Underneath it they felt damp and clammy. The reins came through a slit in the protector, which had a flap on it like a slot in a mailbox. "This thing is probably from a livery stable," Willoughby thought. "It doesn't look any too clean. I hope there are no bugs." She was shrinkingly conscious of Prissie's sharp hip-bone pressing into her side. "She must look a sight with her clothes off—scrawny." A vision of Bobbie and Prissie in bed together arose before her and she wanted to giggle. She transferred her thoughts to her own pleasant affairs.

"Would we have to wait a year? I suppose so, unless some special reason . . . But I could start doing the house over before that—all of it. . . . I wouldn't use her room, of course. I wonder which?" Willoughby let her imagination loose. "And the ring would come from New York and all my clothes—even Paris, perhaps, if Father would leave the mill for long enough to take me . . . Oh, there wouldn't be anything like it in Cleveland! We'd have to have lots of servants for all the parties."

She saw herself receiving before a bank of flowers, holding up the waiting line halfway through, while her French maid helped her put on fresh gloves. She would be like Washington hostesses she had read about, never grasping a hand—letting hers be grasped, steering the bowing guest quickly, skilfully on, her manner composed of just enough charm, mixed with aloof awareness of her own position. "Oh I could do it so beautifully!"

Prissie, who had been doing some thinking of her own, sniffed and said aloud, "I suppose I'll be mistress of that great big house."

"You!"

"Why, certainly, now that Mrs. Thatcher . . . The General—Pa*pa* that is to be—couldn't live alone there after poor Mrs. Thatcher . . . A home for him—a woman's touch." Prissie's pale eyes swam with liquid emotion.

"I wouldn't count your chickens before they're hatched," Willoughby said acidly, and again she realized that Sam was looking at her—"like an alert mastiff," she thought with an inward laugh at his expense, not taking the trouble to examine his expression for any depth of meaning.

Her irritation was short-lived for, with her rosy future so near, even Prissie seemed tolerable. Willoughby slipped back into her dream, but this time she saw herself presiding over the Thatcher table, radiant, vivid, completely eclipsing Prissie, who sat, in this dream, somewhere below the salt and gazed at Willoughby with pathetic envy. With satisfaction untold, Willoughby even went into the details of Prissie's dress. It was blue but so pale that it looked like dirty white in the candlelight, and she wore a baby string of pearls. Her hair was no color at all. Willoughby saw herself in golden velvet the color of her golden hair, and on her neck and wrists and hands blazed all the Thatcher family jewels.

By the time they reached Prissie's home Willoughby was feeling sorry for her and positively kindly toward her—poor little Prissie.

They drew up at the carriage block beside the front walk. The driveway was just straight; no imposing curve in front of the house as at the Fennos'. Willoughby patted Prissie's arm.

"Take care of yourself, dear. I'm so sorry." She turned to Sam to tell him to help Prissie out and see her to the door. It annoyed her only slightly that he was preparing to do so unasked. Prissie disposed of, they drove slowly toward the back of the house and slowly circled the carriage turn-around, like some figures in a stately dance. "How long before she and the General would have an understanding between them? Secret, of course. Perhaps he would say something right after the funeral—unlikely before, though after that kiss he just might, if they were alone together. That would be the real difficulty, probably—but no need to hurry things too much. And in the meantime . . ."

She raised her eyes and looked at Sam, a provocative look, more glowing than she knew because of her secret excitement.

To her surprise she found that he was looking at her and there was considerable intensity in the look, but he was unsmiling.

"Sam, I do like you," she said, thinking not of him but of the seductiveness of her own body so that the whole of her seemed to lift toward him yearningly. As she spoke, she made a graceful gesture toward her own breast, which ended with the palm of her hand upward, held out toward him. There was nothing vulgar about it—a fluttery gesture such as any lady might make, but the same gesture from a flat-chested, sex-less young person and from someone as alluring and as aware of it as Willoughby were bound to produce very different reactions.

The effect on Sam, however, was not exactly what she anticipated. "Do you, now?" He leaned back in his corner of the buggy, slapped the soggy reins on the wet horse and said "Giddap."

They proceeded in silence except for the sound of the iron-rimmed wheels and the clop, clop of the horse's hoofs on the wet cedar blocks, a sound which is like nothing else on earth. Willoughby had not changed her position on the seat since Prissie had left them, so that she was sitting very close to Sam. Now she gave the impression of snuggling intimately and in the heavy, closed-in air of the buggy her perfume rose around them strongly. Presently Sam's arm went around her, under the warmth of her own arm, pulling her toward him, his hand pressing just below the curve of her breast. She put her own hand on top of his, curving her fingers slightly to keep his hand from straying higher and she let her head drop on his shoulder, carefully so as not to disturb the angle of her little hat. And she laughed, a small laugh, full of joy, for she was thinking not only of Hadley but of Mark as well and of what good times she was going to have, safely, with her future assured.

They came to the Fenno gates and Hadley managed the difficult feat of turning in without removing his arm from around her, by taking one of the reins in the hand with which he held her, squeezing her tightly to him in the process. She did not protest, for they were nearly invisible inside the buggy, and she laughed again.

"What *is* the General's first name? Fancy my not knowing."

"Aloysius."

"Oh, *dear!*"

They stopped at the steps. The red carpeting, newly brought out for spring, had turned dark here and there where the rain had soaked in. Sam released her but he kept his arm along the back of the seat and looked down at her.

"You weren't, by any chance, thinking of marrying General Thatcher after Mrs. Thatcher goes?"

"Why, Sam! How could you think a thing like that?"

"You'd be surprised at what I think of you." His arm went around her again, almost angrily, his hand closed over her breast and he tumbled her toward him.

She struggled upright again by pushing with both hands against the side of his leg and leaned against him, looking up at him. "Do you think about me a lot, Sam? Tell me what you think."

"You'd be surprised."

"Would I? Please tell me!"

"All right, you asked for it. I think you're beautiful—the most beautiful gal I ever saw, I guess. You've got a grand air, too . . ."

"The word is *cachet*," she murmured, smiling happily.

". . . and I told you once before you smelled like a lady. You wear fine clothes, too. Most women wear clothes to show them off—you wear 'em to show you off. Anybody'd think you were a lady. I did till I danced with you."

"Why, Sam!"

"No, by God, I knew you weren't before that. I doubt if I'd have talked to you there in that plant room at all if I hadn't known you weren't. You're not even insulted now when I'm telling you you're not."

"You're too exciting. You're more exciting than anyone I've ever known. When did you get this idea I wasn't a lady?"

Sam furrowed his brow in thought and his hold on her slackened, as though his passion had cooled somewhat. Feeling this, she pressed herself against him.

"When? It must have been while I was standing there in the doorway watching you admire yourself in the mirror. I guess I wouldn't even have watched you if you'd been what I call a lady."

"What am I, then?" She was half laughing.

Suddenly he grabbed her wrists and pulled her upright to face him. "I'll tell you what you are if you really want to know. You're a bitch. Now don't pretend to be shocked. I think you're proud of it. You've all the instincts of the girls in the saloons in the mining country that come up to you swaying their hips and wriggling—only with most of them it's just business—with you, it's the way you are. No, don't try to pull away." He jerked her toward him roughly until her fists were pressed against his chest. "You haven't any morals—less morals than a lot of them by a damn sight—but you pretend to have, when there's anything to be gained by it. That's the way you are and, God damn it, I'm crazy about you. I'm so damn crazy about you I can't sleep nights for wanting to get my hands on you."

With an angry shove he pushed her to an upright position and threw her hands away from him. "You think you can play around with me, do you? You think you can manage me and have fun and keep me from going too far. I tell you right now, if you don't get out of this buggy damned quick I'll kiss you and you won't get away from me the way you did last time. I'll kiss you right here in front of your own house and I'll do more than that, I'll give you the kind of experience you've never had before. Now, what about it?"

She was shaking all over. She tore at the rain curtain and scrambled out. She jumped to the ground and her skirt caught on the iron step and tore with a rending sound which mixed with Sam's laughter. She gathered up the length of torn flounce and, turning around, put her head inside the buggy. Sam was picking up the reins and he stared at her with an avid kind of hostility that sent a shiver of excitement all through her. At this safe distance she was entirely in command of herself. She pursed her mouth in the ghost of a derisive kiss, drenched him with a vivid blue look of mockery and laughter, and turned her back.

"Christ!" Sam slapped the reins on the horse's back in such a way that the drooping beast leaped forward with all four feet at once, giving the buggy a terrific jerk.

Willoughby ran up the steps, holding up the torn flounce, and pulled the bell with such vigor that Ellen, taking a Sunday nap in a kitchen chair, woke with a start that unsettled her starched cap. Willoughby never bothered about her keys, since it was far easier and more elegant to ring. She tossed her coat and hat and gloves onto a chair and went into the drawing room. Here John Fenno and Matild and Mark were rather fatalistically awaiting the supper hour.

Fenno lowered his paper and said over it, "That didn't sound like the team."

"It wasn't, Papa. Heaven knows where Joe went. He didn't answer the starter's call. I had to ask Mr. Hadley to bring me home."

"Your dress, Willoughby."

"Yes, Mama, I tore it."

"But, Willoughby . . ."

"How was the exhibit?"

"Delightful."

Mark spoke up with interest. "You really liked those pictures? So old school, most of them."

"Oh, I didn't look much at the pictures. Papa, Mrs. Thatcher is very sick. Bobbie came to call his father home."

"I don't suppose it's anything more than has happened before, do you?"

"Yes, I really do. Prissie said she was sinking fast."

Fenno dropped his paper beside his chair and considered this for a few moments. "If it's that bad, Matild, you and I should go around there. He's one of our directors, you know."

"Now, John?"

Fenno pulled out his watch and snapped open the case. "No," he said, pocketing it again, "right after supper."

Willoughby turned to go upstairs. "Anyway, God knows where Joe is."

For once in her life Willoughby was glad of Lettie's presence, for otherwise her mother's and father's departure would have left her alone with Mark. In that case, Mark would have expected romance or, at the very least, piquant conversation which, after the heady excitement of Sam's love-making, would have been intolerable. Not that Lettie was any more than technically present; still, she was there in the flesh if her mind was elsewhere. Willoughby talked Mark into playing the piano, which he did with brilliance and, gradually becoming absorbed, he forgot to show off. Willoughby pre-empted Lettie's accustomed place in the window, where she could see the lights of the carriage as soon as it turned into the drive, and promptly lost herself in a rich luxuriance of thoughts, happier in anticipation than she was ever likely to be in the most complete fulfilment of her ambitions.

At about nine o'clock the carriage turned into the drive and Willoughby jumped up to go to the door, receiving an offended look from Mark as she passed the piano. She went out to the top of the wet steps to meet them. Her father was coming up, not waiting for the cumbersome Matild.

"Well?"

"All over just before we got there."

"And General Thatcher?" They moved into the hall side by side.

"Composed but curiously vague. It never occurred to me before that he might be a man of strong affections. He's had a lot to bear. . . . Joe says he was right by the door of the hall all the time."

"Joe's getting impossible, isn't he? I have a little headache, Papa. I think I'll go up. Say good night to Mark for me, will you?"

17

THE weather cleared at last and June came in with the cloudless perfection that annually gives Clevelanders the illusion that theirs is a
fine summer climate. Mark stood by the railing at the top of the bank
in front of Fenno and Company and, taking off his hat, daintily wiped
the inside with a silk handkerchief. The morning was hot. He returned
the hat to his head, tilting it well to guard against freckles. Beside him
bravely grew a syringa bush, relic of some farmhouse dooryard, sur-
vivor of the incursion of industry. At the ends of its scraggly but gallant branches clusters of pink blossoms waved, surrounded by a steady
drone of bees from some far-distant hive.

Because of them Mark moved somewhat farther away and gazed out
over the lake, squinting his eyes against the dazzling blue. White sails,
small and large, dotted the surface, and there was one dark streamer
of smoke. He lowered his eyes to the docks below, where a tremendous
bustle of activity centered on an ore boat that was already beginning to
ride high above the water. He frowned at the miniature mountain
range of ore which now, with the new season, was beginning to grow
again, and his frown was critical but without much knowledge. He said
"Hum" in a professional sort of way and searched the tumult below for
Barnes, locating him presently in a knot of shorter men. Barnes' hat
was on the back of his head and a roll of shipping documents protruded from the pocket behind his narrow hips. Mark started the day
whenever possible with a word or two with both Barnes and the superintendent of the mill, for though this was no part of his duty as Secretary, it kept him informed of mill and dock gossip and made him able
to put in his word when Hadley might otherwise be monopolizing the
floor. He watched the swarming Finns on the dock below until Barnes
chanced to look up and Mark beckoned him with an imperious sweep
of his arm.

Barnes took his time but he came, and instead of removing his hat as he would have done in Mr. Fenno's presence, he shoved it even farther back on his head and scratched his forehead.

"We're pretty busy, Mr. Mark. Another boat due tomorrow. Anything I can do for you?"

"I saw you going into Mr. Fenno's office late yesterday. Anything up? I won't be seeing him to get the news till afternoon."

"I dunno, Mr. Mark, but it looks like last year." Barnes glanced over the bank and, as though somebody below might overhear him, he came a step nearer. "They're all excited, as if maybe they were expecting something. Päkkä's kind of hard to understand when he gets worked up, but he keeps talking about somebody called Brodi who's going to see Mr. Fenno about shorter hours and more pay."

"Brodi?"

"Yea, that name's not Finnish. You know who he is?"

Mark was never quite at ease with Barnes. He resented the fact that Barnes never called him "sir" and now he considered again whether he should mention it, but something held him back.

"Yes, I know Brodi. He's always been interested in things like that. So he's going to see Uncle John, is he? He won't get far with *him*." Mark dusted his hands together. "Thanks, Barnes." He'd bet Barnes didn't call Hadley "sir" either, but Hadley didn't know enough to insist on things like that. Hadley seemed to have changed his opinion of Barnes and the way the two of them got their heads together about dock business, you'd think there was nothing more interesting in the world. Mark walked across the cinders carefully, not liking to have his shoes scratched.

Left alone, Barnes stood still a moment, then he pulled his hat down, shoved the roll of papers deeper into his pocket, ran rapidly and with ease down the steps and at once he was gesticulating and commanding in the midst of the crowd below. The matter of hours and wages was no problem of his. Sympathy for the poor devils was one thing but constituted authority was what he was paid to uphold. The army psychology was deeply imbedded in Sergeant Barnes. Keep your feelings to yourself and carry out orders and when responsibility turns out to be more than your allotted share, pass it on to the fellow higher up and let him do the worrying.

Mark went into his office and shut the door. It was a small office, too near the stairs and not as elegant as he felt he, as Secretary of the Company, should have, but at least it had the dignity of a front exposure, like John Fenno's own. Mark always preferred to work with the door shut and as secretively as possible, a contrast to Hadley who could be heard at that moment, loud and good-natured, three doors away.

There was plenty of paper work for Mark to do but he did not attack it at once, for there were other things on his mind. Not this business of the dock hands exactly, but something connected. Last night, as he drove home with his uncle, John Fenno had seemed more than usually taciturn and preoccupied. That was no doubt the result of his talk with Barnes, but what troubled Mark now was that Fenno had said nothing about it to him. Why? A bad symptom and not the first piece of important news about the mill that Fenno had failed to mention. Mark frowned, remembered that he was beginning to get lines in his forehead, eliminated the frown and ran an exploratory finger over the slight remaining ridges. Had Fenno talked it over with Hadley? Mark felt an uncomfortable certainty that he had.

Renewed sounds came from down the hall. "The fellow works at the top of his voice," Mark thought, drawing into himself with delicate fastidiousness. "If the dock hands start real trouble, that will be his look-out. I hope he makes a mess of it—Christ, if he'd only make such a mess of it that Uncle John would throw him out." For a while Mark brooded about the possibility of using the trouble, if it came, to discredit Hadley, but he failed to see just how this could be done. "So Brodi is back of it all. He can't be staying at the boarding house—I'd have known about it."

A slight gleam came into Mark's amber eyes as he considered going to Brodi to appeal to him in the name of their old friendship to withdraw. With Brodi out of the way, the Finns, who were only animals anyway, would come to terms quickly enough. The prospect was a pleasing one and Mark relaxed to think it over. He leaned back and unbuttoned the three bottom buttons of his vest and would have put his feet on the desk except that Hadley frequently did so.

The thing would be to wait until the last moment, until the trouble was about on them and everyone was excited, and then, quite calmly, announce that he had had a little talk with Brodi and that the danger was past. Underplay the part—and Mark saw himself cool and casual in the midst of turmoil. Then he also saw Brodi, black head down like a fighter, compact. He heard the mirthless laugh and stinging comment. The gleam died out, leaving Mark feeling flat and discouraged. "Christ, he wouldn't do it."

Some coup of the sort was badly needed at this point of Mark's career. A bloodless job, this of Secretary, a siding where you might stay for the rest of your life well enough, if it weren't for the vitality, the exuberant masterfulness, the growing sureness down the hall that was steadily gaining more and more of Fenno's confidence. Without Mark realizing it, the worried frown reappeared.

And Willoughby. That affair was not progressing satisfactorily either and she seemed to have become as elusive as quicksilver. Apparently she intended to keep him hanging for, very cleverly, she avoided being alone with him. Anyway, he had had no luck in getting her by herself or even in a responsive mood and she seemed preoccupied and snappish. He had the feeling that she was holding back because she was making other plans, but what on earth could they be? Had she and Hadley been seeing each other? Hard to tell. Hadley would do his damnedest to get her, of course. He admired her and—the boss's daughter! But Hadley was a nobody, and compared to himself . . . Mark smiled a little, tight-lipped smile at the idea of such a comparison.

If not Hadley, who, then? Bobbie Thatcher? But she always treated him as though she felt for him one of those unconquerable physical revulsions that women sometimes have for men who adore them too meekly. But Bobbie had money—or rather, his father had. General Thatcher! A dreadful premonition dawned on Mark, filling him with a cold apprehension. Was Willoughby after the General—just waiting until Mrs. Thatcher should die?

Mark pushed all these thoughts away from him with a quick determination to break this deadlock in which his whole future seemed to be involved. He'd force her to answer him—find some way to make her think about her age—nothing crude to make her angry, but with a sting in it—and then make ardent, seductive, irresistible love to her. He put his hands behind his head, liking the feel of the ends of his hair against his palm. This reminded him to run his hand gently over the top of his head to test the thickness of hair on that crucial spot. It was certainly thinner than elsewhere, but after all that was natural. Nothing to worry about—surely. He leaned back on the soft springs of his swivel chair not very happily. From various directions he felt himself beset.

"Oh, to hell with it," he said after a time, and felt a little better for this puerile thumbing of his nose at Fate. Then he brightened still further and resolved to dedicate that same afternoon to a long drive in the country with Willoughby. "Have another shot at asking her." Out toward Doan Brook, maybe, among June fields, blossom-filled. The spring in his chair complained as he sat upright to thrust his hand in his pocket and pull out his money. Mark was always short of funds.

The expedition would have to be made in the Fenno dog cart, with a lap robe under the seat since grass was full of bugs.

For a while Mark worked somewhat feverishly, mainly at the job of signing papers, which he glanced through as rapidly as possible. At twelve-thirty he got up, pulled his vest down, took out a comb and ran it through his hair and left for a hurried, solitary lunch. Throughout the whole morning no one had found it necessary to seek him out.

He was back again in three-quarters of an hour and, leaving word that he was not to be disturbed unless something urgent occurred, he again shut himself in and prepared to deal summarily with the rest of the stack of papers. That was why he did not hear of Brodi's visit to John Fenno, though the usual inaccurate rumors about what goes on in the front office were flying around the mill.

The new man in John Fenno's anteroom started the rumors, the new man who now replaced old Williams and his alpaca coat and his stooped shoulders. He was polished, soft of voice and small of waist, he handled things daintily and he wore a blue flower in his lapel. Hadley called him "lacy pants" and his name was, inappropriately, Mr. Flint. Not only did he dislike Black Mike on sight but his sixth sense warned him that a visit from a type so unusual in the office of Fenno and Company boded something untoward.

"I don't think Mr. Fenno will see you, Mr. Brodi, unless you tell me what you want to see him about. I'm his confidential secretary."

"Not *this* confidential."

Fenno's door was shut and voices could be heard from its other side. Brodi took *Iron Age* off the center table and sat down.

"I'm afraid I shall have to decline to take your name to Mr. Fenno unless you state your business."

Black Mike lowered his magazine and looked Mr. Flint over from his pale cravat to his delicate shoes, smiled and returned to *Iron Age*.

After a time Fenno's door opened and Thatcher passed through the anteroom with springy step and enigmatic face. Brodi slung his magazine on the table and stalked toward Fenno's door. Mr. Flint beat him by a nose.

"Mr. Fenno, this is a Mr. Brodi. He refuses to tell me what he wants."

Fenno stood by his desk, one hand resting on it, the other playing with his heavy gold watch chain.

"Brodi? I've been hearing about you from Barnes. That's all, Flint."

Mr. Flint would have considered it quite within his province to listen at the door, but he was unfortunately prevented by the arrival of two more directors who took chairs to wait. Around a business office many minor frustrations occur and they are commonly carried to the washroom where they are told in the form of grievances. Accordingly, to the washroom went Flint and, disposing of his frustrations, started the flying rumors. When he went back to the office, he could hear Mr. Fenno's voice, very loud and angry, but no words were distinguishable. From time to time Brodi's voice broke in, not sounding angry but firm and determined. The two waiting directors were rather openly trying to hear.

"Who's in there?" one of them asked.

"A Mr. Brodi, sir."

Mr. Flint fidgeted, fooled with some papers, adjusted the blue flower in his lapel and at length, curiosity being too much for him, announced that he would tell Mr. Fenno that the two gentlemen were waiting.

Mr. Fenno was standing, gripping the high back of his swivel chair in both hands as though he might throw it. His face was very red and there were cigar ashes on his usually spotless vest.

"I'm going to thrash this thing out once and for all," he was saying. Flint's intrusion was obviously resented. "Tell them to wait, Mr. Flint."

Mr. Flint, who could get no inkling about what "this thing" might be, took a quick look at Brodi before he left. Later, in privy council, Mr. Flint described him as "dangerous looking."

"Those dark types—you never know. And after he'd gone, there was Mr. Fenno sitting with his back to the door looking at the lake and I asked him if he'd see the two gentlemen, and he said 'In a minute,' and his voice sounded thick, as though he'd been drinking." Mr. Flint spun the roller towel around to a clean place and patted the backs of his hands with it. "Hot for June," he said.

Brodi started down the steps just as Hadley, returning from a late lunch, started up. They met half way.

"Brodi! Hello. Surprising to see you here."

"It shouldn't be after what I told you in Hudson."

"Oh, that? Really? Been seeing the Old Man?"

"Yes."

Hadley leaned his weight on the banister and a slow smile spread over his face. "And he told you that your demands were 'An outrage, an uncalled-for intrusion, an unspeakable piece of impudence and a violation of the inalienable rights of the employer.'"

Brodi grinned. "That was the general tenor."

"I'm rather inclined to think so myself."

"I didn't convince you, then?"

"You made me think. I'll give you that much. But you can't get away from the fact that the employer has the right to employ labor on his own terms. Labor can take it or leave it—it's a free country. I don't say that, if I were in sole charge here, I might not try out your ten-hour day and some kind of incentive pay to see if, as you claim, it would get more work out of the bastards. What you going to do now?"

"Talk to the Finns through an interpreter. But I can tell you right now there'll be a strike. I came empowered to state that as an alternative to granting our demands. Fenno knows that."

"Look here, how about going somewhere for a drink and talking this over?"

Brodi grinned again. "Talk me out of it, you mean. It can't be done."

Hadley looked at Brodi silently and a little loweringly. It was a reappraisal of the man before him, formed out of Hadley's knowledge of men which life in the mining country had made fairly exact and detailed. Brodi submitted to this scrutiny readily enough, recognizing it for what it was and rather interested than otherwise in seeing the workings of the big man's mind. Hadley came to a visible conclusion and shrugged.

"No, I suppose not." Then something like pleasure crossed his face. "We'll lick you, of course. I think you're crazy—why, you haven't got a chance. I'll be in direct charge and I'll lick hell out of you."

"Maybe."

"By God, it'll be a pleasure. I get fed up with office work and meetings."

"You've got a hard fight ahead of you."

"All right. We've had a small army of toughs here since that trouble last fall. Company guards, we call 'em."

A shadow settled on Brodi. "I don't mean that kind of a fight. Look here, I've been perfectly open about all this. Hell, I've called my shots. Do you intend to fight it clean? Those guards . . ."

"They'll take their orders from me. You'll have a clean fight. We won't start anything rough unless you fellows do. Take my word . . ."

They each stood quietly, estimating the other. Suddenly Brodi thrust out a hand. "Shake on it."

They shook hands seriously, even a little ceremoniously.

Upstairs Mark sucked the tip of a finger to get the ink off it, rose, shot his cuffs and went to the window to look at the weather. The wind had risen a little and miniature waves were attacking the breakwater with the rhythmic swell, crash, hiss and retreat of full-size breakers. Far away great white thunderheads were piled up against the brilliant blue sky, but they seemed no nearer than the Canadian shore. They might not come at all or, if they did, then shelter in some barn might even enhance the atmosphere of romance; a barn full of new-mown hay or last season's hay or whatever sort of hay one found in a barn in June. An excellent afternoon to take off. He picked up his seldom-used baize bag to give the impression of urgent affairs, should he chance to meet anyone in the halls. He adjusted a preoccupied frown, opened his door and went out.

No one was about but there were voices in the stair well. Instinctively he looked over the railing before making his presence known and he was just in time to see Mike and Hadley shaking hands. It was obvious to Mark at once, from their manner, that they were concluding some sort of pact. A pact with the enemy? Mark's agile mind did not pause to question the truth of what he saw. Intrigue seemed a wholly normal pattern of behavior to him. He backed hastily away from the stair rail and went back to his office and stood there, thinking deeply about what he had seen, and the more he thought the more convinced he became that he had stumbled on a valuable piece of knowledge, a piece of knowledge in which John Fenno would be more than a little interested. A piece of knowledge that could be used against Sam Hadley.

Mark missed the final exchange between the two on the stairs.

"All right." Brodi was a little gruff, because he was embarrassed by having betrayed something which might be construed as sentiment.

"All right, fella."

They parted, but on a lower step Brodi paused and turned back.

"Say." He hesitated. "You might just look in on Mr. Fenno. He seemed a bit shaken. I don't think it is anything, of course, but he was pretty mad."

"I'll do that. Thanks." "And that guy's a schoolteacher," Hadley thought, heading toward Fenno's office.

The rain never came. Instead, the heat mounted steadily and by the time Joe had the dog cart around by the front steps it was really oppressive. Willoughby showed no sign of minding it. She was dressed in frothy white with bits of green here and there and a white hat with a pink rose on it and some filmy stuff that went under her chin, which Mark decided was both chic and becoming.

Joe, who did not like Mark, had hitched Mince to the dog cart, knowing perfectly well that Mince never drove easily without Docket beside her to keep her from acting feminine and flighty. Mince's nervous system was not of the steadiest and the light, iron-rimmed wheels of the dog cart made an altogether different sound from the rumble of the heavy carriage, higher pitched and more rattly. As soon as the dog cart turned out of the Fenno driveway she began to be excited and to act as though she were trying to get away from the scary thing which followed at her tail. Mark handled her well enough, but he did it with a tenseness which communicated itself to her through the reins and no doubt gave her the impression that he was frightened also. Willoughby gripped the side rail tightly. She was not really frightened but she did hate Mark's high-strung, ineffectual way with horses.

Because she was just a little nervous, Willoughby almost missed seeing General Thatcher riding alone in the back of the big Thatcher carriage with its top folded down. The first time that she had seen him since the funeral, and she had been waiting and waiting for some sign from him until the excuses she had made for him in her own mind were almost worn out. A month—a whole month and not one word. Just in time she turned up a glad smile, dewy with welcome and eagerness. Mark, preoccupied with Mince, did not see. The General saw her. He tipped his top hat forward, leaned forward himself slightly in acknowledgment of her presence, but his smile, his ebullient manner were lacking. There was more to this formality than the subdued manner of a man who has suffered a recent bereavement. It was a greeting just barely within the bounds of politeness, a patent snub.

Willoughby leaned against the inadequate back of the dog cart. She was trembling. Shock, bewilderment and, finally, indignation shook her. It seemed impossible that he was deliberately being cool to her, impossible that during these weeks he had been shunning her when he had led her to believe . . .

When the first welter of emotion subsided a little and some measure of coherent thought returned to her, she tried to find an excuse, or at least a reason, for the General's behavior. Could she have been mistaken in thinking that the General was attracted to her? "No, certainly not!" she told herself, and her memory found all sorts of proof. "Perhaps he just wanted to keep me away from Bobbie by letting me think —the beast, the perfect beast!" So she blustered to herself, to hide the depth of her mortification.

The dog cart made a precarious turn off the Avenue, Mark sawing on the reins to hold in the now slightly hysterical Mince. Suddenly a wild anger filled Willoughby, an anger so strong that she longed to give it physical outlet. She would have welcomed a violent quarrel with the General and a chance to tell him what a scoundrel, what a little bounder he was. Instead, she had to sit still on this precarious, swaying perch. A spurt of gravel rasped under a wheel as they turned into the side road, the noise grating along Willoughby's raw nerves. She looked at Mark with hatred in her eyes. His white cuffs were sticking out three inches beyond the bottom of his sleeves and he was sitting on the very edge of his seat, pulling on the reins for dear life. The sight of him was, unreasonably, more than she could bear.

"Mark, for the love of God, *be* careful!" All her pent-up feelings were in her voice. Mark flung her a hurt look.

The gravel surface of the road ended in soft dust that muffled the rattle of the iron rims. Mince slowed her pace. She was beginning to tire of her own temperament, feeling the heat. She was flecked here and there with foam flung backward from her mouth, and her hide, wet in great patches from her sweat, gleamed like gray satin. They drove along at a reasonable pace through the unnatural stillness of the muffling dust. Willoughby's thoughts were a welter of hurt anger, Mark's wholly concerned with the dangerous possibility of some farmhouse dog yapping at Mince's unreliable heels. After a time they came to a wooded stretch with no rail fence beside the road. A cart track, deeply rutted, led off between the trees into dense shade. Mark saw this with relief.

"Let's turn in here."

"All right, if you like."

"Hang on, then."

They bumped and jolted over a little ditch and into the ruts of the cart track. Willoughby held on with both hands and bent forward to avoid overhanging branches of the dense maple trees.

"It would be fine if we broke a wheel," she said acidly.

"Then we'd have to stay all night in some barn and you'd have to marry me."

"Not even to save my honor." Her laugh had an edge in it and she cut it off in the middle and looked at Mark sidewise, a look that was both calculating and appraising. Then she laughed again on a quite different note.

Mark was wholly absorbed in the landscape. "What's that shack over there? A sugar house?"

"Probably. How should I know?"

"Let's get out and see. I told Joe to put a robe under the seat."

"We'll have to take Mince out of the shafts. She'll thrash around and break the cart if we don't."

"How do you do that?"

Willoughby gave Mark a look of scorn. A tomboy childhood had resulted for her in many odd bits of knowledge which Mark had never acquired.

"I'll show you, stupid."

Mark climbed with distaste over the high wheel and she waited while he brushed dirt from his clothes. Then she put her hands on his shoulders and jumped down in a froth of ruffles. "Darling," he said, and pulling her to him he kissed her. He kissed her with his eyes shut, searchingly but delicately with an air of inward concentration, as though a part of himself were watching with critical interest his own mounting physical responses to her. She stood still and cold, submissive but wholly unresponsive. Finally, she pushed him away as though she had had enough.

"Let's unhitch, if we're going to. You undo that and that. No, stupid, turn it. Can't you see that little button thing on the end of the whiffle-tree? And knot up the traces or she'll step on them. I'll hold her while you go and see if there's a hitching post by that shack."

Mark went without a word while she held Mince with one hand and did her best to titivate her coiffure with the other. She also bit her lips to give them color and moistened them with her tongue. These performances were almost automatic.

In the stillness Mark's voice startled her. "There's a post with a ring in it right over here."

"All right. Come back and get out the hitching strap."

Mark hung the robe over his arm and led Mince with an outward air of nonchalance but with an inward shrinking and a tingling in his heels when her great hoofs came thudding down so close behind them. While he hitched her, Mince pointed her ears and blew soft breaths at him through velvet nostrils.

The sugar house was not promising. The floor was dirt and the place smelled of dead fires and leaf mold. They went out again and after a little argument spread their blanket under the trees in the deep shadow some distance from a rail fence where the sugar bush ended and a bright, sunlit pasture began.

Mark was tired. He would have liked to lie still with a thin cigar between his teeth to keep off gnats, watching the play of light and shadow and letting his mind speculate about Mike and Hadley and the potential value of his discovery. Willoughby, however, had taken off her hat and fluffed up her hair and was lying back on the robe looking up at him expectantly. Reminding himself of the importance of present business, he leaned down over her, stroking the curve of her neck and kissing it with a great show of gentle tenderness. From time to time he looked deep into her eyes. Gradually he found himself improvising a new character and he became interested. He was creating a Mark full of gentle and considerate devotion, a simple, kindly Mark longing to put his deep love for her at her service. His looks said as much, nor did they at all reveal the anxiety with which he watched for signs of the success of this new approach.

After a great deal of this and very little return from her, he said with a kind of fatigued desperation, "Willie, why don't you marry me? Good God, it's the logical thing to do. Everybody expects it. Time passes. You've got to do something pretty soon, Willie."

"Don't call me Willie!"

"All right, darling, but you ought to think of that phase of it just the same. Then some day the mill will be yours. When a woman owns a piece of property like that it has to be run by a manager picked out by a board of directors and he would never do it quite as advantageously to you as someone who put your interests first."

"How do you know the mill is to be mine?"

"I saw your father's will when I was at Cushing's and I'm violating a confidence to tell you, but I think you ought to know so you can plan your life." Again Mark stroked her cheek with gentle love.

"What about Mama and Lettie?"

"They're taken care of in other ways. You are Uncle John's real heir. But, look, Willie, I know more about the mill than anyone else."

"More than Sam Hadley?"

"Certainly!" Mark flushed. "What I'm trying to say is . . ."

"But you'd be there whether I married you or not."

"No, darling, I wouldn't."

"What do you mean?"

"I've been thinking for a long time"—Mark spoke slowly because the argument had just this moment occurred to him—"that if you won't marry me, I'll go away somewhere. I couldn't stand to be near you, Willie, unless you were mine."

There was deep pathos in his tone. Willoughby looked up at him under her lashes—a quizzical look with a little amusement in it. Not wanting too close a scrutiny, Mark avoided it by gathering her up in his arms, slowly, gently, making himself tremble all over just enough so that she would be sure to feel it. He did not kiss her, but he held her close to his heart and bowed his head over her. "Darling," he said brokenly. "Darling, darling, I love you."

She struggled a little, trying to get her nose out of his shirt front so she could breathe. After she had filled her lungs she said pensively, "Well, I might. I just might."

"Oh, Willie, really?" He almost dropped her in his amazement. "I knew you would," he said hastily, to cover up the amazement.

She sat up and felt of her hair. "I said *might*." For a fleeting instant all the worry and uncertainty that were tormenting her were in her face. She bent her head and, picking up a twig, began to break it almost viciously into little pieces. Mark waited because he did not know what else to do, and after a while she threw the bits of twig from her and raised her eyes to his and his heart leaped when he saw tears hanging on her lashes. He pulled her exultantly into his arms.

"My darling!"

"No, no, Mark." She tried to push him away with both hands on his chest. "Give me a little time—a couple of months. I just don't want to be rushed." And putting her arms around his neck she drew him down, letting herself lie back on the blanket and kissed him passionately and a little wildly, pressing her whole body against him, laughing in a way that made him uncomfortable.

Puzzled by her sudden vehemence and disturbed by the undercurrent of emotions which he could feel in her, he returned her passion, doing his best to make her believe he interpreted her hot kisses, the grasping of her hands, the twistings of her body as she seemed to intend that he should. Actually, there was no desire in him. The sense of the falseness of her emotions combined with the stunning realization that he was apparently close to winning what he had strived for so hard without wanting, dazed him, made his body feel flaccid and his hands clammy.

Perhaps his overwrought state made him preternaturally receptive to impressions. He felt in the midst of his simulated ardors, a tingling in his spine, as though someone were watching them. His hand was down the front of Willoughby's dress. He jerked it out and sat up. On the other side of the pasture fence, about a hundred feet away, stood a man in a floppy straw hat. He was leaning on the fence watching them with most obvious interest. Willoughby sat up too, panting and disheveled. At sight of the man she scrambled to her feet, reached for her hat and began to run toward the sugar house. Mark followed, trailing the robe. Some shouted words reached him. "Hot weather we're having, ain't it?"

On the other side of the sugar house safely out of sight of the man by the fence, Willoughby began to laugh. She laughed and laughed until her cheeks were wet with tears.

When they emerged from the woods, they found a cool breeze blowing and the tops of the trees were bending and swaying.

"It's rained somewhere," Mark said.

"Oh, look. Those horrid little bugs. Every year, this time." Willoughby picked three "Canada soldiers" off her skirt, holding them by their sail-shaped, iridescent wings. "It *is* cooler, though."

They drove in silence, enjoying the freshness. Mince, knowing herself homeward bound, discarded skittishness for a steady, rapid pace. Mark felt safer and so he drove with an air. His yellow chamois gloves were turned back at the wrist and he wore his hat at a rakish angle. He liked the style of the dog cart. Willoughby was as completely out of his thoughts as though she were not sitting gracefully beside him. From time to time he bent down his upper lip and chewed meditatively at his auburn mustache, and his yellow eyes were as cold and calculating as a cat's.

Along the lake shore the fresh breeze was bringing in thousands of the insects like the one Willoughby picked off her crumpled, white dress. The "Canada soldiers" came each year, harmless, lethargic little things with gauzy wings, ripe for death. They floated in and clung to the first object they happened to strike so that few of them got farther inland than the shore line. The advance guard arrived about two o'clock and by sunset every house and tree and standing object was coated with them on the side toward the lake. Their dead bodies covered the surface of the water like a gray carpet that rose and fell with the heave of the lake.

Brodi plucked the little creatures off himself as he walked down Mill Street toward Päkkä's house but after a time he gave up the task as hopeless and when he climbed the Päkkäs' steps he was well coated. Mill Street was quiet, for the Finns had not yet returned from work and the invading army had driven women and children indoors. Brodi took out his handkerchief and, flicking the soldiers away from a small area on the top step of the narrow porch, he sat down. In the fading light the street seemed to him more melancholy than usual. The struggle represented here for a precarious living reminded him of the stunted trees which grew out of the bank by the lake, undernourished, ragged from tearing winds, their roots exposed by erosion. The yellow dog came trotting importantly down the street, saw Mike and swerved from his course to offer greeting. Remembering the dust in the dog's coat Mike refrained from patting him. The dog sat down on the step beside Mike, panting companionably and Mike was grateful for his presence.

After a time the door behind them opened and the tall Finnish woman put her head out, uttering guttural ejaculations at sight of Mike. He pointed toward the mill, trying to convey to her that he was waiting for Päkkä. He did not know whether she understood him but she came out on the porch, flapping her apron at the "Canada soldiers," and began an elaborate pantomime of complicated gestures, talking a stream of Finnish while she waved her arms.

"What?" he said politely. "I don't get it."

Her efforts redoubled and he gave the charade puzzled attention. She seemed to be acting something out and light began to dawn.

"A steam bath! No, thank you, really. Thank you very much, but no." Queer form of hospitality to put you in the shed, pour water over hot stones to cook you pink, beat you with twigs and rub your skin off with coarse sacking. Only honored guests were treated so. He grinned broadly, shaking his head from side to side emphatically. She seemed crestfallen. "It's really most kind of you." He tried to convey thanks in his tone.

She left him with a regretful, pitying look and he sat still, his hands hanging limp between his knees, and the yellow dog sat beside him and panted and dripped sociably. Queer, upright, kindly people, the Finns. Not made for cities and industry and smoke. Päkkä had told him stories about the old country—why on earth did they ever leave it? —about paddling across the lake on summer Sundays to go to the village church and how they all gossiped in the roadway afterward, explosions of hearty laughter, backslapping and the young men in their Sunday best making eyes at the giggling girls. Or flying across the frozen snow behind a team of reindeer, fast, fast.

The light was fading with no glory of sunset hues for Mill Street. In Mike's present mood the scene before him seemed one of hopeless desolation; the shabby cottages, the dreary fields and the coating of gray insects oppressed his soul. Down at the lake end of the street he saw a group of men, black-looking in the dim light and weariness implicit in their slow movements.

Brodi's was not a vacillating nature. To any course of action he gave careful consideration and, when his mind was once made up, doubts did not plague him. But now, watching the weary men approach, his own shoulders bent a little as though the sight of them made him feel the full weight of the responsibility he had taken on himself. One after another of the group of men turned in at some little house and Brodi heard doors open and cries of greeting. The scene was italicized for him intolerably by the knowledge that the welfare of all the families on this street, jobs and even happiness depended to a large extent on the strike, the strike which was now almost inevitable and which would not now be threatening but for him. He clasped his hands and twisted them until the knuckles showed white.

Päkkä turned in at the gate and the yellow dog went down the steps to meet him.

"Mike?"

"Yes, it's Mike."

"You got news? You got news, Mike?"

"Yes, I've got news."

Päkkä dropped heavily down on the step beside him. "Bad?"

Mike sighed. "Yes, I'm afraid so, Päkkä. It doesn't make it any easier that we expected it."

"Then we strike, eh? Like you said?"

"I guess we do."

They sat in silence for a moment, a moment which, for Mike, was outside coherent thought and filled only with Päkkä's heavy breathing. Then Päkkä stood up.

"Come on, Mike. Ve got vork to do."

18

THE Company rig picked up Mark at his boarding house each morning. He had made this arrangement when he became Secretary of the Company, though he neglected to mention it to his uncle. He felt that the appearance of the rig at his door not only enhanced his standing with his landlady, which needed enhancing, but saved money as well. He had no reason to think that his uncle would object to his use of the rig and driver, but he took the precaution of getting out of it at the stable instead of at the front door of the office. The stable was several hundred yards west of the mill, across a cindered field, and as Mark walked over this toward the office building the day after his drive with Willoughby, he saw a great bustle of activity and a long stretch of new wire fence that seemed to have sprung up by magic in the night. The fence was high and exceedingly formidable-looking and it shone like silver in the June sunlight.

"Now what the devil?" he thought. "The strike. It must be that. Hadley doesn't lose any time." And he altered his course slightly to take him toward the center of the fence-building activity. There must be, he calculated, fifty workmen involved and not any of them looked familiar. They had brought in outside labor, apparently. Around this group of workmen stood the Company guards, spaced out at neat intervals. Most of them held short, black clubs. "An ugly lot," Mark thought, looking around for their chief.

This individual was standing at the edge of the bank with his foot on a roll of wire, his broad-brimmed hat on the back of his head and his arm on his knee. He looked like exactly what he was—a small-time ex-police chief who had become "ex" at the instigation of a graft-investigating committee.

"Good morning." Mark's tone was unconsciously conciliatory. "Expecting trouble?"

The chief turned his head aside, placed a stream of tobacco juice scientifically and turned back to look Mark over. Something about the man's face, and especially the eyes, gave Mark an unpleasant chill. The scornful inspection concluded, the chief said "Yea," and transferred his gaze to the docks below. Mark looked downward also.

"Looks quiet enough."

"Yea, but there ain't no ship in now. The *Mackinac Island* put out empty yesterday. Wait till that one gets here—'long about two o'clock, with this breeze." He pointed and Mark saw a white sail in the distance.

"You look for trouble to start then?"

"Then—if it's going to."

"You expecting a rumpus?"

"That's my job, to expect a shindig. If it don't happen, so much the better."

"Will your fence be done by two o'clock?"

"Pretty near. It's a hell of a lot of fence. We been working a gang all night. No gates, though. Can't get gates, it seems, this short notice."

"I suppose your men can handle the dock hands without any difficulty?"

"That's the hell of it."

The fellow's eyes, Mark thought, looked like dead oysters in a face that was both shrewd and cruel. "What do you mean?"

"Orders is, no violence. Orders is we stay this side of the wire and even if them Finns start something, we ain't to beat the bastids up." He spat again to emphasize his disgust.

"Are those Mr. Fenno's orders?"

"Dunno. Hadley gave 'em to me."

"Well, good luck." Mark looked down at the quiet docks. The Finns all seemed to be there; anyway, there were a lot of them. He moved off toward the office building, slim-waisted and elegant, thinking deeply, not so much about the impending strike as about the handshake he had seen on the stairs. The longer he thought about it, the more convinced he became that the knowledge of this handshake with the enemy was so valuable that it might be used to blast Hadley out of the position in which he seemed to be so well entrenched. At the top of the stairs Mark vacillated, inclining first toward Fenno's office and then toward his own. There was no doubt in his mind about how Fenno would receive the news, especially if the breaking of it were adroitly handled. The whole question seemed to be one of timing—could it be used to the greatest advantage now or at some future hour? So he fluctuated until, resolved, he headed toward Fenno's office. Fenno would be sure to be angry if he were not told at once. On the other hand, he was certain to be occupied just now.

"Morning, Flint. Mr. Fenno got someone with him?"

"Yes, sir. Mr. Hadley." Flint's rather prominent eyes traveled all over Mark in a quick inspection, noting details of waistcoat and cravat. In his view Mark was the only gentleman in the organization.

"Directors' meeting still slated for ten?"

"Yes, sir."

Mark went to his own office with the elastic gait of one who finds the world a thoroughly satisfactory place, and when he and Hadley met later at the directors' meeting, he was quite friendly with Hadley, if a little patronizing.

The meeting was a routine one but it lasted longer than it should, because of the threatened strike. The directors plainly enjoyed the excitement and enjoyed giving Fenno advice. They were, of course, against labor organizations of all kinds, deplored the fact that war conditions had so favored their growth that now it seemed impossible to uproot them. Labor unions were un-American, unconstitutional and . . .

"This ain't a union," Hadley said.

He had some difficulty in explaining just what it was, and he rather slid over Brodi's part in the affair.

Mark stroked his mustache and said nothing.

There followed a good deal of strong talk, interspersed with flag-waving, on the part of these frock-coated businessmen until at length Fenno said sarcastically, "I think you can safely leave it to me, gentlemen."

It was then that General Thatcher, who had said nothing up to this point, surprised everyone by advocating the ten-hour day. Not, he made it entirely clear, out of any humanitarian considerations, but purely as a measure to increase efficiency. Hadley, listening to him with extreme interest, noticed that many of his reasons were identical with those Brodi himself had advanced. The General made quite a speech of it and wound up by saying, "Lick the tar out of 'em first and then give it to 'em." These views caused a turmoil of dissent.

After the directors took their leave the atmosphere in the offices grew tenser and tenser and, except for Fenno, Hadley, and the laborers building the fence, very little work was done. The guards seemed to grow more menacing as the day wore on and their clubs were somehow more in evidence. Everyone with a front window peered out of it at the stately approach of the white-sailed ship. Everybody else found frequent business with those who had front windows.

Mark felt the strain to be almost intolerable, and his temper became so snappish that word quickly went about not to essay his shut door. At one o'clock the fence was finished and Mark watched the guards walking along it inspecting the work, while the chief and others shook and kicked the wooden rails which took the place of a gate. Once, standing at the side of his window—there was something in Mark's make-up which habitually made him conceal himself when looking out of windows—he saw Hadley below and made the childish gesture of spitting down on him.

At two-thirty the ore boat docked, and though the windows were too far away for small sounds to reach them, the jar and the creak of her sides against the wet timbers of the dock were felt by all the watchers. Mark, alone behind his shut door, saw the ropes slung over the bollards and then his heart began to beat fast. "It's come. Here it is!"

Barnes was giving the signal to raise the gangplank to the deck and in the half circle of waiting Finns, not one man moved. The order was repeated, shouted, and the shout came to Mark on the breeze. Men on the ship began to run back and forth; others lined the rail. Barnes continued to shout with mounting anger and the Finns stood silent, to all appearances as brutish and stupid as cattle, and Mark watched with an unpleasant gleam in his amber eyes.

Barnes lost his temper. He grabbed something that looked like a shovel from a barrow and threw it down with all his might. He strode forward, elbowing his way through the men, and they made no move to stop him but they turned to stare after him. Halfway to the steps Barnes started to run and then he was lost to Mark's view. By the time his head appeared over the edge of the bank the guards were taking down the bars of the gate and Hadley was running across the enclosure to meet him.

Mark left his window and with every show of haste walked into his uncle's anteroom, past a nervous Flint, and burst into John Fenno's sanctum without knocking. Like everyone else, John Fenno was at the window. He glanced over his shoulder and said, "They're coming up the bank. All of them. They asked for it! We'll drive 'em back to the docks and that will be the end of that."

"Uncle John, I must speak to you about something important. I've been trying to get at you ever since it happened."

"Well?" Fenno did not turn around.

"I saw Hadley and Brodi shaking hands. They had made some sort of an agreement. I thought you ought to be told."

"When was this?" This time Fenno did turn around.

"Not long ago."

"Brodi's behind all this—a friend of *yours,* if I remember rightly."

"No friend of mine any more."

"Hadley wouldn't be shaking hands with *him.* What are you trying to imply, Mark?"

"I'm not implying anything, sir. I'm telling you what happened."

"Hadley's in charge of this, you know. He has instructions to drive the men back to work and have the guards stand over them to see they do work."

"Those weren't his instructions to the guards."

"What do you mean?"

"The chief told me himself that Hadley's orders were not to do anything, not to resist in any way."

Fenno looked at Mark long and sternly from under his brows. Finally he said, "I suppose you are sure of your facts?"

"Absolutely."

Fenno stood still a moment longer, contemplating Mark with dislike; then he walked deliberately to his desk and brought his hand down on his bell. When Flint appeared, he said, "Find Mr. Hadley and send him in." Without glancing in Mark's direction, he strode to the window and stared out. The Finns were now massing on the other side of the improvised gate and the guards faced them, standing a little way back from the wire.

Mark did not look out. He stood on the balls of his feet with his hands thrust in his pockets and bit at his mustache. There was tension in every line of his slim body. Mark would rather not have confronted his rival face to face; that was never the chosen method of one who preferred to work by devious and indirect methods. Now that the situation was forced on him, however, he felt excitement and a sudden wave of confidence in himself.

Both Fenno and Mark heard Hadley's steps in the anteroom and turned to face the door before it was thrown open. Hadley advanced several paces before he became aware of the wall of hostility which confronted him and stopped abruptly.

Fenno walked to his leather chair and let himself down into it.

"Sit down, Mr. Hadley."

"Thanks, I'll stand."

Hadley seized a chair by its back and, tipping it forward, folded his arms along the top and put his foot on a rung. This habit of leaning on the furniture was one of Hadley's many mannerisms that filled Fenno with annoyance quite out of proportion to the cause. As he watched Hadley now, the coolness in his demeanor increased perceptibly.

"Very well. Mr. Sabin just told me that he saw you making some sort of pact with that fellow Brodi yesterday. Is that true?"

"Pact?" Hadley looked puzzled. "I didn't make any pact with Brodi."

Mark spoke softly and with venom. "That's a lie. I saw you."

The chair came down on all four legs with a crash and Hadley started for Mark. Fenno's voice, ringing out, stopped him.

"Mr. Hadley!"

Sam stood still and stared from one to the other like an angry bull.

"Mr. Sabin informs me that he saw you and Brodi shaking hands on the stairs and that you had obviously come to some sort of an agreement. Is that true, Mr. Hadley?"

"Oh, that!" Sam's anger was gone as quickly as it had come. He grinned and resumed his negligent leaning position. "That was nothing. I ran into him on the stairs and he told me the strike was on. We agreed to make it a clean fight and shook hands on it. That was all there was to that."

It was obvious that Sam expected his answer to clear the skies. It did not. Both Fenno and Mark continued to regard him with unmitigated hostility. Fenno was the first to speak.

"May I ask what you mean by a 'fair fight,' Mr. Hadley, and why you considered it within your province to commit the Company to any course of action?"

"Why, sir, you put me in charge of the strike and so long as that's true, I'll fight it fair."

Hadley paused, thinking of Brodi and the straightforward understanding between them, and something about the direct honesty of Brodi's nature made Sam suddenly angry with the two men who faced him.

"If you don't know what it means to fight fair," he said, addressing himself more to Mark than to Fenno, "I'll tell you. It means no rough stuff. It means not using clubs or weapons on unarmed, defenceless

men. It means listening to the other guy's side of the question and telling him yours, instead of behaving as though these men were a lot of
contrary cattle you could drive with whips."

Sam stopped, considerably surprised at hearing himself utter these
sentiments.

Mark started to speak but checked himself, smiling. Things were
going well—better to let them alone and keep in the background, let
Hadley hang himself with the rope they were giving him. Fenno spoke
in the stern voice of a judge.

"Your sentiments are not in accordance with my orders, Mr. Hadley.
My orders were to return the men to work. But the chief of the guards
informed Mr. Sabin that you have issued orders that his men are not to
use force."

"Certainly I did. You can't *make* men work. And in the long run it's
not going to get you anything to break a lot of heads. Talk to the men
or their representatives. Tell 'em why you can't meet their demands.
Explain things, for Christ's sake. Don't just club the poor devils!"

"Mr. Hadley!"

"Mining country language, sir. I'm sorry, but I guess I feel strongly
about this."

Mark spoke and both men turned toward him in surprise, as though
they had forgotten he was there.

"You seem to be extraordinarily sympathetic with the strikers." Mark
appeared to imply far more than his words said and Hadley, leaning on
his chair, glared at him in hot anger. Suddenly the rung of the chair
broke under Sam's foot and Sam looked at it in vague astonishment.
He set the chair down carefully on its four legs and said, as though he
were making an effort to put anger behind him and be reasonable:

"Look here, sir, if I'm going to run this strike for you, I'd better
make my position clear. I don't believe the Company ought to meet the
demands of the men. But I do think, sir, that you ought to see Brodi
and maybe that foreman, Päkkä, and explain your position and listen
to their side. . . ."

"I am under no obligation, Mr. Hadley, to 'explain my position,' as
you call it. I have seen Mr. Brodi once and told him that his demands
are preposterous. I am giving orders, not explanations."

"You can't *order* men to work!"

"Necessity will make them come to terms. The important thing is to
make them realize we will stand no nonsense. They'll go back to work,
all right. The guards must form a cordon around the docks and see to

it that the men return to work. If the men resist and get hurt, it will be their own fault. You will go at once and instruct the chief to drive the men down the bank."

"I'll be damned if I will. If you want to issue orders like that, Mr. Fenno, you'll have to do it yourself!" Hadley's voice was loud with anger.

Fenno slammed his palms down hard on the arms of his chair and pushed himself up to confront Hadley. His face was flushed, and he seemed to be struggling to control his rage, but before he had time to speak, Mark interposed. Having watched this scene with keenest interest, he spoke now in a voice he tried to make calm and judicial in the hope that Fenno would be impressed by the contrast.

"May I suggest, sir, that under the circumstances Mr. Hadley is hardly the person to handle the strike? Perhaps he should be relieved of responsibility in that direction."

They stared at him and Mark supported their looks with a good imitation of quiet dignity. Before Fenno could answer, Hadley spoke.

"I won't give up that job unless I'm ordered to. I gave my word to Brodi that . . ."

Mark raised one shoulder and let it fall again as though to say, "You see?"

Fenno said thoughtfully, "I can hardly undertake to manage the strike myself."

Hadley raised his voice. "Look here. I'll be damned if . . ."

"That's enough, Mr. Hadley. You will do what I say. I should certainly follow Mr. Sabin's suggestion and relieve you of duty in connection with the strike, if there were anyone else who could be assigned to it."

"Uncle John, I know it's hardly within the province of the Secretary, but if I might volunteer my services?"

Hadley threw back his head and laughed. "You!" he said derisively.

Mark gave Hadley a look of burning anger, but he managed to retain his pose of calm superiority. "*I* am entirely in agreement with your orders, sir, and should endeavor to carry them out to the letter."

Hadley burst out. "Look here, Mr. Fenno . . ."

"That's enough. I've listened to too much argument already. Mark is entirely right. You have proved yourself, by your own words, unfit to handle this emergency. Therefore, you are relieved of all duty in connection with the strike." He turned to Mark. "You will take over."

"Very well, sir," Hadley said. "But let me say this. If any dirty work starts—if there is any uncalled-for rough stuff, you'll see me back in this, all right. You'll see me back in this damn fast!"

He glared at the others and left the room, slamming the door. Mark did not trouble to conceal his smile of triumph.

Fenno sent Flint with a message to the chief of the guards, installing Mark in place of Hadley. Mark waited in his own office, somewhat nervously, until he heard Flint's returning steps on the stairway. Then he went down the stairs running and came out on the steps, squinting against the bright sun and the glare from the lake, but looking around his domain with arrogant assurance.

There was nobody near him on the dais of the steps. Some of the guards were looking at him over their shoulders. The chief was way over by the gate and Barnes stood by himself where Hadley had left him. The Finns had lined themselves up along the outside of the wire fence, staring across at the office building. They looked, had Mark been near enough or had eyes to see, a little self-conscious and sheepish. Not a man of them had ever openly revolted against constituted authority before, and it was plain they did not quite know how to act. Had he been closer, the shuffling and embarrassment might have deceived Mark. It did deceive the guards and their chief, but Barnes, wary and worried, recognized this for the merest of surface manifestations. Brodi was there also with Päkkä but, because they were standing back from the wire in council of war, they were not visible from the steps. One wing of the fence cut off the mill itself from the office building and this was lined, on the mill side, with men who had left their jobs to watch the excitement. These were the skilled workmen, members of the Phoenix Lodge, of the United Sons of Vulcan. They were the aristocrats of labor.

Mark beckoned to Barnes with a sweeping gesture of his arm and Barnes crossed the enclosure toward him in the midst of phenomenal stillness, and he walked as though he feared to upset the balance of something.

"I'm in charge here now, Barnes."

"So I understand, sir." A dark flush crept to Barnes' tanned face. You do not challenge a change in command at any time, least of all just before the start of a battle, however much you might like to do so.

Like many a green commander before him, Mark sensed the lack of confidence and it made him bluster.

"I'm going to run things *my* way, understand? Those men are to be driven back to work!"

"They've already refused to work, Mr. Mark. They wouldn't so much as lift the gangplank."

"I saw that. You're altogether too easy on them, but we'll go into that when this trouble is settled. But I tell you now there are going to be a lot of changes around here."

Barnes said nothing. His face was wooden.

"Well?"

"Just what are my orders, Mr. Mark?"

"I told you. The men are to be driven away from that wire, down to the docks, where they are to start unloading that ship at once. If they don't, there'll be some broken heads."

"Perhaps you had better tell them yourself, sir."

"What do you want me to do? Go over to the wire and shout at them? I don't speak their God-damn language."

Barnes' face assumed the stiff, pained and embarrassed look of the experienced soldier subject to the inept orders of a stripling. "Neither do I, sir."

"Then how in hell do you talk to them?"

"Gestures, sir, or through an interpreter when necessary, a foreman called Päkkä. Some of the others speak a little English."

"All right, send him here."

"The chief there is in charge of the gate. He wouldn't take orders from me, Mr. Mark."

"Oh, for Christ's sake, send *him* here."

"Excuse me for making the suggestion, Mr. Mark, but I think I'd have more than just Päkkä in—so more than just him will get it clear what you have to say."

"All right. Let 'em send a delegation. Let 'em send five of 'em. They're to come right over here to me. I'm not going to move from this spot!"

"I'll send you the chief of the guards, sir, but . . ." Barnes hesitated, sketched a gesture toward his hat, glanced up quickly at John Fenno's window, looked suddenly bleak and turned away to cross the enclosure with his long, athletic stride.

The chief took his time and approached with his hat still on the back of his head and a thumb hooked through the belt which restrained his flabby girth.

Mark frowned. "I've been put in charge here."

"Yea, so they tell me. You want five of them bastids let inside the wire?"

"Yes. They're to come here to me. And chief, be careful when you take down the bars that the others don't rush you."

The chief grinned, but his oysterish eyes did not smile. "There's ways for doing these things, Mister. You watch and you'll learn something. They'll arrive scared. Wouldn't want you to get hurt." The look from the oyster eyes touched Mark's cravat, his slim, manicured fingers, his vest, his gleaming shoes. "If they start anything, all you have to do's give us a sign. Just raise your arm and the boys will move right in. Care how we handle 'em?"

"Not in the least. A lesson with the others watching . . ." Mark smiled. "Use your own judgment, chief. I'm sure it's excellent."

"Sure you ain't scared?" The chief let loose a sarcastic stream of tobacco juice on the bottom step and turned away without waiting for an answer.

To Mark, standing on the top step, the next few moments seemed interminable. The guards appeared to be forming a narrow aisle through which the five men must pass from the gate. It was a very narrow aisle, and the guards stood shoulder to shoulder but not so close that their club arms were hampered. Mark watched this maneuver with tense jaw muscles and was surprised to find that he was holding his handkerchief in his hand, drying his damp palms. He put away this betraying sign with haste.

The chief was right about there being a way of doing such things, and twenty years later it became so familiar that delegations of this sort were on their guard against it. Under cover of shouts of "Move on! Move on!" a man got a blow on a kneecap from a club, or a blow in the stomach which doubled him up and made the excuse to urge him on with another blow, perhaps on the point of his elbow but always hidden, even from the next man in line. Päkkä and three companions emerged from this cordon bewildered and angry, and stood in a group, waiting for the fifth man and feeling themselves in enemy territory, cut off by the fence from the protection of their friends.

The fifth man was Brodi and he was no more prepared for this assault than the others. He had, in fact, shepherded the others forward before entering the aisle himself. And to him the guards gave special attention, not because they knew who he was but because he was clearly not a laborer. Brodi emerged in considerable pain but outwardly undamaged. "Come on," was all he said to his companions, and he started off toward Mark, making a visible attempt to control his anger.

For some reason Mark had not considered the possibility of an encounter with Brodi and as he stood there, elegantly slim, he became a hollow shell, his spirit having fled in panic at the approach of this short and belligerent leader who had once been his friend.

Black Mike was in no mood for affability. "What the hell are you doing here? I thought you kept the books. Where's Hadley?"

"Hadley has turned over the handling of this—insubordination—to me." There was no reason for the lie except the vague notion that it might be made to serve Hadley more ill than the truth.

"I don't believe it."

"Damn it, I'm telling you. He's up in the office with the door shut!"

For a minute the five men stood below the steps and gazed up at Mark in silence. Brodi was considering the full extent of Hadley's perfidy and found himself not a little shaken by this action of an enemy whom he had been naive enough to trust. "I wouldn't have believed it of him," he said, to no one in particular.

Mark smiled, a chill and superior smile, and Mike, remembering suddenly their long years of friendship, flushed. Mark said, "We're wasting time, I believe. You're dealing with *me*," and waited for Brodi to make formal acknowledgment of the fact.

Brodi did no such thing. For the first time in his life he was really looking at the friend that the awkward college boy of long ago had admired for his fine manners, waistcoats and knowledge of the world. He made no conscious tabulation of what he saw then or later, but his words were the product of disillusion.

"I'll be damned if we'll deal with you, Mark. Get Hadley down here."

"Hadley is completely out of this."

"All right, then, I'll talk to Fenno."

"Oh, no, you won't."

"Who's to stop me—you?"

Brodi started up the steps.

Mark raised his arm.

The rest of it happened so fast that, afterwards, Mark was never quite clear about the sequence of events, as he afterwards denied with heat that he had given any signal to the guards. But Hadley saw it all from his window above. The guards were on the five men before they knew there was need to defend themselves. Clubs flew. Päkkä and Brodi and the others fought back, but the fight was too unequal and they were kicked, beaten and shoved toward the barrier. All this was in plain sight of the men on the other side of the wire and a great shout of anger arose. The rails of the improvised gate went down with a crash and the Finns poured into the enclosure. At once there was a mêlée of men and guards that rolled, like the crest of a tidal wave, across the enclosure toward Mark. And Mark couldn't face it. He fled.

He fled in panic with some half-formed idea of calling on John Fenno for help. His flight took him through the entrance doors and up the stairs, but before he reached the top he met Hadley descending precipitately with the light of furious rage in his eyes. Mark gave way to him, flattening himself against the wall of the stair well, but Hadley never paused, never gave him so much as a look.

The encounter brought Mark to his senses. He gazed after Hadley as Hadley burst out the door and hurled himself down the front steps and then, slowly, Mark himself descended. By the time he reached the bottom of the stairs there was a gleam in his eyes and a flicker of a smile on his thin red lips. He stood still, just safely inside the front door, and watched. Hadley was taking command. Hadley was issuing orders at the top of his voice, and the pleasant thought came to Mark that he need do nothing at all but enjoy the spectacle of Sam Hadley ruining himself irretrievably. The thought of his own position at the mill, unhampered by Hadley's presence, filled Mark with triumphant satisfaction and a smug complacency. No doubt he himself would have some explaining to do about why he had deserted his post, and he worried about that, but only briefly. He felt the surge of excited confidence that sometimes came to him when he was gambling and the luck was running strong. "Hell, it's a sure thing," he thought.

Hadley was yelling for Barnes and the chief. Mysteriously, Barnes was there, with a "Yes, sir," that betrayed his relief. The chief was retreating scientifically before the onset of the savage wave. Just out of reach of trouble, he was like a dog that barks and snaps at a frothing curler without getting his feet wet.

"We've got to stop this," Hadley said to Barnes, and then, in a shout to the chief, "Get your men out of this!"

"Huh?"

"Get 'em out. Stop the fight."

"Yea? It's all right by me—if we can. Where's the tailor's dummy? Gone to mama? Come on, boys—break it up—break it up. Cut it out, now—the boss says to quit fighting."

A fight of this sort is far easier to start than to stop. The chief's words had little effect, and Hadley and Barnes resorted to the more direct means of grabbing the guards and hurling them out of the fight. It was this more than anything else, the unaccountable sight of Hadley and Barnes apparently fighting on their side, that slowed down the ferocity of the Finns and finally brought the fight to a precarious halt.

The guards were gathered in a belligerent knot, facing a ragged group of strikers that clustered around Brodi and Päkkä as though these two were the magnetic force that held them all together. Hadley stepped forward. The two sides were shouting distance apart now and Hadley shouted.

"Brodi—there's been a mistake here. Order your men back behind the fence and I'll tell you exactly what happened. I told you I'd fight this clean and I meant it."

Brodi stared at him with a black look of anger. After a minute he said something to Päkkä, who turned and faced the men, yelling unintelligible things and gesturing toward the fence with arms and head and shoulders. After some urging and with many backward glances the men began to straggle off. Brodi waited long enough to see them in definite motion and then he turned to find Hadley near him.

"All right, what have you got to tell me, you double-crossing bastard?"

Without waiting for an answer, Brodi swung on him and swung again before Hadley's guard was up. In a second more they were fighting with a deadly grimness and a bitterness made the more intense because of the spontaneous liking each had taken for the other. Each fought to inflict on the other his own hurt and the spectators, the guards, the Finns, the office workers at the windows and the Sons of Vulcan at their private barricade cheered with surprise and delight to find themselves watching a good fight. No one saw anything of the grief that makes a man want to inflict bodily injury on an idol who has fallen.

The blows landed hard. Both men were experienced fighters and they were well matched. Hadley had the great advantage of size and reach, but speed and the surprise attack were on Brodi's side. Hadley's recent sedentary life had not improved his wind, but Black Mike, accustomed to sparring matches with his students, was in excellent trim. These factors balanced out; the spectators recognized it and cheered, and the fight went on, each man trying, and with science, to inflict the maximum damage on the other but fighting as fairly as though there were a referee watching over them.

The fight stretched out and the blows, though placed as well as in the beginning, were slower in coming. They were as forceful as ever, but on both sides there was more effort behind their force. Hadley's breathing became labored and Black Mike, with a cut over his eye which oozed blood, was forced to shake his head frequently to clear his vision. The blows became even more widely spaced and the watchers could see both men breathing hard.

Black Mike went down. He was on his feet instantly, and the blow he aimed at Hadley had renewed power. It caught Sam on the shoulder and spun him around so that he lost his balance and went to his knees. It was the last blow Black Mike had in him and the weight of it carried him down also.

Hadley got to his feet, not quickly, and using both hands to help himself off the ground. He stood there, a little bent, shaking his head as though he were dazed. Mike pushed himself with difficulty to his knees. Hadley looked around as though his vision had cleared, grinned suddenly and held out a helping hand to Mike. The watchers cheered.

Mike took the hand and hoisted himself up, wiped the cut with his arm, and then he too grinned, warmly and broadly. "That's the best fight I was ever in. And say, look here, fella—I'm sorry for the language I used. I don't understand what happened but I'm damned if I don't think that somehow or other Mark and Fenno engineered the whole thing." He held out his hand and Hadley took it.

"I'm damned if I know what happened either, but if you'll come around the corner with me to that joint at the end of Mill Street and have a glass of beer, I'll tell you what I *do* know."

None of this was audible to the watchers, but seeing a good fight over and a draw, they continued to cheer, none the less enthusiastically for being somewhat confused about issues and outcome. Hadley and Mike walked rather solemnly together toward the fence. Someone took down the bars for them and they found themselves surrounded by yelling but friendly Finns. Brodi had to submit to back-slapping from an enthusiastic Päkkä.

"Damn fine fella, Mike. You lick 'em. You lick 'em all. Goddamn fine fight Mike, I tell ya!"

"I guess I didn't win, Päkkä, but I'm going to talk this out with Hadley. Just keep the boys here and keep 'em quiet. Don't let them start anything. I'll be back."

Somebody handed Brodi his coat and helped him into it. Hadley wondered vaguely where his was—back in his office, probably. "To hell with mine," he said. "Let's go."

They walked in silence until they came to the saloon, in silence pushed open the swing doors, scuffed across the sawdust on the floor and sat down at a stained table, smiling and making no attempt to conceal their exhaustion. The beer was put in front of them by a barkeep who showed no surprise at their battered condition, as though such things were usual. Hadley took a tremendous draw, said "Ah!" and, leaning across the table, began to speak earnestly.

"All I know about this mess is that just after your Finns started coming up the bank I was relieved from duty by Fenno. . . ."

"Relieved from duty!"

"Yea, from duty connected with the strike. Seems Mark saw us shaking hands on the stairs and he went and told the Old Man we were fixing something up. I told him what it was—that we just agreed to fight fair and shook on it, but he seemed to think there was some kind of treachery. So Mark put in his oar—said I wasn't a fit man to run the strike—and got himself put in my place. That's all—or all of any importance, except that I went to a front window and watched things. But I could only see part of it from where I stood. I saw all hell break loose. What happened anyway? What set them off? The guards were swinging clubs at you fellows, so I said to hell with Fenno and got there as quick as I could. Then you swung on me!" Sam grinned reminiscently.

Mike grinned in response, but he did not reply at once. He gazed pensively at the yellow tile gutter under the brass rail by the bar. Water flowed in this small moat from a lead spout at one end, but too feebly to wash away the quids of tobacco which spotted the yellow tiles here and there. The bartender polished glasses, and sucked his teeth, and put the glasses among the bottles on the glittering shelves behind the bar. He paid no attention to Sam and Brodi. The brackets on Mike's forehead were deeply furrowed and his stiff brush of black hair looked dusty. The cut over his eye was beginning to swell.

"Mark is a bastard," he said judicially, and sighed for a lost illusion. "You know, I used to think he was about the smartest and most polished man there was. That was back in college days. He had a different suit for every day in the week, and I had just two pairs of pants and had to wear a lumberman's jacket to classes to save my one coat. And he could play the piano and speak French, and he got invited to all the Beacon Hill houses. He's smart, all right, and it's taken me all this time to see through him. I wonder if Fenno ever will. Well, anyway, this is what happened."

Mike told his tale. More beer came and when he had drained the glass, Mike grinned at Hadley. "I shouldn't think your position with Fenno was so good at this moment."

"Hell, no, I'll probably be fired in the morning. If I'm not, I'll quit. I don't like the finances of the Company anyway. The directors are a bunch of dummies preening themselves because they're big guns, thanks to Fenno—all but Thatcher and maybe Cushing, that is. Fenno himself is living back somewhere before the war, thinking it's his own genius and not the country's prosperity that has brought him so far."

"It is his genius in a way."

"It may have been, six, eight years ago, but Goddamn it, times change and fast. He's an autocrat. Hell, if I'm not fired, I'll quit."

"What will you do?"

"God knows. There's no hurry about things—I've got a stake. But let me tell you this—I'll find a way of paying Mark and Fenno back, if it's the last thing I do."

19

H ADLEY shoved back the sheet, raised himself a little and said,
"Huh?"

"Time to get up, Mr. Hadley."

"Oh, yea. Thanks, Mrs. Adams."

He rolled over on his back and put his hands behind his head. No
particular hurry about getting up *this* morning. "Either I'm fired or I
quit," he thought, "and I don't give much of a damn which it is." A
sense of freedom and well-being filled him. He lay on his back, luxuri-
ating. "It's like when school is over for the year and you chuck your
books in the cupboard and run out into the sunshine with a shout—
that's a hell of a way to feel when you're out of a job and don't know
what you're going to do next." He let the pleasant sensation seep
through him.

After a while his feeling of freedom began to be superseded by
anger against Fenno and Mark. Grumbling, he threw off the sheet
and rose, discovering as he did so that he was stiff and sore in various
places as a result of his fight with Brodi. He crossed the floor in his
bare feet, shut the door into his sitting room and dressed slowly, with
angry, emphatic movements. Presently he heard sounds on the other
side of the door which indicated that breakfast was being set out on
his table.

He waited until the sounds abated before he strode in. Steam was
rising from the quantity of birdbath-shaped dishes on the table. He
jabbed his napkin in the second button of his vest and shook out the
newspaper. He was fighting mad and it would have been a pleasure to
pick a quarrel and land a blow on somebody's jaw. He glanced at the
newspaper and bit into a muffin that seemed to have no taste whatever,
and with no mental transition found that it was Willoughby with
whom he was angry, Willoughby to whom he would like to do violence

and whom he wanted with an intensity of desire that made his body ache.

Throwing down the remains of the muffin, he began rapidly cleaning up the contents of the various dishes. "Willoughby, damn her eyes. That's one piece of unfinished business that's not going to be left that way. Christ, she won't even talk to me now I'm out of a job. *Oh, yes, she will. Goddamn it, I'll take care of her!*" He rose, kicked the chair violently out of the way and pulled out his watch. Time to go. Time to go and be fired and tell them all to jump in the lake. He went into his bedroom to get his hat.

His route led through Mill Street but, before turning into the home grounds of the enemy, he hesitated. The place seemed quiet enough, though most everybody appeared to be out on the street or in the front yards. This was obviously not an ordinary day in Mill Street. They were gathered in groups in the road and leaning on fences and sitting on steps, and Hadley's quick survey noted the men that were present. "So the devils aren't at work," he thought, forgetting in his interest and indignation that it was no concern of his. Their attitude toward him, he reflected, might quite possibly be ugly. "Hell, I don't want a fight *that* bad." Then the belligerency of his mood overcame his caution and he started down the street. He walked like a man minding his own business, and as he passed the houses he kept his eyes down, but there was that in his manner which advertised that he would swing on the first man who tried to interfere with his progress.

He took pains not to hurry. His passing created a sensation, though since he knew no Finnish, he had not the slightest idea what they were saying. "They sound like a bunch of monkeys," he thought. A yellow dog with coarse, bristly hair came out of a gate and walked beside him like an escort. He felt the eyes of all those he had passed turn on him. It made the back of his neck prickle.

Their voices did not sound ugly, if you could judge anything by that heathenish sound. Somebody called out something which he thought might be intended for English. "Well, by God," he thought, "I believe the devils are friendly. What the hell? Maybe they liked the fight." He looked around and a girl standing behind a fence smiled at him. He grinned back and she turned away in shy confusion. Two or three of the older women called out to him. "Hell!" he thought, "I'm a hero!" He walked the rest of Mill Street, feeling the buoyant sensation of personal popularity.

When he left Mill Street behind, he found it easy to be mad at these

Finns again, for the enormity of their walking out of a job of work that had to be done seemed to him little less than an outrage. "With the boat right there, waiting to be unloaded. What does Brodi see in them? Stupid bohunks that you have to yell at, like a mine mule. What makes Brodi think they deserve anything better than they've got? Hell, they've got houses and women. You have to fight for what you get in this world—be smart and a fighter—and if you aren't you don't deserve to get it. Look at me and dad. We were smart and we fought until the land turned out to have ore. And nobody was sorry for us— we'd have busted their Goddamn face in if they was." Hadley began to sweat a little, thinking about it. "And when we were out of jobs we didn't think we had a *right* to a job, like Brodi says—we just hustled around till we got one and beat the next man to it because we were smarter. That's the way to live. That's the way life is."

When the lake was in plain view, he slowed his walk and scanned the bright water automatically for sails. There were none, but the breeze was pleasantly cool and he took his hat off, liking the feel of it in his hair. A little farther on he saw the new wire fence around the mill gleam in the sunlight. "Place looks like a prison." As he passed the shop, the clankings and boomings and hiss of steam came out of the building where the Sons of Vulcan were at work. "We'll be having trouble with those fellows next," Hadley thought, forgetting. Near the office building the guards were very much in evidence but no dock hands stood by the fence. The bank was littered with papers as though a Fourth of July celebration had taken place here. Hadley looked down at the docks, but they seemed deserted except for a single figure sitting on a pile of timbers. "Barnes?" A rope ladder hung over the side of the ore boat but she, too, appeared to be deserted.

He stopped walking and looked the whole place over. The mill and everything about it had become very familiar, and it gave him a queer sensation coming back like this as an outsider, queer and not in the least pleasant. He felt as though the place belonged to him, as though they had no right to take it away from him. "The Goddamn sons-of-bitches," he thought, and feeling this epithet inadequate, he shut his teeth hard.

The chief came sauntering toward him. "Morning, Mr. Hadley. Say—I got orders to go to Mr. Fenno's office ten o'clock. Anything up?"

"Probably. I couldn't say."

"I been waiting for you. What you want us to do about them bastids?"

"Nothing now. Wait till you see Fenno."

Hadley climbed the steps. "It's the last time," he thought, "I'll never be going in this door—maybe," and at the thought of the injustice and all he was losing thereby, the full force of his anger returned to him and he mounted the stairs fighting mad.

He strode into Fenno's anteroom and slung his hat on a chair. At sight of him Flint scrambled to his feet and placed himself dramatically in front of Fenno's door.

"You can't go in there."

"The hell I can't." Hadley laughed, for it struck him that Flint looked like a virgin expecting to be raped.

"You certainly can't. Mr. Fenno . . ."

"Move over or I'll take you by the seat of those cute checked pants and chuck you out the window."

Hadley grabbed the door knob and, flinging the door open, burst into Fenno's office, his momentum carrying him halfway across the room before he stopped.

Fenno rose from his chair in all his frock-coated dignity. He looked like a portrait of himself, clear-eyed, straight-shouldered and distinguished.

"Mr. Hadley, I have to tell you that you are no longer a member of this organization."

"Yea? Well, let me tell *you* something." His voice was a shout.

"That will not be necessary. The interview is closed."

"Closed, hell!" Hadley grabbed a chair, banged it down, put his foot on it and rested his arm on his knee.

Fenno watched this coldly without moving, and Hadley, in spite of his boiling anger, felt that he had been a trifle too noisy. "All right," he said in a somewhat lower tone. "I won't argue about whether or not I work here, because if you don't fire me I quit. But there are some things I want to say."

"I am not interested in anything you have to say, Mr. Hadley. I tell you again to leave my office at once."

"Not till I've said 'em."

"It would give me pleasure to have you thrown out if there were anyone in the office capable of doing so."

Hadley gave a short laugh with no mirth in it. "Listen," he said, trying to return to his loud tones. He pointed a finger at Fenno, but he did not go on with what he was going to say. During this exchange Fenno had not moved a muscle, except to clasp his hands behind his back. He stood very straight, his jaw was set and his eyes were burning with anger. Something of the quality of the man and something of his dignity were borne in on Sam. "The Old Man's a gentleman anyway," he thought, and he dropped his hand back on his knee.

"Just let me say this, Mr. Fenno, and then I'll get out. For some reason I've got an interest in this shop—maybe because it's the first job like this I've ever had. Hell, I'm fond of it. . . ." Hadley's tone sounded as though he had made a discovery that caused him some surprise. "I've done a lot of thinking about it, and I believe you're making some serious mistakes that I'd like to tell you about."

This was not in the least what Sam had intended to say, but behind John Fenno's polished exterior there was a staunch integrity of attitude that robbed Sam of all desire to bluster. "He's wrong as hell," Sam thought, "but it's principle he's fighting for," and for some obscure reason this wiped out the last vestige of Sam's wrath. Fenno was speaking and Sam had missed part of it.

". . . my property, to manage in the way I see fit. What few stockholders there are have become so because they trust my judgment. Therefore, since the responsibility is mine, my orders must be carried out without question—and to the letter—by everyone here. On a number of occasions you have . . ."

"That's old ground, Mr. Fenno. It's agreed I quit. But I want to say this. You're too extended. These contracts with Cooke aren't paid up and there are a lot of other outstanding accounts. That's fine if business stays as hot as it is now, but if we have hard times, like some people seem to think . . ."

"That's a matter of opinion, Mr. Hadley."

"And another thing. We—you—the Company needs some specialists. Technical men to keep up on the new methods of making steel that are coming in so fast, and somebody who knows something about—I don't know how to say it—about labor, hard times, politics, things like that that affect business. This little labor trouble doesn't amount to *that*. The strike will fold up in a couple of days. But it's a symptom, maybe, of something bigger that's ahead of us and that we ought to be trying to find out about. And then there's this. Times are changing. You built up this business, but it's going to take different qualities than yours to keep in the swim the way things are getting to be. Competition is going to be tough. So tough it will have to be the chief concern of the head of a business like this. I've met a lot of younger men in iron and steel and they're like me, fighters, with no holds barred. You're a fighter too, but of a different sort. You're too much of a gentleman for what's coming—and so are all the men on your board but Thatcher."

"You seem to forget, Mr. Hadley, that I built this business up. During the war I foresaw the coming demand for iron. I saw clearly that the country would be clamoring for it and that the post-war expansion of industry would be like a tide—a tide which, taken at its flood—a tide in the affairs of men." John Fenno was speaking slowly and his eyes had a faraway look. Sam had the curious illusion that he was listening.

Abruptly Fenno turned his back on Sam and walked to the window. He stood with his back to the room, looking out, and his voice rose to its normal pitch. "As I say, I foresaw all this. When I returned after the war, I bought this property. I borrowed money again and again, and each time I did so the business grew and the loans were completely paid off."

Fenno came to a full stop and turned around to face Sam. His hands were still clasped behind his back. "I see no reason why I should justify myself to you, Mr. Hadley. The facts speak for themselves."

"I'll grant you the past, Mr. Fenno. It's the future I'm talking about."

"I think we can conclude this interview. I am not interested in what you have to say."

"All right, but I'm going to finish by saying that I'm one of those who's going to give you the competition I was talking about. I like the steel business and I'm going to stay in it. Right around here," he added, thinking about Willoughby. "You'll do everything you can to prevent that or to get me out one way or another. Fair enough. I don't blame you. I don't know yet what I'm going to do, but I'm smart and I'll get there, and when I do I don't expect any quarter from you and you can't expect any from me. We'll be in each other's way before many years and we'll fight it out."

"For the last time, Mr. Hadley, will you leave my office!"

Sam took his foot off the chair and suddenly he smiled. "So we're enemies, Mr. Fenno, or will be. Will you shake on it?" He held out his hand.

John Fenno said nothing at all, nor did he take his hands from behind his back, and his eyes continued to regard Sam with the same burning hostility. Sam shrugged and left the office. Resentment and much of his original anger filled him, and he resisted with difficulty a childish impulse to relieve his feelings by slamming the door. He picked up his hat. Flint was bent over his desk, very red in the face.

"The little sneak was probably listening," Sam thought, and started toward his own office to collect his things. He stopped by the stairs with his hand on the rail. There was nothing in his office that he wanted— nothing that belonged to him but a few pencils. "Leave 'em for the next guy." He was curiously loath to go into his office again because of an unformulated fear that the ink spot on the floor, the torn blind and the scratches on the desk top made by the heels of his shoes would prove too articulate. The stiffness in his joints did not seem to have been helped by his walk, and he began to be aware of a headache. The trouble was, he felt more like smashing something than going peacefully on his way.

A door opened behind him and light steps hurried down the hall. Sam did not turn around and the steps stopped suddenly and then retreated, almost running. That would be Mark—scurrying back to the safety of his office like a fox to his lair. Hadley did not turn around but every muscle in his body tightened. "If that bastard had said one word . . ." After a minute he started down the stairs, letting his weight land heavily on each step.

Out in the air and sunshine something of a burden seemed to have been lifted from his shoulders and he felt detached enough to be astonished and a little amused that he had let Mark escape without a good thrashing. "I wouldn't have done that a year ago. All this high society must be getting me.

"Well, that's that," he said, half aloud, and started off briskly, as though he had some idea where he was going. This business of having nothing special to do was, at the same time, both pleasant and unpleasant. He thought about going to see Willoughby but—"Hell, you can't go call on a lady in the morning. She's probably not even up." But there was also a feeling which he could not have explained that he wanted her to hear he was no longer with the Company, before he saw her again. He didn't mind telling her—it was rather that he wanted to give her time to decide what her attitude toward him would be. He felt that he might even enjoy dealing with that attitude when he saw her. "She'll probably try to slam the door in my face," he thought, striding purposefully along.

When he had walked as far as the horse-car route, he got on one and rode downtown. At the back of his mind was the idea that, when he got there, he might drop in to see Thatcher. It was not an intention, just a thought that could be decided on later. He got off the car in the center of town and looked around him as though he had never seen the place before.

General Thatcher would be pleased to see Mr. Hadley.

"Sit down, my boy, sit down. I'm glad to see you."

Thatcher reached out a hand across his table desk without rising. "He looks two feet taller in here," Sam thought, sinking into the chair across the desk that the General indicated. "I wonder why." Sam did not realize that the chair he was using had been put there rather than at the side of the desk precisely so that visitors could not see the General's dangling legs or the deep cushion on his chair. It was the same arrangement as in the General's library at home, and whether its greatest virtue was in impressing visitors with the little man's dignity or bolstering his self-esteem was a moot point. The General's smile hid the look of speculation in his eyes.

"You've come to see me about something to do with the mill, Sam?"

"Yes and no, General. Fact is, I'm not working there any more. I was fired—but if I hadn't been, I'd have quit."

"You don't say? How did that come about? I'm sorry to hear it— I really am." Hadley had the feeling that the General meant what he said.

"Well, sir, it's like this." Hadley told him the story of the strike. He did so in some detail, and he took pains to tell it exactly as it happened without coloring the facts in anybody's favor. He could not himself have said why he was trying to be so honest. Maybe it was because he wanted to look at things squarely himself and talking to the General helped. His brow was furrowed with his effort to be impartial, and he stared at a chocolate-colored rose on the General's elegant carpet while he talked, unaware of the keen interest with which the General studied him.

When he told about the fight, the General laughed and Sam glanced up quickly, puzzled, but the General made no comment and Hadley looked back at the burgeoning rose and went on with his story.

At the end of it Thatcher put his fingers together like a church steeple, in the immemorial way of people about to pass a considered judgment.

"I will have to say that I think Mr. Fenno was within his rights. After all, he does own the Company and so the responsibility is his. On the other hand, nothing is to be gained by violence."

The General's face assumed a serious expression and his eyes a faraway look, and Sam knew without anything being said that he was thinking about the war. He came back into the present as though he had shut a door on something. "I should say that Mark's talents were not along the lines of handling men. But that is neither here nor there. What do you propose to do with yourself now?"

"I haven't the slightest idea." Sam grinned broadly. "I'll stay in the iron and steel business, though."

"Take your time to look around, then. Don't hurry. You have quite a sizable account with us, if I remember rightly—enough to count heavily in your favor in making any new associations. Enough to set you up in a small way on your own."

"I nearly was in business for myself last year," Sam said reminiscently, and told Thatcher the story of the Lake Furnace Company.

The interest in the General's eyes deepened but the only comment he made was, "I always did think Fenno didn't tell the Board the whole story of that transaction." Then his voice took on the animation that told Sam the interview was at an end. "Well, Sam, anything I can do for you—anything the bank can do for you—let us know. Keep me posted about your plans. Come in any time. Any time. I'm really sorry you've left Fenno and Company, but never mind that now."

Sam stood up and the General reached across the desk to shake hands with him.

Out in the street Sam again had the feeling of aimlessness, and this time he was sure he did not enjoy it. "Imagine not having a thing you hafta do," he thought. "So now what? Go see some of the boys in the industry? No, let 'em come to me. They'll get the news I'm available fast enough," and Sam smiled at the face-saving euphemism. "Brodi. Sure—I promised him I'd tell him about the row with the Old Man. Now where did he say he was staying?" Sam began searching himself for the scrap of paper on which he had written the address.

Brodi, it developed, was spending the summer in a boarding house a notch or two down the social scale from Sam's own, but it was on a pleasant street, shaded by maples. The dense shade was grateful and Sam idled along. The street seemed strangely quiet, almost deserted, with only a few children and dogs about, and Sam wondered why until he remembered that almost his only experience of city streets was in the morning and evening when they were full of people either rushing to work or slowly coming home again. "Lord Almighty," he thought, "I mustn't take the first job that comes along just for the sake of being at work again."

Sam found Brodi upstairs, just shutting the door behind himself. His hat was in his hand.

"Hullo," Sam said. "Goin' out? I won't keep you. Just thought I'd look in since I promised to tell you the news."

"Hi, fella. Come in. I was just going to Mill Street but a few minutes won't make any difference. Come in."

They entered a shabby room that was chiefly occupied by a deal table that looked as though it might have been borrowed from the kitchen. The table was covered with papers and small white cards, such as are used in libraries, with neat writing on them. Even to the casual glance there was order in the mass, as though the undertaking were progressing along workmanlike lines.

"You been working, I see."

"Yea. It's a funny thing—you'd think if people *knew* how laborers lived—had the absolute, unarguable facts about their lives—that they'd get so indignant they'd do something about it. But now I'm not so sure they would. I don't know any other way to go about it, though, than to cram the facts down their throats. Mankind was certainly created with very little instinct for worrying about the misfortunes of others —and the more fortunate a man is personally, the less he concerns himself. Is there any news? Have you seen Mr. Fenno?"

"Yes, and he fired me before I had a chance to quit." Hadley swung a chair around and sat down.

"Fireworks?"

"No." Sam's tone was faintly astonished. "It's a funny thing—I was mad as hell at him when I went in, and I'm mad still when I think it over, but he's so damned dignified that you can't call him names the way you would an ordinary guy."

Brodi grinned. "Don't let it worry you. You probably got the idea across."

"What's new about the strike?"

"Nothing. I went back there after I left you yesterday. By that time the guards had orders to drive the men down the bank to the docks. They tried to do it, too, but most of 'em slipped through the line the guards made and just went home. Those the guards did round up had to work or get kicked around, but there weren't many of them. This morning Päkkä came around to see me and he said nobody reported for work. I'm going around to Mill Street now. He said the Finns on the dock at Farabee are out too—on their own. I didn't have a thing to do with that."

"You'll be licked."

"That may be."

"Then why did you stir up all this mess, anyway?"

"Same as I told you. Two reasons. There's a chance of getting better conditions, though I admit it's slim. There's a better chance that when the hard times hit, wages won't be cut, or not so badly, because of the trouble now."

"But you yourself?"

"Oh, I aim to make a career of bettering labor conditions. This was a poor sort of start, I admit, but the teaching is getting to seem more or less temporary. This is a start."

"There won't be much money in it, I should say."

"Not much."

A silence developed and Brodi, his brows deeply furrowed, stared out the open window at the encroaching maple leaves. Sam stared at Brodi.

"Do you know either of the Fenno girls?"

Brodi brought his gaze back inside the room. "Yes, both of them. One of them is quite a remarkable girl."

"I'll say she is! Jesus, what a gal!"

"Oh, I didn't mean that one."

"The other one? The one that looks like a wet kitten? What's remarkable about her, for Heaven's sake?"

Brodi told him the saga of the census of Mill Street, and Sam was clearly puzzled.

"I don't get it. In the first place, I'm damned if I can see why you care. They're just a lot of hunky laborers, anyway you look at it. And I don't see the sense of those questions anyway, but if Fenno finds out she's been meeting you on Mill Street, he'll have your blood—and hers too."

"Oh, the Mill Street part of the job is done."

"But you're still meeting her?"

"Oh, sure. She has a right to know how the compiling and the article are getting along. She's smart—I wish my students were half as smart. . . ."

"The other one, the one called Willoughby—now she's something." Sam was experiencing the common desire to talk about an infatuation.

"I don't like the type."

"Oh, you'd have to beat *that* out of her. I don't know why, but that gal gets me. She . . ."

Sam's voice was drowned by the long, eerie scream of a locomotive whistle. The roaring, rattling train rushed toward them, the violence of the noise swelling until it seemed to fill the little room, shaking it, bursting it apart and then draining out slowly leaving the atmosphere shattered.

"Jesus! I didn't realize you were that near the tracks, Brodi. How do you get any work done?"

"It is disturbing."

"Say, why don't you move over to my place? There's an empty room, I think, and Mrs. Adams keeps things so quiet even the dog barks in a whisper."

"I might, at that."

Suddenly they were both embarrassed, as though they each recognized that acquaintanceship and liking were on the point of changing into friendship, and the acknowledgment of this fact made them self-conscious. Neither was sure, now that the issue had suddenly and mysteriously formulated itself, that he wanted the invasion of his mental privacy that friendship implied.

Mike said, a little stiffly, "You're probably too high-toned for me."

"We're not high-toned." Sam stood up and picked up his hat. "Well, I'll be going. Hope I didn't keep you."

"No. Awfully glad you came in. I hope you'll do it again."

They walked downstairs together to the front door, slowly, as though reluctant to leave each other's company. At the door they came to a halt.

"If you haven't anything better to do when you finish on Mill Street, why don't you just walk over to my place and *look* at that room?"

By mid-afternoon Sam decided that Brodi was not coming and he was strangely disappointed. "I like that guy," he told himself. "Damned if I don't." Sam was miserable. He had read everything in his rooms, done his accounts and made a desultory effort to straighten up his bureau drawers. Now there was nothing to do but just sit, or go out—and there was no place to go.

When someone pounded on his door, he knew at once that it was Brodi and he jumped up and threw it open.

"Hullo. I'd given you up." Then, noticing an air of excitement about Black Mike, he said, "What's happened? Come in."

"By God, we're going to get *something* out of them." Mike threw his hat on the table and sat down.

"You don't say? You don't mean to tell me Fenno's given in?"

"No, not yet, but he will!"

"I don't believe it!"

"Well, listen. You know the other concerns in town which have ore docks don't like Fenno any too well. They're afraid of him. The shipping companies hate him too since he started building his own ships. Well, listen to this. When I got to Mill Street I found two of their men and a man from Farabee offering thirteen cents to the Fenno hands. Same hours but a cent an hour raise. They were hiring them right and left, though the Farabee fellow told me that they didn't really need the men—just wanted to put Fenno in a spot so he'd be short of ore at the end of the season and would have to buy from them or the shipping companies at fancy prices—and believe me, they'll hold him up."

"Well, for gosh sake! Somebody ought to have figured something like that would happen. *I* ought to have!" Hadley laughed. "Fenno can't afford to lose those men. He'll have to meet the raise. So what then?"

"Then I went and got hold of Barnes and told him what was happening. When I left he was heading for Fenno's office on the double quick. Fenno can hold his own men if he doesn't do any more than meet the new wage though, because their homes are near the mill."

Both men fell silent and stared at each other eloquently.

20

"OH, WILLOUGHBY, you're not taking the carriage *again?*" Matild's voice came complainingly down the stair well.

Willoughby's mouth drew to a hard line and she jerked at her gloves, pulling them on, but she said nothing.

"Willoughby, do you hear me? When Lettie goes out . . ." Matild's voice took on the dreary sing-song in which she carried on the accounts of her grievances. "She never takes the carriage, and you're always out, both of you." Matild sounded as though she might be going to cry.

Willoughby picked up her purse from the hall table and moved soundlessly, save for the rustling of her taffeta pleats, toward the front door. *"Oh, why doesn't she shut up!* Just because she wants to drive out in the country and buy currants from that woman. She can buy her old jellies from somebody else, already made."

On the front steps a wave of summer heat engulfed Willoughby and added to her irritation. She had no idea where she ought to go—where she was likely to find him. *"You'd think I'd meet him somewhere in two weeks of just driving around!"* Joe was drooping, half asleep on the box. He had been waiting some time in the hot sun.

"Joe!"

He straightened up slowly, taking his time about it.

"Where to, Miss?"

"Past the Union Club—and drive slowly when you get there."

She raised her ruffled parasol with a whoosh of silk. He might be coming out of the club or standing on the lawn, talking, as so many of them did after lunch. She would just happen to notice him, with blue-eyed surprise, and offer to drive him back to the bank.

When she reached the Club, she saw many businessmen on the porch and talking in groups in front of the building. She looked them over with care. She even leaned forward to look, and her heart was beating fast, but there was no sign of General Thatcher. She was surprised to discover that her hands were trembling so that her parasol shook a little. There was Sam! Hadley saw her too and started to break away from the group of men he was with, but she gave him a bow of such distant formality that he flushed angrily and turned his back on her.

The carriage proceeded slowly down the Avenue and Willoughby was so lost in her own thoughts that she forgot to notice her surroundings. After a time Joe spoke with a tone of long suffering.

"Where to now, Miss?"

"Oh, let me see." Her hand went to her throat where it touched her string of pearls and she almost smiled at the idea it brought to her. "The bank, please. And hurry."

The pearls would be a good excuse. *"I was just leaving my pearls in the vault, General. Is it really you? I am so glad to see you."* She planned the meeting in detail down to the least flutter of her eyelashes, but beyond the first meeting her mind did not go. From there on she would rely on charm, and she had no doubt—no, not any doubt at all —that it would serve her well. There must be, and of course there would be, some explanation for his long silence and for his odd behavior that day their carriages passed wheel to wheel.

When she came out of her day dreams, she found that the carriage was turning down an unimpressive side street.

"Joe, why don't you keep on the Avenue? I don't want to go down here."

"Avenue's torn up, Miss, next block."

"All right, then, since we're heading that way anyway, drive me down to the lake and back." "He might not have finished lunch," she thought. "I'm early for my appointment," she added aloud to stop Joe's curiosity.

The streets they drove through were pleasant and tree-shaded, but the houses were not as good as those on the Avenue or some of the other streets that ran from east to west. Willoughby knew nobody who lived in them. Most of the women seemed to have been driven out to their front porches by the heat, and Willoughby enjoyed the sensation which she and the beautiful carriage caused. She was as aware of every detail of that picture as though she were one of the onlookers. The silver on the harness, Mince and Docket's perfectly matched coats, her own graceful and languorous pose, even the Dalmatians trotting by the rear axle, all pleased and relaxed her and dulled the edge of her driving worries. She arched her wrist in its lavender glove over the handle of her tiny parasol and tilted her head slightly to improve the line of her profile. She found even more pleasure in impressing those she considered her inferiors than those of her own social class.

When the street reached the bluff above the lake, it made a loop and returned into itself. In the center of this loop, civic spirit had created a plot of grass, two crescent-shaped beds of wind-blown petunias, a shade tree of sorts and a bench. A man and a girl sat on the bench, their backs toward the approaching carriage. They sat rather close together, for one end of the bench was taken up with a pile of books, and the man was apparently reading aloud to the girl. As Willoughby looked idly at them they appeared to find something funny in the reading, for they turned toward each other and laughed merrily like people certain of enjoyment in each other's company.

"Why, it's Lettie!" Willoughby forgot her graceful pose in her astonishment—"and that Mr. Brodi!"

"Joe, stop," she said imperiously and in a hoarse stage whisper as though they might hear her. "Don't go any farther. Turn right around here—and hurry."

She watched the two with held-in breath while Joe was turning around in the narrow street, but they were too absorbed to see anything but themselves. Willoughby sank back against the cushions. "The little *sneak*. So that's the way she goes to the library for a book!" Willoughby felt highly outraged. "I'll fix *her*." A smoldering kind of anger burned in her all the way to the bank, and with it a memory of the happy look on Lettie's face that hurt her as much as though it had been an intentional mockery of her own unhappy state.

There were always loiterers around the door of the bank. Willoughby swept past them as though they were not there, but she felt their glances traveling all over her and she had the gratifying thought that she was like a beautiful queen that men hungered for but could not reach. The queenliness was still in her manner when she looked around the lobby, picked out a man at a desk who seemed to be some sort of manager, and walked haughtily toward him.

"I am Miss Fenno. I want to see General Thatcher, please."

The manager rose and bowed, as though being spoken to by Miss Fenno were an honor.

"If you wouldn't mind waiting, Miss Fenno? He is engaged just now and it may be a little while. Perhaps you have some other business in the bank you could attend to while he finishes?"

"I'll leave these, I think." Willoughby touched the pearls with one finger and moved off, rather grandly to hide her excitement, toward the part of the bank which housed the safety-deposit boxes. This was at the end of a long corridor and one of the doors on that corridor led, she thought, to General Thatcher's office. All these doors were shut.

She left her pearls and came back, loitering. Just as she passed one of the doors it swung open suddenly. A man with a lawyer's bag under his arm was hurrying out, but Willoughby paid no attention to him, for she found herself looking into a very ornate office and straight at General Thatcher, who was sitting in a high-backed chair behind a long table. Their eyes met. Willoughby made a gesture of pleased surprise and started forward, but instantly the General dropped his eyes to the papers before him as though he had not seen her, and then the strange man with the lawyer's bag shut the door. She was left alone staring at its walnut panels.

The snub was plain. Whatever lingering hope there may have been in her mind after the previous rebuff, it was now dispelled. Pain and despair and hurt pride overwhelmed her. Until this minute she did not know how much she had counted on the General and his wealth and his position. She felt as though her whole world were in ruins and she saw the panels of the door blurred and distorted through her tears.

Steps in the corridor behind her brought her to herself. Some men passed her, hurrying. They both glanced at her, but she kept her head turned away and groped blindly in her flounced cuff for her handkerchief.

She went into the lobby of the bank with her head held high, and she would have walked past the manager's desk without stopping, but he rose and stood waiting for her.

"Excuse me, Miss Fenno. I was misinformed. General Thatcher is not in the bank. Would you care to leave a message?"

"No, certainly not!"

She walked down the steps and through the group of loiterers without even being aware of them. She climbed into the carriage, flounced down on the fawn-colored cushions and raised her parasol with such a vicious gesture that the silk of the lining split. Angrily, she threw it on the floor.

"Take me home. The shortest possible way." She wanted more than anything in the world to be alone, away from curious eyes, able to give vent to the emotions which filled her.

For once Willoughby let herself in with her key, and she went upstairs treading as lightly as she could. She was in no mood to see anybody. She felt as brittle as thin ice and so little in control of herself that she felt she might go all to pieces if she had to contend with the slightest thing. The whole world seemed turned against her, and Willoughby, who never in her life had felt defeated, now had no more fight left in her. She shut the door of her room, pulled off her hat and threw it with her purse and gloves on a chair. The hat slipped to the floor and she let it stay there. She went to the windows and closed the folding shutters until the room was as dim as twilight. Then she threw herself across the bed and lay face down. She did not cry; she did not even think coherently. She simply gave herself up to hatred and despair.

After a long time she heard the front door slam and knew that her father had come home. He called her name from the hall below but she did not answer. He did not call again and, listening, she heard the distant slamming of the study door. She rolled over on her back and pushed her hair off her forehead and rubbed her cheek where the pattern of the counterpane had made a red mark. Then she stiffened and lay rigid, for a strange sound was coming from the next room. Someone was singing. Willoughby raised herself on one elbow to listen. The voice was clear and fresh, and the melody as burbling and happy as a summer brook. There was unmistakable joy and love of life in the singer. Lettie! How strange that Lettie, the dreary, frightened soul, should sing like that!

Willoughby felt the strangeness as an affront. She slid to the edge of the bed and stood up and, as she listened behind her closed door, this happiness was nearer to breaking her down into tears of grief and self-pity than anything else. She did not let herself cry but she nursed the vindictive anger which began to boil up in her. She opened her door and slipped out into the hall. Lettie's door was open and Willoughby stood unseen and watched her. Lettie was sitting at her dressing table, tidying her hair with little pokes and pats, and Willoughby caught glimpses in the mirror of a radiant smile. The song broke off and Lettie pulled three daisies carefully out of a vase on the dressing table and tried them in her hair, first here, then there, studying the effect.

The daisies finished it. Willoughby could stand no more. Disheveled as she was, she went down the stairs, moving quickly and with a purpose, but walking as though she were on thin ice. She opened the study door a little way and put her head in.

"May I come in, Papa?"

John Fenno lowered his newspaper and his features softened.

"Yes, yes. Come in. I called you but I got no answer. I thought you were out gadding."

"No, Papa. Listen." Willoughby sat down on the edge of the tufted sofa and rubbed one of its cobble-like bumps with the palm of her hand. The sofa made her think of Mark and the thought passed quickly through her mind that she would have to see Mark soon.

"Papa—you'll have to do something about Lettie. She's been meeting that Mr. Brodi in secret."

Anger replaced the tempered geniality of Fenno's expression. The effect was rather like the rolling up of majestic, dark thunderheads.

"How do you know this, Willoughby?"

"I saw them today—down by the lake sitting on a bench together. He had his arm around her," she added untruthfully. "I've been suspecting for some time that something or other was up, but I didn't know what it was or of course I'd have told you at once. I think that's pretty disgraceful. Don't you, Papa? She told Mama she was going to the library."

John Fenno uncrossed his legs and stared in angry silence at nothing. Willoughby plucked at a button of the couch. The button came off in her hand, and she looked at it in surprise and threw it on the floor.

"What are you going to do about her, Papa?"

"What? Oh—send your mother to me. His interference at the mill was bad enough, but this . . ."

Willoughby rose with alacrity. She was feeling very much better, as though she had things in her grasp once more. On the stairs she met Lettie with the daisies in her hair and gave her a look of loathing. She opened the door of her mother's room without knocking and Matild, who was sitting in her chair doing nothing, started guiltily.

"Father wants to see you. Right away." Willoughby spoke as she might to a bad child who was being sent off to receive a spanking, and she smiled when she saw the alarm flare up in her mother's eyes. Then she went into her own room and, sitting down at her little desk, wrote a note to Mark. When the note was sealed and handed to Ellen to give to Joe for immediate delivery, she merely sat, waiting and listening. After a time Matild came stumbling up the stairs, sobbing and gasping.

Willoughby and her father had dinner alone that night, and Willoughby sat in her mother's chair. John Fenno alternated between gloomy abstraction and an attempt to convey to her by a sort of somber pleasantness of manner that he felt gratitude to her for being unlike her sister and her mother. He even stood aside to let her precede him into the drawing room for coffee and, drinking quick sips from his little cup, told her things about the mill, taking her into his confidence, talking to her like an equal.

"That fellow, Brodi, is a ruffian," he said, setting his cup back in the saucer with a smart clatter just as the door bell rang. "Who can that be?"

"Mark, dear. He's coming to see me."

"Mark seems to be doing all right as Secretary but I would just as soon you didn't give him too much encouragement until he's been at it a little longer."

"It's been more than a year, hasn't it?"

"Yes, but it takes more than that for a man to prove himself. I wasn't wholly satisfied with something he did during the strike, but he said he couldn't help himself. In other ways, I'll have to admit he's been a good Secretary. I'm going to my study."

He rose and Willoughby rose also. She slipped her arm through her father's and laid her head for an instant on his shoulder. In the hall they could hear Ellen opening the front door and Willoughby spoke in a low voice.

"I can handle Mark, you know. I always could, Papa. There are lots of advantages in someone you can handle, especially for a person like me. Remember that, dear."

Fenno gave her a swift, questioning look as though he suspected that she might mean more than her words said. He made motions with his lips, seeming about to speak, but he said nothing. How like himself she was—in her own way. And when she showed him affection as she was doing now, it seemed to fill his very bones with love for her. She patted his shoulder and gave him a little shove.

"Here's Mark. Go along, dear."

He went and she turned back to greet Mark, all smiles.

Mark had come in as though on a crest.

"Hullo, Willie. I got your note. Delighted—but I'm full of curiosity about why you asked me to come."

He reached out for her but she eluded him and went to sit down at the piano. She felt she could not look at him just now.

"I thought it might be nice to have some company." Her fingers began to wander over the keys.

"All right—fine, but don't play, my girl. If any playing is to be done, it's going to be done by me."

Willoughby brought her fingers down on the keys in a crashing chord and launched herself into a spirited gavotte. After a few bars she stopped and began rapidly turning the pages of the music on the rack in front of her as though she were hunting for something. Then she spoke over her shoulder, and her voice was high and a little breathless and unlike her ordinary tones altogether.

"I really asked you to drop in because I thought we might announce our engagement—if I can get father's approval. We might announce it on my birthday."

"Willie!"

"For the love of *God* don't call me Willie! That's weeks away and everything depends on him anyway. I think I can bring him around, all right, though he won't like it, so you'd better leave him to me. He told me tonight he's going to New York in a couple of days and I think it would be smart to wait until he gets back before I say anything. You might be quietly looking for a ring, though. A big one."

21

WILLOUGHBY drove to the depot to see her father off, and as he was about to get out of the carriage, she patted his hand affectionately.

"Good-bye, Papa dear. Bring me something nice from New York."

He got out of the carriage and turned to look at her. How pretty and all-of-a-piece she looked, sitting there, and suddenly his affection for her stirred him almost intolerably so that he longed to give it some expression, but he only gazed at her silently for a moment.

"Don't keep the horses standing on the hill," he said finally. "Don't hitch, Joe. I'll carry my own bags." Without more words he turned into the wooden Bridge of Sighs that led to the tracks.

His bag was the least of the burdens that John Fenno carried to the train. The foremost of these was worry about the new order for rails that had come in without any payment for the old—the reason why he had this hot and disagreeable trip ahead of him. Cooke. The fellow was never there, and doing business with what Thatcher called "that crowd" was like fighting a man who kept leaping away from your blows. "Hitting air," Fenno murmured, and was suddenly a victim of the memory of his elation on that private train. That had come to be a bitter memory which he put away from himself whenever he could.

The porter was taking his bag and saying something deferential about the heat. Fenno followed him down the aisle of the stuffy car without comment and sat down stiffly on the green plush seat, his hands resting on his knees. A bad time to be taking this trip, leaving Mark cock of the walk. Fenno refused to admit even to himself that he missed Hadley, but the plain truth was that Mark, now filling Hadley's place, was not making an able general manager, though he had done well enough as Secretary. "The young popinjay gives himself too many airs," he thought. "More interested in his own authority than in getting things done. Causing antagonisms where none existed before."

And dock hands were suddenly scarce. Barnes said that his competitors were to blame. Maybe—but probably it was that fellow, Brodi . . .

Brodi and Lettie. Fenno's mind shifted to another anxiety. That business was Matild's fault, really. Couldn't she see what was going on under her nose? His grievances welled up in him as they always did when he thought about Matild, filling him with bitterness. After a time he gave a profound sigh and, taking out his watch, held it in his hand, waiting to see if the train started on schedule.

Back at the Fenno house Matild also was filled with bitterness. She watched from Lettie's customary place in the window as the carriage departed for the train, and the minute it turned into the avenue she dropped the curtain and made for the stairs. As a usual thing, Matild's angers were like the spluttering of a damp firecracker, ineffectual and soon over. But for the past two days her resentment had been kept alive by Willoughby's jibes and John Fenno's silences, and in addition to her anger there was a deep, festering hurt because of the alliance of these two against her.

As she pulled herself laboriously up the stairs by the hand-rail, however, a kind of triumph superseded her anger. They were gone and, for an hour or so, she would have the house to herself, she and poor Lettie, shut in her room. Poor Lettie. To be secretly on Lettie's side gave Matild the feeling of getting back at "them." She had not seen Lettie or even spoken to her through the door for two days, but she had a pleasantly miserable feeling that they were martyrs together. As she climbed the stairs she panted a little from the excitement of her defiance.

She went straight to Lettie's door and threw it wide. "You may as well come out. They've gone." Her tone spoke more of her defiance than of her pity.

Lettie came to the door looking as though she had no more tears to shed, and stood there doubtfully and a little vaguely. Matild blinked at her. Lettie looked white and drawn, and she looked older. It was really this last that brought back to Matild with a rush all that she herself had suffered not only now but for years past and, staring at her daughter, her faded eyes swam with tears. Lettie, who had been focused nowhere, looked at her mother as through a clearing mist, astonishment at what she took to be her mother's sympathy taking the place of her own sorrows. Her face contracted with a sudden spasm of gratitude and she bent swiftly and kissed the little pouches in her mother's cheek. The action was so unexpected that it all but stopped Matild's breath.

She gazed at Lettie for an instant with slack mouth; then she covered her face with her hands and burst into sobs and, turning away, she stumbled clumsily toward her own room. It was with Lettie's arm around her that she sank into her little rocker.

Lettie knelt beside Matild and clung to her while Matild wept. Matild pulled Lettie's head down on her bosom, clasping her tightly and rocking back and forth, taking an almost hysterical comfort from the feel of her child's body in arms that had been empty for years. She patted her daughter as though it were Lettie who needed comfort, and brushed her hair away from her forehead and covered her face with kisses.

A year before Lettie would have shared her mother's tears, for then she had as much need as Matild for the love and comfort that would have resulted from bridging the gap between them. Now she no longer felt the little girl's desperate need for a mother's arms. But Matild did not realize any of this; to her Lettie was still that little girl.

After a while Matild's weeping died away into sobs that sounded peaceful and fulfilled, and Lettie pushed herself out of her mother's embrace and sat back on her heels.

"What are they going to do about me, Mama?"

"Oh, Lettie, we have to go to a resort soon's your father gets back—and leave *Willoughby* to run the house for him! Then you have to go to a country school in the East somewhere."

Matild saw Lettie stiffen under the shock of this news, but she paid no attention to that because she felt the urgings of a sudden curiosity, mixed with the astonishing discovery that her own daughter's plight was as romantic as any story book.

"Lettie, who *is* this man, dear?" There was no reply. "Lettie, your mother is speaking to you. I said, who *is* this man, dear?"

"Didn't Papa tell you?"

"No—that is, yes, I suppose he did, but I didn't quite catch the name and . . ." Matild did not want to finish her sentence by telling her daughter that, after the things John Fenno said to her she did not dare ask, not even at night in the dark when his long form was stretched out beside her.

"He's Michael Brodi, Mama. You remember him. He came here to breakfast with Mark about a year ago."

Matild drew down the corners of her mouth in thought, then she brightened. "You mean that man with the hair like a black doormat?

He made your father angry about something at breakfast. Do you like him very much, Lettie?"

"Very much, Mama."

"Well, dear, you'll just have to give him up. Your father would never let you . . ."

A stubborn expression settled on Lettie's face, and Matild regarded it with a look of strain.

"Now, now, dear. You mustn't make any trouble. You must be Mama's good little girl. Wasn't that the bell?" Fright sounded in Matild's voice. "It must be Willoughby back from the station. Oh, Lettie, get back to your room quick. Here, kiss me first."

Lettie scrambled to her feet and bent to kiss her mother, not on her pursed-up mouth but on her cheek.

"I won't give him up, Mama. You can send me away to school for years and years but I just won't."

She rushed back to her room and collapsed on the bed in tears, because she was suddenly overwhelmed by the futility of saying you won't give up something which you do not possess.

The ring at the front door signalled the arrival not of Willoughby but of Mark, come to endure the rigors of the sewing room cot once more in the interests of protecting the ladies. He passed his bag to Ellen with a curt, "Here, take it up," and went directly to the decanter of whisky on the dining-room sideboard. There Willoughby, returning, found him when he was halfway through his second drink.

"My bride!" he said, and raised his glass to her in a mocking salute. She stiffened and he saw that he had struck the wrong note. He set down his glass and took her in his arms and said in a different tone, "My dearest Willoughby." He kissed her gently and without passion in several places. Then he remembered something. "Tonight," he whispered, "in Uncle John's study?" He felt it was expected of him.

She disengaged herself and turned to leave the room. "No, not until we're married, Mark," she said over her shoulder. "If ever," she added. She sounded reproving and virtuous. He tossed off the rest of his drink in indignation. "To hell with her."

The next day Lettie went out. She went quite openly with her hat and gloves on, making no attempt to be stealthy, though she did pick a time when she felt pretty sure that she would not be seen. Because of her reconciliation with her mother it did not seem right to sneak out. The ethics involved in this were complicated, but ethics they were and on their account she walked slowly, though her heart was beating fast, and shut the front door with only a little less than the normal amount of noise. She did not draw a full breath, however, until she had turned the corner, and then she gave herself up to the tumult inside her. "Oh, Michael, Michael," her heart cried, and she hurried desperately.

The door of Mike's boarding house, which was also Hadley's, was opened by the kind of maid whom no amount of scolding could make to look anything but grubby, and that Mrs. Adams supplied the scoldings was evident in the girl's frightened, sullen air. She was about Lettie's own age, and she looked more accustomed to tramping through the dirt of a barnyard than across Mrs. Adams' spotless floors. She fixed her eyes on Lettie's scar. Lettie gritted her teeth but did not turn her head.

"Mr. Brodi ain't t'hum," the girl said firmly, and started to close the door in Lettie's face.

"Oh, wait a minute, please."

"Mrs. Adams ain't t'hum, either. Anyway, she don't allow no girls."

"I'm different. You can see that." Lettie tried the experiment of smiling at her. "This is your first job, isn't it?"

"Yes." Lettie's smile seemed to terrify her and she retreated a step, a strategic advantage which Lettie seized by advancing so that it was no longer possible to shut the door in her face.

"It's all right. I'll wait."

The scared look deepened. "There ain't no place to wait. Mrs. Adams don't allow nobody to use her sitting room."

"Then I'll wait right here in the hall." Lettie shut the door behind her with an air of determination.

"Land, Miss, I'm busy. I can't stay here and watch you."

"It's all right, I tell you. I won't steal the spoons," Lettie said grimly.

"Well—I got work to do." She left, with two or three doubtful backward glances, and presently the rattle of the stove shaker could be heard from the back of the house.

There was no place in the hall to sit down and the doors leading off it were shut. Lettie tried to think what to do, but all those shut doors and this strange place began to frighten her. Whenever she heard a noise from the street, she thought it was Mrs. Adams coming home. "Oh, Michael, please come," she whispered with desperate intensity. "Please come before Mrs. Adams does." And then the breathtaking thought occurred to her that if she could find Michael's room, she would be safe there. "At the back," he had said. "A little room upstairs at the back." She began to mount the stairs stealthily.

More shut doors and a long uncarpeted hall in which her steps sounded alarmingly. "They'll think I *am* stealing if they catch me," and the thought nearly sent her fleeing down the stairs again. "Michael, Michael, Michael," she whispered to herself over and over again, as though his name were a talisman to keep away harm.

She tried a door but it was locked. So were the second and the third, but the fourth yielded and she peered in. The room was very small indeed. It had just one window, a single chair, a camp bed that looked as though it might have been bought at a Quartermaster's sale of surplus Army goods, a boarded-up fireplace with a tiny stove in front of it, bright with its summer coat of blacking and, taking up most of the remaining space, a table. The table was pulled close to the window and littered with papers, and with a strange, sweet thrill of excitement she recognized her own writing on some of them.

She came softly into the room, shutting the door behind her. Just inside the door she stood still. Michael's room! His shoes under the chair, his clothes hanging on the wooden pegs, the dent in the pillow which his head had made. She looked all around her at everything, and she felt choked with emotion, a little like awe, a little like being alone in a church. The images broke up into rays and stars because she saw them through her tears. "Michael, Michael, I love you so." She stole across the room to the wooden pegs and, picking up the sleeve of a shirt, a rather dirty shirt that should have been in the laundry, she laid it against her cheek. Minutes ticked away while she stood there.

She did not hear Michael's step on the stair or his emphatic tread coming down the hall. The door flew open and she dropped the shirt sleeve. With his coming a little beauty departed and more reality moved in.

"*Michael!*" She ran to him and threw herself on him.

In that brief instant before he had to support her onset he had the impression of a thinner, whiter Lettie, who was intense to the breaking point. She was weeping wildly and talking in broken, incoherent phrases. Finding her here in this state was a shock to him, and he followed his first impulse without thought, which was to put his arm around her protectingly and let her cry. He could make nothing at all of what she was saying. Her arms were around his neck and her young body was pressed heedlessly against his. After a minute he stopped trying to listen to her, for he felt the warmth of her stealing through to him and he became aware of her firm young breasts and the long curves of her legs behind the wires of her hoops. His own body began to respond to her so that before he realized what he was doing, he was holding her close to himself, giving in to the feeling of her, letting her stir him.

He came to himself with a sense of shame and astonishment. "Jesus, she's only a kid." And he tried to loosen her arms and to look into her face for confirmation of her innocence of purpose, which he knew needed no confirming.

He found it, the wet, griefstricken look of a hurt child and, unreasonably, he himself felt hurt and put in his place and mature.

"Lettie, Lettie," he said, trying to contend with all this. "What's the matter? Has something happened?"

She pulled away from him then and looked at him reproachfully through a smear of tears, and for the first time she spoke coherently.

"I'm trying to tell you, Michael. They're going to send Mama and me to a resort."

He almost laughed and then, abruptly, it did not seem funny at all. He felt very far indeed from laughing at her. Instead, a wholly new sense of protectiveness and responsibility seemed to possess him, tinged with a feeling of closeness to her that he knew was a residue of the warmth that she had so unexpectedly stirred in him.

"Lettie," he said, but he got no farther. A peremptory banging on the door startled them and Mrs. Adams' agitated voice called, "Mr. Brodi, open the door at once."

"Oh, good Lord," he thought. He went to the door and opened it, but just wide enough to step through, and closed it carefully behind him.

Mrs. Adams was very angry. Her lips were drawn in a straight line, her crown of iron-gray hair quivered, and her bony hands, clasped one over the other, shook a little.

"Yes, Mrs. Adams?" She was so little that even Mike could look down on her, but she seemed like a fighting cock—no wonder Sam was in awe of her. Mike noted that she had the kind of springy hair which looked as though each strand were endowed with its own individual energy.

"I never heard of anything like it in all my life, Mr. Brodi. You get her out of here this minute. . . ."

"Listen, Mrs. Adams, it's all right. She's a nice girl—she's in trouble."

He paused, horrified. "I don't mean *that* way either." He was beginning to get angry himself. "The poor kid's had a shock. Something has happened." He controlled his anger and tried to sound reasonable and to convey the impression that Lettie was only a child. "She's little Miss —but never mind names. She doesn't know she's done anything wrong in coming here. She just brought her trouble to me because I'm older." He felt silly and unconvincing.

"All the more reason, Mr. Brodi, if she doesn't know what she's doing, why she should leave at once."

"I quite agree with you, but I can't send her out in the street in the state she's in. She's crying. Mrs. Adams, listen. I'll take her home myself as soon as I can. In the meantime, I'll leave the door open and you can sit in a chair over there by the stairs."

A heavy tread was coming down the hall and they both turned to see Hadley approaching them.

"Afternoon, Mrs. Adams. Hi, Brodi. I was looking for you."

"Hadley, for Lord's sake, will you . . . ?"

"I'll thank you not to swear, Mr. Brodi."

"I beg your pardon, Mrs. Adams. Sam, Lettie is here, in quite a state over something. She came by herself and I'm trying to convince Mrs. Adams that it's all right and that I'll take her home as soon as she's calmer." "If he laughs," Mike thought, "or looks knowing, I'll bust his face in."

Sam did neither. He looked considerably concerned. "She's a nice girl, Mrs. Adams. I know her and if Mike Brodi says it's all right, it is."

"I'll have her out of here as soon as I can, Mrs. Adams."

The irate woman looked from one to the other and both men felt like small and delinquent boys under her gaze. "She's crisp and wiry," Mike thought, "and about as warm-hearted as winter sun on a rock pasture. She reminds me of all the disciplinarians I ever met."

"See that you do." Without a word more, Mrs. Adams turned her back on them and marched rigidly down the hall.

"Well, see you later." Sam was visibly embarrassed.

"Yea." Mike was embarrassed too. He went back into his room, leaving the door open a careful foot, and at once some of the shame and all of the astonishment at his physical response to Lettie returned. She was leaning on the table looking out of the window, but he knew that she was seeing nothing. She did not speak, but whether this was because she was still struggling with her tears or because she had sensed his ill-timed impulse to laugh at her, he did not know. He put his hand around her arm.

"Lettie, come and sit down and let's talk about it. You have to tell me what happened, you know."

He led her to the cot bed as being the only place in the room where two people could sit down together. He took out his handkerchief and started to give it to her but changed his mind and mopped at her tears himself. He did it gently, with one hand under her chin, holding her face up to him. Her eyes were closed and he saw how the lids quivered and how the lashes were stuck together with tears. Her lids were delicate and thin, and they seemed to him not so much to shutter her eyes as to veil them, softening rather than blanking out her expression. With an end of his handkerchief he blotted a tear from the corner of her mouth and saw with an inner disturbance how sensitive and vulnerable her lips looked. He had never noticed these things before. Perhaps he had never really looked at her, or perhaps, like everyone else, he had seen nothing but that outrageous scar. Just now she looked like the very essence of grief.

Would so sensitive a face be an equally delicate recorder of the subtleties of happiness and joy? He had seen her happy—her face had a way of lighting up when they met or when she told him about some antic of Shamrock's, but he found he could remember nothing beyond a general impression of childish pleasure. The feeling that he had missed the nuances of Lettie's emotions broadened into the uncomfortable conviction that he was missing other essential meanings in life around him, meanings to which Lettie was sensitized. He had let himself become blunt and dull. Curious how this girl was always opening his eyes or giving his complacency a jolt. He sighed. These wanderings were not getting him on with the business of giving her the benefit of the suppositious mature aid and counsel for which she had come to him.

"Lettie." He tried to sound as old and reliable as possible, but his harried expression and the furrows on his brow betrayed the extraordinary assortment of emotions he was experiencing. "You must tell me what happened."

She opened her eyes then, tragic and large. "Oh, Michael, she's found out about it and she told Father I've been *bad!*"

"But, good Heavens, you haven't, Lettie. And you have a right to your own life."

"I know, Michael, but she told Mama and Father—and Father'll believe *anything* she tells him, and they tried to make me promise never to see you again and I wouldn't, and they're going to send me away to this summer resort until school opens and then I'm going to a very strict school and—oh, Michael—I can't live without you and the work and—and Shamrock."

Her grief and the breathless length of her sentence overcame her, and she twisted sidewise and threw herself down on the pillow. Instead of crying, however, she lay there completely limp and, looking down on her, Brodi sighed again. He knew that, like a child, she felt that by telling him she had shifted her burden to him. "All she wanted was to make me understand how bad a fix she's in now. Poor kid, she's sure I'm infallible and that I can straighten everything out. Oh, good Lord, I only wish I could. The whole awful mess is my fault. I warned her, sure. I told her what the consequences would be, sure. And what does that mean? I knew damn well that, when you're young and some desire conflicts with hypothetical consequences, the desire always wins. It's apt to at any age. Hell, it did with me because I wanted her work and the fun of having her around. Now what do I do?" He looked down on her lying there, her unscarred cheek on the pillow, one hand beside her face. She looked exhausted by grief, and so young. Because the sight was so poignant, he turned his back on her and began to pace the room.

A small voice from the bed said, "Michael." He whirled around. She was still lying with her cheek on the pillow, but she had gathered up a wad of it into her hand as though it were something to cling to. Abstractedly, he noticed a little gold ring on her finger. It was set with a turquoise—a childish sort of ring. Probably she wore it from habit. He'd never seen it before.

"Michael," she whispered. "Come over here, please."

He went to stand by the bed, his hands still thrust deep in his pockets. "No, sit down, Michael."

He sat tentatively and with reservation.

"Michael." She squirmed around on the bed until her face was hidden, and for a long time she said nothing more. Then he felt her quiver with resolution and the hand which still held the pillow clenched spasmodically.

"Michael, I thought perhaps you and I—I thought perhaps we could get married, Michael." She hurried on as though she had felt his shock. "I could cook for you, Michael—I don't know how, but I could learn—and sew buttons and . . ." She was racing on, low-voiced, intense and eager, as though by the outpouring of words she could stave off refusal.

"And I'd be there all the time to help you with your work." She sat up suddenly and stared at him with enormous eyes. "Oh, Michael, please. I'd just slave for you, I'd work so hard."

Michael stared at space, adjusting himself to the impact of her words. He felt as though someone had put a cold wet sponge at the back of his neck. The sensation transformed itself into prickles all through him and finally drained out his fingertips, leaving behind a feeling of weakness. "Lettie, for Heaven's sake," he said helplessly, and he rose again to go and stand by the window. The palms of his hands felt clammy. He stood there a long time, trying to cope with the full realization of what he had done to Lettie, and with the picture of his own colossal selfishness in having used her work and her companionship at such a cost to herself. "But, Lord," he thought, "I didn't mean this to happen. She only thinks she's in love, of course, but . . ." And even as he built up this defense the conviction of its falseness increased his remorse. Lettie's affections, once given, would not easily be deflected, and the fact that they were unfounded, that her idea they could live happily ever after was as silly as one of her romances, would not mitigate the hurt in the slightest. He drew a deep breath and, leaving the window, went to sit on the edge of the cot beside her.

"It wouldn't work, Lettie," he said somberly.

"Yes, it would."

She was lying on the pillow again and she spoke with a kind of strangled intensity, but without opening her eyes, as though she were afraid to look at the world outside her own imaginings. As he looked down at her the quality of her youth again touched him and stirred him to an unfamiliar gentleness. In Mike's life gentleness had previously been associated only with his mother when she was old, and sometimes with young, furry animals. Now the intensity of the feeling was irresistible and he raised a hand that trembled slightly and put back the damp hair from her forehead.

She twisted around and kissed his hand. He took it away and she sat up and, leaning against him, put her head on his shoulder.

"Lettie, Lettie, it wouldn't do, dear." His arm was around her and he patted her back with awkward emotion.

"You called me 'dear'! Why wouldn't it do, Michael? We work well together and we like the same things and we have fun. It *would* work, Michael."

His arm tightened around her once, convulsively, and then he stood up and went to stare out of the window. She said nothing but he could feel that all of her being was centered on him. He was still aware of the enervating tenderness that she stirred in him—a desire to protect and cherish. Suddenly he whirled around, but he did not look at her. He let his gaze travel around the room, over his books, his bags, the toilet articles on the dresser, the papers on the improvised desk, the shoes protruding from under the chair; over all his bachelor things, a long stock-taking of his life.

"No, Lettie." The words were not audible. His lips never moved. He went slowly toward the bed. She was smiling at him. Smiling! He was almost shocked, "Lettie!"

She rose to her knees and flung her arms around his neck. She was still smiling, a rather wonderful smile it seemed to him, but her mouth was quivering with tears.

"Oh, Michael. I knew you would!"

"Now, Lettie . . ."

He was sitting on the bed. She had thrown herself across him and he found himself cradling her in his arms. For some reason it was hard to say any more. The light in her face did queer things inside him. Her lashes were still stuck together with her tears, and this trivial thing unnerved him. He held her close to him and, trembling with a gentleness that was almost overwhelming, he kissed her.

After a minute he pushed her away from him, not quite roughly, and sat with his head in his hands. She did not speak to him or touch him. They stayed this way for some time and then he moved his hands across his forehead and upward over his hair, dropping them, finally, to hang limp between his knees. He had to clear his throat before he spoke, and his voice had little resemblance to his normal tones.

"Would you like to get married right away, Lettie? I suppose if we're going to, that's the way it ought to be."

PART FOUR

22

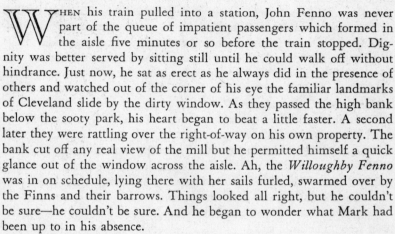

WHEN his train pulled into a station, John Fenno was never part of the queue of impatient passengers which formed in the aisle five minutes or so before the train stopped. Dignity was better served by sitting still until he could walk off without hindrance. Just now, he sat as erect as he always did in the presence of others and watched out of the corner of his eye the familiar landmarks of Cleveland slide by the dirty window. As they passed the high bank below the sooty park, his heart began to beat a little faster. A second later they were rattling over the right-of-way on his own property. The bank cut off any real view of the mill but he permitted himself a quick glance out of the window across the aisle. Ah, the *Willoughby Fenno* was in on schedule, lying there with her sails furled, swarmed over by the Finns and their barrows. Things looked all right, but he couldn't be sure—he couldn't be sure. And he began to wonder what Mark had been up to in his absence.

After this momentary excitement he felt very tired, as he often did these days, suddenly and without sufficient cause. He glanced quickly around, but everyone was standing in that absurd queue and all the other seats were empty. He shut his eyes. He found these financial fellows at Cooke's curiously wearing. They made him feel almost old, though in spite of their flashy clothes some of them, he felt sure, were older than himself. They made him feel self-righteous too, and irritable and conscious of how different he looked in his somber black coat. But they'd knuckled under, all right, and been much more respectful than last time, probably because they owed him money. They'd made all sorts of promises. How did he know they'd keep them? He'd have enjoyed telling them to take their orders elsewhere, but there was the Lake plant all set up for making rails. Perhaps it would be wiser to look for new business somewhere else, but looking for new business seemed like a tremendous, overwhelming effort—and he used to be keen on it. If Mark were worth his salt . . . The train was coming to a halt with a series of uncomfortable jerks. Fenno opened his eyes.

On the platform he followed the boy with his bags, keeping his eyes straight in front of him lest he encounter the eyes of someone he knew. He hated chance encounters. Perhaps Willoughby had come to meet him. The thought warmed him and took away some of the battered, angry feeling that his encounter with the minions of Cooke and Company had given him. His mind's eye saw her sitting in the carriage, bathed in sunlight, smiling at him, and he walked a little faster, feeling pride and comfort. He slipped his hand in his pocket and felt the smooth leather of a jeweler's case. A pretty thing—he hoped she'd like it. No sense in waiting for her birthday—give her the pleasure now.

Out on the street in the noise and confusion of carriages and drays and people, all struggling with the steep incline, he did not see Joe standing deferentially until Joe spoke to him.

"Afternoon, sir."

"Joe. Where's the carriage?"

"Over there, sir. I've got my eye on the carriage from here. Team don't like trains much."

Fenno looked and his heart sank. There the carriage stood, neat and glossy—and empty. Fenno trudged toward it and the two Dalmatians watched him with a kind of tired interest, as though they knew that his arrival meant the end of their respite.

Joe gathered up the reins and the whip, and half turned toward the back seat. "The mill, sir?"

Fenno considered. He had intended going to the mill as a matter of course—it was only three o'clock—but she not being here to meet him left him feeling gloomy and morose. He needed her, though he did not put it to himself in so many words. He wanted to sit back and be fed by her vitality, her style. A long sigh escaped him. "No, home," he said to Joe's waiting back.

He let himself in with his key and paused to listen to the quiet house, feeling the strangeness of the week-day afternoon. Then he walked heavily into the drawing room. It was empty and looked as though it were waiting. He seized the needlepoint bell-pull by the gilt pear which hung on the bottom and jerked it, hating the ornate mechanism. Nora appeared and looked startled.

"Miss Willoughby," he said, forestalling any expression of welcome. "She's out, sir. Till dinner time, she said."

Fenno turned his back on Nora and went to his study. The others, he supposed, were upstairs. Well, he didn't want to see *them*. He eased himself down into his familiar chair, letting it bring him some measure of comfort. He sat there for a long time without moving, but after awhile he took the morning paper off the table beside him and held it in front of him, sometimes reading, sometimes giving himself up to gloomy thoughts.

He had taken, lately, to worrying about her safety when Willoughby went out, imagining runaways and street accidents. Absurd, of course —but still, you never knew. Mince and Docket were safe enough. Or were they? Joe said they shied at trains. Perhaps he should replace them with a stodgier team. He resolved to talk to Joe. Then he remembered that she had not the carriage to use and that she was out in Heaven knew what kind of contraption, and his heart gave a great thick bound of anxiety. He told himself angrily that there was nothing to fear and he concentrated on a paragraph in his paper, reading it twice without its having any meaning for him.

When, a little later, he thought he heard someone come into the drawing room, he rose quickly and went to investigate, keeping one hand on the little box in his pocket. It was only Matild. He found her sitting on the middle of the *tête,* clutching the edge of it as though she expected it to decamp from under her. How worn she looked. Old. Much older than himself, though, in point of fact, she was younger by a year. He made a noncommittal noise in his throat and said that he supposed Lettie might as well come down for dinner—they couldn't keep her locked up forever. Then he took his accustomed place in front of the hearth and told her about his plans.

"I've made arrangements for you and Lettie to leave for Poland Springs day after tomorrow. I called on Mrs. Tilden and she recommended Poland Springs, but her manner was most peculiar. Have you done anything to offend her? I'm sure we were generous enough when Willoughby was with her."

"No, John. I'm sure not. She never answered my last letter."

The look of strain on Matild's face deepened. She was having a struggle with herself about whether to tell her husband that Lettie had been away from the house for hours and that she had only just come home a little while before John himself must have arrived. And Matild was sure Lettie had seen that man, for she had come home all shiny-eyed and kissed her mother with a real show of affection and high spirits. Matild looked at her husband's commanding figure and decided to say nothing. After all, Willoughby had been out herself at the time, so she knew nothing about Lettie's absence. She couldn't tattle. Matild's face set in stubborn lines. John Fenno looked at her with patent distaste and went back to his study.

He had been on the point of asking her about Willoughby, but his fear of betraying himself was, for the moment, greater than his fear for her and that fear, he told himself sternly, was preposterous. No reason at all to suppose that she was not all right. The thing was, in all probability, only another symptom of whatever it was that was the matter with him these days. Not that he was at all prepared to admit that anything was the matter. He took a cigar out of his humidor and went through the elaborate ritual of lighting it, thinking about himself. There was nothing the matter, really, beyond getting tired a little more quickly than he once had. Whatever it was seemed to be in the mind, shadows, a vague feeling of not dominating affairs at the mill and even here at home the way he once had, effortlessly. Why should it take effort now? Well, if it did, he'd take a new grip—a hard-fisted grip. He broke off this train of thought to listen intently.

He rose and went into the drawing room. There she was, as radiant as ever, and Matild was nowhere in sight. He had her to himself, then. A kind of peace settled on his heart.

"Papa." She bent forward and kissed his cheek. "Was it a nice trip, dear?"

"Nice!" The perfume of her was sweet and warm. There was no man good enough for her! At least, she seemed to think so, and it probably was true. Well, that suited him all right.

"Those horses," he said. "Would you say they were perfectly safe? Reliable?"

"What horses, dear? Mince and Docket? Of course. What an idea! What made you think of that?"

He muttered something about accidents, which she did not try to hear. She seemed restless, wandering around the room, picking things up and putting them down again, almost as though she were worrying about something. "There isn't anything she could be worried about," he thought. Presently he remembered the little jeweler's box in his pocket, and he was about to take it out and give it to her when he heard Matild and Lettie on the stairs. Later would do, when he could have her to himself again.

Dinner time arrived. The Fennos never talked much at the table except for Matild's occasional attacks of garrulity. Boredom and fear of sharp sarcasms ruled what conversation there was. Tonight Lettie ate her dinner in complete silence, but it was not her usual, unhappy silence. John Fenno watched her covertly, and it appeared to him that her mind was busy and that those present at the table played no part in her thoughts. She seemed to have escaped somewhere and, though he phrased to himself no such fanciful thought as this, he was angered. He felt a perverse need to break into her private enjoyment.

"Lettie!"

She dropped her fork with a clatter and stared at him.

"I have informed your mother that you and she will leave day after tomorrow for Poland Springs. We will then find a suitable finishing school for you and you will not come home again before the school opens."

A very strange look indeed came on Lettie's face, but before he could think about its meaning, the door-bell rang stridently, jangling along everyone's nerves. They all sat still and stared toward the hall. Even Matild turned around to stare, and Ellen rustled in from the kitchen, rustled past them and out to the door.

Ellen came back looking flustered. "It's Mr. Brodi to see you, sir. He says he'll wait till after dinner."

Fenno rose from his chair. "Tell him to leave the house at once. No, wait. I'll tell him myself."

Before he had time to leave the table, Mike appeared in the dining-room archway. He looked about him swiftly, walked to Lettie's side and, putting his hand on her shoulder, spoke low enough so that only she could hear.

"Get your things and wait for me outside in the buggy."

Lettie rose and Fenno roared at her.

"Keep your seat, young lady. Mr. Brodi, you will leave this house at once!"

Lettie cast a terrified look from one to the other, but at a nod from Mike she fled precipitately and, in the moment of silence which followed, her feet could be heard pounding up the stairs. Mike was the first to speak.

"If you will come into the other room, Mr. Fenno, I have something to tell you which concerns your daughter."

"You have no concern with my daughter whatsoever."

"I think you had better come." Mike's tone revealed all the hatred he had for the man who stood so commandingly at the head of the table.

"I have no intention of bandying any words with you."

"Very well. I wanted to spare the ladies the shock of the news, but if that's how you feel." Mike fought with his pocket and brought out a stiff document. "Lettie and I were married this afternoon. There's the certificate, if you care to examine it." Mike threw the paper down on the table in front of Fenno. "Everything's in order."

Upstairs, Lettie was scurrying around in a frenzy of hurry. She clapped her hat on her head and jabbed the pins into place. She pulled open drawers and slammed them shut. She dove into the wardrobe and backed out, dragging a small traveling bag which she had packed furtively just before dinner. With this and her purse and gloves clutched in her hand, she cast one last and somewhat wild look around her room and hurried out.

Downstairs they were shouting, and she could hear her mother crying. Then Willoughby's voice rose sharp and sarcastic, but her words were drowned by the shouting. Lettie felt frightened and she ran for the back stairs. The kitchen door was open, but there was not a sound on the other side. "They're all in the pantry listening," she thought, and she let herself out of the back door, thankful that no one had seen her. She started for the driveway but changed her mind. The drive was directly below the dining-room windows and the chance of being seen was altogether too great. She ran around the other way, feeling guilty and excited and happy all at once.

A buggy stood by the front steps. It was hitched to a benign-looking dappled gray horse who pricked up his ears with interest when he saw her and turned his head to watch her as she hoisted her bag to the floor of the buggy. Then she put her purse and gloves on the seat and started back around the house the way she had come. This time she ran as fast as she could toward the carriage house. The great doors were shut, as they always were when Joe and the stable boy were in the kitchen having their supper, and the two Dalmatians and Shamrock set up a terrific barking when they heard her struggling with the latch.

"Oh, hush!" she whispered. "Please hush."

She pulled the heavy doors open a crack and slipped inside. The Dalmatians sniffed at her and went to lie down on their straw beds, but Shamrock jumped on her and reached a long wet tongue for her face. She dropped to her knees and put her arms around the dog. "Oh, Shamrock," she whispered in an ecstasy, "we're going to live all together, you and Michael and I." The tongue caught her squarely on the face and she stood up, laughing. Shamrock began to lope around the carriage house for the sheer joy of motion. He had grown big and rangy, but he was still predominantly legs, and in spite of a voracious appetite his ribs showed.

Lettie went to the long row of pegs where the harness hung and began hunting for Shamrock's collar and leash. It was hot in the carriage house, hotter than outside. Shamrock sat down in a mote-filled shaft of sunset light and panted. In the stable beyond, Lettie heard Mince and Docket moving around in their stalls. The carriage house smelled doggy and homelike, and the carriages looked peaceful with their shafts turned up in the air. Lettie was filled with a wistful love of it all. "I'll miss Joe and Ellen—and of course, Mother," she thought, and then she found the collar with the leash attached and these thoughts were forgotten in the excitement of fastening the collar around the wriggling Shamrock.

"There," she said, and straightened up. "Come on, Shamrock."

The dog made a joyous bound for the door and almost upset her. She had a difficult time restraining him while she fastened the door behind them. They rounded the house at a headlong pace. "Oh, Shamrock, *please* don't bark," Lettie said. The dappled horse was more interested than ever and Shamrock's desire to make friends was so ebullient that he had to be dragged to the steps of the buggy.

There Lettie was faced with a strategical problem of the worst sort. The wheel was high and it blocked the narrow entrance to the buggy, the more effectively since the horse, who wore no check rein, moved around as far as he could to watch, pushing the wheel even closer to the buggy step. Shamrock was in a scatter-brained dither of pleasure. He had no idea what was wanted of him and no intention of trying to find out. Lettie finally tied him to a spoke of the wheel and, going to the horse's head, led him carefully to the other side. This left a fine wide entrance, but before she had finished untying Shamrock, the nag's curiosity was too much for him and he moved back to watch.

Lettie started all over. She got the horse firmly planted again and she even took time to stroke his nose hurriedly. "Now *please* stay there," she implored, but as soon as she turned away from him he moved back. "Oh, dear, Shamrock, what am I going to *do?* I guess I'll have to lift you over the wheel."

She bent and, putting her arms around Shamrock's middle, she lifted him. He hung in her arms as limp as a half-filled sack of grain, and his legs stuck out at preposterous angles. One of them went between the spokes of the wheel instead of over it. "Oh," she said, close to tears, "can't you help a *little?*" She set him down again and took a fresh grip and by a tremendous exertion hoisted him over the wheel and more or less inside the buggy. He promptly tried to get out again, but she forestalled him and clambered in herself without any regard for her clothes, which were covered with dust from the wheel. She sat on the seat and gasped and fended off Shamrock, who had climbed on the seat beside her and was trying to lick her face. Then, as though he were suddenly sick of clowning, Shamrock lay down on the seat with his huge paws hanging over the edge, put his nose down, heaved a tremendous sigh and was instantly asleep.

Lettie sat still with her hands in her lap. After awhile a secret and very lovely expression came into her eyes and touched the corners of her sensitive mouth. She put her hand inside the collar of her dress and drew out a narrow white ribbon from which hung a plain gold wedding ring. She worked with the knot until it came loose, slid the ring off the ribbon and slipped it on her finger. Then she folded her hands in her lap and sat very still and straight, smiling.

The front door banged and Michael came running down the steps. Lettie leaned forward, an expression of concern replacing the gentle smile. All the lines on Michael's face seemed to have become deeply bitten-in, and the way he moved showed traces of violent anger. He came quickly around to the far side of the buggy, unsnapped the half-round cement anchor from the horse's bridle and, swinging it in his hand, started to climb in. Shamrock rose to greet him and suddenly Michael smiled.

"I'd forgotten all about Shamrock," he said.

He dropped the anchor to the floor, picked up the reins, and they started off at a good pace. Michael kept silent and the lines on his face were deep again. Presently, he drew a long breath, turned toward Lettie and smiled. She returned his smile, a little timidly but happily.

"Was it bad?" she said. "Father, I mean?"

"Bad enough. I don't think he knows you're with me now. I don't like being clandestine but it's better than dragging you into a row."

"Was Mother upset?"

"It's a funny thing, but I think she is pleased, really. I'm afraid she'll have to take the brunt of it, though. But let's forget all that. Do you realize, Mrs. Brodi, that you have work to do? You have to plan our lives. You have to decide where we're going to live—it better be Hudson, I think—and you have to set up housekeeping for us and . . ." An amused expression crossed Mike's face. "And Shamrock, here. You're going to be a very busy woman, Mrs. Brodi."

Lettie giggled.

Presently the soft look came back to her face and she stretched out her hand. "See, Michael—I put it on. And I'll never take it off again."

Late that night Matild lay on her side of the big bed. The place beside her was empty. She was tired beyond all normal fatigue, tired to the point where her muscles could no longer relax, frozen as they were with tension. She had been lying here a long time, ever since John Fenno had sent her upstairs from the dining-room table in order that he might deal with his problems undisturbed by her wails and protestations. She waited now in fear and misery for his judgment on herself, certain that his blame and the full weight of his wrath would fall on her.

With nervous apprehension she had kept track of the events downstairs by the sounds they made. Thus she knew when Brodi left by the slam of the front door, which seemed to shake the bed on which she lay. After awhile there followed a violent cadenza on the piano that meant Willoughby was alone in the drawing room. The notes were like an angry outburst, a repudiation, a denunciation of everything but self and a release from emotion that had become too strong to be contained. The wild notes reminded Matild of Willoughby as a wilful and intractable child who vented her angers by seizing her pinafore with both hands and jerking until the material tore right up the front. Matild sighed profoundly, feeling the martyrdom of mothering a child over whom she had never had any real control. The cadenza broke off unfinished, the notes still vibrating in the air.

Willoughby was trying to make up her mind. "If I wait to ask him whether I can marry Mark until he's had time to think about this affair of Lettie's, he'll just say Mark isn't good enough—and he isn't!" she added parenthetically and with bitterness. "Father will say he's always had great ambitions for me—oh, I can just *hear* him. He'll say he's counting on me, all the more now that Lettie has disgraced us by marrying a nobody. He'll talk about all he's done at the mill being really for me and in the end he'll forbid me and that will be the end of that."

Willoughby clutched the edge of the piano stool with both hands and swung back and forth. "But if I ask him now, before he's had time to think much—he does look tired and Lettie is a blow to him—if I coax him and call him 'Daddy'—he might, he just might. I'll call him 'Daddy,' " she thought, and then she stopped thinking and watched the picture in her mind. She saw General Thatcher in his office looking straight at her and away again without a sign of recognition. *"Oh!"* With one swift motion she rose. She held her chin high and her resemblance to her father was striking. Upstairs Matild heard the staccato sound of her heels as she walked toward her father's study.

John Fenno held a paper in front of him because it was his immemorial custom to do so after the close of the evening meal. He did not read, for his mind was engaged in a kind of gloomy stock-taking. It was one of those moments when a man's life, his ambitions and accomplishments, have turned to bitterness, when his hope for the future and his pride in the past seem to him nothing but delusion and futility. When Willoughby entered, he lowered his paper. He did not smile but his big frame made a slight, quick movement that was almost a betrayal of his eagerness for companionship and understanding.

"Come in. Just reading the paper—it gets worse every day. I don't see why a city of this size can't have a first-class news sheet." He threw the paper on the floor beside his chair and rose stiffly. "I was going to pour myself some sherry. Have some?"

"Yes, thanks, Papa."

She watched her father in silence while he took the stopper out of the heavy glass decanter and poured the sherry into two fragile, V-shaped glasses which he took from a rack in a wooden box on the table. He carried a glass to her carefully, his eyes on the amber-red liquor, and when she reached out to take it, she noticed that his hand was trembling. She sank gracefully down on the edge of the couch and then, because her memories made this particular seat distasteful, she rose and perched on the arm of his chair. They sipped their sherry in silence and once he raised his hand and patted her knee awkwardly, withdrawing it again and seeming once more to close himself in the shell of his dignity.

When they had finished their drinks she rose, took his glass and put it with her own on the table. Then she came to stand in front of him.

"Daddy—there is something I want very much."

He looked at her a trifle anxiously and she thought she saw in him an absence of force, as though his scene with Brodi had used up so much of his vitality that he could no longer conceal its lack.

"What is it?" he said in a tired voice. "I usually try to give you everything you want."

"Then give me this! I want to marry Mark, Papa."

"Mark!"

"Yes, dear."

There was a silence in which John Fenno seemed to grow stern and remote. He stood, seeming to tower, and she faced him.

"Willoughby, this is preposterous."

"I don't think so, Papa."

"I had always assumed that some day you would marry, Willoughby, but it must be somebody better than Mark."

Willoughby walked to the window and stared out. Over her shoulder she said, "Show me somebody better and I'll marry him, Papa."

Fenno considered this, standing with his hands clasped behind his back. "Young Thatcher might have been better," he said finally. "His expectations, at least, are excellent and there are other business reasons . . ."

"He makes my flesh creep." Willoughby turned and walked back to her father. "Besides, dear, if I took him away from Prissie, it would make quite a scandal." Her tone was light and bantering and his manner rejected this frivolity.

"Mark has no money of his own."

"I know, Papa, but the mill will make enough for both of us and some day we would have a lot."

Fenno shot her a somber glance from under his lowering brows. "Some day the mill will be yours," he said slowly.

"I know, Papa. And then the board would appoint somebody to run it who might not have my interests at heart the way Mark would if we were married. The way Mark wouldn't have if we weren't," she added in a lower tone.

Fenno gave her a look of surprise in which there was a trace of sardonic pleasure at her acumen. Willoughby went over to his desk and leaned with her back against its edge, facing him, her hands grasping the wood on either side. This position forced her hoops out in front of her in an ugly line and she straightened up to improve the contours of her figure. "Besides, there isn't anybody *but* Mark now that Mr. Hadley's gone."

Fenno began to pace the little room with his hands behind his back. Finally he stopped in the middle of the floor and said gloomily, "Mark is a weakling."

"I know that, dear, but *I'm* not." She went over to him, accentuating a little the rustling of her dress, and put her hand on his lapel. "I'm like you."

Standing so close to him, she was startled by his appearance. "Why, he's old," she thought, noticing how the indomitable lines of his face seemed to sag, and her fancy took a wild flight into the future. She'd miss him when he was dead—really miss him, but it was clear to her that there were compensations and a freedom when you no longer had a parent over you. Because these thoughts made her feel guilty, she gave his lapel a little tug of affection. Her gesture seemed to bring him back from some far place and he concentrated burning eyes of suffering on her.

"I want to do the right thing, Willoughby. You're all I've got."

She bowed her head and considered his tone rather than his words. "That settles Lettie," she thought. "The little fool." Then she realized that, in him, this was a moment of weakness and she seized it.

She put her head down on his shoulder and said, "I *want* to marry Mark." She said it pleadingly, like a little girl. John Fenno did not move, but she sensed his capitulation and his great unhappiness. She did not want to deal with these emotions or even to look closely at their effect on herself. She was, in fact, just barely ashamed of her consciousness of her own strength and of a new attitude toward him which no longer contained respect.

"Daddy dear . . ." She paused to let this expression of affection sink in. *"You"* can make a success of anything. You can make a success of me and Mark. Besides, if we make big, grand affairs out of the engagement party and the wedding, it will take people's minds off Lettie. You wouldn't want them thinking that both your daughters were marrying against your wishes."

Again she saw in John Fenno's eyes the expression that seemed to say he was goaded beyond endurance. "He's always controlled everything," she thought, "and now he's losing his grip." John Fenno turned away, as though he himself knew that his eyes betrayed too much. She smiled a little.

"Poor daddy," she said.

Upstairs Matild knew when the conference was ended for, with her preternaturally sharpened hearing, she heard the distant closing of the study door. She held herself rigid, feeling that now her turn had come and her husband's anger would shortly crush her. In the dark, her face was a mask of dread and misery. The steps which came up the stairs, however, were light and they were accompanied by the faint rustling of Willoughby's taffeta gown. For a brief moment of bitterness Matild hated her daughter with all the vehemence of which she was capable. Willoughby's door shut behind her, a calm and confident closing, and she began listening again, with heightened apprehension.

A long time passed and Matild drifted into a miserable state between sleep and wakefulness. She never lost consciousness of what it was she feared but she fell a prey, also, to nameless, unidentified terrors. They rose up all around her and once she nearly screamed. She came wide awake, then, to find herself clammy with sweat.

She drifted off and again the terrors claimed her. She had no idea of time but when, at intervals, she came to the surface of consciousness, she knew it must be very late. Outside the window shutters she felt the strange, rustling quiet of a world deserted by humans. In her over-wrought state, her husband's steps on the stair were ominous and doom-filled beyond all reality. His steps were heavy and slow, and each one struck a blow at her heart.

When he turned the handle of the dressing-room door instead of the one behind which she lay, she gasped. After that there were no sounds at all for some minutes, as though he were standing still in the dark, and Matild lay on her back, feeling the thumping of her own heart. She heard him strike a match and begin to move around in the process of undressing. But how slowly he moved, with hesitations and fumblings that seemed, even to her frightened mind, strange and un-natural.

She knew each stage of his undressing by the sounds he made, even though there were queer silences between them. She heard the ward-robe door open and close again, and knew he was sliding his night shirt over his erect form. Then followed the hollow sound of his blowing into the lamp chimney and the thread of light under the door disappeared. She stretched herself even more tautly and her heart began to beat fast, so that she had to breathe in shallow gasps. She was steeling herself for the opening of the door between the rooms. It did not come. Instead, she heard the sudden loud creaking of the springs in the dressing-room couch. She opened her eyes wide with surprise and waited for further sounds. Was he going to sleep there? He had never done so before.

After awhile the knowledge grew in her that he was lying stretched in the dark, as tense and wakeful as herself. She seemed to feel his presence through the walls. The realization that he was not coming to share their bed even in anger took a long time to complete itself. When it did, she suddenly heaved herself over on her side and, burying her face in the pillow, burst into sobs which she tried with all her might to smother and keep silent.

23

THE hot nights of July gave place to the cooler nights of August. Morning found the cobwebs, which lay like patches on the lawns, white with dew and the song of the cicada grew strident. All nature stood at the height of her perfection. Each blossom, each tree seemed to have rounded out its full year's growth, to have reached the greatest possible culmination of beauty and, as though any further effort were gratuitous, there the season paused. Golden day followed golden day in confident splendor. No rain, no wind came to mar this perfect maturity and so sure, so serene a world seemed to have lost all memory of such recurring catastrophes as black frost and destruction.

September came with no change in the blue of the sky or the abundance of the earth. A week passed and then one day a tiny cloud appeared far out over the sparkling lake. Few people remarked it, so intent was everyone on enjoying this golden age, but hour by hour the cloud grew and toward evening a wind began to blow, bowing and swaying the tree tops. Leaves which had seemed secure on their twigs forever began to fall, revealing a weakness none had suspected, and lay yellowing on the lawns. By morning the rain had come, driving down in silver lances that laid the perfection of the flower beds in a ruin of torn petals and bent stalks.

Something similar to all this was happening in the economic world. The richness of a golden age hung in the air and so great was the abundance that many people believed the recurring blight of hard times would never come again and that the cycle of the economic seasons was forever suspended. Then the tiny cloud appeared. The money market remained tight and in industry the backlog of orders decreased, though such things alarmed but few. New capital was, mysteriously, a little harder to raise and there were other signs for those who, like Brodi, scanned the economic skies.

On Friday, the eighteenth of September, 1873, the storm broke. At eleven o'clock in the morning, Jay Cooke and Company closed its doors. The evening papers in Cleveland carried no story of this disaster and, except for a few financial men who heard the news in the afternoon by wire, Clevelanders knew nothing at all about what had happened until they opened their *Leaders* the following morning. Businessmen, therefore, went to bed on Friday night secure in their belief in the indefinite continuance of prosperity or, if not quite secure, then not unduly troubled by the signs and portents of the times. They awoke on Saturday to a changed world in which fear dominated.

The failure of Cooke and Company was disastrous enough in itself, for the firm's interests were woven all through the economic structure of the country, but far more disastrous was the doubt and mistrust that grew in everyone's mind about the soundness of banks and businesses of all kinds. Men reasoned that if the great colossus could fall, then why not others. Men of substance who, on Friday, had met in faith and fellowship, on Saturday met guardedly and with restraint in their manners, each wondering whether the affairs of the others might not secretly be rotten to the core. These were frightening speculations and they spread like prairie fire. Panic was in the air, prompting men to sudden, drastic and ill-considered actions, and fear bred fear until fear itself became the mainspring of the disaster.

John Fenno did not read the news, for the *Leader* was late and he was forced to go grumbling to the office without a paper. While Nora was clearing off the breakfast table, she heard the folded paper hit the front door with a whack and she went at once to get it, but by that time everyone was upstairs, so she took it to Mr. Fenno's study and left it on the table. Matild seldom looked at the papers. Willoughby, who usually read the headlines and a paragraph or two before turning to the advertisements, was in the sewing room standing on a sheet, enduring a fitting of a dress she hoped to wear that evening to the first ball of the fall season. Probably the events of the day would in no way have been changed had she read the news, since none but John Fenno could have estimated its effects on his fortunes.

The morning, therefore, passed peacefully enough. Upstairs, Willoughby stood on the sheet and fretted. The gown was made of grayish pink tulle, and it had a garland of pale lavender violets over one white shoulder. Violets and their silvery leaves were scattered here and there over the cloudlike skirt, and in the evening Ellen would pin more violets in the cascade of curls on the back of Willoughby's head. Having to stand still was an annoyance. She glanced with contempt at the wretched woman kneeling, with her mouth full of pins, on the rumpled sheet. Willoughby sighed and shut her eyes in order to summon up a vision of herself, glowingly alive, in her new gown.

She was crossing a great room lit by the sparkle of crystal chandeliers, fully aware of the thrilling grace of her carriage, and Hadley waited for her. As she approached him in this dream room, her blood began to run hot with her physical awareness of his body. She knew that, when she reached him, he would take her roughly into his arms, master her, force her to surrender herself to him. Without her being aware of it, her mouth opened softly and slackly and a shudder passed over her body which made the wispy little woman look up questioningly.

Willoughby opened her eyes. The day dream had been startling in its vividness and she awoke breathless but determined that, engagement or no, she would translate it into reality. "Just once," she thought. "Mark needn't know. Mark needn't ever know." Her body grew warm and eager, and her heart began to beat as though she were already on the verge of violent passion.

The excitement stayed with her, filling her with a thrilling vitality and wiping out all customary boredom. In this exalted state she ate lunch with less bickering than usual and prepared for a trip downtown to get her pearls from the bank to wear to the party. She dressed herself carefully, put on her hat, went into the hall and called loudly for Ellen. Hearing her, Matild waked with a start from her nap.

"What do you want with Ellen?"

Willoughby opened the door of the darkened room. "I'm going to the bank for my pearls."

"Can't you get along without Ellen? She has to iron my dress." Matild spoke crossly from the tumbled bed. Matild liked to escape into sleep. Willoughby had long recognized in this a self-indulgence and, for some not very obscure reason, it made her feel virtuous to disturb her mother's sleep.

The room smelled of sleep and of Matild's dress hanging over the chair, and Willoughby backed out. In the fresher air of the hall she said loudly, "I can't go around alone like just anybody. It's time I had a maid of my own."

Matild heaved herself clumsily to one elbow. "Willoughby. Come back here!"

Willoughby advanced a reluctant step, holding her breath.

"You haven't got that new French hoop on, have you?"

"What if I have?"

"It isn't decent. It shows you all down the front. You can't go on the street like that."

Willoughby shut the door with a bang and went downstairs, closing her ears to her mother's shouted comments.

All the way downtown she rode in an aura of pleasurable enjoyment of her own elegance, bowing to the right people and contriving not to see the wrong ones with a skill that left them only a suspicion that they might have been snubbed. At the bank she performed the difficult task of getting out of the carriage with grace and without looking at her feet. There were quite a few people standing around on the sidewalk in front of the bank and most of them turned to watch her. She walked among them with her head up and an amused, withdrawn expression on her face, intended to convey that here went a lady of the world so surely to the manner born that she need not too blatantly bear the manner. The performance was sufficiently subtle to conceal its own art. The folds of her gray broadcloth dress were pulled tight across the flat hoop, making it easy to imagine the curves of her fine body underneath, and gathered into a great bunch behind, which in no way retarded the grace of her movements. She was conscious of every inch of herself.

There were more people than usual in the bank also, and they seemed to be milling about in a rather peculiar way. She noticed them without much interest as she turned into the long corridor which led to the safety-deposit department. In this normally deserted place she was surprised to find a small crowd of men, and as she waited her turn she looked them over in boredom. She was mildly astonished to see that most of them held packets of bank notes or greenbacks in their hands, some openly, some with a furtive air. Others had the hunched-up but bulky look that made her suspect they carried sizable sums in their pockets, and they all seemed to exude unfriendliness, as though each man wished he were alone.

Her turn came at last and as she followed the elderly guard, she asked idly and without much interest why all these men were putting money into their boxes when they could get it from the tellers whenever they wanted any.

"They're worried about things, Miss Fenno. The failure of Cooke and Company, you know. They've been coming in like this since morning, but they shouldn't be worried. The bank's perfectly sound."

She let the velvety pearls slide through her fingers, loving them, before she gave them to Ellen, who had to stand on tip-toe to clasp them around Willoughby's neck and slip them inside the gray collar. Then Willoughby frowned, remembering about Cooke and Company. Her father would be angry—with all those contracts.

"Come on, Ellen," she said. "That's all."

They were halfway down the corridor when a door next to General Thatcher's office swung open, almost blocking their passage. It swung toward Willoughby, so she could not see who was on the other side and she was about to go around when she heard a familiar voice.

The words, as much as the voice, arrested her. Sam Hadley, surely. Her heart began to race. He had just said, *"Fenno will get the surprise of his life."*

Sam! She signalled Ellen to stop. Hadley appeared to be standing with his hand on the knob at the other side of the open door, concluding a conversation with someone inside the room. The corridor was empty for the moment, except for herself and Ellen, and so she listened without pretense.

A strange voice speaking, apparently from inside the room, said, "Frankly, I'm astonished that General Thatcher was willing to let you buy control of the Company without Fenno's knowledge."

"It's a chance a man takes when he puts control in the hands of a bank."

"That's true, but even so, Thatcher's a director, and I feel sure that he wouldn't do it if he didn't know Fenno was too deeply involved with Cooke to pay the loan. We're sound enough here, but just the same, Thatcher probably feels we wouldn't be doing our duty if we didn't make our position as liquid as possible."

After this the door was partly shut, as though Hadley had stepped back into the room, and Willoughby strained to hear his words.

"Just one thing more. I mentioned to Thatcher that I'd rather tell Fenno about this myself."

"If he comes into the bank, we'll have to tell him."

"He won't come in today, I'd take a bet. He'll be too busy trying to get enough directors away from their own troubles to hold a meeting. Thatcher's the last person he'd want to see." Hadley laughed and his companion joined him rather feebly.

The door opened wide again and Willoughby heard Hadley say, "All right, then. I'll see you people in a day or so."

Hadley came striding out into the corridor with never a glance behind him. Two men, who looked as though they might belong to the bank, were walking rapidly down the corridor toward them. They gave Hadley preoccupied nods and ignored Willoughby. They wore worried frowns and as they passed her one of them said, "It would put us in a better position if we could sell about half a million governments but, Christ, with the Stock Exchange closed indefinitely and things as they are, who knows what governments are worth?"

That meant nothing to Willoughby; in fact, she scarcely heard the words for she had taken the sudden decision to catch up with Sam's retreating figure. "He's bought control of the Company," she thought, hurrying after him. "What on earth does that mean?" The words had an ominous sound but her absorption with her own affairs, her excitement at encountering Hadley, were so great that she did not try to find an answer to her own question.

"Sam!" she called. "Sam!"

He turned around and stood still, obviously amazed to see her there and, watching his expression, she felt sure he had no idea she had been listening. He looked a trifle annoyed, perhaps, but not suspicious. She slowed her pace and came toward him with her hand held out, smiling.

"Speaking of angels!"

"Hello." He took her hand and dropped it.

She thought, "He's mad at me," and she did her best to turn on the full radiance of her beauty. Aloud, she said sweetly, "I'm *so* glad to see you." She clasped her hands over her tiny purse with an affected gesture. "I've *missed* you, Sam."

He grinned but said nothing.

"Sam," she went on, letting a little pleading creep into her voice, "I have the carriage outside. Why not let me drive you wherever it is you want to go?"

He looked startled and then, in rapid succession, he looked a number of things which she did not bother to try to fathom. Instead, she lowered her eyes and said softly, "You know I like you very much, Sam."

At that he laughed, loudly and uproariously, and the sound echoed in the corridor. "What can be the matter with him?" she thought. "He can't really be mad at me." She said in a hurt tone, "What on earth is so funny?"

"Never mind. I never did think you were good at jokes. But if you want to drive me to the mill, why, sure, sure. I've got some business there. *You* driving me to the mill—that's all this day needs to top it off, all right." Again his laugh rang out, and it frightened her a little. "Listen, gal, I've got to see a man here first. Meet you outside in a few minutes."

He turned and left her and she stood still, gaping at him. How big he seemed. She followed his retreating figure slowly down the corridor. "Control" seemed to her a queer word to use. Her father, and no one else, had control. He wouldn't sell that to anybody, and nobody could sell it for him, so what on earth could they have been talking about?

Her train of thought was broken by the discovery that there seemed to be a great many more people in the lobby than when she had passed through it before, so many, in fact, that it was difficult to make her way through them. She looked around for Sam but he was nowhere to be seen. Long lines had formed in front of the tellers' windows, keeping their formation in spite of the milling, shoving crowd, like currents in the sea. The people in these lines were plainly uneasy and anxious, and impatient to move forward. The tension in the air was so unmistakable that Willoughby stood still in astonishment, and some of the contagious anxiety affected her, though she could not have given it a name or assigned it a cause. Rising up on tip-toe, she could see that all the tellers had great quantities of bills stacked up in plain sight, and they were paying them out rapidly, but they seemed to be talking earnestly to each person in turn. The sound of excited voices was ear-splitting and this, as much as anything else, was contributing to the visibly growing panic. Before she knew what was happening, Willoughby found herself wedged in among the people, with her access to the corridor shut off.

The crowd made one of those sudden movements which are as impersonal, as regardless of an individual, as an earthquake, and therefore terrifying. Willoughby felt herself swept irresistibly forward and she began to push and shove against the bodies around her, trying to free herself. Fright closed her throat. A person is never more alone than when in the midst of a density of terrified people, fighting for survival. She raised her fists to beat on the backs in front of her, not caring whom she hurt if she could save herself from being crushed.

"Willoughby, Willoughby."

Somewhere a voice was calling her and she looked wildly around.

"Willoughby! Over here by the pillar."

She turned her head and saw Bobbie Thatcher standing on the base of an ornamental column, which raised him above the crowd enough to keep him from harm. He was holding to the column with one arm and reaching the other out toward her over the intervening heads. She grabbed for this as she might for a life preserver and, partly through his efforts, partly through hers, she reached the base of the column.

While Bobbie fended off a would-be usurper with more fight than she thought he had in him, she clambered up. Immediately, she began to straighten her hat and tidy herself and he put an arm around her to keep her from slipping.

"Oh, Willie, Willie," he said in an agonized tone, gazing at her. "He does look like a dying calf," she thought, and the look annoyed her so that some of her poise began to return to her.

"What on earth happened?" she asked crisply, freeing herself expertly from his encircling arm.

"Oh, Willie—are you all right?"

"Of course I'm all right. What's going on?"

"A run. Papa's coming out to make a speech in a minute. Oh, Willie, I love you more than anyone in the world."

Willoughby laughed disagreeably. "And so you got engaged to Prissie."

"I couldn't help it, Willoughby. Honestly I couldn't—but I'll never love anybody but you."

Bobbie sagged into a kind of desperate, weakling misery and Willoughby turned away in disgust. From the opposite side of the lobby something that looked like a flying wedge of men in frock coats was driving through the mass of people toward the center. The crowd seemed to be focusing on it. "Look there," Willoughby said. A chair appeared from nowhere, was held high for a moment and disappeared again. Then General Thatcher, helped by many hands, rose up and seemed to find a footing on the chair. He gained his balance and raised his arms above his head. He stood there stony quiet, but something electric seemed to emanate from him, commanding and controlling the people. Everyone faced toward him, but Willoughby saw that the queues weaving through the crowd were unbroken. "Listen," she said, catching some of the excitement.

General Thatcher's voice boomed out, startling in its volume. "I am the president of this bank." He had the kind of authority that expects to be obeyed, the kind of authority that compels obedience, and Willoughby had again the impression that a strange personality had taken over the body of the bouncing little General. The people in front of the tellers' windows ceased to shove and the tellers stood still with their hands full of bills.

"I am the president of this bank. I have only this to say. The bank has plenty of money. Come and get it. Get all you want. We'll pay every single depositor the full amount. The bank will not close its doors. That's all."

He stepped down and vanished. Talking broke out everywhere and the tellers' hands began to move again, counting bills. For Willoughby the interest in the scene was over and she started to speak, but Bobbie said with a long sigh of relief, "I think he's stopped them."

The crowd seemed to be thinning out and quite a number of people were moving toward the door. The queues wavered, and here and there someone stepped out of line. The run was over almost before it had started.

"Were they all getting their money out?"

"Yes."

"I think we can get down now."

"Wait a minute and I'll help you."

When she was safely on the floor again Willoughby said, "I've got to hurry. I'm meeting someone."

"I'll see you to the door." There was still enough of a crowd to make walking difficult.

A thought struck Willoughby. "Bobbie, what does it mean when someone buys control of a company?"

A slow flush of misery crept over Bobbie's face up to his white eyelashes. "You've heard about it," he said dejectedly.

"Yes, but what does it *mean?*" Good Lord, how he showed his emotions.

He seized her hand. "Oh, Willie, I'd have tried to stop it if I could. They've sold him out. He doesn't control the mill any more. Sometimes I *hate* my father!"

"You mean father has sold the mill?"

"No— Oh, Willie, he owed money to the bank and now he can't pay so the bank took the mill—control, that is—and sold it to Sam Hadley."

Willoughby stared at him a minute blankly. "You mean he doesn't have the mill *or* the money?"

"It isn't quite as simple as that, Willie. I'm sure there will always be a place for your father . . ."

Willoughby wasn't listening. Her mind had grasped the essential facts and was speeding on from there. The things she was beginning to understand made her feel weak and trembly, and the floor felt like sponge under her feet. "Why," she whispered, "we'll be *poor.*"

"Willie?"

"Leave me alone!"

She turned her back on him and walked away, very erect, and he stood watching her, swallowing and swallowing while his Adam's apple pumped up and down.

The sunlight hit her full in the face like a blow, and she stood still. There was Sam, leaning against the carriage door, huge and confident. Her hand stole out and she laid it flat on the wall for support. Sam! Sam owning the mill. Sam in control. She straightened up, stretching her figure to its full height. She lifted her chin and controlled the trembling of her hands. She smiled, and her smile was full of radiance. She came down the steps toward him like a queen. A plan was already taking form in her mind.

"Sam!"

"Hullo. I took you at your word, and here I am." He opened the carriage door and held it for her.

"This is lovely," she murmured, giving him a quick, provocative look through her lashes as she stepped in, and there was no sign of her swift and calculating thoughts.

He stepped in beside her and, turning sidewise, looked her over from head to foot, deliberately. "You look fine." His stare was cold and amused.

She reached out and touched his knee lightly with the tips of her fingers. "I'm *so* glad to see you."

"Yea? Say, didn't you have a maid with you?"

"Oh, I lost her in the crowd. Never mind her. I thought perhaps you'd like a little drive, Sam. I'll take you anywhere you'd like to go."

He laughed at this and she glanced up at him again with a faint and rather wistful smile. For an instant they looked straight at each other. Her eyes were carefully questioning; his, bold and probing. Each was trying to see the other's thoughts and their expressions hardened subtly, the one toward the other without either one relinquishing any detail of external manner.

Hadley broke the spell. "All right. I've got to go to the mill, but I'd just as soon not get there too quick. Let's go." He leaned back sidewise on the soft cushions. She was surprised to find she was trembling a little in response to the violence in their relationship that both felt and both so elaborately concealed. She tightened her grip on herself and, smiling sweetly, swayed a little toward him.

"Sam, let's run away from everything for a while. . . . Joe, the park, please."

During the drive through the city they talked very little, without noticing their own silences. On the exterior, Willoughby appeared all soft sensuality, but inside she had hardness and determination. Understanding very little of what had happened, Willoughby magnified the catastrophe until she was convinced that complete poverty was imminent and irrevocable. To her mind no disaster could be worse, but she wasted no time in lamentations, even in her own thoughts. In disaster the only thinkable course for a nature such as hers was survival, and the cost to others made not the slightest difference. The whole of her—vitality, will and brain—was engaged in saving herself.

Once she stole a look at Sam. He was staring off into the distance and smiling at his own thoughts. Seeing his abstraction, she studied him carefully. For the first time Willoughby was looking squarely and appraisingly at him. What her mind saw, with shock, was not the uncouth admirer with a big body capable of giving her thrills. It upset her to realize that, had she looked earlier and with more attention, she might have seen a great deal more than this. She saw now that he was capable of swift, and even ruthless, action and she perceived, if somewhat dimly, that he was strong and that the characteristics she had labeled "nerve" and "presumptuousness" came from his confidence in his own ability.

This realization gave Willoughby pause, but only briefly. Her goal was now clear in her mind and she set about reaching it, sweeping all other considerations out of the way. She drew a deep breath, fortifying herself, and looked up at him with wide, admiring eyes.

"Sam, I think you are the most exciting man I know." She said it a little breathlessly, as though her words were tremulous with passion. All physical desire for him, for the moment at least, had fled.

He laughed and his bold eyes traveled all over her. They were driving slowly through the sooty park, and a warm fall wind blew in the tops of the trees. Out on the dazzling lake little whitecaps flecked the surface and crashed against the breakwater in showers of spray. A curl of Willoughby's golden hair came loose and blew across her lips, and she opened them and bit the curl in her teeth, laughing. He seized both her hands and drew her violently toward him. She struggled free and, still laughing, raised her arms to pin the curl back in place. The gesture brought her body erect and her well-rounded breasts strained against the gray cloth of her bodice. She saw Sam's eyes dwell on them, burning. A shiver ran up her spine and she could not have said whether it came from apprehension or excitement, but she prolonged her gesture ever so little.

"Joe," she said, "drive down to the beach."

"I daren't, Miss. The team's afraid of the engines."

"All right, then, go as near as you can and we'll walk."

Hadley helped her over the shining rails with his hand under her arm and the back of his hand pressed against the curve of her breast. "Just like Nora and her young man," she thought, "on her Sunday off!" But she did nothing to resist and he kept his hand there after the rails were passed.

Sand filled her shoes and the brisk breeze buffeted her. She laughed and faced it, thinking about the new French hoops that concealed her figure so little in the front. The wind blew the hair back from her face and she leaned into it, like a figure on the prow of a ship, very much aware that Hadley was watching her and that she could count on his making the next move. It came at once. His hand under her arm jerked her around roughly. They were standing on the deserted beach but in full view from the park on the bank above them, and without a word he pulled her after him into the shelter of a clump of bushes that were struggling to grow in the side of the clay bank. Still roughly, he drew her down beside him on the sand, holding her tightly against him and pressing his mouth on hers.

For a time she lay quietly in his arms, thinking her own thoughts, but then the physical desire which he had always been able to arouse in her flared up. She returned his kisses with a reckless passion, swept away, forgetting herself and the purpose for which she was here, forgetting everything but her overwhelming longing for this man.

Sam felt her desire and it released all the restraints in him. Kneeling over her, his breath coming quickly, he struggled with the buttons on her bodice. At this Willoughby regained a little of herself, enough so that the shrewd and calculating in her took control once more. She struggled to free herself and Sam, astonished, hurt and angry, finally let her go. She scrambled to her feet and they faced each other and for an instant their true feelings were in their faces. Then she hung her head and took a step toward him.

"Not that. Not unless you are going to marry me, Sam."

She did not raise her eyes. This was her gambler's throw and, as the silence lengthened out, suspense tightened her nerves so that blood sang in her ears and blurred her sight.

Sam spoke in a strangely hushed voice, huskily. "Do you want to marry me, Willoughby?"

"Oh, yes, Sam, yes! Let's get married now—at once!" She threw herself on him.

He pulled her arms from around his neck, stepped back and held her by her wrists. "Did you hear something at the bank? God Almighty, answer me! Did you hear something at the bank and rig this up because I got the mill? Answer me!"

He began to shake her. His fingers bit into her wrists and he shook her until he really hurt her.

"Sam, don't. Don't, Sam." She tore herself out of his grasp and burst into tears of defeat and nervous collapse. For once in her life she wasn't acting.

"Jesus!" he said very low. After a moment he took hold of her arms firmly but, this time, not roughly enough to hurt her, and pulled her hands away from her face.

"Willoughby, listen here. Did anybody at the bank tell you I'd bought control of the mill?"

She shook her head and looked sullen and tearful, like a child, and she began to sniff and sob again because she was afraid to trust her voice for fear she could not make it sound truly convincing.

"Do you know what I'm talking about? Do you know what it means —to buy control?"

This was safer. "I don't know what you mean—control. Papa controls the mill." She was still relying on the tearful manner.

Sam put his hand under her chin, raised her face and looked at her searchingly. She had the sense, or the artistry, not to try to look candid. She merely continued to look aggrieved, hurt, and her mouth pouted.

He took away his hand. "I'd like to know what you're up to," he said thoughtfully and a little resentfully.

"Sam, I'm not up to anything—don't you see?" She moved close to him, burying her head in his chest so that he could no longer see her face. "If you want to know the truth, I've never been able to forget you since that first kiss." Suddenly she threw her arms around him. "Sam— Sam," she cried, and she pressed her body against him with wild, frantic passion.

For a while he resisted her and then she felt him begin to tremble. "Christ," he said. "Christ!" There was suddenly a white-hot intensity in his passion that made her exult. At that she struggled free, pulled out a handkerchief and began composedly to wipe her eyes, not looking at him.

"All right," he said. "All right. I don't care whether you're lying or not. I think you probably are—and I don't care. I don't care about a Goddamned thing but you. If you want to get married, all right!"

"Oh, Sam!" She stood off a little way, not risking his embrace. "Why not now, Sam? Why not right away?"

He thought a minute, and she held her breath.

"I'll have to tell your father about this first."

"No, don't tell him!" Panic filled her. "Don't tell him. He'd stop us."

"Oh, no, he won't."

"But Sam, you don't have to tell him till *afterwards.*"

Hadley did not reply and after what seemed like a long time to her she looked at him questioningly. He saw her look and grinned. The grin was so unexpected it unnerved her a little.

"I guess I do," he said. "It's a funny thing, but I guess I do." He went on almost as though he were talking to himself about something which he found astonishing. "I couldn't do *that* to him without giving him a chance to fight back. Business is another matter." He seemed to be thinking about this, smiling a little as though this were a joke on himself. By and by he looked up. "Don't worry. I'll manage *him.* Where do you want to get married? And when?"

"The City Hall?" Now that the strain was over, she was shaking. She wanted to get back to the carriage and sit down. "See Father first, if you have to, but right after that. Can we? Right away—today?"

"Sure. All right, the City Hall." He pulled out a watch. "Listen, I'll go to see your father now, if you'll drop me at the mill. You'd better not wait there. I'll meet you at the City Hall at five. There isn't much time."

"Don't forget to bring witnesses," Willoughby said sweetly. Except for a slight shakiness in the knees, Willoughby was herself again.

24

As HADLEY mounted the front steps of Fenno and Company he looked around him with proprietorship. "I can't believe it," he said half aloud, and then, "Damned inefficient arrangement, hauling the ore up the bank by team. I'll put in narrow gauge." These and similar reflections carried him as far as Fenno's anteroom, where Flint barred the way, looking, Hadley thought, rather like a fancy, pop-eyed Pekinese. "One thing's sure—you're fired," he said to himself, grinning at Flint.

At sight of Hadley, Flint was shocked and flustered. "I'm sure he won't want to see *you*, Mr. Hadley."

"He'll see me," Hadley said easily. "Tell him I'm here."

"Mr. Cushing is with him now."

"I thought Cushing finally resigned."

"He did, Mr. Hadley, when Mr. Fenno took those new contracts from Cooke. But something seems to have happened. If I were you, I wouldn't wait."

"Something *has* happened," Hadley said, settling down in a chair. He was not one to dramatize himself but, nevertheless, it pleased him to walk in like this with no fanfare and wait in seeming humility.

After awhile the door of Fenno's office opened and Cushing came out. When he turned around and caught sight of Hadley he started, flushed like a schoolboy, opened his mouth to speak, shut it again and, with one quick gesture, brushed his glasses from his nose. They swung back and forth, like a pendulum, on their black cord, while Cushing blinked at the misty void in front of him. Then he scooped them up, settled them on his nose, gave Hadley one sharp-edged look and hurried out without a word.

Hadley rose slowly and went to Fenno's door. Something in the atmosphere seemed to have paralyzed Flint, and Hadley turned the handle of the door and entered with no protest from that quarter. John

Fenno was sitting in his big swivel chair with his back to the light. His shoulders were stooped a little. His eyes were sunken and his hands rested flat on the arms of his chair, as though they constituted a weight too great to lift. The sun was streaming in behind him, but he gave the effect of sitting in deep shadow.

Hadley came a little way into the room and stopped. "I see you know," he said quietly.

Fenno neither moved nor spoke.

"He's at bay," Hadley thought, and was astonished to find that his own heart was beating fast. "He's not going to ask for quarter." There was something noble, something unquenchable about the once-erect figure in the chair, and in that minute Hadley was nearer to liking Fenno than he had ever been before.

A straight chair with a high back stood close to Hadley. He reached out and, drawing it to him, he folded his arms along its top and put his foot on a rung, as he might have on the brass rail of a bar. .

"Look here, sir," he said. "I don't want to put you out. I'd like to have you stay—in a position of honor, as Chairman of the Board. I need—the mill needs you." Hadley was too tough-grained to feel unhappy, but he had come far along a new path in the past year and he was experiencing no enjoyment.

Fenno raised his head and squared his shoulders and one hand left the arm of the chair.

"No!"

"Look, Mr. Fenno, I'd rather you didn't answer now. Take time and think about it. Talk to the Board."

Fenno's flash of animation was brief. He seemed to have sunk downward, as though some inner support had collapsed. Hadley waited a moment and then went on.

"I hate like hell to tell you this, Mr. Fenno, but there's a special reason why I'd like you to stay with us as Chairman of the Board. Willoughby and I are going to be married."

Once, during the war, Sam had stood on a hillside talking to his superior officer. The valley below them was calm and peaceful under a blue haze of autumn, and far off to the left of them they could see the Confederate encampment, grayish tents dotting the banks of a tiny river. They were not talking about anything much; just letting the sunlight and peace penetrate their tired bones. Suddenly, the captain's body had jerked strangely and as Sam turned to see what ailed him, he crumpled slowly to the ground.

Fenno's body had jerked just as the captain's had, but he did not crumple. Instead, as Hadley stepped forward, he turned his swivel chair around to face the lake, his back to Hadley.

This mute appeal for privacy touched Hadley and he stood still, gloomily staring at the chair's unrevealing back. After awhile he said, "I really want you to stay with us, Mr. Fenno, and I hope that's the way you'll see it."

He expected no reply and he got none. Only one sleeve of Fenno's coat was visible, the rest of him hidden by the high back of his chair. Hadley was shocked to see that sleeve trembling. He turned toward the door, walking noisily so that Fenno would be sure to hear him and know that he was alone. With his hands on the knob he paused, thought a minute and then turned the knob and went out.

Flint was sitting at his desk with his hands under it, somewhere, out of sight. He stared at Hadley with fright in his eyes. "Now where the hell," Hadley thought, "did he find out? Is everyone going to be afraid?" He suddenly felt lonely.

He was almost at the hall door before he remembered something and came back. "Got a piece of paper?" he asked Flint.

"Yes, sir."

A tablet and a slim pen were held out to Hadley. He took them and wrote: "We are going to be married at the City Hall at five today. We would like to have you there, sir." At the bottom of this he scrawled a large S.H., folded it and handed it to Flint.

"Wait about ten minutes and take that to Mr. Fenno. I suppose it won't do any good to tell you not to read it."

The hall was empty of people and Hadley stood still, slid his hand almost affectionately along the banister rail and looked all around him. "Jesus, I can't believe it," he thought with wonder. Then he grinned. "I suppose, to do the thing right, I ought to throw the Old Man out of his office, put my feet on his desk and pound a bell. It's all different from what I thought it would be like, but, by God, there's one little job I'm going to enjoy!" With an air of determination he started down the hall toward Mark's office.

When, without warning, the door burst open, Mark started, and when he saw that the intruder was Hadley, his anger flared. Mark's eyes were never cold, and just now they were full of amber sparks of hatred. He put down the pen hard, splattering ink.

"What the hell are *you* doing here?"

"If you didn't shut yourself in, as though work were some kind of crime, you'd know. Probably everybody but the night watchman knows by this time."

"What are you talking about?"

Hadley planted his foot on the seat of a convenient chair, leaned his arm on his knee and pointed a thick finger at Mark. "Listen," he said, "I bought control of this place today. You and Lacy Pants there"— Hadley jerked a thumb in the direction of the ante-room—"are through. Get it?"

Mark's eyes narrowed to slits, then, with one fluid motion, he jumped up.

"I don't believe you!" His empty swivel chair swung up and down, the spring complaining.

When Mark leaped up, Hadley put his foot on the floor. His fist closed and his right shoulder drew back, though he hid these motions instinctively by the turn of his body. But Mark was not a fighter. The two men stared at each other, Mark's face full of hatred, Hadley's reflecting his contempt for the slim man with the long fingers and the catlike eyes. Hadley was the first to break this brief silence.

"All right. Clear out quick. I'll be wanting this office for somebody else right away. Somebody who used to be a friend of yours. Tomorrow I'm taking over. This afternoon"—an inward sort of smile spread over Hadley's face—"this afternoon I have something else to do."

With that he turned and walked out, leaving Mark still standing there. In the hall he let himself indulge in a very pleasant feeling of satisfaction. "That," he thought, "was something I *really* enjoyed." He looked at his watch and went clumping downstairs in a hurry, to summon the Company carriage.

From the mill Hadley had himself driven straight to the Brodis'. This was not his first visit to their humble quarters. These consisted of two rooms in a boarding house which, unlike Mrs. Adams', catered to married couples. He knocked on the door and waited, smiling a little at the sound of scurrying inside. Presently the door was thrown open by Lettie. When she saw who it was, a pleased smile lit her face.

"Mr. Hadley! Do come in."

"You were going to call me Sam. Remember?"

Lettie blushed. "Sam. Please excuse the awful mess things are in," she went on, making way for him. "We're packing to go to Hudson. School opens Monday and we were going today, only Michael has been so interested in"—she took a special breath—"in the current economic devolopments," she brought out proudly. "He only got back from downtown this minute. I'll tell him you're here."

She walked across the small room to a door, and as she did so she implied, as might an actor crossing a stage, a passage through long corridors and stately chambers. Sam smiled at her back. Sam was not ordinarily a prescient person, but he thought, watching her, "She'll always live in a palace so long as she's happy. I'm darned if I don't think Mike's in luck." Sam was right. Lettie's propensity for romantic imaginings could, at her will, transform her surroundings, and she was fast developing an extraordinary ability to discover beauty and charm and enjoyment in whatever her surroundings might be. This was like finding, at long last, an outlet for a talent.

"Michael, Sam is here."

"Fine. I'll be right out." Mike emerged, putting on his coat. "Hullo, Sam. It's here. This is it. This is the beginning. You've heard about Cooke, haven't you?"

"Yea." Sam grinned. "I've heard. Listen to me, you two. I'm marrying Willoughby. Right away—in less than an hour. At the City Hall. I want you two to be witnesses."

Lettie sat down suddenly on the edge of a trunk. "My goodness me!" Then she giggled. "For goodness' sake. Willoughby! Well, I never."

"I'll be damned," Mike contributed. There was a glint of amusement in his bright black eyes.

"We'll have to hurry," Sam said, and he sounded ever so slightly aggrieved.

Lettie jumped up. "My goodness! I can't go in *this* dress!" She made a dash for the bedroom, slamming the door behind her.

"Listen, fella," Sam said, sitting down on the top of the trunk Lettie had just vacated. "I want to talk to you especially." The trunk had a rounded top and Hadley shifted to a more stable seat. "It's like this. They've got the nervous jumps at Thatcher's bank. I thought they might have and that they might be darned glad to convert what looks like a bad loan into some ready cash. So I went in and offered to take the Fenno and Company stock off their hands. Thatcher snapped it up. So—I own control. What do you think of that?"

Brodi threw back his head and laughed. "I think you're a damned dangerous fellow to know. Congratulations. How does it feel to be a big gun?"

"A lot different from what I thought. I've just come from the mill and, Jesus, I'm sorry for the Old Man. I asked him to stay on as Chairman of the Board."

"Will he?"

"I suppose so, when he's had time to think it over. Then I went around to Mark's office and fired him. *That* was a pleasure! What I'm getting at is this: How about your coming with us in Mark's place? I tell you"—Hadley's voice became earnest—"I've got to thinking we need somebody like you for two reasons. First, I've got a feeling I'd like to try out some of these labor ideas of yours and find out if there's anything to 'em. Then, too, I don't mind telling you that what's happened to Cooke has scared the hell out of me. I have an idea we're still in for a lot of jolts. It's going to take a while for business to get over what's happened, but all that's too far out of my line. I've just got sense enough to know that it's going to affect me, but I need an expert to talk these things over with and to tell me what to watch out for. What about it? We could make the salary right, I should think."

Brodi did not reply at once. After a minute he smiled, and it was both a smile and gravely serious at the same time, the kind of smile that is the peculiar characteristic of the intellectual and is never seen on the faces of those who are predominantly men of action. Such a smile often unduly impresses the latter type. With Brodi the recently acquired mannerism was wholly unconscious.

"I appreciate that, Sam. Thanks. But no, I can't do it."

"Why not, fella? I need you. By God, I do!"

Brodi shoved his hands in his pockets and began to pace the little room. After two or three laps he came to a halt in front of Hadley and rocked back and forth on his heels.

"I want to keep on with my writing."

"That isn't the real reason," Sam said shrewdly.

"No, it isn't. Listen. You're one of the big guns now. There hasn't been time for it to affect you any, yet. But it will. It will never make a Fenno out of you, but in your own way you'll get the point of view of the top and, though maybe right now you'd deny it, gradually you'll forget what it's like to be in the ranks—if you ever knew," Brodi said parenthetically and grinned. "Little by little I'd find myself working *for* you, not *with* you. This is especially true because you aren't really a liberal and you are going to find yourself sympathizing more and more with the other side."

Hadley started to interrupt and Mike held up a hand. "No, let me finish. I know you don't agree with me, but it's true. I appreciate your offer." Mike paused and, when he went on, it was with a faint trace of embarrassment at the necessity for expressing sentiment. "There's no reason why we can't stay friends, fella."

"I wish to hell you'd do it."

"No, I'm going to stay on the outside." Suddenly Brodi grinned again. "And if I don't like the way you handle labor, I'll fight you with everything I've got."

Hadley looked puzzled and serious. "Jesus, I never know what you're going to think about anything. Listen here. . . ."

He got no farther. The door of the other room burst open and Lettie came out.

"Will I do, Michael? Michael, will I do?"

"You look fine."

"We'll be crowded in the rig," Hadley said, "Come on."

While they drove to the City Hall they talked very little, restrained by the alien presence of the driver. Hadley was lost in serious thought and Mike felt sure he was reviewing their conversation. Presently Sam's expression changed to one of somewhat fatuous pride. "He's thinking about Willoughby now," Mike thought, liking him. They mounted the steps and stood just inside the door of the City Hall, feeling vague.

"Where were you to meet her, Sam?"

"Darned if I know. We just said City Hall."

Hadley seemed to Mike a trifle awestruck and to have lost some of his powers of locomotion. He grinned. "I know how it feels," he thought, and from then on he unobstrusively took command.

"We're blocking the way here," he said. "The room you want is down that corridor, second door on the left. Lettie can show you. We know all about it." Lettie smiled as though he had said something delightfully witty. "Lettie and you go on and keep them from closing up. I'll wait for her here."

To his surprise, he did not have long to wait. "She gauged it nicely," he thought. "Kept Sam waiting but got here before the place closed up." He stood at the top of the steps and watched her collect her ruffles and climb down from the hired hack. "Cinderella out of the pumpkin," he thought. "She's gorgeous, but Sam's welcome to her." Willoughby turned to pay the driver, raking over the coins in her purse daintily, with her gloved finger. "If I were a gentleman, I'd go down and pay it for her."

She was dressed in a wonderful and daring color that was somewhere between yellow and orange, and her gown was trimmed with embroidered autumn leaves in dark orange and brown and, here and there, a little green. The details were lost on Mike, but he saw that the dress made her golden hair look like a maple after frost. "She'll cost Sam more than he thinks," and he went down a few steps to meet her, resenting the stares that everyone in the neighborhood turned in their direction.

If she felt any uneasiness at seeing Mike instead of Hadley, she concealed it admirably.

"Why, Mr. Brodi, what brings *you* here?"

"I'm a witness, I guess. Sam's gone to make sure the clerk doesn't leave. Lettie's here too."

"My sister! Really?" Willoughby laughed. "I suppose you're my brother-in-law. I hadn't thought about it before."

"Turn down here," Brodi said.

They walked on in silence, while Willoughby enjoyed the sensation she was creating in the dirty passage of the City Hall and Brodi nursed anger at himself for being aware, every time he met this tall beauty, of the shortness of his own muscular body.

He opened a door and stood back, letting her enter. "I wonder how long it took her to develop a walk like that," he thought, watching her fluid motion and seeing in his mind's eye Lettie's bumpy bounce, loving it.

Willoughby floated forward. "Sam, and Lettie. Imagine my sister coming to my wedding." She looked Lettie up and down in the way that had always made Lettie cringe and flush and droop with gawky misery. Lettie giggled. Suddenly Mike felt as though someone had opened a cage and let a captive out. "She's free, praise God, she's free," and he wanted to shout. This toughened product of a hard world felt weak in the knees and excited and soft at the core, as though that giggle were of import incalculable.

That, is perhaps, the reason why Brodi, afterwards, found he had no very clear-cut impressions of the ceremony which followed. The clerk, who had the mediocre but stubborn look so common among public servants of all ranks, was annoyed at their arrival, for his register was already in the safe and he was being put to the trouble of getting it out again. Nor did Brodi remember the clerk's face, though he did remember the small cloud of dust that arose when the clerk slapped the register down irritably on the counter behind which he stood. Mike remembered, too, the glare from the tall, uncurtained and very dirty windows and the smell, the sour, animal smell, that seems to pervade all buildings dedicated to public use.

The little party moved up toward the counter, Willoughby and Sam in front, Lettie and Mike behind them. The clerk began to speak in a nasal and irritated voice. Mike did not listen because just then Lettie turned up her face and smiled at him and he was filled with the necessity for returning her smile in such a way as to do her the honor he felt she deserved.

Willoughby was self-possessed and aloof, and Mike hated her. Then he forgot her because of something which sounded in Hadley's voice. This was a deep earnestness, a gravity, and hearing it, Mike saw a little deeper into his friend's character. A kind of dignity seemed to have invaded the dirty room, redeeming the hurried, undignified business of the marriage. Brodi glanced at Lettie to see if she felt it also and, finding that she did, his rejoicing went far beyond the need of the occasion.

There was no wedding ring, everybody having, in the hurry, forgotten the necessity for such a thing. Sam dislodged with difficulty from his own finger a battered article with a cat's-eye setting, and they were married with that. The clerk dipped a pen and held it out, shoving the register toward them.

"Well, folks, you're married," he said, sinking his irritability in a kind of professional jocularity.

They signed, Hadley first and then Willoughby. Then she pulled the cat's-eye ring off her finger and held it out to Sam.

"Here, you'll have to get me a *nice* one right away."

Sam took it, looking first dashed and then confident and amused. Mike noticed that he did not put it back on his finger but dropped it into his pocket.

That was all. Willoughby and Sam said good-bye to the Brodis on the sidewalk. Willoughby was still haughty and aloof. Just as Mike and Lettie were turning away, Sam put his hand on Mike's shoulder and walked a few steps beside him.

"Listen, fella. I wish you'd reconsider what we were talking about at your place, but if you won't maybe you'd let us pay you for your opinion about things now and then, when we need it. Sort of like a doctor—consulting."

Brodi took a few seconds to think. "I could do that. Yes, sure, I'd be glad to do that."

"Fine."

The two men shook hands while the two women looked on.

As this scene was taking place on the sidewalk, Fenno was letting himself into the big house. He had a great deal of difficulty fitting the key into the lock of the front door and no realization that Joe was standing watching him or any memory that Joe had just helped him out of the carriage and up the front steps. The door seemed very heavy as he pushed it open, and his eyes adjusted slowly to the dimmer light within. He stood still, to listen, but he heard only a strange ringing in his ears, like eerie and distant bells. Then he found himself leaning on the hall table without being able to tell whether a great deal of time, or none at all, had elapsed.

He straightened up and squared his shoulders and then, with infinite daring, he took his fingers away from the support of the table top.

"Must see a doctor," he said aloud, thickly.

He walked into the drawing room and as he did so, the mists cleared and everything came back to him. He pulled out his hunter with shaking fingers and compared the time carefully with that of the ormolu clock on the mantle shelf. Five-thirty. So it was probably done by this time. Over. Matild must be told. Where was Matild? Upstairs, probably. She liked to take her corsets off. His mind's eye, however, saw a Matild of long ago, plump and pretty, with a mouth that showed traces of a stubbornness which must be conquered. Genteelly poor, this girl was, but she had an aristocratic name that appealed to him more than her soft body. Fenno was not aware, for the moment, that time had been at work on this girl. He'd have to tell her, but just now talking to her seemed a tremendous effort. "Let her wait," he thought. "Let her wait." And then he found himself in his study again, with no sense at all of the time that had elapsed since he had stood in the drawing room. This did not trouble him greatly. Rather, he felt that the disruption of connected time was something to be mused on, a point on which to fasten attention in surrounding mists. He heard the front door slam and then Ellen's voice was saying, "Mr. Mark wants to see you, sir." He knew it was Ellen with perfect and pleasing clarity.

He felt the leather of his chair under his hands, just as he had always felt it. He ran his hand along the seat stealthily, because the feeling gave him confidence.

"Tell him to wait, Williams," he said in a very loud voice. "Tell them all to wait."

When Hadley had left the office, Mark continued to stand, staring at nothing, his mustache twitching and his amber eyes flickering. "It's Uncle John's fault," he thought. "The whole thing's Uncle John's fault and he'll have to fix this. By God, he'll have to fix something up for me quick. He got me into this mess."

Mark went straight to the Fenno house, where he paced around the drawing room impatiently until Ellen came back. Ellen said, "Mr. Fenno says to wait, sir," and so Mark was forced to wait and to try to put on the semblance of calm. He sat on the *tête* with his knees crossed, and swung one foot up and bit his mustache and looked at his nails without seeing them. "He certainly owes it to me to find me something good," he thought. "After all, I'm going to be his son-in-law." With every passing second the strain of waiting mounted until Mark felt brittle with nerves. Then he remembered the decanter.

He rose at once and went into the dining room, where he stood beside the sideboard and drank the whisky straight. There was no glass handy so he drank out of the decanter, folding his red lips around the crystal top. He dribbled some of the third swig on his cravat, but he did not bother to wipe it off. Courage was beginning to fill his veins, the courage he needed to tell the Old Man a thing or two. The liquor, however, did not seem to be affecting him at all. He couldn't feel it. By the time he had downed the fourth drink a subtle change had come over Mark. Nothing about his appearance had altered, really, but he looked coarser and older and things that had lain hidden under his polished exterior were now, for the first time, reflected in his face.

His brain, however, was crystal clear. Willoughby, he saw, was still his trump card. Because of her, Fenno would certainly help to fix him up in something good. And Willoughby would want him more than ever. "I'd be a regular lifeline to her," he thought. But did he want Willoughby? He considered this, holding the decanter in both hands and leaning one elbow on the sideboard, standing gracefully with his feet crossed. He looked like a fashion plate gone slightly blowzy. The answer was plain enough. It was "no." "Only till I get fixed up. She's damn important to me till I get fixed up but then—to hell with her!"

He was so preoccupied that he did not hear the front door open or know that anybody but himself was in the front of the house, until he looked up and saw Willoughby and Hadley standing in the hall and staring at him in astonishment. He set the decanter back in place, harder than he intended, and bowed to them.

"Charmed," he said. "Simply charmed. May I ask what the hell you're doing here, Hadley?"

He came out into the hall as he spoke, and he was amused to note that Willoughby did not seem at all pleased at finding him there. She turned her back at once and walked haughtily into the drawing room. Hadley did not bother to answer and both men followed Willoughby. It was then that a devastating thought came to Mark. Willoughby and Hadley! "That would solve all her problems," he told himself, and he looked from one to the other while his knees grew weak and a wave of apprehension went through his slim body.

For a while nobody said anything. Willoughby threw her purse and gloves on a chair, but she kept her hat on. She began to wander around the room, poking at ornaments with her finger. She came to a halt by the piano and turned around to face them.

"I suppose Papa's not home yet?" she asked Mark.

"He's home. He's in his study. I wanted to see him, but he sent word to wait."

"Mama?"

"I don't know. Upstairs, I suppose. Why?"

Willoughby ignored him. "Sam, I *wish* you'd come on. I still think it was a crazy idea, coming here. I could buy what I need." It sounded like an argument that had been going on for some time.

Mark's irritation began to rise. "Hadley, I wish you'd get the hell out. I want to talk to my uncle and I want to talk to Willoughby. If your being here is nothing else, it is certainly bad taste."

Hadley made an angry ejaculation and was about to speak when Willoughby interrupted.

"You may as well know," she said, leaning back against the piano and twining her fingers in the fringe of the "throw." "You might just as well know. Sam and I are married."

"What?"

"You heard me!"

Mark took a forward step and all color drained from his face, leaving a spatter of pale freckles curiously prominent. Then slowly, very slowly, he began to collect himself. Finally, he smiled, tight-lipped. When he spoke, it was to Hadley.

"You married *her?*" He indicated Willoughby with a jerk of his head.

"Yes, if it's any business of yours."

"You poor damn fool. Of course it's my business. Willoughby and I were engaged to be married. Did she remember to tell you that?"

Hadley flushed, and it was perfectly clear to Mark that his blow had struck home. Mark came a step nearer to Hadley.

"No, of course she didn't tell you. And let me tell you this . . ." Mark pointed a pale and slightly trembling finger at Hadley. "Let me tell you this. You've been had. The only Goddamn reason that girl would marry you is because she must have found out you got control. I know her. She trapped you into it. You'll be the laughing stock of the town. Why, you Goddamned fool, she isn't even a . . ."

Something ominous in Hadley stopped Mark and, without actually moving, he seemed to retreat.

Whatever Hadley might have done at this point was forestalled by a scream of rage from Willoughby. She leaped forward, her face contorted. For whatever it was she intended to do to Mark, she had no time. Her action transferred Hadley's attention from Mark to herself. He seized her by an arm and jerked her back. He held her to his side with one arm around her, pinioning her arms to her side.

"Shut up. Both of you!"

He did not say it very loudly, nor did he have to say it twice. The room was absolutely quiet, except for the heavy breathing of all three. Sam took his arm from around Willoughby but he clamped his hand over her wrist. When he spoke, his voice was perfectly calm.

"That's enough of that. What you say may or may not be true. I don't care. That's past. She was her own boss then, but she's my wife now, and I'll take the responsibility for whatever she does. I'll take the responsibility for keeping her in order." He turned to Willoughby and gave her arm a slight tug. "You heard that little speech?" he inquired, almost gently.

She stared at him, wide-eyed and silent. He grinned at her.

Mark shrugged one flexible shoulder. He thrust his hands in his pockets, pushing his coat back at a devil-may-care angle. He turned his back on them and sauntered out of the room. Out in the hall he paused. In the dining room beyond, Ellen and Nora were beginning to set the table for dinner and the faint clink of silver and glass came to him like sounds from another world. He idled over to the hall table and picked up his hat, the elegant hat from the first-class hatter, and held it upside down in his slim, gambler's fingers. He read the name of the first-class hatter carefully, as though it were something of the greatest import. He put the hat on his head and peered into the mirror, adjusting the brim here and there, with the utmost care, until it lay at a flawless angle. The tiles of the vestibule scratched under his feet and the noise seemed to him to fill all space. He opened the front door and stepped out.

Back in the study John Fenno sat very still. In a minute, he knew, it would be necessary to attend to something old Williams had told him about, but now everything seemed so exceedingly peaceful that he did not want to move. His swivel chair seemed to be rocking him gently up and down of its own volition. There was no way of telling how much time had passed. He thought about pulling his hunter out to look, but he remembered that his hunter was exceedingly heavy. Let it go. He felt better, though, much better. He even knew that this was his study and not the office, and that old Williams was long since in the accounting department. "It's some sort of attack," he thought. "Just some sort of attack, like that other one. I really will have to see a doctor." But he had no memory of how he had come to the study, and this bothered him.

There were voices somewhere and he remembered that he was wanted. He summoned his resolution and pushed himself out of his chair. It was easier to stand up than he had expected, though he felt giddy and sick to his stomach. "Too many cigars," he thought. "That's probably the whole trouble—too many cigars." Before he had taken more than a few steps he found that he had a headache, a far worse headache than he had ever had in his life before. He opened the drawing-room door, but the pain was so great he had to hang onto the door frame.

No one ever knew how much of the conversation he may have heard. No one knew, among the emotional tensions in the drawing room, just when he had opened the door.

Willoughby and Hadley followed Mark's departure with their eyes and then they turned to look at each other, silently, estimating, sizing up, preparing for conflict. Something, a sound, perhaps, or the feeling of a presence, made them whirl around. Fenno was standing very straight, with a terrible straightness, but he was hanging onto the door frame with both hands.

"Willoughby," he said. It was the last articulate word he ever spoke and it was a dreadful sound. Willoughby cried out, and ran to him.

25

THE months slipped by, and with their passing, the failure of Cooke and Company began to appear in its proper perspective; that is to say, less as a cause of the catastrophe than as the first visible symptom of an unsuspected disease. When the extent of the disaster was finally brought to light and the necessary adjustments made in business and in industry, it was found that a national disaster of this sort is but the sum of hundreds of thousands of individual disasters. Almost every family in the country was to some degree affected and many were forced to make for themselves new patterns of living.

The Fenno household was one of these, though the great house gave few external signs of the change within. The sun, shining on the ornate façade, revealed that the white had dimmed a little, and the struggle to keep the birds from roosting on the carved acanthus leaves seemed to have been abandoned. No red carpet decorated the front steps and the window boxes were empty of everything but last year's stalks.

These things were signs of neglect and of what Matild liked to describe as their "straitened circumstances." The inside of the house was changed also, but here the change was so much a matter of atmosphere that the physical details of worn upholstery and smudged wall paper were incidental. The house had mellowed, a thing no house can do unless the attitude of those who live there is right for mellowing. The tick of the grandfather clock was more audible, for old clocks are not so much dependent on quiet as on peace for the dispensing of their curative philosophy. The drawing room was softened and its sharp stylishness blurred, but less by the fading of its colors than by a sort of film of living. Books with worn bindings lay on tables and the single vase of flowers gave evidence, not of art, but of an honest love of flowers. Pieces of furniture, moreover, had invaded this room that were never part of the original scheme, having wandered down from the attic like poor relations come to sit at a party.

Matild raised her head to listen, blinking her eyes against the sun which came through the drawn-back curtains. A faint thumping could he heard from upstairs and she pushed her sewing off her lap and, rising, swayed out into the hall. Her ample figure was uncorseted.

"Coming, John," she called placidly. "Coming," and she began to climb the stairs. She was rather more agile about it than she had been a year ago, for the flabbiness of her short figure had hardened somewhat. On the landing, by the long window ledge full of plants, she paused for what was to be just a little minute, to touch the velvety bell of a fuchsia blossom. There was a tender pleasure in the way she bent over the plants and a soft smile crept into the pale eyes that had more light in them than formerly, and dented the corners of a mouth less prone to droop.

Her hand left the fuchsia blossom, wandered and came to rest cupping the serrated leaf of a rose geranium. The plant still looked a trifle denuded, she noticed, for they had used so many of the young leaves to put in the bottom of the jelly glasses before the pale gold apple jelly was poured in. Here, in the strong light from the window, the strain was evident among the pouches of Matild's face, but a softening process had taken place, and it was plain that the look of strain was now largely a habit of the muscles, as though they retained a memory of things almost forgotten by the spirit.

The renewed pounding of John Fenno's stick on the floor ended Matild's communion with her plants. "Coming, dear, coming," she called, and she paused only long enough to touch the fuchsia blossom with one short finger and watch it swing back and forth on its stalk before she climbed the last of the steps and entered the bedroom where he lay.

"You wanted me, John?"

She looked down inquiringly on the pale, stern but still handsome figure stretched out on the bed. Then she smiled and, until this past year, there had not been such a smile on her face since those days when her babies were little. It was a maternal smile, full of proprietorship. John Fenno had not looked at Matild for years, but had he done so now, as she bent over him, it might have seemed to him that he was seeing dimly, as in the depths of an old, silvery and clouded mirror, a faint image of the girl of long ago. Some of the proprietorship in the smile did reach him, however, for he shut his eyes and turned his head away, but before his eyes closed there was in them a look of helpless fury. John Fenno's spirit still blazed.

"What was it you wanted?" she said.

With his head still turned away he made a strange, animal sound in his throat. Her hand stole out and she smoothed the turned-down edge of the sheet and gave the counterpane a gentle tug. Sometimes it was so very hard to understand him.

"What, dear? Watch? It's right there beside you. It's just half-past three. No?"

He opened his eyes and glared reproachfully at her. She answered his look with a soothing, conciliatory pat on his shoulder. At this his big frame seemed to tremble with a deep anger which Matild disregarded as she might the querulous frettings of a child. The fact was, Matild no longer feared her husband, and in this lay the clue to the change which had taken place, not only in Matild herself and in her appearance, but even in the atmosphere of the house. Matild was happy.

"Weather?" she said inquiringly. "Was that what you wanted to know? It's quite warm for October, really. Indian summer—Indian summer," she repeated, liking the phrase. She looked to see if she had guessed right and met the smoldering eyes. "Oh, dear," she said. "I think you'd better write it down," and she handed him a tablet and pencil from the bedside table and pushed up the pillow behind his head.

Waiting for the slow, clumsy writing to be finished, she thought, "How he hates it all. But he couldn't do without me for a minute." A warm glow of pleasing satisfaction filled her. "Not for a minute. Not for a single minute." It was almost like having one of her dear babies back again.

She took the tablet from him. "Oh," she said brightly. "Water. I should have guessed. I'll just get you some fresh—nice and cool." And she swayed away toward the tap in the hall cupboard. She brought the glass back, dripping, and the water looked so good she took a little sip before she sat down on the bed to hold him up and help him drink, even though she knew he hated to have her do a thing like that. So private he had always been about all his possessions and about all his thoughts. He put his lips to a clean place on the glass, gulped thirstily and motioned her peremptorily away.

She drew her little rocker up beside the bed, sat down and folded her hands in her lap. Her wrinkled lids lowered drowsily and she slipped off into a vacuity of peace and contentment. From time to time she opened her eyes and looked at the bed. Usually John Fenno lay on his back, staring at the ceiling, his face bitter and hard, but now, when she looked again, his eyes were on her with such an expression of hurt and misery and bafflement that she rose and took his hand.

He let her hold it and once he even tightened his fingers on hers, making her heart swell with pity and warmth until it almost choked her. Then he thrust it away petulantly and the old, fierce light came back. His spunk pleased her.

"That's right," she murmured approvingly. "That's right."

He shut his eyes, as though against something his spirit could not bear, and she went back to her seat. While he lay there with his eyes shut, she studied his face with interest. How strange his skin looked since the stroke, transparent but taut, as though all its elasticity had gone. Today his yellowish pallor was tinged with gray, and she wondered hazily if this foreboded any change in him. She sighed with a melancholy that was not wholly unpleasant.

Sometimes his prostrate figure made her think of a great oak in her mother's back garden that had fallen one stormy day when she was a little girl. The tree looked so stricken, lying there, that she had cried for it. With time, the stricken look that had touched her began to vanish, for with each passing year the firm outline of the huge trunk blurred a little, rotting here and there, sinking closer to the earth, gradually losing its identity in the soil. The realization that something like this was happening to John Fenno brought her sadness, but no sharp sorrow. For her, less grief would accompany his death than there had been in his life. Gentle melancholy has a soothing touch. After awhile Matild slept.

She woke again to find his eyes on her, burning and angry. They were directed, seemingly, to the collar of her dress and, still half asleep, her hand went up to discover the cause of his black gaze. Her fingers touched a small pin at her throat. A startled look came on her face and for a moment all the old strain and guilt were there.

The pin was a lovely thing, a snowflake in diamonds with a large diamond sparkling in the center. Matild had loved it from the moment she found it, so surprisingly in a drawer in John Fenno's dressing room. She was "redding up" his drawers, after his stroke, extending the boundaries of her kingdom to include this room, as she had, later, extended them to the whole house. Here she came on the little box with the name of a New York jeweler on the outside. She pressed the catch and there the snowflake lay, glittering on its velvet bed.

Several weeks passed before she opened the drawer again and took it out of its box. It must have been bought on that last trip of his, she thought—for her—though she did not really believe this last. She pinned it on, pretending, and after that she wore it often, though never in her husband's presence. "I just forgot," she thought, covering the pin with shaky fingers and gazing at her husband with a kind of fascinated horror.

The fire of anger burned brightly in his eyes and then, by degrees, a dreadful resignation took its place, a look so full of unhappiness that she forgot the pin. "He's thinking of Willoughby," she thought. "I can always tell when he's thinking of Willoughby."

Somewhere a door opened and footsteps approached the room. Matild's unstable attention shifted to them. "Lettie," she thought placidly. A comfort, a real comfort to have them living in the house. Lettie's head appeared around the door. She glanced inquiringly at her mother. Matild looked at the bed, saw her husband's eyes were again closed, and raised a finger to smiling lips. John Fenno had heard Lettie. He raised a hand and beckoned without turning his head, and she came in and stood beside her father's bed. "She's beginning to show her condition," Matild thought. "I wonder how John will take it when he finds out."

Lettie understood her father's attempts at speech far better than her mother did and she interpreted easily the guttural sounds which came from his throat.

"Michael's still at the mill. I'll tell him you want to see him as soon as he gets back."

Michael was teaching no longer. Most of his time was given to writing, and in the preliminary work for this Lettie had a growing share. The rest of his time, and the more lucrative part, was spent as consultant at the mill. At first, Fenno had resented Brodi's presence so bitterly that the fact that he was living in the house was kept a secret. In time, however, he had come to accept this defeat, as he had been forced to accept so many others. Sometimes, nowadays, Brodi brought him news of the mill. John Fenno had not wanted to listen but, with wisdom, Mike had asked his advice on this and that. The answers were laboriously written and usually useless, for Fenno had no understanding of the exacting demands of the new era. Mike was quick to see, however, that the mere asking of advice returned to Fenno some measure of his self-respect. Sometimes, while they were communicating laboriously on these subjects, the figure on the bed stretched itself out and became commanding.

Lettie went slowly downstairs, taking each step with care. As she went, her lips moved, for she was repeating a poem to herself. Matild had passed on to her daughter her belief that the life of the unborn could be influenced for good if its mother thought only high and beautiful thoughts, and so Lettie was learning many poems. When Black Mike heard about this he laughed uproariously and harshly, but then he stopped laughing and looked at Lettie with that surprising gentleness of his. "If it gives *you* pleasure, do it," he said, and Lettie, who was exceedingly preoccupied these days, did not notice that Michael looked at her as though she had gone a long way from him.

Lettie wandered slowly into the drawing room and smiled as Shamrock rose from the hearth to meet her, swinging a tail that was now fully feathered. She sat down in the middle of the *tête*. All her motions, these days, were careful and temperate.

Shamrock barked once but Lettie did not start. "That's Michael," she said dreamily.

Michael's feet were thudding up the front steps and Lettie's smile deepened. She was thinking that Michael expended so much energy on everything. "And I used to, too," she thought, "before I learned to save it for *him*."

The front door slammed and the battered felt hat hit the hall table with a soft plop and Michael was in the room with her. He seemed to her so full of energy that the air around him quivered. "He's sweet," she thought, which was probably the most inappropriate adjective that had ever been applied to Black Mike.

"Hullo, my gal."

"Hullo, Michael dear."

He came over to the *tête* and stood there, looking down on her, and she turned her face up to him. The furrows in his brow deepened because it seemed to him that her skin was so transparent and even her hair was lifeless, as though the vitality of every part of her were being drained away to supply the processes of creation. She was smiling up at him, but the smile seemed to come from far away. Because this look made him feel alone, he reached out and rumpled her hair to bring her back to him.

"Oh, Michael," she said, still smiling, but she came no nearer.

"I wonder," he thought, "if she ever will. I wonder if she ever will again."

26

W ILLOUGHBY was dressing for one of the chic little dinners for which she was beginning to be known, or rather, Suzanne, her maid, was dressing her, when she heard a tap on the door.

"It's me—Sam."

"Don't come in now."

"All right, but I just wanted to make sure you got the Brodis for the party tonight, like I told you."

"*As* I told you, dear." Willoughby took a deep breath on which to launch an evasion, and apprehension widened her eyes. In spite of Sam's direct order, she had not invited the Brodis. The Brodis would have spoiled everything. "You *can't* have people like that at a smart party and it's stupid of Sam not to see it," she had told herself, and the invitation was never written. Lettie and Black Mike had never seen the inside of her small but very stylish house and it was her intention that they never should. The door opened and Sam put his head in. She frowned at him.

"I said, don't come in."

An expression of pleasure came on Sam's face and he stepped inside the room. Willoughby sat at her dressing table, her body covered in the filmiest of lace, while her maid did things, daintily, to the back of Willoughby's headdress. The sight of Willoughby obviously drove from Sam's mind all other thoughts and he advanced on her. Willoughby snatched a towel from the dressing table and held it over her breasts.

"Go away, Sam. What will Suzanne think?"

"All right. All right." Sam's voice was good-natured but, as he turned away, he gave the maid a look of dislike that might have alarmed one who felt less secure in her mistress' favor. The door closed and Suzanne raised her hands in an expressive French gesture as she met Willoughby's eyes in the mirror. Both women smiled. The crisis was postponed and Willoughby gave herself wholly to Suzanne's ministrations.

Suzanne was an important part of Willoughby's life and her most prized achievement. She was little and French and snobbish and rude to guests and Willoughby felt that all these things were infinitely chic. Suzanne was hard as nails, with a yellowish face, black, shiny shoe-button eyes and little, grasping fingers. Her bulges were tightly corseted and in her tight black-satin uniform she looked so smooth and sleek that she seemed wet; looked, in fact, rather like a black and glistening tadpole to which a bit of lace apron had been added. Suzanne spoke almost no English and Willoughby never ceased to be pleased when guests innocently addressed a request to her only to receive a douche of voluble French. Willoughby's own French was very bad, but Suzanne and Willoughby understood each other more fundamentally than by language and the basis of the understanding was not so much that each had something to give the other as that each had something to take.

Willoughby lingered until she heard Sam go down the stairs and the first guests arrive. She wanted to put off explaining to Sam as long as she could. Thought of the impending scene spoiled the dinner for her, the delicious, fashionable dinner. When Sam had finally realized the Brodis were not coming, something hard and implacable had appeared under his affability and she began to be afraid that she had at last gone too far. As the dinner progressed the fear grew into panic, the more unbearable because she never in her life had been afraid like this before, and she tried desperately to hide it by glittering talk and sparkling manner.

By the time her guests left she had recovered sufficiently to transmute her fright into an unsteady anger. "I'll ask the people I please," she thought, listening to the loud voices full of the forced gaiety of departure which were coming from the hall where Sam was seeing out the last of the guests. Sam always saw their guests all the way to the front steps, but Willoughby went no farther with them than the drawing-room doorway. She stood now in the middle of this small but elegant room and surveyed the debris of her party. "This is *my* life," she thought. "Sam has the mill but this is *my* life. He shan't interfere." She looked around her lovely room with the special, wholly feminine aliveness of a woman in her own home, a sight no man ever sees if his presence is known.

When Sam returned she was standing with her back to him, blowing out the candles with which the room was lit, and she began to talk with a breathless casualness. "Don't you think candles are chic, Sam? Did you see how simply astonished everyone was? Now they'll all go home and buy candles because *I* use them!"

Sam was silent and after a moment her chatter died and she turned to face him in the light of the only lamp in the room. "You're so quiet, Sam. Didn't you enjoy the party?" Something about him brought back all her fears and she said it placatingly.

"Where were the Brodis?"

"They couldn't come. Too bad, isn't it?" she added sarcastically.

"Yea?" He said it softly and strolled across the room to stand in front of her.

"Yes," she said, not hiding her anger. If he found out the truth, all right.

Suddenly he seized her roughly by the shoulder. There was a blacker anger in his face than she had ever seen there before.

"You're lying to me!"

"Sam!"

His fingers bruised her and he shook her a little.

"Sam! Sam! Please—you're hurting me!"

"Listen to me," he said, not relaxing his grip in the slightest. His voice sounded mature and commanding, so that she had the sudden sensation of confronting, not the familiar Sam, but someone of more stature and dignity than she had ever faced before.

"Listen to me, Willoughby," he said. "If you ever lie to me again— ever, about anything, you'll never see me again."

"Sam, for Heaven's sake, can't you see what *dowdy* people they are?" She gave a sudden twist and slipped out of his grasp.

"Dowdy! Jesus Christ!" He took a quick forward step and seized her wrist, holding her, though she tried to pull away from him. "Dowdy! Why, that's incredible. Is that all you see in them? Haven't you sense enough to see what he *is*? Haven't you sense enough to see he's a coming man? Why, I'd rather work with Brodi at my right hand than any man I know. He's got more brains than any of us. He'll be a big man some day and I'm proud to be his friend. I want him for a friend more than any man I've ever known. And all you can think of is to say that they're dowdy. Christ! And your own sister. Can't you see the stuff that's in her? No," he said, with less anger. "I suppose you can't. Sit down, Willoughby. We're going to have a talk."

Sam pointed to a flimsy chair which stood in front of an inlaid French desk and Willoughby sank into it without a sound except the rustling of the stiff brocade folds of her gown. Her eyes were wide and terrified and she was listening less to Sam's words than to the implacability of his tone and to the beating of her own heart. Sam drew up an arm chair and, sitting on its edge, leaned his arms across his knees and let his hands droop. All the anger was gone from his voice now, but there was a calm sternness in his manner which was not like anything she had ever seen there before. She shivered a little and drew into herself.

"Willoughby, we've been married a year now, and you are the head of my house. I have given you plenty of rope. I wanted to see what you would do with it—what you would make of yourself. Well, I've seen! You've grown more selfish and self-centered all the time. All you care about is clothes and parties and style and things that will feed that conceit of yours. You don't care about me, except in bed, and even there the only thing you want is your own satisfaction. We'll try it for one year more—understand me? I'm giving you one year. You've got to make yourself over, do you hear? If you can't, we're through."

"But Sam . . ."

"I'm not interested in whether you think you can or can't. You've got to! Now, then—you got some paper in that thing? Paper to write notes on?"

Willoughby held a lace-edged handkerchief to her trembling lips and nodded without looking at Sam.

"All right. Get it out and write a note to Lettie and ask them to dinner. I don't care what night but make it soon. And don't you make it haughty-sounding. And tomorrow you ask the swellest people you know to meet them. Hurry up."

Willoughby silently took up paper and her pen with the slim mother-of-pearl handle and began to write. As she wrote, tears of misery welled to her eyes and she wiped them away with her frilly handkerchief. Hadley stood looking down on her, silent and stern and a little sad. When she had finished she reached out a shaking hand for an envelope.

"Wait a minute. Let me see that."

Sam read the note carefully and slowly and tossed it back on the desk. "All right." He stood in silence while the envelope was sealed, watching while she lit the desk candle and held the spluttering stick of wax in the flame. She groped nervously for her silver seal and in silence he handed it to her and watched her press it into the wax. "Now give it to me." He put the note in his pocket and turned to leave the room.

"Sam!"

He stopped and stared at her with cold eyes. She rose and rustled toward him. "Oh, Sam!" She threw her arms around his neck and put her head on his shoulder. He stood without moving, his hands hanging at his sides, and slowly she began to press her body against his while she tried to pull his unyielding form toward her. Finally he reached up and took her arms from around his neck and pushed her away.

"Christ!" he said in disgust.

He picked up the lamp and left the room.

Willoughby stood still for a moment in the darkness and then she followed him as he mounted the little stairway with heavy tread. He went straight to Willoughby's dressing room where a dim light burned. Suzanne rose, blinking, from her seat in the shadows. Suzanne never looked tired; only a little harder and yellower as the evening wore on.

Sam glared at her. "Like a lizard, an evil lizard," he said under his breath, and aloud: "We don't want you. Get it? Get out. Scat. Go away. No want."

Suzanne turned her shoe-button eyes on Willoughby. "It is necessary to undress Madame."

Suddenly Sam's restraint broke and his voice rose to a roar.

"No! I've had enough of you—do you hear? Get out. Get out for good. You're through. Fired!"

Suzanne shrugged very delicately and gave Willoughby a look full of meaning.

Willoughby waited to get into their bed until she was sure Sam was asleep. The Hadleys' bed probably caused more gossip among the women of Cleveland than anything else connected with this gossip-attracting pair. In the first place it was French, and to Cleveland women there was something scandalous in a bed's being French. Then, it was neither mahogany nor walnut, but made of a strange blond wood. When Willoughby explained that it was pear wood they resented it because they thought she was making fun of them. Pear wood, indeed! The head and foot boards were upholstered in blue brocade like a parlor chair, which was perfectly astonishing, and the counterpane, instead of being a decent white, was also blue brocade. The bed became a symbol, and a virtuous housewife, like Prissie, thought of it and became more self-righteous than ever.

Willoughby and Sam now lay in it back to back. Sam slept, nerveless and at peace. Willoughby's thoughts were busy with stocktaking. "What can I *do?*" she thought desperately. "I can't budge him. I've got to have more money, and he says, wait till hard times are over—wait—wait—wait. I can't wait. And now this. Now I'll have to put up with all his grubby friends. And Suzanne! I *can't* get on without Suzanne. He wants to make me lead *his* life and I have a right to my own. A right! And he acts like a workman, lounging in his chair and unbuttoning his coat. Oh, it's cruel—cruel."

Willoughby wept, scalding, slow, bitter tears of misery while Sam's breathing rose and fell in placid evenness. After a long time her tears stopped and she stared, wide-eyed, into the darkness. She thought her heart was breaking and that no one had ever suffered so much. She thought with longing of the old house and of her father. "*He* loved me," her heart cried. "Oh, *daddy—daddy,* why can't you help me now?" And then, with her longing for him, a great loneliness filled her, crowding out all other emotion. "There is not one person in the whole world who really loves me," she thought and believed that her thought was true.

Sam stirred in his sleep, rolled over and threw his arm across her body. She lay still, feeling its weight. "I could never throw it off," she thought. "I might try, but I could never throw it off. He'd never let me—unless he left me." When a struggle is useless, there is comfort in the knowledge that one does not have to fight. After a while she, too, slept.

She awoke with a start to realize that the room was gray with the end of night and the dawn wind was blowing. Someone was pounding on the front door urgently, insistently, as though they had been pounding for some time. The bell was ringing too, filling the back regions of the house with clamor. Willoughby sat up, threw her hair back and shook Sam's shoulder.

"Sam! Sam!"

"Huh?"

"Sam, wake up. There's someone at the door."

Sam came awake slowly. "Let Suzanne answer it," he said when consciousness returned.

"She won't. You'll see. And the other girls won't do her work. They hate her."

Sam swung his feet over the side of the bed and the process seemed to bring him wide awake.

"Say, Willie." His voice was serious with no trace in it of their quarrel, and she looked up, startled. "It could only be one thing. It had to come sometime. You'd better get up and start dressing."

27

A<small>ND</small> now, sir, if you would be good enough to lend me a hand?"
Michael turned from watching Hadley shepherd the last of the
black-swathed figures from the Fenno drawing room.

"Certainly. What . . . ?" How oily-lugubrious the fellow was, and
with the tallowy complexion that seems to belong to the ministrants
of death.

"The coffin lid, sir."

They stooped for it where it rested, leaning against the dais which
held the coffin, in front of a bank of flowers and greenery which covered the mantle. The lid was unexpectedly heavy and Mike suppressed
the thought, as inappropriately cynical, that the housings of Fenno's
death, like those of his life, showed quality and circumstance.

With the lid poised between them, Michael looked down on John
Fenno, lying there in such unnatural peace. He tried, in this last second,
before that face became forever only a memory, to comprehend a character so dissimilar to his own. Proud, ah! Defiant, angry, uncompromising still, the features somewhat blurred as though seen through a
veil of futility, and their dignity augmented now by death. An effigy
in wax, carved by the spirit—with what tools? With hate and ambition,
but with human cravings too, these last, perhaps, plainer now than in
life—in that still face that bore so strongly the stamp of despising its
own weakness, despising even its own death. The unctuous young man
was lowering his end of the lid and Michael hastened to do likewise,
feeling it settle into place with a small jar that seemed to reverberate
through his senses in widening circles. A lifetime of passion and one
small jar to close the account. But the passion went on in all those lives
created and conditioned by this still form.

Michael stood back, listening to the scraping of the screws. It was
now three days since he had opened the door to Willoughby and Hadley, hastily summoned, and looked with interest to see what cracks

might have appeared in Willoughby's polished surface. So far as he could see, there were none, and he found himself hoping, fatuously, that there might be one or two underneath, invisible.

"Is he still . . . ?" Hadley had said, and Mike nodded, watching Willoughby strip off her gloves with perhaps a trifle more than her usual care.

When this was finished, she said, "He doesn't want to see me." This was not a question, or at least it was said with no rising inflection, but Mike felt the questioning nevertheless and he would have given a good deal to be able to gauge its import. Hope? Fright? Relief? Or, perhaps, merely the conventional feeling that situations which tend to force a person's true nature out into the open should, at all costs, be avoided. Mike did not answer her, and the three of them stood there in silence while the two men watched Willoughby's eyes travel with interest around this room which she had not seen for so long a time.

Then Mike had been summoned and he mounted the stairs with the alacrity which the wishes of the dying are always able to command. "I'll have to read his eyes," Mike thought, entering the familiar room which had now become more than a room.

"You wanted to see me, sir?"

The eyes smoldered. There was a little pause and Michael said, "You want me to do the best I can for them? I'll try, sir." And then, because he did not quite want to name Willoughby, he added, "For all of them," though it was in his mind that Willoughby was being looked after with great competency.

The burning eyes held his for a second longer and then the fire died out. "He's letting go his hold," Mike thought, watching a film come across the eyes. A moment more and it seemed as though John Fenno no longer saw beyond the film. Mike hesitated, trying to make a final compliance with everything that John Fenno was. Would he want to be left alone—just now—just at this ending? Mike looked down on the long form on the bed and his brow was deeply furrowed with the effort, so unusual with him, to see into another's character. "He'd think of death as an indignity," Mike thought. "He'd not want anyone to see," and Mike tiptoed from the room. Outside he found Matild waiting for admittance and, taking her gently by the arm, he led her away.

"Again, sir, if you please."

Mike started. Two corners of a flag were being held out to him. He seized them and helped to spread the flag over the coffin. One forgot this soldier phase of Fenno's life, but it must have meant something to him, since he was moved to leave directions for a military funeral. Some hidden idealism, some hero, worshipped in secret, perhaps, whose influence Fenno may have felt through all these years. On a sudden impulse Mike took the long cavalry saber and the cap from the hands of the oily young man and himself arranged them with care, on the flag.

If such a hero there were, Fenno had never revealed him. Sherman? Mike himself had wired the news of the death of his former staff officer. There had been no reply. All the newspapers had carried copies of a long telegram of condolence from the Secretary of War to Mrs. Fenno, but this Mike put down to a politician's acknowledgment of Fenno's industrial eminence. This view was nicely borne out, Mike reflected cynically, by the fact that the telegram was released to the newspapers but never actually received by Matild. No, there must have been some intensity of emotion, perhaps never fully acknowledged even to himself. And Mike rearranged once more with conscientious care the silver chains hanging from the sword.

Even more strange, certainly, that no one had heard from Mark, but Michael had the conviction that no one ever would have news of him again. A telegram sent to an address left with his landlady had brought no word in return. The address was in a city with a harsh Western name, but Mark might be anywhere by this time. The West was the natural destiny of men like Mark.

Later, in the church, the vague meaninglessness of ritual dulled Mike into a kind of intellectual drowsiness. The sonorous words of the Order affected him as might the droning of a bluebottle fly on a window pane, and he suffered from daze and from a sense of the unreality of everything save the feel of Lettie's hand in the crook of his arm. He seemed to be existing in a world of shadows in which the fact of death itself had no more meaning than the mote-filled gules of colored light which slanted across the apse and stained the bishop's bulbous sleeves. *"O teach us to number our days that we may apply our hearts unto wisdom."* No greater significance lay in the words than in the hands held out over the coffin, pale, almost effeminate and consciously graceful hands emerging ghostlike from stiff ruffles and black bands. The whole ritualistic business made Mike feel alien.

In the fresher air of outdoors, life seemed somewhat more normal. He found himself in the second carriage, sitting on a hard and narrow seat alone with Lettie. By leaning out of the window a little way and screwing his head around, which he tried to do with dignity, he could see half of the file of soldiers, two of the four white horses which drew the black caisson and part of the caisson itself and the flag-draped coffin. He could just manage to see also, by foreshortening his vision as much as possible, a horse bearing what he presumed to be John Fenno's cavalry saddle and his boots, reversed in the stirrups. Theatric touch, that. The horse, a borrowed cavalry charger probably, was a stranger to him. He hoped Lettie hadn't seen those boots. He stole a glance at her. The long thick veil was raised and he received in return one of those rewarding looks which had been their chief means of communication and assurance during these last trying days. His heart bounded in response and he could not restrain himself from reaching out swiftly to touch her. She returned his touch gently, but he knew her thoughts were back in her early childhood when her father was still an untarnished ideal.

Beside the grave and in front of the pile of clay, now so decorously covered with flowers, the honorary pallbearers took their stand and Mike watched them with carefully hidden cynicism, as they dressed their line awkwardly. "They're here," he thought, "to lay John Fenno in his well-appointed grave and to close their account, I suspect perhaps not wholly regretfully, with that forceful, dominating and egocentric associate." Their look of substantial dignity seemed to him a little marred by embarrassment because they were being forced to think briefly of success and achievement in relation to death and a clay pit on a peaceful hillside. How carefully they seemed to blend deference with a little show of restlessness and a faintly impatient air of being unwilling that this ceremony for one of themselves should detain them too long from their urgent affairs. They all looked a little liverish and a little tired from living through an era. Mike turned away, disliking the sight exceedingly.

The bishop came forward, holding out his pale, tapering hands with the prayer book in them, and paused, collecting attention. The silence deepened and in that somewhat charged moment there was a commotion on the roadway and many eyes, Mike's among them, turned that way. A livery stable hack rattled up, halted vibrantly, the door burst open, and a figure in a long overcoat emerged backward, dragging into the open a great wreath of rhododendron leaves tied with red, white and blue streamers. In the silence he straightened up and, with a quick birdlike turn of the head on the scrawny neck, surveyed the multitude. Mike felt his pulses quicken and his nerves tingle, and he knew, without taking his eyes from that electric figure, that everyone there present was similarly stirred. A quick gesture swept the hat from the still reddish hair and hooked the great wreath over one arm, and Mike felt, rather than heard, in the people massed about him, the gasp of recognition. More than a hundred people watched this man with the weatherbeaten face as he walked toward them. He came slowly with a kind of lambent dignity, unassuming and proud, casual and intense, commanding and humble, and Mike, who was watching this approach almost without breathing, knew that he was living through one of the unforgettable moments of his life. Sherman placed the great wreath at the foot of the coffin gently, straightened and stepped back and back until he was lost in the crowd.

With this retreat it seemed to Michael that the lavish, tawny afternoon began to fade, drawing a veil of time and distance over the scene, and when the prelate spoke, his voice full of soft blendings and velvet sympathy, it was like a voice heard in memory from the past. It was the fruity, almost theatrical, but cultured voice of a churchman used to administering a rich and consciously picturesque religion to a rich and substantial congregation, and its mellowness robbed the words it spoke of any connection with damp earth and decay. But though it rose in organ tones, faded and rounded out again, the effect was, for Michael, diminuendo. He saw as in some blurred, receding vision an officer lift the saber and the blue cap from the coffin. Far off, though right before him, he watched the strange motions of the six sergeants folding the flag, their gestures stiffened and formalized by custom. He watched the flag passed from hand to hand jerkily and received by the officer with a wooden bow. He heard the click of heels, saw the officer advance, bow again and hold the flag, the cap and the saber out, stiff-armed, toward Matild. Without himself feeling emotion, he heard her gasp, saw her clutch at them through her long veil, saw the flag slip and open out, spilling its red stripes downward. He saw Hadley stoop and retrieve the flag, and felt Lettie withdraw her hand from his arm with gentle pressure, to take the cap and saber from her mother.

"More than a man has gone," Mike thought. "An era too. The crash of this prosperity—a real ending. Nothing will ever be quite the same again, though in time the country may be richer and even, conceivably, better. But the ideals, the dreams and the standards of that era, even its evils, have no longer any significance. Just at this moment, on this sunny hillside, we are still caught in the past, making this strange, dead tribute to the dead, but in a few minutes some of us will escape into the present. Willoughby and Sam will escape to rough-hew their destinies; Lettie and I have our life and our work ahead of us." He turned and took the heavy saber and the cap from her, crooking his arm once more for her hand. "But these others, many of them for the rest of their lives, will have no more vitality and importance than shadows from the pages of a history book moving through the brain. The line of self-important pall bearers. Matild, the great general—shadows, their era gone, the things they lived and fought for, history."

Still feeling as though he were looking at some scene already past, Mike watched the six sergeants lift the coffin with the canvas bands, swing it slowly forward and, straining and red-faced, lower it into the open grave. He saw the bishop produce from the folds of his vestments a small and immaculate trowel and watched him scrabble for dirt under the evergreen boughs.

"Ashes to ashes, dust to dust . . ."

Loose earth fell in a clattering shower on the coffin and Mike heard a sigh from the congregation, like a gentle wind in the tree tops, of muted, cultured distress.

The crisp command came muffled to his ears. "Attention. Right face. Forward by files. Halt!" The gleaming muskets were pleached above the grave and the sound of the shot poured out over the valley, sending back echoes as though shattering itself against the barrier of the hills.

Mike bent his elbow to hold Lettie's hand a little tighter. He felt her eyes, invisible under the concealing veil, turned on him, and his heart stirred.

"And now, in the name of the Father, Son and
Holy Ghost, Amen."

Michael closed his eyes in the humble feeling of the awareness of life which is sometimes a form of prayer with the unreligious. When he opened them again a moment later, some of the gold had gone from the autumn afternoon. Dusk would follow and then night, and with night would glow again that light in the sky, the light shining up from white hot steel and iron. John Fenno had contributed more than a little to the brilliance of that light. Just now it was dimmed by hard times, but it would glow—and Michael had a sudden and stirring faith in his prophecy—in future prosperity, more brilliantly than ever.

When Michael's mind returned from these wanderings he saw that a bugler stood at the head of the grave. Long, limpid notes floated out, filling Michael's heart with the intolerably moving knowledge of the sadness of beauty, the loneliness of human life, the heartbreaking finality of death. He felt the pressure of Lettie's hand on his arm, and with the slowly fading notes of the bugle the sadness in his heart faded also.